DAY OF TERROR

The newscaster was reporting that at least three aircraft, perhaps as many as five, were believed to have been hijacked. It occurred to the General that the White House, the Capitol Building, and other government offices would be potential targets of a coordinated terrorist attack.

The answer to the question of where the next strike would occur came more promptly than he expected.

The Pentagon on the Potomac was the most secure building inside the strongest country in the world. At 0940 a hijacked airliner crashed into the west exposure of the five-sided building. General Kragle was knocked sprawling out of his chair. He gingerly picked himself up off the floor. Agent Thornton was on his hands and knees, coughing from the shock and from the acrid smoke and haze suddenly smogging the room. The General pulled him to his feet.

"I'm all right, General," Thornton said. "What the hell happened?"

The General threw open the door to a wall of smoke filling a hallway littered with ceiling tiles and other debris. Flames illuminated the far end. His big, booming voice assumed natural authority.

"People, listen to me. Follow my voice. We're getting out of here."

America had received her wake-up call.

Also by Charles W. Sasser

DETACHMENT DELTA:
PUNITIVE STRIKE

DETACHMENT DELTA

OPERATION IRON WEED

CHARLES W. SASSER

AVON BOOKS
An Imprint of HarperCollinsPublishers

This is a work of fiction. Names, characters, places, and incidents are products of the author's imagination or are used fictitiously and are not to be construed as real. Any resemblance to actual events, locales, organizations, or persons, living or dead, is entirely coincidental.

AVON BOOKS
An Imprint of HarperCollins*Publishers*
10 East 53rd Street
New York, New York 10022-5299

Copyright © 2003 by Bill Fawcett & Associates
ISBN: 0-380-82059-5
www.avonbooks.com

First Avon Books paperback printing: April 2003

Avon Trademark Reg. U.S. Pat. Off. and in Other Countries,
Marca Registrada, Hecho en U.S.A.
HarperCollins® is a registered trademark of HarperCollins Publishers Inc.

Printed in the U.S.A.

10 9 8 7 6 5 4 3 2 1

*This book is dedicated to Craig Roberts,
army buddy, police partner*

AUTHOR'S NOTE

While this novel is a work of fiction with no intended references to real people either dead or alive other than the obvious ones, discerning readers will make obvious connections between recent history and events in this book. These are intended. For example, I have used the tragic terrorist attacks of 9/11, the War on Terror, and the subsequent actions in Afghanistan as a setting for the adventures described.

This is the second book in the Detachment Delta series dealing with the U.S. Army's elite Delta Force and counterterrorism. The first book, *Detachment Delta: Punitive Strike,* centered upon events prior to September 11, 2001. The second continues with America's War on Terror and the Kragle military dynasty that spans three generations of warriors. A comment made by Jennifer Fisher, my editor at HarperCollins, applies as well to this current saga as it did to the first: "There was an eerie sense of wondering what was fact and what was fiction. . . ."

For thirteen years I was a member of the U.S. Army Special Forces (the Green Berets), and therefore have some understanding of covert and SpecOps missions. I hope to continue this merging of fact and fiction to create stories that may very well reflect the *real* stories behind counterterrorist operations by the United States.

Finally, I want to make clear that my rendering of certain high-profile characters, such as former President John Stanton and Senator Eric Tayloe in this volume, are largely creations of my own imagination or are interpretations necessary to the plot.

CHAPTER 1

West Bank, Israel

Israeli armor consisting of Merkava main battle tanks, boxy armored personnel carriers, and HUMMV all-terrain vehicles thundered onto the Lutheran church compound in Beit Jalla shortly after midnight. Rifle fire rattled sporadically from where Palestinian security forces occupied positions on nearby Virgin Mary Street. Bullets thucked into the high mud walls surrounding the church and orphanage. A pair of tracers streaked overhead, bright in the darkness and looking as big as baseballs. Major Dov Landau unassed his troops and dispersed them to defenses around the wall and on the top floor of the rectory.

"Major Kragle," he said to the American army officer, and pointed toward a five-story church hostel that was still under construction. "We're emplacing a machine gun and observation post on the roof. It can become a bit targeted. Care to join me for a look at the situation?"

"That's the reason I'm here, Major. You Israeli boys are the experts in counterterrorism and urban fighting."

"We've had a half century of surviving it," Landau said matter-of-factly. "The Arabs leave us no choice."

The Israeli troop commander was short, and as squat, solid and implacable as one of his tanks. He led the way across the churchyard at a jog, followed by a soldier lugging an M-60 machine gun by its carrying handle and wearing a helmet equipped with night vision goggles. Major Brandon Kragle fell in behind an ammo-bearing rifleman with a filled sandbag under each arm. As an American observer sent over by the elite counterterrorist U.S. Army 1st Special Forces Operational Detachment—Delta, he was unarmed except for a 9mm Sig-Sauer sidearm Landau had handed him before the convoy departed Jerusalem.

"Just in case," Landau had said. "Frigging Palestinians would love to knock off an American."

The bishop and other church staff were removing sleepy children from the orphanage and herding them across the darkened churchyard toward a basement beneath the rectory. A young woman looked up as she hurried past with a baby wrapped in a blanket. Brandon recognized her from that morning. She was a tiny, well-built girl of about twenty-five or so with long sunburned hair and, he remembered, bright emerald eyes. He towered over her by at least a foot.

"I know you," he said.

"Yeah? We're going to have to stop meeting this way, Major." She kept going, disappearing in the night with the children.

Brandon had met her, or at least had *seen* her, that morning at army HQ in Jerusalem. The first thing he'd noticed were her remarkable eyes. They reminded him of Gypsy Iryani, who'd died the previous year on a Delta mission into Afghanistan with him. In other respects—her long sunbleached hair, her wide mouth and small perfectly-formed nose—she was an opposite of the redheaded, freckled Gypsy. But the eyes. He turned and looked after her because of the eyes. It was almost like Gypsy had gazed out of them at him.

Her ass in the tight-fitting jeans was nearly as spectacular as her eyes. Unlike everyone else in the tactical operations center, she wore civvies—jeans and an open-neck shirt. She seemed to command respect and a certain authority, which nettled Kragle, who disapproved of women in military combat positions, especially in positions of authority. He'd acquired that attitude from his old man, General Darren Kragle.

"Who is she?" Brandon had asked Major Landau.

"Off limits," Landau said. He laughed. "All we know is that she says to call her 'Summer.' "

"Is she a Sabra?"

"I don't know if she was born here or if she's an import. I suspect she may be American. She showed up about six months ago. She's effective when it comes to gathering intelligence. Rumor is, if you're a terrorist and the Ice Maiden sleeps with you, you can expect to be dead by the next day."

"*She's* the one!" Brandon said, looking at her with new interest. "She set up old Mustafa. He was sixty-four years old. She slept with him!"

"And he's dead."

Abu Ali Mustafa, one of the top five figures in Yasser Arafat's hard-line Palestine Liberation Organization, had organized seven suicide bomb attacks against Israelis during the past six months, including a blast at a pizza parlor in central Tel Aviv that killed six civilians, two of them children under four years old.

The green-eyed woman had set him up for the kill. He and others among the PLO leadership were at a secret meeting in nearby Ramallah on the West Bank. Summer, with her inside knowledge, pointed out the location on the second floor of an office building. Two Israeli helicopters fired a pair of rockets through the windows, decapitating the old villain and killing two others.

That was two days ago. That night, the Palestinians retaliated. Firing from Beit Jalla's hilltops, across a small valley, they hit thirty-one apartments and a synagogue in the Israel neighborhood of Gilo. A young girl was killed, and a man and an old woman were hurt. Israeli troops responded by seizing parts of the Palestinian town and fortifying positions with sandbags. Mosque loudspeakers called on people to take to the streets and resist. Sporadic gunfire, sometimes heavy, popped and banged from throughout the town's nighttime streets.

"Why bother with the small snakes like Mustafa?" Brandon asked Major Landau now. "Why not start with the head of Yasser Arafat, the old cobra himself?"

Major Landau shrugged in a pained way. "There are those of us who would like to," he said. "Your previous President Stanton treated him like a world leader, and now our politicians are afraid of world opinion if we target him. Politicians are the same everywhere, my American friend. They consider before anything else their own political survival. Power is a potent aphrodisiac."

He paused, sighing out of some deep sadness. "There are so many snakes surrounding poor Israel. Your country, my friend, has not yet experienced daily life under terror and attack. But there will come a day, I predict, when you will."

Brandon had heard that before. It was a day the General had also been predicting for years. Few in America listened to him. After all, America was protected by her seas, he thought, and by her . . . by her seas.

He cast a final glance toward where Summer and the orphans had retreated into the rectory basement. He decided he would have to get to know her better. Something about her, something more than the eyes and her tight jeans, intrigued him. He climbed the stairway of the unfinished hostel with the little band and its machine gun. Major Landau led the way with a muted red-lensed flashlight.

He turned it off. "We're here."

The entire fifth floor was without interior partitions, except for the open plates and supports. Their footfalls echoed in the emptiness. The outer walls were of mortar and stone, which provided cover from sniper fire. Major Landau found a ladder and moved it beneath a half loft's peak window. They climbed the ladder, with the machine gun and ammo, to a small loft platform. While the gunner set up for action, Brandon stood to one side of the window and looked out over a town crouched in total darkness except for a blaze somewhere to the south, sputtering sparks into the night sky.

Amplified voices through nearby mosque loudspeakers sounded like racing go-carts as they exhorted people to go out, for Allah's sake, and kill something. An Israeli patrol came under attack to the east. Rifle and automatic fire surged and ebbed for a long mad minute before it subsided into isolated gunshots. A machine gun banged out a long exclamation from a vacant lot on a hillside a block or so over, near Virgin Mary Street, which was no virgin when it came to violence. Red tracers floated across the little valley separating Beit Jalla from Gilo. Bullets whacked and chewed indiscriminately at the Jewish town across the stillness of the valley. It apparently didn't matter to the shooter what he hit, as long as the target was Israeli of whatever age, gender, or size.

"Have you located him?" Major Landau asked his gunner.

"Not yet." He was adjusting his sights while the assistant gunner packed the bipod legs with sandbags and fed the gun a belt of ammunition. Then both were still as the gunner peered out over the town through night vision goggles.

Landau removed his helmet with its NVGs and handed it

to Brandon, who put it on. Buildings, streets, and people flitting in shadow leaped out of the darkness, all in a liquid green light. Muzzle blast from the flickering Palestinian machine gun almost blinded him, its intensity magnified through the NVG lenses. He squinted.

"Do you see the machine gun?" Landau asked him.

"Vacant lot to our eleven o'clock, behind the wide building with the big billboard . . ."

"Okay, I got it now," the machine gunner said.

There was a hush as he completed ministrations to his weapon, muttering, "Okay, okay . . ." He took aim and fired a three-round burst, loud and ringing in the loft. One of the rounds was a tracer. Brandon watched it streak down into the town. He heard the rounds impacting, echoing. The Palestinian machine gun went quiet.

"He's down?" Landau asked.

Brandon returned the helmet and NVGs. Landau adjusted the lenses and grinned. "Good shooting," he said.

The sector went quiet after that. The American major and the Israeli officer sat with their backs against the wall and spoke in hushed tones about urban warfare, terrorism, counterterrorism, and the reopened Palestinian uprising. Major Kragle mostly listened. Colonel Buck Thompson, commander of Delta Force, had sent him over on a two-week observation tour to study Israeli tactics in a sustained terrorist environment. No better classroom on terrorism existed in the world.

"The Palestinians' key weapon is suicide bombers," Major Landau said. "They strike everywhere, killing civilians in order to intimidate the population. It's a sad time. Judaism and Islam both call for burial with haste. You can have morning coffee with your wife, hear news of a bombing at midday, identify her mangled body shortly thereafter, and then see her buried in the earth before the sun sets. My father is an old man whose job is to bury people. He says that in all his life he has never seen anything like this year. We are a state under the threat of constant terrorism and death."

He broke off to readjust the weight of the submachine gun resting across his lap.

"But we have known little else throughout Jewish history. It should be plain to everyone that our Islamic enemies mean to wipe us off the globe and to kill or run off every Jew. Did you know that Israel does not appear on any of the maps of our enemies?"

Brandon wondered if Americans had the courage and fortitude to endure under such conditions.

The soldier on watch at the window stirred. "Major Landau, we have movement down there."

Brandon and Landau gained their feet and copped a quick look out the open-paned window just as a blossom flared in the street below. A rocket-propelled grenade streaked up out of the darkness toward the loft.

"Jump!" Landau shouted.

Brandon had been conditioned to act instantly. He leaped into space, tumbling toward the floor below. Blast and flame from the explosion caught him in midair, slamming him against the floor, stunning him.

When he recovered, groaning, fire crackled in the loft, illuminating the level. Someone bent over him.

"You're alive!"

He blinked and recognized the girl Landau called the Ice Maiden.

"We need to get out of here," she said. "Can you get up? I'll help you."

Still dazed, Brandon murmured, "The others . . . ?"

"They're all dead," she said in an emotionless voice.

"Jesus!"

"He's dead too. A long time ago."

CHAPTER 2

Boston

Jordan R. Kragle, ambassador to Egypt, currently on a leave of absence, pushed his wife in her wheelchair up the ramp of Concourse C at Boston's Logan Airport. Marge Kragle, known to almost everyone as Little Nana, peered like a withered sparrow out of the roses festooning her lap.

"I'm being smothered!" the old woman chittered. "Where'd all these—these—" She was distressed by her inability to recall the word. "—these *weeds* come from?"

At the top of the ramp the Ambassador pushed her out of the path of pedestrian traffic and knelt next to her wheelchair. He patiently supplied her with the right word. "They're *roses,* Marge."

Little Nana's private nurse looked away from the disturbing scene of the tall, distinguished-looking diplomat kneeling at the feet of his tiny, uncomprehending wife in one of the busiest airports in the United States. Theresa was plump, in her forties, with crooked teeth and lots of dyed-red hair. She pretended to study the schedule monitors on the wall.

Jordan Kragle thought he detected a glimmer of recognition in his wife's faded blue eyes, but it vanished as quickly as it appeared. He ached for her to look at him with real awareness and cry out in that mock scolding way that had become family humor among the Kragle clan: "Jordan! Where are we off to this time? The Russian Steppes?" Little Nana always said "Russian Steppes" to indicate anywhere remote and exotic to which Jordan's postmilitary diplomatic career had taken them. She had been unable to travel with him for the past five years because of Alzheimer's disease.

The waspy little woman's features softened. A trembling hand as transparent as an X ray reached out and touched the kneeling man's silver hair. "You are nice-looking," she said. "Who are you?"

The Ambassador swallowed a lump of disappointment. "I'm your husband, Marge. Jordan. I send you roses."

The hand recoiled. "My husband had dark hair. He was killed during the war."

"I wasn't killed, Marge. We have three sons. Remember? Darren, Mike, and David. Darren's a general in the army. Mike is a journalist. David—"

David was the one killed in war. In Vietnam.

Little Nana glared, unresponsive and confused. How well Jordan knew the heartbreaking symptoms of Alzheimer's: steadily increasing memory loss; speech, judgment, and muscle coordination becoming impaired; outbursts of rage and tears for no apparent reason; the body gradually deteriorating and made susceptible to other diseases and infections; the victim eventually growing incapable of caring for herself. Most died from pneumonia and other infections.

Little Nana's mind was more than off track; it skipped randomly from track to track. "Doctor," she scolded, "my room is down this hallway. Take me there right away."

Jordan patted her hand. She snatched it away. He stood

erect, a tall man in his late seventies with a mustache as silver as his hair. He covered his eyes with his hand a moment to let the pain of seeing her like this subside.

"Mr. Ambassador?" Theresa said gently. "The gate's down this way. The flight's scheduled to leave in a half hour and there's a line at security."

"Yes, yes. Of course." He began to push his wife again. "A car will meet Marge and you at LAX and take you directly to the hotel," he said to Theresa.

"Yes, Ambassador. You've already given me the information."

"This meeting in Washington is a must. Otherwise, I'd go with you now."

"We'll be fine, sir."

"I should arrive in Los Angeles about eleven tonight. Did I give you my flight number? Never mind. I'll come directly to the hotel. Marge needs her sleep. We have an appointment with Dr. Schlefstein at nine tomorrow morning. He's reputed to be the world's leading authority on Alzheimer's. He's treated President Reagan and . . ."

His voice trailed off. They had spent the past two days at the Alzheimer's Institute of Advanced Medicine in Boston. Tests were called inconclusive, as always, and ended with a recommendation that Mrs. Kragle see yet another specialist, this one on the other side of the nation.

Although Alzheimer's was incurable, the Ambassador refused to accept it as hopeless. He took regular leaves from his post to seek promise and hope, like plants sought sunshine and rain. He had whisked Marge all over the globe seeking treatment, a cure—but clouds continued to cover the sun and it never rained. Only their deaths could prevent his trying to restore a last glimmer of recognition in his wife's eyes.

Theresa placed a hand over his on the handle of Little

Nana's wheelchair. She squeezed. How could he stand one disappointment after another, over and over?

"I know I shouldn't get my hopes up," he said.

"Sometimes hope is what keeps us going," Theresa said, tears brimming in her eyes.

Two Middle Eastern men crossed directly in the wheelchair's path. The Ambassador swerved the chair to avoid colliding with them. The young men stepped nimbly aside, but not before Little Nana's roses spilled all over the floor.

"A thousand pardons!" Jordan exclaimed, subconsciously reverting to Arabic because of the men's appearance.

"It is we who should seek pardon," the taller of the two men replied in Arabic. "Please? Let us help."

They knelt to help collect the scattered blooms under Little Nana's stern gaze and rambling tongue-lashing.

"She is ill and does not mean it," Jordan apologized.

"We deserve it," said the first man. He stood and carefully returned the roses to their protective covering. He was neatly dressed in slacks and a sport shirt. He wore glasses, had a mustache and a groomed little beard, and looked about thirty. He bowed politely.

"You speak excellent Arabic," he complimented. "Are you Islamic?"

Jordan switched back to English. "I'm Jordan Kragle, ambassador to Egypt."

"That explains your facility in our language. Permit me to introduce ourselves. I am Marwon al-Shahhi. He is Hanza Alghambi."

The second man wore a business suit. He was shorter, younger, with dark penetrating eyes and a pencil-line mustache. He shook hands but he still did not speak. He seemed nervous.

"The least we can do is aid you after almost causing a collision," Marwon said. He insisted on taking Theresa's carry-on and helping them through security. "We're taking the same flight, United Airlines 175," he said when the Ambassador gave him their gate number.

The little group arrived in time to hear the advance boarding call for handicapped persons and children traveling unattended. A flight attendant helped Theresa with Little Nana. Marge had nodded off. Jordan kissed her tenderly on the forehead. She jerked awake and looked at him.

"Jordan?" she said, and his heart leaped. It was only a glimmer, but it was something. Then the light faded. "Who are you? Go away! Go away!"

The attendant pushed her out of sight down the loading ramp behind a small boy and girl, obviously brother and sister, who held hands for moral support. Little Nana did not look back. Theresa turned and waved once.

Marwon touched the Ambassador's sleeve. "We go with Allah," he said.

CHAPTER 3

The Pentagon

The meeting to talk about establishing a National Homeland Security Agency to combat terrorism had dragged on since 0600 in an oak-paneled conference room of the massive Pentagon building in suburban Arlington, Virginia. It showed no signs of letting up. General Darren E. Kragle, commander of United States Special Operations Command (USSOCOM), loathed meetings that went on and on and never seemed to get anywhere. This one had been a floater around D.C. since at least February—and still nothing had been accomplished other than the changing of members now and then. Once politicians took hold of something, they worried hell out of it like a toothless dog with a rubber ball. The rubber ball never got chewed up, it just got slimy as it was mauled around, until after a while nobody wanted to touch it.

General Kragle's father, the ambassador to Egypt, was on his way to D.C. after he had put Little Nana and her nurse on a flight from Boston to Los Angeles. The General knew that the old man would never give up on a cure, and he wanted to meet his father and spend the day with him. The Chairman of the Joint Chiefs of Staff stepped on that idea.

"General Kragle, I realize you have a thorn in your butt about long powwows," General Abraham Morrison said.

"Particularly political ones," the General agreed.

"But anything that comes out of this—"

"*If* anything comes out of it, sir."

"All right, *if* anything comes out of it, USSOCOM will be directly impacted. You've said it yourself—that SpecOps will carry the next war."

"We're already in the next war, sir. With terrorists. If we don't realize that and do something about it, terrorists will be stacking up American casualties in front of the nation's capital."

"Tell that to the members of the NHSA committee."

"I have. They scratch their nuts and yawn and ask for more money."

The General settled for making a late lunch date with his father and arranging to take the afternoon off. The Ambassador had a meeting at the capitol with the Foreign Relations Committee at 1100, anyway. When the General arrived early at the Pentagon, he was both surprised and delighted to discover that Senior FBI Agent Claude Thornton had been added to the membership of the Homeland Security Exploratory Committee. The black Mississippian stood patiently and alone outside the locked door of the conference room, waiting. He broke into a broad grin, white teeth flashing against his dark ebony complexion, when he spotted the General. He shook hands warmly.

General Kragle boomed, "What are you doing in this den of thieves, Claude? Damn. I figured a guy like you who spoke raghead would be in Cairo until they toted you feet first back to Mississippi."

Thornton chuckled. "Feet first is the only way this black boy is going back to the mint julep state. I got in last night. You can call me the head nigger MFIC of the FBI's new National Domestic Preparedness Office. That falls under the Homeland Security Act."

Thornton had a blunt, mocking manner that matched the General's in many ways and contributed to their friendship. The agent was solidly built, in his late forties, very dark-skinned and with a shaved head as smooth and black as a bowling ball. He stood six feet tall. The General topped him by six inches and ten years. He was square-jawed, tanned, and his salt-and-pepper crew cut and mustache were strictly within army regulations. The General wore class B greens with ribbons in rows from the middle of his chest to almost the top of his shoulder. Although authorized to wear the Congressional Medal of Honor, the nation's highest award for valor, which was generally worn by itself, he thought it pretentious and extravagant and therefore wore it at the top of his other medals.

"Do we have time for me to buy you a cup of coffee?" Thornton asked.

The General laughed. "This is D.C.. Everything runs slower on government time. Let me show you the way to the canteen."

Their heels clacked in step and echoed in the near vacant corridor. The Pentagon's reduced peacetime staff on the night shift had not yet been replaced by the career daytimers. The two men indeed had some catching up to do. They hadn't seen each other since they dissolved the secret tactical operations center in Cairo following the successful completion of Operation Punitive Strike.

The General started it: "How's the wife?"

"She's doing fine since she took off with the Cairo press attaché and moved to Oregon."

"Christ, I'm sorry, Claude."

"I'm not. Claude Junior was accepted to the Naval Academy. He started in the fall. I'm as proud of that boy as you are of yours. How are your sons doing, anyhow? Both of them are brave men."

"All *three* of them are," the General corrected with gruff pride.

"I didn't meet the younger boy, the one in the navy. He was in Osama bin Laden's jail."

Navy Journalist Second Class Cassidy Kragle had been one of three captives seized by al-Qaeda terrorists during the bombing of the USS *Randolph* in Aden Harbor. General Kragle, Thornton, and Ambassador Jordan Kragle manned an underground TOC in Cairo to support Delta Detachment 2A when it parachuted into Afghanistan to rescue the hostages. Major Brandon Kragle commanded 2A. Sergeant Cameron Kragle insisted on going along as a team member; Cassidy was his brother too, after all. In spite of the cowardice Cameron had shown during Desert Storm by running from the enemy in battle, he had been beyond brave on Punitive Strike. So far as the General was concerned, all three sons had been real Kragles.

"Cassidy decided the army *was* big enough for the both of us after all," General Kragle said. "He took a discharge from the navy and enlisted in the army. He's attending the Special Forces Q Course at Bragg now, on his way to volunteering for Delta Force. Remember the other hostage, the female sailor?"

"Sure. Kathryn . . . uh . . ."

"Burguiere. It's *Kragle* now. Cassidy married her. They're expecting my first grandchild in January."

"I find it hard to picture you as a grandpa."

"I'll be a better grandpa than I was a father."

"How about the other boys?"

"Brandon's in Israel. He'll return Friday. He's getting practical training with the Jews on counterterrorism. I suspect it's something he'll be needing more sooner than later."

They turned down a junctioning corridor toward a cafeteria out of which exuded rich odors of frying eggs, bacon, and freshly brewed coffee.

"I had my doubts about Cameron," the General admitted, "but he came through big-time in Afghanistan with 2-Alpha. He received the Silver Star for his stay-behind op. Brandon recommended him. The boy is now a commissioned captain in the Army Chaplain Corps. A certified sky pilot. He's been assigned as chaplain to Delta Force."

Both men got coffee at the line in the canteen. Thornton paid. He said, "It looks like Delta Force is becoming a family fiefdom."

General Kragle laughed his booming laugh. "Special Operations is in the Kragle blood," he said. "I was with the 5th SF in Vietnam. Charlie Beckwith and I built Delta when all the skyjackings started in the 1970s. My old man, the Ambassador, was with the Alamo Scouts during World War Two. *His* gramps rode with Quantrell's Raiders. I expect Cassidy's kid will be in SpecOps if it's a boy. What else can a Kragle do? We're from a long line of Irish warriors."

David Kragle, the General's brother, was killed while fighting with the 1st Air Cavalry in the Ia Drang Valley in Vietnam. The other brother, Mike, was wounded near Khe Sanh before going back as a CPI war correspondent to win a Pulitzer.

"After the deal we pulled with Punitive Strike," Thornton said as they sipped coffee at a table, "I'm lucky my black ass wasn't skinned and tacked up on a wall next to your white ass."

The General chuckled. "When you're right and you got 'em by the balls, Claude, their hearts and minds will follow. We had 'em by the balls too after President Stanton ordered our own C-141 shot down. But it's a different administration now. The voters finally came to their senses and kicked that bunch of grafters out of the White House."

"Think anything will change, General?"

"Interns won't be wearing knee pads and giving blowjobs in the Oval office john."

"Damn!" Thornton said with mock disappointment. "Just when I was thinking about becoming the first niggah President too."

"Other than that," the General said, "nothing ever changes in Washington. The same damn endless meetings and bullshit. One of these days, Claude—and you can mark this old soldier's words—America is going to get a wake-up call."

CHAPTER 4

"Intelligence," explained the CIA Director to the military and civilian officials gathered around the thick oaken table at the Pentagon, "is gathered in many ways." The room had oaken walls as thick as the table; it exuded the air of a bomb shelter. "The CIA has its network of spies and informants. The FBI has its counterterrorism agents. The National Security Agency has telephone and computer taps. The military has satellites and spy planes—"

"And the knee bone is *not* connected to the thigh bone," interrupted General Kragle impatiently. Everyone in the room understood the intelligence-gathering system and how fragmented it was. He glanced at his watch: 0830. Over two hours and the talking went on.

"Exactly the point I'm making," the CIA chief agreed, unruffled. "The knee bone is *not* connected to the thigh bone. Each department protects its own interests like red wasps guard their nests. The CIA has attempted numerous times to organize the various agencies to coordinate action against threats to the United States. For example, in July the State Department issued a strong warning of terrorist actions, another USS *Randolph* or embassy, but there was no unified response. A strong Homeland Security Agency would eliminate redundancy and internecine conflict and coalesce efforts—"

Senator Eric B. Tayloe, Chairman of the Armed Services Committee, slammed the lid on his ever-present briefcase and shot to his feet. "I question the wisdom of authorizing an NHSA to employ active, proactive, and covert powers over citizens," he asserted. "If the Hart-Rudman Commission proposal is accepted, it will transfer Customs, the Border Patrol, the Coast Guard, the FBI's National Domestic Preparedness office—together with all of FEMA and parts of a dozen other agencies—into a new superagency presumed capable of mounting an instant and seamless response to terrorism. Civil libertarians, with good cause, must raise constitutional concerns about it. Security agencies do not always show a tender regard for working within the framework of the law. Any terrorist strike on the U.S. could involve the suspension of constitutional liberties . . ."

And so the endless debate continued.

"Potential adversaries cannot hope to be successful against us in traditional military terms," put in Representative MacArthur Thornbrew, who served on the House Armed Services subcommittee. "They must look for nontraditional methods of attack—like terrorism, information warfare, and the use of chemical and biological weapons. Unless we take steps now, America's future may well be one of continuing assaults against us and our way of life, such as those against the USS *Randolph* last year, against our embassies in Africa in 1998, against U.S. troops living in the Khobar Towers in Saudi Arabia in 1996, and against the World Trade Center in New York in 1993—"

Senator Tayloe was back on his feet, his face reddening. "When John Stanton was president, he warned against such actions. The military is one of our problems. DOD's focus on international war has exacerbated the likelihood of terrorist attacks at home. Hot spots around the globe, as related to U.S. military actions overseas, are apt to cause terrorism . . ."

You little shithead. General Kragle dropped his chin on his chest and kept his silence with a supreme effort. His primary mission on the exploratory committee was to listen and take notes. The CJCS would speak for the military and for USSOCOM.

The General lifted his head and glowered at the senator. To him, the tubby little man looked as though he had spent his entire life so far protected by his mother. He was a card-carrying member of what Kragle called the "blame America first" crowd. Back in the 1980s when Daniel Ortega and the communists took control of Nicaragua, Senator Tayloe had led the stampede of left-wing American politicians to Central America to kiss commie ass. The General never forgave him for that, nor for pushing the prosecution of Colonel Ollie North in the Iran-Contra affair.

"The military has developed its own strategies of counter-terrorism quite independently of other agencies' plans," Tayloe continued stubbornly. "I'm speaking here specifically of USSOCOM—Delta Force, Special Forces, and Navy SEALs. Will they submit to following a plan laid down by authority other than their own?" He stared directly at General Kragle. "I don't think so," he concluded, biting his words. "Not judging by recent events."

Kragle knew he was referring to Operation Punitive Strike. The short hair at the base of the General's neck prickled like nails driven into his skull. General Morrison warned him with a look not to rise to the bait. Claude Thornton looked down at his notepad.

A man of action, not of talk, General Kragle scribbled furiously on his pad in order to tune out the discussion and the little senator's high-pitched voice. He knew the meeting would go on like this for hours. Toward the end of the day, perhaps far into the evening, someone would comment that a lot had been accomplished and recommend that they adjourn and re-convene tomorrow at 0600. It was like the movie *Ground Hog Day*, in which the same day kept replaying itself.

The outer door opened and a uniformed aide slipped into the room and whispered to Secretary of Defense Donald Keating, the bespeckled, craggy-faced man who chaired the meeting. Keating's lips tightened. The room fell expectantly quiet.

"Gentlemen," Keating gravely announced, "I've just been informed that an airliner has crashed into the World Trade Center building in New York."

The mood in the conference room tightened like a coiled spring.

"It's unknown yet whether it was an accident or whether . . ." The Defense Secretary left the sentence dangling.

The coiled spring released in an explosion of speculative chatter.

"I've asked that a TV set be brought into the room," the Defense Secretary said over the conversations.

The television arrived and the officials crowded around to watch televised chaos. Both Fox and CNN aired live action of the towering twin structures of the World Trade Center. Smoke and flames enveloped the top floors of the north tower. Panicked and desperate people, among them a man and woman holding hands, were leaping from windows to avoid the even more ghastly fate of being consumed by fire. The talking heads were as stunned as the viewers.

"The facts are still unclear," reported Fox anchor Shepard Smith. "All we know at the moment is that an American Air-lines Boeing 767 has crashed into the 110-story north tower of the World Trade Center in lower Manhattan—"

"There are no commercial flight paths over the Trade Center," Claude Thornton noted. He looked grim.

"No one is going to deliberately fly a jet into a skyscraper," someone else remarked.

"It's called martyrdom," General Kragle said. "Terrorists drove themselves and a boat full of dynamite into the side of the USS *Randolph*."

"But . . . but something like this—it's crazy. It has to be an accident."

Events on the tiny screen continued to unfold like a horror suspense movie made for TV, as if it were *The Day the Earth Stood Still*.

Millions of horrified people around the world watched as a second airliner suddenly appeared. It flew low and straight toward the other tower. It banked slightly, straightened . . . and crashed into it. The force of sixty-five tons carrying 14,000 gallons of high octane fuel drove the plane deep into the building. A fireball blew out the floors. Terrified people were immediately hanging out the windows and leaping to their deaths against the concrete of Manhattan.

"My God in heaven!" Senator Tayloe cried.

Little Nana and Theresa had taken off from Boston's Logan Airport about an hour ago on a United flight bound for L.A. For his own peace of mind, General Kragle stepped into the hallway and cell-phoned his father. The Ambassador was on his way from Boston to Washington in a rental car.

"I just now heard about it on the radio," the Ambassador said. "Your mother should be almost to Chicago by now. How about Brandon? Isn't he flying into New York?"

"Not until Friday."

"What's your take on it, son?"

"This has Osama bin Laden's fingerprints all over it. I tried for eight years to get the previous administration to send out a Delta team to assassinate the sonofabitch. Assassination

wasn't politically correct. Instead, they spent millions more
trying to close down Bill Gates and Microsoft than they did
to stop terrorism. Maybe the new President will listen after
this."

"He's about to make a public statement now," the Ambassador said.

"Call me when you get to Washington, Dad."

The General made another phone call, to MacDill Air
Force Base in Tampa. He ordered USSOCOM to full alert,
then returned to the conference room. He felt nearly as helpless as when he had been a prisoner of war in Vietnam. While
the Special Operations forces of USSOCOM would be
needed later, there was little he could do at the moment except watch the boob tube sketch out a scenario from a Holly-
wood thriller.

No one in the conference room appeared to have spoken or
moved during the few minutes he was gone. All eyes were
glued to the TV screen. A voice-over of the President of the
United States was being broadcast from an undisclosed location. His voice was firm and resolved.

"Today," he said, "our nation saw evil. Thousands of lives
were suddenly ended by evil, despicable acts of terror. We
have been attacked like we haven't been since Pearl Harbor.
Freedom itself has been attacked. I assure you, freedom will
be defended. America has stood down enemies before, and
we shall do so this time. This conflict was begun on the timing and terms of others; it will end in a way and at an hour of
our choosing."

His words seemed to generate energy. The conference
room exploded into a buzz of urgency. In one corner, the
CJCS was on a red phone with the Joint Chiefs. Defense Secretary Keating, his face leaden and his lips compressed, conversed on another line with the Secretary of State. Everyone
else jumped on his cell phone. General Kragle rang secure

lines to the commanders of the army, navy, and air force Special Operations commands, giving them a heads up on possible future actions. He kept an eye tuned to the television screen while he talked, from which he learned that the plane that struck the north tower was an American Airlines flight. The second aircraft was from United.

Again he thought of Little Nana.

Shepard Smith was reporting that at least three aircraft, and perhaps as many as five, were believed to have been hijacked. It occurred to the General that the White House, the Capitol Building, and other government offices would be potential targets of a coordinated terrorist attack.

The answer to the question of where the next strike would occur came more promptly than he expected.

The Pentagon on the Potomac was the most secure building inside the strongest country in the world. At 0840 a hijacked airliner crashed into the west exposure of the five-sided building. General Kragle was knocked sprawling out of his chair. He gingerly picked himself off the floor. Agent Thornton was on his hands and knees, coughing from the shock and from the acrid smoke and haze suddenly smogging the room. The General pulled him to his feet.

"I'm all right, General," Thornton said. "What the hell happened?"

The General threw open the door to a wall of smoke filling a hallway littered with ceiling tiles and other debris. Flames illuminated the far end. His big, booming voice assumed natural authority.

"People, listen to me. Follow my voice. We're getting out of here."

America had received her wake-up call.

CHAPTER 5

NEW YORK (CPI)—In the most horrifying attack ever launched against the United States, terrorists crashed two hijacked airliners into the World Trade Center on Tuesday, bringing down both 110-story twin towers. Millions witnessed the deadly calamity on television as another commandeered airliner slammed into the Pentagon and a fourth crashed in a mining pit outside Pittsburgh. It is speculated the fourth plane was heading for the White House.

The death toll at the WTC could reach as high as 6,000 persons. Over 20,000 people work in the twin towers. More than 100 are believed to have perished when American Airlines Flight 77 crashed into the Pentagon. None of the 266 people aboard the four airliners are believed to have survived.

Passengers aboard the hijacked planes who managed to make cell phone calls described similar circumstances. Four or five Middle Eastern-looking men wearing red headbands and armed with knives stabbed flight attendants, cut throats, threatened passengers, and then took command of the planes. Terrorists apparently took over the flight controls themselves.

American Airlines Flight 11, with 92 people aboard, left Boston's Logan Airport at 6:59 and slammed into the north tower shortly before 8:45 A.M. United Flight 175, carrying 65 passengers, left Logan Airport for Los Angeles at 7:14 and crashed into the south tower at 9:03. American 77, with 65 people, departed Washington's Dulles Airport and crashed into the Pentagon at 9:43. United Flight 93 carried 37 passengers when it plunged into a Pennsylvania field, killing everyone aboard.

Consolidated Press International correspondent Mike Kragle, who would submit his story before any other reporter in America, had been in his office in the north tower when the first air strike occurred. The sound he heard was like a military missile—a high, shrieking sound, a roar, and then an explosion. The shock knocked him to the floor.

Terrified people began evacuating the building. Workers with their clothing ripped and their lungs filled with smoke and dust stumbled down flights of stairs to the streets below. Most of those trapped in the floors above the strike zone perished. Many leaped to their deaths rather than die in the conflagration.

Having reached the street below, Kragle watched the second airliner crash into the south tower. He didn't know at the time that his own mother, seventy-six-year-old Marjorie Ann Kragle, was aboard the flight. Nor would he learn until later that a second relative, General Darren Kragle, his brother, escaped death at the Pentagon when it was struck by the third plane and suffered only minor injuries.

The two towers collapsed into rubble by 10:30 A.M. Ankle-deep gray ash, like dirty snow, filled the streets for blocks around.

Defense Secretary Donald Keating was attending the meeting at the Pentagon to establish a National Homeland Security Agency to combat terrorism when the attacks occurred. He was on the telephone with the Secretary of State when American Flight 77 tore into the western side of the building, sending up a huge cloud of smoke that was visible for miles.

Officials were still fighting the fire Tuesday night and were still not sure of the number of casualties.

Washington, D.C. reacted as if it were under siege, for the first time since the British burned the White House in the War of 1812. The White House was evacuated. Secret Service snipers with automatic rifles sealed off a two-block perimeter. Other federal buildings were evacuated, restaurants shuttered, department stores barred. Washington police carried rifles, and the city took on the silence of a grave.

Officials across the world condemned the attacks, but in parts of Iraq, Iran, Libya, Egypt, Afghanistan, and Pakistan people took to the streets to celebrate. In the West Bank city of Nablus, thousands of Palestinians chanted "God is great!" and handed out candy.

CHAPTER 6

Collierville, Tennessee

The Farm, settled during the French and Indian Wars, had been in the Kragle family for over three hundred years. The original log cabin still sat in the woods out behind the main house, protected from the elements underneath an open barn-like shelter. The core of the main house was over a hundred years old. Add-ons over the generations had doubled its size around the edges, lending it the appearance of an aging ante-bellum dowager with a make-over that never quite covered the wrinkles and liver spots.

Groves of towering pecan and sweetgum gave the Farm the homey flavor that endeared it to the family. Although the past two generations of Kragles rarely used it, there was no chance of it being sold. An elderly couple, the Blakes, occupied the back rooms of the big house and preserved the front half for the occasional Kragle passing through. The Farm was now used primarily for infrequent weekend or vacation retreats, for traditional family weddings, and, as today, for burials in the family plot.

Little Nana's memorial ceremony had been delayed in anticipation of Major Brandon Kragle's arrival. He was the last of the immediate clan still missing. The General's house-keeper, Gloria, had spoken to him twice by cell phone, and was assured that he was on his way by car. Then she called him again just to make sure. She paced among the small crowd of mourners on the front porch, never taking her eyes from the narrow lane to the highway down which the major would surely arrive momentarily.

In fact, Gloria was more than merely the General's house-keeper. She was family. Rita Kragle had died at childbirth with her son Cassidy. Gloria, young then, never married, and fresh off a black Georgia sharecropper's farm, became mother to the three rowdy Kragle boys. It was a full-time occupation, which she embraced with love and warmth. All three boys took to calling the black woman "Mama," a ti-tle that guaranteed more than a few curious glances when-ever they went out in public. Out of deference to the General, Gloria finally encouraged them to call her something else. The boys came up with "Brown Sugar Doll" or "Brown Sugar Mama," although Gloria was far too dark to be called brown.

Presently, a rented Ford appeared. Gloria was the first to recognize the tall man in army dress greens and green beret who got out of the car. She hugged Cameron and Cassidy in her excitement, then sent up a howl of joy that set everyone to grinning as she flew across the yard on her stubby legs to throw her fully two hundred pounds into Brandon's arms.

"Now," she cried through tears of relief, "all my boys be home!"

Brandon swung her in a tight circle that lifted her feet off the grass. "Brown Sugar, you is getting so pretty and so *skinny*."

"Oh, pshaw and dumplings!" She blushed. "You just be saying it 'cause it's true." She felt him all over for broken bones. "Is you sure you is all right? If them Palestines had hurt my boy, why, I don't know what I do—but it be a terrible thing to behold."

Brandon chuckled. "Lucky for them Palestines I'm all right, Sugar Mama. Just a few scratches and shook up a bit. A pretty Jewish girl named Summer patched me up."

"Humpf!" Gloria snorted. "That Summer be winter if she don't take care of my boy. It be just terrible, *terrible*, what be going on with Little Nana and all. I swear the prophecy be near. Jesus done getting ready to come back like He say He would."

She darted a suspicious look at a young man of Arabic appearance coming off the porch with the others to greet Brandon. He was small, almost delicate, with a dark complexion and a narrow face. He wore army greens and the maroon beret and patch of the 82nd Airborne Division. With pointed inference, Gloria blazed. "Them furriners be right here amongst us. They done kilt all them people in New York and Little Nana, and they almost kilt the General and Mr. Thornton at the Pentagon. I don't see why we has to let furriners come here, and I don't see why any of you has to go overseas, Brandon, and let them shoot at you over there."

Brandon hardly blamed Gloria for being wary. Following the terrorist attack, people all over America were cautious of anyone who wore a turban or who might have once worn one. It didn't matter if he was in uniform and wrapped in Old Glory.

Brandon shook hands with his silver-haired grandfather, who looked distinguished, solemn, and inordinately sad all at the same time in a business suit. The General, his father, came in dress greens, as did his younger brothers. Uncle Mike wore a safari jacket and a tie and carried his ever-present old Canon AT-1 camera, which had helped him win a

Pulitzer in Vietnam covering the war for Consolidated Press International. Among the hundred or so relatives and friends, Brandon spotted Claude Thornton, the black FBI agent from Egypt; Colonel Buck Thompson, Delta Force commander; and Sergeant Gloomy Davis, the sniper from Brandon's Troop One. Rather than shake hands, as the others did, Gloomy embraced his tall CO, ignoring the formal line usually drawn between enlisted and officer. Gloomy and Brandon had been through too much together to stand on ceremony. The wiry little Okie's mustache seemed to droop more than ever, and his doleful blue eyes camouflaged, as always, a dry sense of humor.

"The rest of Troop One would have showed up, boss," Gloomy explained, "except they've been hog-tied to Wally World on alert." Wally World was what the troops called the Delta Special Operations Training Facility at Fort Bragg, North Carolina. "Rumor has it," Gloomy went on, glancing at Colonel Thompson, "that the Delta troops are about to get orders putting us right in the middle of the President's war on terror. Is that right, sir?"

Colonel Thompson shook his head noncommittally and deferred to General Kragle, who also declined to answer.

"We didn't think you were going to make it out of Israel," Cassidy said to Brandon. "Who's this Summer?"

"The Ice Maiden." Brandon laughed. "I'll probably never see her again. The problem was, I couldn't get a direct commercial flight out of Jerusalem. The U.S. is diverting all air traffic to Canada or sending it back to where it came from. I finally caught a military hop."

Kathryn clung shyly to Cassidy's arm. She looked decidedly pregnant. The first time Brandon saw her in Afghanistan, she looked like a teenage girl, although drawn and near catatonic from prison, deprivation, and abuse. All bobbed brown hair and big brown frightened eyes. Now she was a woman, with longer hair, high, attractive cheekbones, and full lips. Her pleasing plumpness was more pronounced during this fourth month of her pregnancy. Her baby would be the first of a new Kragle generation.

Brandon smiled at her and would have whipped her into his arms for a hug except that she was pregnant and looked ill. "Congratulations. On the baby, I mean."

"We've seen the ultrasound," she said. "It's a boy. We're naming it after you. After all, if you hadn't come when you did—" She broke off, unable to continue. She was being raped in the prison shack by an al-Qaeda terrorist when Delta Detachment arrived to rescue her and Cassidy.

"Are you all right, honey?" Cassidy asked her now.

"Just miserably pregnant." She sniffed. Her eyes were red and her cheeks had a grayish pallor. "I think I've caught a cold or something. I just became a little dizzy. I'm all right now."

Cameron introduced the stranger from the 82d Airborne. "Brandon—Major Kragle—this is Sergeant Rasem Jameel."

Sergeant Jameel saluted smartly.

"Rasem is converting from Islam to Christianity," Cameron explained. "I'm tutoring him, with God's help. He's my most irreplaceable volunteer at the base chapel."

Even when they were kids, Cameron had always brought home stray people instead of stray dogs and cats.

"I am originally from Saudi Arabia, which is ally of America," Jameel volunteered. He had a thick accent. "I am now American citizen and have been a soldier for three years."

Discussion naturally turned quickly to the upcoming war and how far America's response to the attack should and would go. War fever and a renewed sense of patriotism and excitement infected the Kragles, as it had also swept the nation. In the drive up from Fort Bragg, Brandon was amazed to see American flags flying in front of homes and on the streets of every town through which he passed. Americans were mad and ready to go to war. Each of the Kragle men expected to be involved in some capacity, from Uncle Mike itching to cover another conflict for CPI, to Cassidy eager to graduate from the Special Forces Q Course and go on to Delta.

"The United States has more than two hundred antiterrorism agencies," the General said. "Somewhere in that bureaucracy there had to be prior intelligence on what happened last Tuesday, but it was so caught up in politics and red tape that it couldn't be accessed. After this, I predict a National Homeland Security Agency will be operating within another week. Claude, I don't envy you feebies trying to run down the terrorist network. That raid was well-orchestrated. That's not done without a complex support network."

The black agent looked tired. He had spent long hours day and night since the attack overseeing an FBI evidence squad in the rubble of lower Manhattan.

"I've been asked to work with the Attorney General and a Homeland Security director as soon as one is appointed," he confided. "Gloria is right about one thing—our immigration policy is a shambles. We've literally welcomed terrorists who have set up combat cells within the United States."

"This may have all been prevented if we could have taken out Osama bin Laden at the al-Qaeda camp when we were in Afghanistan," Brandon interjected. "We missed him by one lousy day."

"Bin Laden is only one head in the terrorist hierarchy," Ambassador Jordan Kragle said. It was obvious he spoke from the emotion of having lost his wife to terrorism. "The Taliban in Afghanistan has harbored him since 1989. He'll have to be taken out first. Then we'll move on to others, which I think we will do. I'd be real nervous if I were Gadhafi in Libya or Saddam in Iraq. If the previous President had had the guts *this* President has, we wouldn't be having Marge's funeral today."

Unable to sit on the sidelines, with the war having become personal the instant United 175 plowed into the south tower, the Ambassador had already telephoned the President, volunteering for duty. Considering Jordan's long service in Cairo and his reputation among Muslim states, the President asked him to head a diplomatic commission to build an international coalition of nations to support America's declared war against terrorists. Jordan would be emplaning for Cairo almost immediately after his wife's funeral. Stopping those who had initiated these atrocities was the most loving thing he could think of to do in his dead wife's memory.

The Kragles were a male clan except for Kathryn and Gloria. The women soon interrupted the war talk and moved the entire assemblage toward the family cemetery at the edge of the large meadow behind the log cabin. Cameron led the way, carrying Little Nana's family Bible, his head bowed and his lips moving in prayer. Except for Cameron, who was tall and blond and took after his mother, the Kragle men were all tall and dark-haired.

Gloria wore a long dress as black as her face. She took turns clutching the arms of "her" boys, holding onto them as long as she could, afraid if she let go they would be gone. Tears streamed down her round cheeks. She had been virtually the only female influence in the lives of the General's three sons.

Brandon and his brothers had received little opportunity to become closely bonded with Little Nana. She was always off in the "Russian Steppes" with the Ambassador on some foreign assignment or another. In her later years, because of Alzheimer's, she hardly recognized any of her grandchildren. They showed up at her memorial more out of family respect for the Ambassador and a sense of duty than from any close feeling for the old woman.

In fact, the Kragle brothers had received little opportunity to become closely attached to their own father, since wars and military assignments kept him away from home so much. Gloria was the one who actually raised them, was always there to wipe their noses and get them to bed on time and off to school, and to root for them at football and basketball games.

"Oh, how your daddy love your mama," Gloria always said in explaining the General's frenetic life. "That man worship the very ground Rita walk on. That be why he never get married again. His heart was done pure-dee broke when she die and we come to bury her out at the Farm. He done never got over it. Sometimes I think he drive himself so hard so he don't never have to think about her."

The General was walking ahead with the Ambassador. He kept a hand of support on Kathryn's elbow. Young Cassidy, on the other side, clutched her hand. He resembled a much younger version of the General. Kathryn sniffed and stumbled. Both men reached to catch her.

Some men, Brandon thought, were better with grown sons than with young sons. The General was like that. Certainly, the three boys were at least somewhat closer to him now than they had ever been growing up.

The funeral home had set up an awning inside the growing family plot, underneath which a hole had been dug to bury the urn made of beautiful polished wood. It was unlikely anything of Little Nana was actually inside the urn. New York City had given out the urns for the thousands of persons so far confirmed dead in the World Trade Center tragedy. Each contained dirt from the mass graveyard at the site. Most victims would never be found. They simply vanished in the inferno, leaving behind pictures, belongings, and holes in the lives of their loved ones.

Little Nana—or what was purported to be Little Nana—was being buried next to her son David, with a plot on the other side reserved for Jordan. The next two graves contained Rita and Uncle Mike's Eurasian wife, Brigette, whom he brought back from Vietnam.

Cameron gave the invocation, saying the right words and occasionally reading passages from those underlined in red pencil in Little Nana's Bible. A tear snaked down the Ambassador's weathered cheek, but he stood tall and broadshouldered and otherwise composed between Cassidy and the General as what was purported to be his wife was consigned to the hereafter. The Kragle men handled grief and turmoil with poise and control. It was a family trait.

"It be hard for the Kragles to love," Gloria whispered, weeping quietly between Brandon and Cassidy, "but they do love hard when they love."

Kathryn collapsed while a cousin led the mourners in "Rock of Ages," Little Nana's favorite hymn. She looked red-eyed and puffy-faced. Cassidy walked her back to the main house early.

It occurred to Brandon that Little Nana's memorial services might be the last time they would all be together, considering the rapid unraveling of events that would undoubtedly scatter them all over the globe in harm's way. The war was temporarily on hold, but it was brewing and bubbling, waiting to spill out of the caldron in all its fury.

CHAPTER 7

Rampart Range, Colorado

Sergeant Gloomy Davis opined in his somber, deadpan manner that this was the strangest clusterfuck of would-be horse wranglers he had witnessed in one place since Arachna Phoebe jumped off the Beaver River Bridge back in Hooker, Oklahoma. Full of stories about his cowboy days in Hooker, he paused to provide ample opportunity for someone to ask, "Why, Gloomy, what kind of clusterfuck was it when Arachna Phoebe jumped off the Beaver River Bridge?"

Instead, the seven other soldiers of Major Brandon Kragle's Troop One detachment piled off their horses and collapsed in the high mountain meadow, too bushed to be enticed. A cold, late September wind whistled across the red face of the setting sun, howled around Bison Peak, and flattened the tops of prairie grasses growing autumn golden in the meadow. There was the feel of snow in the air. There would be another hoar of frost by morning if the wind died. The horses and mules snuffled and stamped their feet in anticipation of a freeze overnight.

For the past week the detachment had ridden horses and dragged pack mules around Colorado's rugged Rampart

Range between Pike's Peak to the south and the South Platte River to the west and northwest. Colonel Buck Thompson's orders had been simple but deliberately vague when he called Majors Brandon Kragle, Dare Thompson, and Keith Laub to his office at the Delta compound at Bragg.

"Consider this a premission warning and the beginning of isolation," he said. "Each of you commanders pick the best men out of your troop and designate them as follows: Major Kragle, you will be Detachment 1-Alpha; Dare, you're 2-Alpha. That leaves 3-Alpha for Major Laub. You'll sky up for Fort Carson, Colorado, day after tomorrow at 0400 hours. There, your detachments will be separated for specialized training. You won't be in contact with each other again."

"Sir, if this is a mission, what can we expect?" Laub asked.

"You'll receive a full mission briefing once you return and go into isolation at Fort Carson." He grinned tightly. "Have a good time in the mountains, boys. By the way, instruct your men *not* to shave or get haircuts. I want to see beards when I meet you in Colorado. Good luck."

The only thing the wranglers who provided stock for 1-Alpha were told was that eight men from back East needed to be trained to work with horses and mules in rough, mountainous country. The stock ramuda should consist of the rankest horses and the mules should be of a nasty disposition. The strangers must become cowboys—and become cowboys fast. Slim and Toothless, appropriately labeled, were in turn amused, perplexed, and amazed when the detachment showed up in worn flannel shirts, boots and faded jeans purchased from Goodwill. There was purposefully little about them to indicate the military, except they carried weapons and high-tech communications gear. The wranglers had been told to ask no questions.

The first couple of days had been one continuous rodeo. Ice Man Thompson's bald-faced dun bucked him off six times the first hour and averaged once-an-hour buck-off after that. Thumbs Jones vied for second place in the buck-off category. Mad Dog Carson's mule kicked him with both hind feet squarely in the solar plexus and sent him flying. After catching his breath, and before the mule could bray much more than twice, the Dog clambered up off the ground, growled "Fu-uck!" and kicked the mule in *its* solar plexus. That cemented a mutual respect, if not exactly affection, between the two.

"You are such an *animal*, Mad Dog," Winnie Brown complimented him.

"Fu-uck you very much, Winnie Pooh."

As a week in the mountains drew toward its end, every man of detachment 1-Alpha had learned to ride nearly as well as Gloomy Davis, who claimed he was literally born in a saddle. Ice Man hadn't been tossed off in two days. The detachment was a rugged, hairy-looking bunch. It was evident to the Colorado wranglers that while the easterners might have been novices with horses—all except the moroselooking comic with the droopy mustache—they were no tenderfeet when it came to the outdoors. To a man, they were perfect physical specimens, at home in their environment. Slim and Toothless were consumed with curiosity.

"You fellas ain't city slickers," Toothless fished. "You fellas are good in the woods."

Good in the woods was one of the criteria by which Brandon had selected the detachment's seven enlisted men. All except Mad Dog, Winnie Brown, and the team's top kick and second in command, Master Sergeant Roger "Mother" Norman, had accompanied him into Afghanistan on Operation Punitive Strike.

At forty, Mother Norman was the oldest man on the detachment. His beard was growing gray around the edges of a thick burnt-orange bush that stuck out in all directions like a porcupine's quills. He was short and muscular and in good physical shape, notwithstanding that the biceps of his left arm had been shot away in Iraq during Desert Storm. In order to remain with Delta Force, he had conditioned what was left to be as strong as any other man's good arm.

John "Mad Dog" Carson, the detachment's communications specialist and a sergeant E-6, had replaced Sergeant Rock Taylor, who was killed during the Punitive Strike mission. The Dog, as he was also called, was of medium height but twice medium width, and his long arms hung almost to his knees. He had to walk sideways through some doors because of his shoulders. His massive chest and back were covered with hair as black as his beard and the hair on his head. He was twenty-eight years old and considered the best dih-dah in SpecOps commo.

Sergeant Theodore "Ice Man" Thompson, no kin to Colonel Buck Thompson, was an average-looking man with brown hair and brown eyes. The team's weapons specialist, he had been North Carolina middleweight kick-boxing champion three years in a row. He seldom spoke more than two words an hour.

Skinny, lank-haired Sergeant 1st Class Winfield "Winnie" Brown, the team's intelligence specialist, had attended Harvard for a few semesters and often affected a scholarly speech pattern that made him sound stilted. He knew his business, however. In his thirties, he had transferred into Special Forces and then into Delta from a civil affairs outfit that specialized in prisoner interrogation and enemy force analysis.

Mad Dog jokingly referred to the detachment's black demolitions man, Sergeant Calvin "Thumbs" Jones, as the team's "token." Thumbs was tall and was actually a high yellow and not black at all. He derived his nickname from having blown off half his left thumb in a demo accident. His favorite saying was. "There are few of the world's problems that can't be solved with a few sticks of dynamite."

Sergeant T. B. "Doc TB" Blackburn, the detachment's medic, was a furry bear of a kid not much past twenty. His fledgling beard, though black and thick, clung soft to his broad cheeks. Thumbs, Mad Dog, and Ice Man threw him to the ground—it took all three—and the Dog gave him a mock shave by licking his cheeks.

That morning, Gloomy had dropped a young buck deer with one shot at a range of more than eight hundred meters, drilling it dead through the heart and lungs with the .300 Winchester he called Mr. Blunderbuss. In its protective case, Mr. Blunderbuss was seldom out of the sniper's easy reach. The two Colorado hands marveled at his marksmanship.

"That was something, *really* something," Toothless exhorted, lisping through his missing teeth. He slapped his battered Stetson against his leather chinks. "By jovey, I ain't never seen nobody shoot like that before."

"*Who* are you fellas?" Slim chimed in. "No kidding, *who* are you?"

Mad Dog leered at him. "No kidding, Slim. If we told you, Gloomy'd have to kill you too."

Nightfall was near, and the purple cold dusk of the mountains was settling. Doc Blackburn and Thumbs Jones finally got up off the meadow and began gathering dried firewood from a nearby aspen grove. Ice Man built a fire, while Mad Dog and Major Kragle radioed in a sitrep. Winnie and Mother Norman unstrapped the muley deer carcass from one of the mules, laid it on a poncho, and began butchering it. Gloomy helped the two wranglers feed the stock and hobble them so they could graze in the meadow without wandering off too far. The team worked quickly and efficiently, as they had been trained to do.

Soon, the fire blazed warmth against the night, and the troops had strung their poncho hooches. An owl inquired from the distant timberline and received answer from a pack of coyotes down in the river bottom. The sweet aroma of roasting venison filled the air. After gorging themselves on fresh meat, Slim and Toothless withdrew to their bedrolls. Horses moved around just outside the firelight, grazing. Mad Dog watched them.

"We got all this high-speed shit like satellites, desert FAVs that can climb like goats on four wheels, and airplanes that fly and bomb without pilots," he said, drowsy from a full belly and the warmth of the fire. "So what're we doing? Riding horses like the fucking cavalry. Major, are we about to have an Apache uprising or something?"

Gloomy poked the fire with a stick, feeling contented and at home. "You missed Punitive Strike," he said. "Mujahideen in Afghanistan ride horses."

TERRORISTS OPERATE WORLDWIDE WEB

WASHINGTON (CPI)—According to Claude Thornton, head of the FBI's National Domestic Preparedness Office, the FBI has identified most of the nineteen hijackers who commandeered and crashed four airliners on September 11. Thornton also said that authorities in the United States, Germany, France, England, and Egypt have arrested 150 terrorist suspects linked to the al-Qaeda network run by Osama bin Laden, a fugitive Saudi Arabian multimillionaire.

Bin Laden first came to prominence fighting with Afghan "holy warriors" against Soviet troops in the 1980s. Since then he has declared a

jihad, or holy war, against the United States and
has built a complex terrorist organization with
tentacles that reportedly reach into sixteen
countries around the world, including the United
States. He is believed to be behind a number of
terrorist actions against U.S. interests, including
the bombing of the USS *Randolph* last year and
the destruction of U.S. embassies in Africa.

Bin Laden is currently known to be headquartered in Afghanistan, whose ruling Taliban government protects him. Taliban spiritual leader
Mullah Mohammed Omar said Afghanistan would
react with force if the United States attempts another armed invasion. He was referring to a U.S.
Army Delta Force detachment raid on an al-
Qaeda camp last year to rescue two American
hostages taken when the USS *Randolph* was
bombed in the port of Aden. Seventeen American
sailors were killed in that bombing and three
were taken hostage, one of whom was subse-
quently executed before he could be rescued.

FBI agents are tracking the dead hijackers'
bank accounts, communications, and travel tick-
ets which connect hotels, rental cars, and airplane trips to plotters in Europe, the Middle East,
and the United States. Mohammed Atta, a Saudi
on the first plane to crash into the World Trade
Center, is believed to have trained in Afghan
camps run by bin Laden's inner circle.

Also linked to these camps are Marwon al-
Shahhi and Hanza Alghambi, who were among
five terrorists who commandeered United Airlines Flight 175 that flew into the south tower of
the Trade Center less than a half hour later.

Several of the hijackers were trained as pilots in the United States. Others claimed in their visa applications to be pilots, airplane mechanics, students, or tourists. Many claimed to work for Saudi Arabian Airlines, a government air carrier. Some of the men left little trace of their time in America. Others have been here for years. They blended into the everyday life of America as "sleepers," biding their time until they received orders to strike.

A manual called *Military Studies in the Jihad Against the Tyrants*, recovered during an investigation of Osama bin Laden, instructs anyone willing to "undergo martyrdom" to "act, pretend, and mask himself behind enemy lines," to smile at taxicab drivers and "crave death." Foreshadowing the actions of the 9/11 hijackers, it gives precise instructions on how to use weapons with blades, such as striking at lethal spots in the ribcage, in an eye, on the back of the head, and at the end of the spinal column.

The manual includes a passage at the end promising salvation to those who die "for the sake of Allah." It concludes: "Utter your prayer seconds before you go to your target. Let your last word be, 'There is no God but God and Mohammed is His messenger.' Then, *inshallah*, you will be in heaven."

The President of the United States ordered a freeze Monday on the assets of twenty-seven organizations with suspected links to terrorism, including those controlled or under the influence of Osama bin Laden. He is also considering military options.

Former President John Stanton cautioned the
President to be careful in considering retaliation.
"The President is talking about a war on terror-
ism," he said in a speech delivered at Harvard.
"No country has ever taken on terrorists and
won."

CHAPTER 8

Fort Carson, Colorado

Looking weather-beaten and rugged in jeans, soiled chambray, or flannel shirts, some of them wearing ball caps or Stetsons, the bearded men of Major Brandon Kragle's Detachment 1-Alpha drew curious stares from the two MPs stationed at the gate of the high-wire fence that enclosed the premission isolation facility at Fort Carson, new home of the 10th Special Forces Group.

"You boys must be some bad mojos to be caged up like this," one of the MPs smirked.

Mad Dog sprang at him with a savage growl. The startled MP jumped back. The team laughed and filed into the building. The MPs hurriedly closed the gates and locked them.

Delta Force's deputy commander, Lieutenant Colonel Doug "No Sleep" Callahan, was waiting inside.

"Looks like we intend to be here awhile," Thumbs Jones commented, looking around at the first floor, which was filled with weight-lifting equipment, a sparring ring and other workout gear. There was a movie screen and a large-screen TV at the end of the open room. A locked door led into a classroom.

"It's far preferable to sleeping on the ground," Winnie Brown said.

"Nah!" Mad Dog scoffed. "It takes practice to be real miserable."

"At ease, lads!" Brandon interrupted.

"Thanks, Major." Colonel Callahan was there to settle the team in prior to the mission briefing. He indicated a stairwell. "Your living quarters are on the top floor. Major Kragle and Sergeant Norman will occupy the two individual cadre rooms. The rest of you dirtbags will have to sleep in the open bay. The rule is—one man to a bunk."

"Do sheep count, sir?" Thumbs Jones inquired innocently.

"You're all *animals*," Winnie Brown cried in a falsetto voice, pretending offense.

"Hoo-ya!" Mad Dog agreed.

Delta troops were high-speed, hard-drive people. They worked hard, played hard, and either way had a lot of energy to work off.

"A plan of the day is posted on the bulletin board," Colonel No Sleep said. "The routine goes something like this: Reveille at 0400, followed by an hour of PT, breakfast, the rest of the morning in the classroom with area studies and target folders, midday meal, firing range in the afternoon or small unit drills and demolitions, evening meal, followed by commander's time."

"Sir, what's our destination?" Winnie Brown asked.

"You're the intel sergeant."

"My supposition is Afghanistan or Iran."

The colonel smiled. "I suggest you all go upstairs, shower and clean up. You stink like the horses' asses you've been associating with for the past week or so. There are toilet articles and fresh BDU uniforms on each bunk. No razors, though. Let those beards grow. Colonel Buck and General Kragle will arrive for your mission briefing at 1100 hours."

"I could sure use a piece of ass," Thumbs rumbled as the team dispersed to the top floor.

"Ask Gloomy to find you a good-looking sheep," Mad Dog suggested.

After a shower, Brandon felt clean and refreshed in desert loam-and-sand BDUs, if not exactly clean-shaven. He quickly went through mail Colonel No Sleep was thoughtful enough to have brought out from Bragg when he came. One plain envelope with no return address was postmarked "Israel." Puzzled, he opened it. A pair of military dog tags on a chain fell into his hand. The accompanying note was brief and in a fine, legible script.

Major Kragle—

You left these on the table when we were examining you for further injuries. 9/11 was a shock around the world. I have spoken with Major Dov Landau's widow. You were the last one to see him alive in Beit Jalla. She was touched by your graciousness in writing her. So was I.

                                        Summer

No last name. No return address. She had a nice ass, and green eyes that reminded him of Gypsy Iryani. Her hands were gentle when she helped him remove his shirt in the basement of the rectory to patch up minor shrapnel and burn wounds and check for broken bones. Troops carried Major Landau's body down from the loft, along with the mangled corpses of the two Israeli machine gunners.

"You were the only survivor," Summer had said. "You must have extraordinary karma."

Brandon grimaced as she'd applied antiseptic to a cut on

his chest. "Maybe it helps to have a brother who's a chaplain," he replied.

He wanted her to keep touching him.

"If you do this kind of thing often," she said, looking at him with those incredible eyes that thrilled and saddened him simultaneously, "you're going to need all the pull you can get with the Big Guy."

She smiled. It softened the strong, stern lines of her face in a way that attracted him from somewhere deep inside, like from an old memory. He hoped it wasn't Gypsy's. She stepped outside for something—and never came back. He left Israel without seeing her again.

Brandon exchanged a few words with his father before the mission briefing began. The General filled him in on events with the rest of the family. The Ambassador was en route to Turkmenistan and Tajikistan via Russia, to forge a strong alliance around Afghanistan and to arrange for military strike bases along the border. Uncle Mike went to Washington, D.C., to write CPI pieces on the political aspects of 9/11 and the President's War on Terror. Cassidy had almost completed the final phase of the Q course to qualify for his Special Forces tab, after which he would put in for Delta.

"Kathryn can't seem to shake the flu," the General said. "The doctor says he's never seen such a persistent strain of influenza. Cameron requested assignment to an active mission. I asked Buck to turn him down. A chaplain doesn't belong on the front lines in SpecOps."

Brandon concurred.

The General paused. "Son . . . ?" Concern furrowed his brow. Of his three sons, Brandon was most like him in his dedication to mission and love of the army. "The President has issued a finding, as I knew he would, and is about to authorize a covert mission. Three of them, in fact, initially."

"I understand, sir. We're going back to Afghanistan."

"Yours is the only troop with on-ground experience."

"Sir, I would have it no other way. Don't worry, I can handle it. We'll be all right."

The General nodded. He shook hands with his son. "Major Kragle, prepare your men for mission briefing."

Brandon returned a crisp salute. "Yes, sir!"

The classroom came equipped with eight desks, a podium, chalkboard, view screen, a large world globe, and maps and photos on the wall covered with flannel drop cloths. A bound volume entitled *Afghanistan: An Area Study*, along with a target folder marked *Operation Iron Weed*, SECRET, lay on each desk. With the General and Colonel Thompson were young, brainy-type captains and lieutenants from the G shops of Ops, Intelligence, Supply, Commo, and Medical, who got up in turn with laser pointers to present their portions of the briefing. No one in the detachment expressed surprise at 1-Alpha's objective destination. Winnie Brown had predicted Afghanistan all along.

Colonel Buck got up. "It is expected," he said, "that the United States will use all forces at its disposal to rid Afghanistan of the corrupt Taliban government and Osama bin Laden's al-Qaeda terrorist network. Special Forces will target on various elements of the Taliban and al-Qaeda. Operation Iron Weed is Delta Force's share of Operation Enduring Freedom, America's overall War on Terror. Detachment 1-Alpha—your detachment, Major Kragle—has been dedicated to the capture or neutralization of Osama bin Laden."

A hush filled the room and lasted for several minutes. Then, to a man, the detachment stood up and cheered.

"When do we insert?" Team Sergeant Norman asked.

Colonel Buck looked to the General for guidance. General Kragle nodded to go ahead.

"That depends," Buck Thompson resumed. "The President has not yet announced the day and hour of our reprisal. Special Forces in general and Delta in particular are selected and trained to be flexible, mobile, and deadly efficient. At the appropriate time, Iron Weed will be activated and flown to a strike base near the Afghan border. The detachment will be linked with assets who speak the language and know the country. You will be inserted into a preselected AO to work with mujahideen of the anti-Taliban Northern Alliance. You will maintain commo and receive support from an SFOB headquartered within the theater."

"So that's the purpose of the horses and mules?" Gloomy Davis asked.

Thompson smiled. "In the Hindu Kush horseback has proven to be the fastest mode of transportation. You will need to move through and behind enemy lines as well as with advancing forces. You will blend in with the native populations—thus the need for beards—and take to Osama bin Laden's trail."

He paused and stepped back from the podium in deference to the General.

"You will follow bin Laden's trail wherever it goes, with the support of intel from SFOB and other sources," General Kragle began. "Since, technically, deliberately targeting the bastard is a political assassination and against U.S. law, your mission calls for capturing him if possible in order to bring him to trial. However, in the words of the President of the United States, bin Laden is a wanted criminal, gentlemen, and he is wanted *dead or alive*. Ordering you to kill him is, again technically, an illegal order which I cannot issue and you cannot obey. However, the best thing that can happen is that he die in combat."

The team understood. Gloomy Davis absently stroked the case that contained his deadly Mr. Blunderbuss.

Colonel Buck took over again. "In the meantime, until H-hour is announced, each of you will be expected to memorize the Afghan area study and maps and every other aspect of Osama bin Laden contained in your target folders. The 'Shake' is how he is coded and will be referred to from now on. Consider him a dead man walking. I want you to know how he thinks and feels, how he walks and talks, who his closest associates area, the names of his brothers and sister, sons and daughters, and the last whore he slept with. I want you to know everything about the man, including what it smells like when he farts. That kind of knowledge is how we're going to catch him."

Major Brandon Kragle looked around with pride at the determined, confident expressions on the hairy faces of his men. These were tough, intelligent soldiers who would literally go anywhere, anytime, to do any damned thing. Exactly as Colonel Charlie Beckwith and then–Major Darren E. Kragle had intended when they founded the elite counterterrorist force.

The General had the last word.

"It's an extremely hazardous assignment," he acknowledged, looking directly at his son. "It's a whole lot like a snail crawling across the edge of a razor blade. He can make it okay as long as he doesn't make a mistake and slip."

STRIKES LAUNCH 'ENDURING FREEDOM'

KHANABAD, UZBEKISTAN (CPI)—Land-based U.S. air bombers struck at least three Afghan cities Sunday night in the opening salvo of Operation Enduring Freedom against international terrorism. Fifteen bombers, including B-2 Stealths and 25 other strike aircraft flying from U.S. aircraft carriers, began the attack after nightfall. American and British ships and submarines also launched more than 50 Tomahawk cruise missiles from positions in the Arabian Sea.

The strikes began in Kabul. Electricity went off in the city for more than two hours. Second waves of bombers targeted Taliban military headquarters and the home of Taliban leader Mullah Mohammed Omar in the southern city of Kandahar. Explosions destroyed radar facilities and the control tower at the Kandahar airport. Also targeted were hundreds of housing units built for members of Osama bin Laden's al-Qaeda terror movement. Other loud detonations erupted near Farmada, a bin Laden training camp about twelve miles south of Jalalabad.

The United States has amassed a military force of nearly 30,000 troops, more than 300 warplanes, and two dozen warships in the region surrounding Afghanistan and Iraq. In an unprecedented move, Pakistan granted the U.S. permission to overfly its territory. The former Soviet republic of Uzbekistan also provided an airfield for U.S. use near Afghanistan's northern border. Troops from the U.S. 10th Mountain Division have already been deployed to this forward position.

About an hour after the U.S. strikes, Northern Alliance forces in control of Bagram Air Base fired rockets at Taliban forces that occupy the mountains surrounding Kabul. The Northern Alliance controls roughly five percent of Afghanistan and has been fighting the Taliban for years.

The Taliban has ruled almost all of this impov-

erished nation since 1996, imposing upon the
Muslim population its own strict version of Islamic law. Women are banned from working and
must cover their faces and bodies in public. Men
and women are not allowed to mix. Girls attend
school only until they are eight years old. Men
have to wear beards and pray in the mosques.
Most forms of entertainment, ranging from music and movies to even the flying of kites, have
been banned. Possession of a Christian Bible can
lead to the death penalty.

In a rare interview with Consolidated Press International, Taliban leader Mullah Omar declared Afghan Muslims would fight to the death.
"With the grace of God, the American rockets
will go astray and we will be saved. We shall be
victorious."

A veteran of the Soviet war with Afghanistan,
Lt. General Ruslan Aushev, warned that America
was undertaking a war it cannot win.

"You can occupy it," he said, "you can put
troops there and keep bombing, but you cannot
win."

The last Soviet soldier left the country in
1989, ending a ten-year occupation that resulted
in 15,000 Soviet casualties. Between 1830 and
1920 the British Empire fought three major wars
in Afghanistan. It suffered heavy losses and brutal massacres at the hands of highly independent
tribesmen. Several thousand British and Indian
soldiers, women and children, and thousands of
camp followers were slaughtered by Afghan fighters in 1842 as they attempted to retreat through
deep mountain passes.

The U.S. military must deal with the same nightmare geography that defeated previous invaders: high mountain passes, deep ravines, cliffs honey-combed with caves, bitter cold, and tough guerrilla fighters who know the terrain. Military analysts therefore believe Special Operations commandos, not large ground forces, will be deployed to capture or kill plotters of the terror attacks against America.

U.S. Special Operations Command is based at MacDill Air Force Base in Tampa, Florida. Approximately 29,000 troops serve on active duty, and another 14,000 are in the reserves. They are trained in a wide array of missions, including psychological warfare, sabotage and kidnapping, small-scale strikes on strategic targets, reconnaissance, fighting terrorists, and training and equipping indigenous forces in foreign lands.

Special Operations is composed of: Army Special Forces, commonly known as the "Green Berets," of whom there are 5,000 in five active duty groups. The 5th Group has been specifically trained for operations in the Middle East;

Navy SEALs. Approximately 2,200 SEALs operate out of bases in Coronado, California, and Little Creek, Virginia;

Army Rangers. The 75th Ranger Regiment has about 2,000 soldiers in three battalions;

Marine Force Recon. A small unit indigent to the U.S. Marines skilled in short- and long-range reconnaissance;

Delta Force. A supersecret counterterrorist unit based out of Fort Bragg, North Carolina, it functions in small, mobile groups and is highly trained in reconnaissance, hostage rescue, and counterterrorist operations.

Also included in SpecOps are Army Long Range Reconnaissance (LRRP) units; the 16th SOAR (Special Operations Aviation Regiment); Air Force support units; psychological warfare units; and various others.

USSOCOM has already received its deployment orders. Covert operations are under way.

"If you're going after rats," said General Darren E. Kragle, USSOCOM's commander, "you have to be willing to go into the sewers."

CHAPTER 9

Fort Bragg, North Carolina

Chaplain Cameron Kragle stood at the window of the plain white World War II–era building he had converted into a chapel on Smoke Bomb Hill. Cold rain fell straight down so hard in leaden sheets that it drummed on the roof and almost drowned out the grind-and-pound of the ancient offset printing press Sergeant Rasem Jameel was operating in the other room. Through the rainfall Cameron could barely make out the giant figure of the Iron Mike Special Forces statue downhill among the giant pines near the headquarters of the U.S. Army Special Operations building. Colonel Buck Thompson had offered him a building for a church inside the Wally World compound, but Cameron turned him down. He thought it best to open his ministry to the other Special Forces and airborne types at Bragg. Besides, his congregation of Delta Force troopers was so small it might well fit into a large closet. Young, tough SpecOps warriors seemed to fear nothing, not even God.

He was hardly aware that the printer quit running until he heard Rasem in the chapel with him. He knew by the sounds that the Saudi immigrant-turned–U.S. soldier was straightening the rows of chairs that served as pews, arranging the pulpit and preparing communion service for Sunday's worship. Rasem was his most loyal convert and follower, next to Kathryn, who attended church faithfully since her marriage to brother Cassidy nearly a year ago.

Even pregnant, Kathryn made herself available to help Rasem and him with the bulletins and appointments and other chores required in running an army chapel with only a volunteer staff. She hadn't shown up this afternoon, however, to assist with getting out the nationwide armed forces mail ministry the chapel shared with televangelist Brother Billy Dye. Cameron blamed it on the weather.

He also blamed the weather for the feeling of melancholy that seemed to hold him captive. Shadows from rainwater on the windowpane crawled across his squared Kragle face as they crawled deep within his soul. Like worms of doubt. He lowered his handsome head with its short-cropped blond hair and muttered a prayer. Then he looked up again, out at the rain, and the worms still crawled.

Cameron had wrestled periodically with the doubts in his faith ever since he was a kid and Gloria led him and his brothers by their hands to their first Sunday school classes. Over the years, he had vacillated from unquestioning faith in God to agonizing indecision about mankind and man's place in the universe. His doubts produced guilt. Guilt brought on bouts of melancholy.

This had been his worst year. Not quite a year ago, Gypsy was killed in Afghanistan, and nothing could have prevented it. Not Brandon, not himself, not God. He and Gypsy would have been married by now. Even though she loved Brandon as much as she loved him, she would still have married him because he knew she could not stand to hurt him. Brandon was tougher; he could take the hurt.

Cameron saw Gypsy's face floating in the rain when he

was in these moods. He shook his head to clear his mind. He closed his eyes in another prayer, but when he opened them again she was still there.

Why couldn't he be more like his brother Brandon? he asked himself. Brandon with his direct-action mentality, with his unswerving Kragle moral code of right and wrong, with his ability to live life without questioning what it was all about. No wonder Gypsy Iryani had loved Brandon too.

He knew it had to be more than the rain and memories of Gypsy that brought on the rainy day mood so completely. It was also Little Nana's death and the collective deaths of thousands at the World Trade Center, the Pentagon, and in the final airliner crash in Pennsylvania. It was the War on Terror, which had just started with air strikes against Afghanistan. Brandon was already involved, away now on a mission so secret that even the General wouldn't talk about it.

Rasem came and stood silently with him, looking out the window. After a while he said, "I have completed the printing, Chaplain Cameron."

"Huh? Oh, thanks, Rasem."

Rasem was silent for another moment. "In Islam," he said, "each human person has a direct relationship with God and there suffices no need for an intermediary. You have such a relationship with our God. I see it. Muslims pray five times a day, but you pray more often. Does God ever answer?"

Rasem expected an answer.

"God is the greatest of all mysteries and, at the same time, the greatest of all realities," Cameron said, and for him it was true. God was his staff and his bread. "God is the infinite mystery behind all reality—and the absolute reality behind all mystery. Neither the phenomenal universe nor the invisible universe can satisfactorily explain God. Before all other being began, God already was. He eternally *is*. This human race and the anthill in which we exist are surrounded by mysteries deep and vast, awesome and haunting, impenetrable and elusive. The biggest mystery is that inexplicable supermystery that is and always will be—God. Yes, Rasem. God answers if you will listen."

Then, knowing this, he wondered why he still had doubts. How could he ever doubt God? Everything that occurred in anyone's life was a part of His plan.

The telephone rang loudly. The church was small, consisting only of the sanctuary and a small office off the raised stage of the pulpit.

"I will answer it," Rasem offered.

Cameron turned from the window. His eyes passed across the dark royal-purple curtains against which a huge Christian cross blazed in gold. Not real gold. A slogan above the cross—GOD IS GOD IN ALL LANGUAGES—reminded him of his hope to reach out with God's help to meet the spiritual needs of all soldiers, regardless of their faiths.

Rasem stepped to the office door. "It is Mrs. Kathryn," he said.

"Cameron," she said when he took the phone. Her voice sounded thick and pained. "I'm sorry I couldn't help with the mailings today—" She broke into a fit of coughing. Her voice hoarsened. "Cameron, I don't feel well at all. I've gotten real sick. I didn't want to bother Cass—"

"I'll be right over."

He hung up the phone, concern for his sister-in-law replacing other thoughts of the celestial.

"She's ill," he told Rasem.

Rasem looked stricken. He was quite fond of her. "I will take care of matters here, Chaplain. I will stuff the envelopes and take the mail to the post office."

"Pray for Kathryn," Cameron said as he jerked on his army slicker and ducked out the door into the rain.

CHAPTER 10

Camp MacKall, North Carolina

The rattletrap Ford truck stacked with crates of live chickens eased to a stop, brakes rubbing, on the rural North Carolina road. An elderly man wearing faded farmer overalls and a battered straw hat got out of the truck. He looked up and down the muddy road, squinting into the sun at the moment it dropped out of the lowering rain clouds and below the horizon. Purple shadow immediately crept across the soaked landscape.

Satisfied, he walked to the edge of the road and picked up a stone from a pyramid of three arranged next to the bar ditch. He tossed it into forest that bordered the road. It knocked showers of water from the trees.

Almost immediately, six wet, scroungy-looking young men responded to the signal and scrambled down out of the sand hill pines. They wore military BDUs mixed and unmatched with various items of civilian apparel. All were armed with M-16 rifles. Two carried rucks on their backs filled with "explosives."

The farmer shook hands with one of the men, "Cool Hand

Luke," and led them all to the back of the truck. "Hurry. Get in."

Sergeant Cassidy Kragle exchanged looks with Sergeant Bobby Goose Pony, his half-Arapaho buddy from New Mexico. He looked at the truck. "All right. Get in *where*?"

The farmer grinned, obviously enjoying himself. He removed the truck's end gate to reveal a space underneath the chicken crates and concealed by the sides of the truck.

"Get in, quick," he urged. "They patrol the roads."

"They" in this instance were the "Pineland enemy." The farmer was a local resident who with others in the vast rural area of North Carolina's sand hills to the north and west of Fort Bragg and Camp MacKall formed a loose association known as the "Pineland Auxiliary." Civilians really got into the Robin Sage exercises the final weeks of phase three, Special Forces Qualification Course. Some of them sided with the "Pineland enemy" while others, like the farmer, sympathized with the bands of "resistance fighters" struggling to overcome an oppressive government. Cassidy and Goose Pony were members of SFQC, Class 7-01, under final testing to win their SF tabs. The other four fighters were "guerrillas" commandeered for their roles from the 82nd Airborne Division. There was so much spying, treachery, and deceit going on during Robin Sage that it was sometimes hard to tell the good guys from the bad.

"I know this fella. Get in," urged Cool·Hand Luke, speaking in the contrived pidgin English of the guerrillas. "Him with us."

"And the chickens?" cracked Goose Pony.

"Them with us too."

The truck reeked of wet feathers and chicken shit. Cassidy shrugged. What the hell. He had already gone through more shit than this in order to get this far toward winning the green beret. He was over six feet tall but lanky enough that he twisted himself like a pretzel around the shorter, stockier Arapaho as the resistance fighters crowded into the truck bed beneath the poultry. The farmer literally squashed them into the space with the end gate.

Chicken shit plopped down on them like large intermittent raindrops. The odor mixed with gas fumes as the old truck geared up and rumbled down the road was nauseating. Cassidy thought he heard the old man laughing at the wheel.

"Maybe I'll change my name to Bobby Goose Chickens," Goose Pony complained.

Goose Pony and Cassidy had been buddies since SFAS. Pony, at thirty, was a little older than most SF candidates. Like Cassidy's brothers Brandon and Cameron, he was a Desert Storm veteran, having fought in the Iraqi War with the armored divisions. Cassidy's own combat experiences in Afghanistan after his brothers rescued Kathryn and him from the terrorists provided a basis of friendship between the two veterans despite their age difference.

"Everybody calls me Goose Pony," he had introduced himself on the first day of SFAS—Special Forces Assessment and Selection. "It would have been Bobby Goose Three Pony, but the white man came and took the ponies." He pondered Cassidy's name. "Kragle? Isn't that the USSOCOM's name, the big boss in the sky? Any kin?"

"None," Cassidy lied, although Pony would later discover the truth.

It was bad enough that some of the training cadre knew General Kragle was his father and that he had to work twice as hard as any of the other candidates in order to overcome his name. Cassidy wouldn't have it said that he earned his tab and made it to Delta because of his old man. Not that the General would show him any partiality in the first place.

"Too bad," Pony said. "I could use some pull. I want to go to Delta."

That mutual ambition strengthened the bonds between them. Both were also 18 Charlies, the engineering MOS specialty, which meant they had also attended phase two together. Now, nearly a year after they first met, they were still together and stuck in the back of a rattletrap truck underneath a flock of caged chickens none too particular about their toilet habits.

Worse yet, it began to rain again, a slow, cold drizzle. It got dark fast with the cloud cover and the disappearance of the sun.

A road checkpoint stopped the truck. The insurgents held their breath collectively as the old farmer cut the engine and two Pineland OpFors, also played by 82nd paratroops, questioned him. They walked around to the back of the truck.

"Whatcha got in there?" one of the OpFors asked.

"Can'tcha smell 'em?" the farmer asked.

The OpFor were suspicious. They rattled the cages and peered down through them into the darkness of the truck bed.

"Harold, go get a flashlight."

Cassidy fingered the trigger of his M-16. A couple of shots—blanks, of course—would put these guys out of commission. On the downside, it would alert other OpFor that the insurgents were up to something.

Suddenly, the clouds opened, as if on cue. Rain drummed hard on the truck cab, pounded the muddy road, and reminded the OpFor of the poncho hooch shelters they had erected next to the road barricade.

"Forget the flashlight," the first enemy said. "Not even the green beanies would ride in that shit. You can go," he said to the farmer.

The truck moved on. Water turned filthy and disgusting

with manure sloshed in the truck bed around the passengers.

"The shit you get me into," Goose Pony muttered to Cassidy.

No one ever claimed earning the coveted green beret was easy or pleasant. Like Barry Sadler sang in "Ballad of the Green Beret"

> *Silver wings upon their chests,*
> *these are men, America's best;*
> *One hundred men will test today.*
> *But only three win the green beret . . .*

Of the 236 students who started Class 6-01, only seventy-eight successfully finished. Cassidy's 7-01 was nearing that attrition rate. He wouldn't fail, however, not even if he had to drag himself across the finish line with one leg gone. Kragles never quit. The General always said winning was in the Kragle genetic pool.

Cassidy had had a tough year, especially for a young man newly wed. The Afghanistan experience made him want to join his brothers at Delta. To get there, he got out of the navy and immediately reenlisted in the army. There was Army boot camp, and then on to airborne training at Fort Benning, followed by selection for Special Forces. The Navy Cross awarded him as a result of Afghanistan had helped in the selection process.

Brandon and Cameron gave him a heads-up on what to expect. Both had passed the Q course at the tops of their respective classes.

"Teaching you to think and act and fight and lead and *survive* while doing it, that's what the course is all about," Brandon counseled. "We're the most useful, resourceful, and dangerous group of warriors on the planet—but we are not aggressive and confrontational like the SEALs. We are agile and flexible. Agile men are seen as rebels, mavericks, misfits, not 'Big Green Machine' garrison material. We're the quiet professionals that Mother Army doesn't want to know about unless there's a war. Lock us out of sight during peacetime— but we'll be the first called when the balloon goes up. Most of all, we're survivors who'll still be standing and fighting back after insanely tough or deadly encounters."

Obstacle courses, grueling runs, pounding rucksack marches, land navigation and fieldcraft, "situation and reaction" problems . . . sleep deprivation, limited rations, and unbelievable physical exertion . . . Nearly a third of the recruits washed out during SFAS, even before phase one. Only those worth the money and effort were sent forward.

Phase one taught the survivors how to plan, conduct, and lead squad-size patrols and to accurately navigate cross-country in a combat environment.

Phase two for Cassidy and Goose Pony consisted of engineering and demolitions school at Bragg. Other students went on to become medics, commo specialists, weapons experts, ops and intelligence specialists.

Phase three took up the Special Forces core mission—unconventional warfare in all its various aspects.

Kathryn and Cassidy joked about how her getting pregnant must have been by divine intervention since they had spent so little time together.

"We're gonna make it, Kragle," Goose Pony finally decided. "We're on our way downrange."

"Did you have doubts, Pony?"

They had less than two weeks left to completion. The day Cassidy took off for Little Nana's funeral at the Farm had not been counted against him. He was still in line for honor grad. He could endure the rain and the misery and the chicken shit sloshing underneath his nose for that length of time. His rite of passage was almost over.

The farmer slowed the truck when he approached the target, a bridge that had to be "blown" in order to cut off the Pineland enemy when the guerrilla elements linked up with invasion forces in another few days. He stopped the truck long enough to let the resistance fighters out of the bed. It was still raining hard. Full night had fallen. The truck rumbled on across the concrete bridge, its lights quickly disappearing.

The guerrillas set up security on both ends of the target while Cassidy and Goose Pony rigged explosives on the bridge's structure and supports. They passed fuse lengths up to the bridge surface and paid it out down the road to trees at the near end. Cassidy attached the end of the fuse to a hell box and prepared the electrical charge. Far side security folded back to rejoin the band.

"Vehicle coming!" a guerrilla warned.

Headlights were coming down the road through the black rain. Cassidy gave them one glance and then set off the charge. Blinding flashes and sharp explosions split the night as grenade simulators detonated underneath the bridge, doing no damage to the structure but making a big bang.

"Pull out!" Cassidy shouted. "Mission accomplished."

The band of insurgents dashed uphill through the pines and dived for cover and concealment as the vehicle arrived. A sergeant got out of the HUMMV and stood in his own headlights so his white referee's armband could be seen.

"Kragle!" he called out. "Get down here. Front and center."

Another soldier got out and also stood in the light, a tall man wearing a slicker. He pulled back his hood to reveal his face and blond crew cut. Cassidy recognized Cameron. Chaplains never came to the field except to deliver bad news.

CHAPTER 11

Afghanistan

A dozen strong, the armed band climbed in the coming dawn, breathing hard from exertion. The trail continued to rise steeply toward the top of a barren ridge, visible only as a craggy knife's edge against the lightening sky. An overnight dusting of snow swirled furiously in a bitter wind originating from somewhere in the Arctic regions of Russian Siberia. Except for thin pockets of accumulated snow, the country this high was predominately brown and rocky, with scrubby evergreens in the canyons and, it was said, demons in the elevations.

Major Brandon Kragle's eight-man Iron Weed detachment wore traditional Afghan garb, like the four mujahideen who met them on the drop zone—loose goat hair pantaloons, long sweeping robes, turbans, and heavy quilted or sheepskin coats. It had all been provided by the welcoming party. The clothing, plus the beards cultivated during mission training, merged the Americans as seamlessly into the terrain as any of the nomads, farmers, and tribal shepherds who dwelt in these mountains and valleys.

An observer would have had to get close to see the

weapons and heavy combat rucks, and even closer to find that the strangers' knowledge of Pushtu or Dari went little beyond asking which way was north and requesting food. Even then, the observer might not have been overly suspicious. These mountains were full of hostile tribesmen waging war on each other. An observer was wise to keep his distance.

Not two hours previously, a C-130 Hercules painted flat black flew low over the mountains in the deeper darkness before dawn. It disgorged from its rumbling belly a single stick of paratroopers so hastily that all eight parachutes blossomed almost simultaneously. The jumpers landed together in a small alpine clearing designated during mission planning as LZ Fire Ant. It was always an unspoken fear among men who do such things in dangerous foreign lands for a living that they would be deposited in the wrong place or that their contacts and assets would not show up.

Neither eventuality occurred. Four armed Afghans appeared almost immediately. Brandon folded up the detachment into a defensive perimeter, weapons ready. Two of the mujahideen waited in the rocks as lookouts while two approached. One was quite small in silhouette, appearing in the darkness to be no more than a boy. He carried a carbine, a CAR-15.

"Where has my bird gone?" he asked, reciting the recognition question.

Brandon gave the correct response: "He has gone to his cage."

"Good. I'm your interpreter. Call me Ismael."

Brandon couldn't help himself. "Ismael? I suppose this is Captain Ahab?" he said, indicating the second Afghan.

"This is Hafiz Saeed," Ismael said patiently. He spoke perfect American English without an accent. "He's a Zarbati, the elite of the Northern Alliance forces, and a member of the Jijak tribe."

The boy's voice was low and throaty, like it was just now changing with puberty. Even in the darkness of a snow cloud cover, Brandon saw that he was barely into his teens and beardless. He appeared slightly built even in his robe and heavy sheepskin coat. The top of the turban he wore low above his brow and over his ears reached no higher than the American's chest.

"How old are you anyhow?" Brandon asked, curious.

"Old enough to understand not to stand on an open DZ yapping."

Brandon accepted the putdown. No need to piss off the locals. Besides, the kid was right. He had probably been fighting in these mountains since he was eight years old.

The detachment cached air gear and uniforms where they would not be easily discovered. Ismael showed them how to tie their turbans in a certain way to indicate their ethnic group, in this case Jijak. The Pushtus, he said, were to the south and east along the Pakistan border. Many of the Pushtus were sympathetic to the Taliban and bin Laden's al-Qaeda.

"There's one rule while you're in these mountains," Ismael said. "Don't trust anyone completely."

"Not even you?"

Ismael hesitated. "That's up to you. Even I don't come with a guarantee."

Brandon's lips curled. He twisted his fingers in the neck of the kid's robe and drew him close. "I come with a guarantee," he said. "I know you had to have been cleared for this mission, but if you fuck my men over in any way, I guarantee to wax your ass."

"Fair enough." Ismael responded without emotion, seeming unoffended. "I think we'd better go. We have a long walk."

Brandon had learned from previous missions that trust in anyone outside the team bred carelessness.

The mujahideen were hardy men accustomed to the bitter Afghan terrain and climate. They set a brisk pace. Two of them ranged out ahead on point while a third fell back on the trail to watch for trackers. Brandon dispersed Ice Man to the rear and Gloomy Davis with the two guerrillas on point as additional security for the detachment. Ismael remained near the American commander.

The sky gradually brightened.

"Where are the horses?" Winnie Brown complained. "We endured saddle sores and mule skinning only to find ourselves pedestrian strangers in a strange land?"

Training in the Colorado Rockies had helped with altitude conditioning, but nothing fully prepared an outsider for the brutal Hindu Kush. Ismael called a rest break after full light.

"It'll take you and your men a few days to acclimatize to the altitude," he said. "It always does."

Brandon confirmed his first impressions about the kid in the daylight. He looked fifteen years old, tops, except for large brown eyes that somehow made him seem almost ancient when seen from a certain angle. A lock of coal-black hair fell from his turban across his brow. He was more tanned than naturally brown-skinned like most Afghans.

"Don't let my youth deceive you," he said. "I can, and will, do anything that's necessary."

"Have you killed a man?"

"I have killed *men*."

He said it in a way, not boasting, that caused Brandon to believe him. Maybe this kid is older than he looks, he thought.

"How far are we from the guerrilla base camp?" Brandon asked, changing the subject.

"Not far."

The terrain became too rough for horses, even if they'd

had them. The trail was less than a foot wide in a few places. They inched across those areas by hugging the upside cliff while the mountain at their feet fell abruptly away into a canyon hundreds of feet deep. A dislodged stone seemed to fall forever before it struck bottom.

Mad Dog struggled under the load of a full ALICE pack that contained a PRC-137 SMRS SATCOM radio and accessories in addition to ammunition, bedding, and other personal supplies. The rest of the team switched off carrying his backup radio, the old reliable "Turkey 43" which bounce high frequency signals off the upper atmosphere to almost anyplace in the world. Cell phones and individual Motorolas for close range communications completed the detachment's commo complement. Commo in the field was a team's lifeline. With so many systems functioning as backups for each other, Iron Weed should have little problem talking to the SFOB in Khanabad, Uzbekistan, or even farther than that in an emergency.

The team experienced an anxious moment on a narrow section of the trail when Mad Dog stumbled and went off balance. He teetered precariously over the brink of an abyss that dropped into impenetrable shadows. It appeared he was about to plunge after a dislodged showering of stone and gravel.

He caught himself at the last moment. "Fu-uck this place and the horse it rode in on," he growled.

"We're almost to the top," Ismael said, unmoved. "It's easier going after that."

"As compared to what?" Doc TB asked.

"It's not Broadway," Ismael said.

The team of eight Delta soldiers carried the firepower of an average infantry platoon. In addition to his M-16 rifle, Thumbs Jones humped a supply of C-4 explosives and a twelve-pound PAQ-10 GLTD—a laser target designator that sighted, ranged, and designated targets up to six miles away for strike aircraft. Gloomy Davis, naturally, carried Mr. Blunderbuss in a case secured to his ruck. He was married to the sniper rifle. Mad Dog, Doc TB, and Winnie Brown were each armed with an M-16 rifle, Winnie's equipped with an M-203 40mm grenade launcher. The reticent Ice Man Thompson let an M-60 medium machine gun do the necessary talking for him during an action. The team's leadership, Major Kragle and Team Sergeant Norman, each had a stubby MP-5 submachine gun slung across his shoulder.

Every man in the detachment was also laden with a pistol, hand grenades, knives, and any other weapons he considered essential and could stow in his pack. Brandon had chosen a 9mm Sig-Sauer semiauto pistol and sheathed it to his web gear along with the Ka-Bar combat knife his grandfather, the Ambassador, used with the Alamo Scouts in World War II. On his wrist he wore the latest GPS—global positioning system.

It was full daylight by the time they reached the top. The cloud cover was burning off, promising a clear, bright day. A miles-wide valley opened below their feet. Ismael pointed out a sprawling earth-colored city along a river in the haze of distance.

"Kabul. That is the Royal Palace," he said, pointing, "and that is the Kalola Pushta Fort to the north. Farther north is the Bagram airfield, which the Northern Alliance holds."

He continued by indicating the location of al-Qaeda training camps and Taliban militia bases to the south. He pointed out army bases, the international airport and military airfields. He clearly knew the city.

"Kandahar to the south and west is the home base and birthplace of the Taliban," Ismael said, in a lecturing tone Brandon found patronizing and therefore irritating. "Mullah Omar and Osama bin Laden have headquarters in Kandahar and Kabul. Kabul is under threat now and will be the North-ern Alliance's first target. We—the Americans," he corrected, "have been bombing it almost daily. We have reliable intelli-gence that bin Laden has a headquarters in Kabul."

Brandon looked sharply at him. It stood to logic that Is-mael and at least the leadership of his mujahideen band had been informed of their mission. It was a lot of trust to place in the hands of ragtag guerrillas who appeared to change loyal-ties a lot more frequently than they changed underwear.

"How reliable?" Brandon asked.

"Our orders were to find bin Laden and keep him under surveillance," the kid said, as though answering Brandon's unspoken question. "Don't you think it's reasonable to as-sume that your arriving here has something to do with bin Laden?"

He grinned, proud of his logic.

"We can find bin Laden," he said then. "Getting to him now . . . ? That may be a little harder."

Daylight American air strikes began while the guerrillas were walking the high ground. It seemed that it had been planned for their viewing. Dozens of high contrails in the sky converged over the city. It consisted of heavy airpower, B-52s and B-2s, their 2,000- and 5,000-pound bombs glinting in the morning sun as they plummeted toward targets in and around the city.

"Hijack *them* babies, cocksuckers!" Gloomy Davis ex-horted.

Bright flashes sparked like strings of giant firecrackers. Dirty smoke billowed and continued to rise and spread until it covered the city. Rumbles of thunder rolled across the flats and trembled the ridge from which the Deltas and their mu-jahideen escort watched. It was a spectacular and humbling show.

Precision strike aircraft followed the B-52s in waves, F-16

Fighting Falcons and F-15 Eagles. The U.S. had complete air superiority. Most Taliban antiaircraft guns and SAM missile sites had already been knocked out during night attacks.

Iron Weed plodded south, following the military crest of the ridge while bombing continued. Kabul lay out of sight by mid-morning and there was no more land thunder. Hafiz Saeed the Zarbati, who seemed to be in charge, halted the march in a grove of stringy evergreens in a field of boulders. The trail led out of the boulders and down on the other side. Saeed sent a man forward to announce their arrival. Brandon watched him exchange a few words with a sentry who came out of the rocks. From beyond came the whinny of a horse.

"Expect a mixed welcome," Ismael said, suddenly very grave. "Understand that these mujahideen are not helping because they love McDonald hamburgers, Nike shoes, and Britney Spears. They're being paid money and offered supplies to provide you a base of operations and limited assistance. Understand but for that they'd just as soon cut your throats and take your weapons and packs tonight while you sleep. Those are the facts. Accept them."

How did this kid know so much? Brandon wondered. He was Afghan, but he talked like an American.

"You have another problem. Bek Gorabic is an asshole. He hates Russians, English, Americans, and anybody else that isn't Jijak and Muslim as much as he hates the Taliban. He's commander. However, Abdul Homayan and his band blundered into a Taliban ambush that killed more than half of them. The rest fled into hiding here. Bek and Abdul are personal rivals and enemies. There's a power struggle over which man will end up in command."

"Great," Brandon said, sarcastic.

"Look, Major Kragle—"

"How did you know my name?" Teams on mission inserted sterile—without rank, insignia, or names other than their first.

"Never mind now. You've got other things to worry about," Ismael said in the overbearing lecturing tone of a tutor to a pupil. "Afghanistan is full of tribal loyalties and rivalries. You have to live with it. If you can't handle it, sir . . ."

The kid squinted in the direction of the guerrilla camp.

"If you fuck up, Major, your first fight is going to happen down there at that camp."

CHAPTER 12

The scenario seemed to come directly from the Army Special Forces playbook. At least once a year the teams engaged in war games during which "A" detachments inserted into a "hostile" country, linked up with guerrillas, established rapport with suspicious guerrilla chieftains, and then trained and led the guerrillas in operations behind enemy lines. Classic SF training, the reasoning being that if you trained for the toughest missions, the routine ones came easy.

A game of the ancient Afghan sport of bushkazi was under way when Brandon led 1-Alpha into the guerrilla camp. Horses' hooves thundered as about a dozen whip-wielding riders fought a running duel up and down and across a dusty, snow-swirled field contained in a deep bowl of surrounding rock pinnacles and hogback ridges. The game involved no-holds-barred combat waged at full gallop, the objective being to wrest control of a goat carcass from the rival team and carry it across a goal line. Blood and hair flew, not all of it from the dead goat.

Tribesmen armed with Russian Kalashnikovs, American M-16s, and weapons from several other nationalities cheered excitedly from the sidelines. They looked gaunt and worn, as though they had not eaten well in recent times. They were almost in rags. Brandon counted twenty-six men either playing the dead goat game or watching. A platoon-size element. There was also one woman in sight. At least she appeared to be female; she was covered head to toe in a faded black burqa.

Brandon halted the detachment on a slight knoll where the trail entered the camp and overlooked it. Ice Man nudged him. "Major," he said, putting a lot into the only word he had spoken all morning. He nodded toward where a Chinese-made Pika gun and a pair of Chinese 62mm mortars were arranged outside the entrance to a cave. Goat skins provided a covering for the cave opening.

It seemed peculiar to Brandon that the guerrillas should all be armed while in camp. Just as peculiar was the way the Afghans, though obviously curious, kept their distance and watched the strangers from the edges of their eyes. They appeared to have been alerted for action.

The team automatically spread out to obtain fighting room. Saeed and the two other Afghans from the DZ welcoming party joined the spectators on the field, distancing themselves from the newcomers until things were resolved. Ismael remained with Brandon.

The woman in the burqa turned and disappeared into the cave.

"Cunts who wear their own bedsheets really turn me on," Mad Dog cracked.

"Did you hear about the stray B-52 bomb that hit the only whorehouse in Kabul?" Gloomy Davis asked, then followed with the punch line after the appropriate timing. "It killed seven camels and three sheep."

Doc TB blinked. "What?"

"Think about it," Winnie Brown said.

Shortly after the woman disappeared into the cave, the skins parted and a stocky, bow-legged man of about forty stepped into the wintery sunlight. White ran down the chin of his black beard, as though he'd been drinking bleach and spilled it. He wore a heavy sheepskin coat soiled and stained almost black, and a red and green turban that covered his eyebrows. He shifted a U.S. SAW—a 5.56 light machine gun, or Squad Automatic Weapon—from his left hand to his right. His breath made little puffs of exclamation in the cold air.

He shot the Americans a long, unfriendly look, sizing them up, before he shouldered his weapon and swaggered to the sidelines of the bushkazi game.

"That," whispered Ismael, "is Bek Gorabic."

"Real glad to see us, ain't he?" Thumbs Jones muttered.

Mother Norman kept watchful eyes on the scene below. "What the hell have we walked into here, Major?"

"I feel like a chicken thrown into a pen full of Oklahoma coyotes," Gloomy said.

Ismael kept up a running commentary in a low voice. "Bek's weakness is in titles and horses. He was an officer in the government and had a title when there was a king, before the Russians came. Most of the horses belong to him. He's an old horse thief, worse than the Comanches. Call him 'Commander Bek' when you talk to him, and admire his horses. For now, it's best we wait here. Let Bek break the standoff. It's more respectful unless you want a showdown."

"Why the hell would I want a showdown?" Brandon snapped. "We need these people."

"If you kill Bek now," Ismael coldly responded, "it will save trouble later."

Brandon reserved his reply. This whole thing was getting edgy, like it was about to blow up in their faces. And the mission had just started.

The game of horsemen and dead goat continued at a furious pace. One man was knocked off his horse and limped off the field of battle while his mount, a sorrel with a rack of bony ribs, stampeded toward a corral built into a copse of trees next to a stream.

These were savage men, not the least of whom was the kid Ismael, who talked of killing like any normal teenager might discuss going to a movie. Brandon half expected to see Genghis Khan come riding up the mountain at the front of his hordes. He recalled old lines from Kipling's "Young British Soldier":

When you're lying out wounded on Afghanistan's plains.
And the women come out to cut up what remains.
You roll to your rifle and blow out your brains . . .

Russians had had intimate experience with the fabled mujahideen brutality during their ten-year Afghan war. Captured Russian troops, their stomachs ripped open, were left to die while the blazing sun baked their innards. In Afghanistan, the Russians, said you saved the last bullet for yourself.

"That is Abdul Homayan," Ismael said, indicating a tall, red-bearded man in a quilted coat of indistinguishable colors. "He is pro-American as long as it suits him and serves his purpose. Right now I think it serves his purpose."

The red-bearded man had ignored the strangers until now. The bushkazi appeared to be winding down now that one team had gotten the remains of the goat across the opposite goal line. Abdul stood, looked toward the Americans, and nodded. He said something to two of the men nearest him. They casually made their way toward a teepee of stacked firearms and stationed themselves near it.

Just as casually, Ice Man slung his M-60 machine gun with the muzzle pointed downrange. Safeties clicked off as the detachment got ready.

"Easy, lads," Brandon cautioned.

"Sir, I make the odds three to one or better," Mother Norman said.

"Watch Bek," Ismael advised. "Abdul is siding with you."

Bek made no move until the game on the field ended, the horses and men lathered and winded and the goat carcass torn into bits, its blood splattered on the players. He turned then to look full at the Americans and stood there silently with the SAW slung on his shoulder, his right hand resting firmly on the butt of a holstered revolver.

"He's making it personal between you and him," Ismael warned tersely. "Don't hesitate if he goes for his gun. Drop him."

What the hell was this, Brandon wondered, *High Noon*? It occurred to him that he was being used to settle a political rivalry within the guerrilla band. He resented it, and he resented Ismael, but the hands were already dealt. All he could do was play the cards.

"Kill only Bek," Ismael encouraged. This kid had a mean streak in him. "Don't miss your first shot, Major. If Bek is allowed to return fire, it may embolden his backers to fight."

"Get this straight, Ismael," Brandon blazed between his teeth. "There'll be no shooting or killing unless it's necessary."

"It may be necessary, Major."

"I'll make that decision."

"He's ready for us to come to him," Ismael said, his voice stretched thin with tension.

Brandon took a deep breath and loosened the Sig-Sauer in its holster, a gesture he wanted Bek to see.

"Sergeant Norman, keep the team here. Stay ready."

"Yes, sir."

"Ismael, come with me. I'll need you to translate."

The blowing of the horses, the soft footfalls of the approaching Americans and the boy, and the sigh of cold wind among the rocks were the only sounds. Brandon stopped halfway to Bek.

"Let him come the other half of the distance," he explained.

No one on either side moved for what seemed an interminable time. Brandon stood with his hand loose and not far from the butt of his Sig as the impasse drew itself out. Bek looked confused.

Abdul the red-beard was the first to break ranks. He strode forward until he faced the American from only a few feet away. He nodded to show his approval of the way Brandon was handling things. After a moment, two or three other men came forward. Curiosity brought up others one or two at a time. Bek was still dangerous, but Brandon watched the confrontation being defused.

Finally, the only way left for Bek to preserve the appearance of leadership was to walk forward himself. He paced up the little knoll, his hand still on the butt of his weapon, and stopped in front of Brandon. He glared at Abdul.

He was almost a head shorter than the American, but made up in breadth what he lacked in height. He was thick and coarse and his huge head appeared even larger because of the beard with its skunk stripe down the center. His eyes were shrewd and pushed deeply into flesh like those of an old boar hog. His teeth were broad and yellow through the beard when he spoke in Darik, the language of the north and the Tajik tribal associations. It sounded aggressive and Oriental to Brandon's ear.

"Translation?" Brandon asked Ismael.

"He says he's glad to see the Americans have brought him weapons."

"Funny man. Tell him the weapons belong to us, but we will use them to fight with him against the Taliban."

"Ha!" Bek sneered when it was translated. "We do not

need the infidels to fight our war for us. We are warriors here and we are winning."

"Is that why you've been stuck in the mountains for years while Mullah Omar and Osama bin Laden are warm with their women in the cities?"

Bek stiffened. "You come into my own camp and insult me!"

"It's no insult, Commander Bek. It's the truth."

"We are many in these hills and we are strong."

"You're stronger with American warplanes and other things we can provide."

Bek thought that over. Greed narrowed his eyes. His jaw jutted and he thrust his huge head toward Brandon.

"I do not like Russians and Americans and other infidels," he rumbled. "Here, I am in command. I will kill any who disputes it."

He gripped his pistol by way of emphasis. Abdul stepped forward, flaring. "Be a fool, Bek, and if the American doesn't kill you, I will. Listen to him. He makes sense. We need what the Americans can provide."

Ismael translated for Brandon almost in real time. He was good. The listening mujahideen shuffled and got ready. It wouldn't take much to ignite the whole mess. The camp seemed almost equally divided between Bek allies and Abdul supporters.

Bek eased off. "Be careful how you speak, Redbeard, for my patience with you grows thin."

"Patience is all you have, Commander Bek," Abdul replied. "You have fighters and you have weapons and horses. Yet, you hide in these mountains like rabbits and do not go down to fight."

"My men have fought bravely!" Bek bellowed in his defense. "We killed the tank only last week."

"The tank was already dead, and guarded by only two Taliban."

The whites of Bek's eyes flashed red with barely subdued rage. In another moment the two sides would be clashing, with Delta caught in the middle. Brandon stepped carefully between the two chieftains.

"Tell them," he said to Ismael, "that we weaken each other when we fight among ourselves. We have a common enemy. You've already received goodwill payments of weapons, food, and other supplies. There's more."

The other Afghans listened eagerly. America had lots of food, lots of guns. Like soldiers everywhere, the mujahideen traveled on their stomachs. Their stomachs gravitated toward the visitors. Bek looked around, unable to miss the ambivalence on the faces of his soldiers. But he had made his stand and could not appear to be weak and back down. He thrust his great head toward Brandon.

"Your mission, whatever it is, must not compromise my men," Bek challenged. "I am responsible for them and will not martyr them for nothing. What *is* your mission? I am the commander. I should know."

"It'll be explained in time," Brandon promised. How was it that Ismael, a mere translator, knew of the detachment's target and the other guerrillas did not? he wondered.

"When will we receive more food?" Bek demanded.

"There'll be an airdrop as soon as we reach an agreement and approve it."

Bek snorted. He was not satisfied, but he seemed to understand that he had pushed the situation as far as he dared. He did an abrupt about-face and headed toward the cave, followed by a small coterie of his inner guard. The remaining Afghans relaxed and gathered around the Americans, curious and jabbering now, and looking over their equipment. Abdul said something before he and some of the men strode off to take care of the horses.

"What'd he say?" Brandon asked Ismael.

"You won't get another opportunity like that," the boy told him. "Bek is treacherous. He'll go along, but don't trust him. He won't face you again, but watch your back constantly and sleep with one eye open. You should have killed him when you had the chance."

CHAPTER 13

Tampa, Florida

Given the time difference between Florida and Afghanistan, it was early afternoon in Kabul and only a quarter after three in the morning in Tampa, according to the grandfather clock in General Darren Kragle's office on the upper floor of his home. The General rubbed his face wearily. Dressed in a faded robe over his pajamas, slumped in the chair behind his cluttered desk, he looked old and haggard, an appearance the youthful haircut and Florida tan failed to supplant in the dead of a long night.

He scooted his chair to face the picture window and away from the television turned to CNN. It was black outside except for neighbors' porch lights and, in the distance, the red and green running lights of a fishing trawler creeping into Tampa Bay. Gloria padded in with a fresh pot of coffee. She wore a robe and house slippers in the shape of long-eared bunnies; Cassidy had given them to her. She had applied straightener to her kinky hair and a black dye to cover the expanding gray, over which she wore a red head rag that the boys always teased made her look like Aunt Jemima.

She poured two cups, took one and slid the other across

the desk to the General. When he didn't respond, she sighed expansively to make sure he knew she was back and sat down heavily across the desk from him.

Without looking, General Kragle shook his head to her unspoken query. There had been no word yet.

Of the three Delta detachments inserted into Afghanistan under Operation Iron Weed, only Major Brandon Kragle's 1-Alpha had not yet reported in to the SFOB in Uzbekistan. Major Dare Thompson's 2-Alpha and Major Keith Laub's 3-Alpha had both radioed in a "Bingo," meaning a successful linkup with their Northern Alliance counterparts. Thompson had been assigned to run down Mullah Mohammed Omar, the Taliban leader; Laub was tasked with rescuing four American women missionaries imprisoned for proselytizing Christianity. One-Alpha's mission was considered the most risky of the three. Killing Osama bin Laden—and he surely would be killed—meant a significant political and propaganda coup for Enduring Freedom. For security purposes, each of the three detachments operated independently and knew nothing of the others' missions.

The SFOB promised to patch-in a SATCOM to the General as soon as it received 1-Alpha's code word denoting a successful entry and linkup.

The waiting was getting to Gloria. Finally, she could take it no longer.

"It don't seem fair to me, Darren, that you sends my boy back to them Afghanites when he done just got out the last time by the hair of his poor neck," she accused, wagging her deadly finger at him. "Here we done lost poor Little Nana and Kathryn so sick and all—"

"Gloria, do you think Brandon would have had it any other way?"

That subdued her, temporarily.

After a moment, the General got up to put his arms around

her. "I'm sorry for snapping at you, Sugar Doll. It's just that—"

"It be my job to understand the Kragle men," she said, sounding put upon. "Sometimes it has took a lot of understanding too."

It had been a long, sleepless night for both of them. In addition to waiting on the call from SFOB, they remained in frequent telephone contact with the base hospital at Fort Bragg, where Cameron and Cassidy kept vigil.

"Sir, the doctors still haven't made a diagnosis," Cameron explained. "They've called in a pulmonary specialist from Walter Reed. I understand you're under a lot of pressure and have responsibilities with the war, but maybe you should be here. Kathryn's not doing well. She's in God's hands. We're praying for her."

"Gloria and I are flying up first thing in the morning."

"Cassidy needs you, sir, even if he doesn't know it or won't admit it."

"Let me speak to him."

He stared absently at the TV screen while he waited for his younger son to come on. News and commentary twenty-four hours a day. Agent Claude Thornton, director of the FBI's National Domestic Preparedness office, and MacArthur Thornbrew, recently appointed NHSA chief, were being grilled by a noisy gaggle of reporters and talking heads. The General had seen it twice tonight already, but he watched it again.

The *New York Times* correspondent in particular seemed incensed over the FBI's roundup and detention of more than 150 Middle Easterners on immigration violations, an action the *Times*, in an editorial, called racial profiling.

"Such detentions are essential at this time," Agent Thornton argued in response to a question. "We are looking at the possibility that more than four airplanes were initially targeted for hijacking. It's increasingly clear that terrorist networks that conduct these kinds of acts are harbored, supported, sustained, and protected by a variety of rogue governments. The 9/11 attack seems to be part of a larger plan that includes various sorts of other terrorist acts, not only the hijacking of airplanes."

"What sort of acts?" a reporter demanded. "There is a rumor that a Florida man has come down with a condition that might be the result of bioterrorism."

MacArthur Thornbrew stepped to the podium. "We had rather not comment at this point."

A CNN talking head imposed himself upon the screen, raising an eyebrow. "The government," he intoned, "is being disturbingly secretive. One of the things such secrecy deprives citizens of is knowing just how far and energetically the government will go into shaving away constitutionally protected activity."

A segue then gave equal time to what the General contemptuously referred to as the "blame America first" crowd. Antiwar protestors were marching down Pennsylvania Avenue to the police barricades that surrounded the White House, chanting, "No more war!" and "Give peace a chance!" They thrust up signs declaring WAR WILL NOT BRING OUR LOVED ONES BACK and DEMAND PEACE. Protestors occasionally ran through the streets, shouting and throwing bottles, forcing police in heavy body armor to keep up.

Their complaints, presented to the cameras, were familiar:

"The nation's in grief. I'm in grief. But adding more victims to the list is not going to do anyone any good."

"Who on earth is a bigger terrorist than Uncle Sam? It's insane. Clean up home first. Straighten out America."

"I wish the people of Afghanistan victory against the U.S. forces of imperialism."

Disgusted, General Kragle watched speakers climb onto

police barricades to address the protestors. Among them was Senator Eric B. Tayloe, who had opposed the forming of a Homeland Security Agency in committee and was now protesting the War on Terror and the roundup of illegal immigrants.

"What concerns me very much is the saber-rattling and the calls for vengeance," he shouted, speaking through a bullhorn. "You don't bomb a city or a country for an event like this. You use clever, intelligent, undercover operations to get the criminals and punish them. Then you try to understand the underlying causes of crime."

The General glared at the screen.

Former President John Stanton was back in the public eye, tarnishing the dignity of the presidency, in the General's viewpoint, by appearing in street theater. God, how he must miss being the center of attention, Kragle thought, watching Stanton standing before the cameras, his bottom lip trembling and his eyes teary, which the General believed was contrived. The sonofabitch had been unsuccessfully impeached for perjury before he left office, he thought, but he still should have been charged with murder for his role in shooting down the American C-141 over Afghanistan during Punitive Strike.

"There is a vast and growing divide in this world of ours," Stanton was saying. "A divide between the haves and the have-nots, the rich and the poor, the comfortable and the wretched. It is from the desperate, angry and bereaved that these suicide pilots come."

Bristling, the General still cradled the telephone receiver, waiting for Cassidy. "Asshole!" he spat at the TV.

"Amen," Gloria said.

Cameron came back on the phone. "Sir? I'm sorry, Cassidy wants to speak to Sugar Mama."

The General handed the receiver to Gloria without comment. He knew she had been a better mother to his sons than he had been a father. Would Cassidy never forgive him his failings?

He turned off the TV set. He'd seen enough. While Gloria talked to his younger son, giving him comfort, he stared out the window into the night. USSOCOM could not afford the luxury of permitting his personal life to interfere with his duties, no matter what it cost him. He had the SpecOps side of the war to conduct. Iron Weed elements were already in-country. The 75th Rangers were ready to jump off. Marine Force Recon was aboard ships in the Arabian Sea. SEAL teams and Green Berets had gone into isolation to prepare for clandestine ops behind enemy lines.

It was the Irish curse of the Kragles passed down from fathers to sons that they be warriors marching off when the drums beat. It seemed they had no other choice. Their family and personal lives inevitably suffered.

Gloria hung up the phone after a few minutes. She came up behind the tall man and reached both hands up to his shoulders. "I understands," she whispered.

And she did. The Kragle men bore their losses and hurts alone, stoically. Duty and mission always came first for them. It had to be that way.

Two more phone calls came in before dawn. The first was the expected call from the SFOB in Uzbekistan. Gloria was packing for their flight to Fort Bragg. She came running in. The General smiled and nodded. Major Kragle's detachment had safely linked up with the guerrillas.

"Praise the Lawd the boy's all right!" Gloria cried, bursting into tears.

The second call came from Cameron.

"Sir, we have a diagnosis. It's bad news. Kathryn has inhalation anthrax."

THE SECOND ATTACK: BIOTERRORISM

WASHINGTON (CPI)—The wife of a U.S. Army Green Beret is believed to be one of the first victims of a suspected bioterrorist attack against America following the 9/11 assaults against the World Trade Center and the Pentagon. Kathryn Kragle, 22, was diagnosed with inhalation anthrax at the Fort Bragg hospital in Fayetteville, North Carolina. She is listed in critical condition.

More than 200 Americans are believed to have been exposed to or infected by anthrax since the first case was discovered in Florida earlier this week. Four people have died, the first deaths in the United States due to anthrax in more than 25 years. There have been only three cases of inhalation anthrax in America in nearly a century.

MacArthur Thornbrew, chief of the National Homeland Security Agency, said the U.S. mail appears to be the common denominator. All victims, with the exception of Kathryn Kragle, have handled or received letters filled with powdered anthrax. The source of Kragle's case continues to puzzle authorities.

In Washington, the staff of Senator Eric B. Tayloe, who opposes the War on Terror, opened mail containing what is referred to as "weaponized" anthrax, a particularly virulent strain of the bacteria. Three Capitol Hill workers, members of Tayloe's staff, have tested positive. They are expected to recover with prompt treatment.

The letter addressed to Senator Tayloe was hand-printed in block letters with a return address of a nonexistent private school in Newark,

New Jersey, as were all the others. All contained virtually the same message: "This is next. You cannot stop us. We have this anthrax. You die now. Are you afraid? Death to America. Death to Israel. Allah is great."

It was dated the same day as the September 11 attacks on New York and Washington.

"There's a battlefield outside this country—and now there's a battlefield inside the country," said Senior Agent Claude Thornton of the FBI's National Domestic Preparedness Office.

As devastating as the 9/11 terrorist attacks were, national security and public health officials warn that bioweapons, which are invisible and next to impossible to trace, could cause far more deaths among ordinary Americans than the thousands dead or missing at the World Trade Center and the Pentagon. A government study estimates that 200 pounds of anthrax spores released upwind of Washington, D.C., could kill up to three million people.

The bacteria has sparked a nationwide panic. Without warning, citizens won't know until hours or days later that an attack has occurred. All three branches of government have responded to the attack. Supreme Court justices are camped out in borrowed quarters. Lawmakers have dispersed around the city. The White House and other federal buildings are locked down and under quarantine.

The flulike symptoms of inhalation anthrax include fever, malaise, fatigue, and sometimes a dry cough. A period of improvement may follow, but then a decline sets in—difficulty in breathing, sweating, and bluish discoloration of the skin. The first symptoms usually occur within two to ten days following exposure, but may not appear for up to seven weeks. However, if not diagnosed and treated early, the patient can go into shock and might die 24 to 36 hours after the severe symptoms set in. The disease is fatal in 80 to 90 percent of cases unless treated early . . .

CHAPTER 14

Fort Bragg

Sergeant Cassidy Kragle refused to leave his wife's bedside even to change out of the scroungy BDUs he wore when his brother pulled him from Robin Sage. Kathryn opened her eyes once and looked at him. Her lips moved. She was trying to speak. Cassidy bent near, holding her hand and gently stroking her hair.

"Our . . ." It was an effort for her to speak. "Our baby . . . ?"

She looked at him without recognition then, the way Little Nana had looked at them. Kathryn had hardly moved since. She lay in the ICU with tubes and monitors trailing from every orifice, her face pale and drawn. An unearthly bluish cast at the temples spread slowly across her brow and down her cheeks.

Now, Gloria sat with Cassidy. The room was tense and silent except for the hum of life-support equipment. Hour after hour they held vigil at the young woman's bedside—the plump black woman with tear-swollen eyes, and the tall gaunt young soldier already coping with grief the Kragle way. Sorrow, pain, and anger stretched his face as tight as a mask. He kept everything else inside, including his tears of fear and dread.

Doctors and specialists assured him they were doing everything they could for her. The anthrax had simply had too much time to build up inside her body.

The General entered quietly with cups of coffee. Gloria took hers gratefully, nodding her thanks. Tears streamed down her cheeks. Cassidy continued to stare into his pregnant wife's still face. Occasionally he moved closer and bent over her to make sure she was still breathing. The General stood behind his son's chair, listening to the hum and the silence. He blinked and rested one huge hand on Cassidy's shoulder. Then he left the coffee and quietly went out again.

Cameron and Sergeant Rasem Jameel were in the waiting room with FBI Agent Claude Thornton. The clan was starting to gather again, as it had for Little Nana's funeral. Uncle Mike caught a flight out of Uzbekistan for the U.S. that afternoon. The Ambassador was returning tomorrow from a trip to Europe and Asia. Brandon had purposefully not been notified of Kathryn's condition. There was nothing he could do, and he could not be jerked off Iron Weed. Kragles understood the necessity of total concentration on mission.

Thornton flew in from D.C., not only because he was the General's friend, but because bioterrorism fell within the jurisdiction of the Domestic Preparedness Office. He spent most of the day supervising efforts at the base post office and the main post office in Fayetteville, attempting to determine if either had been contaminated with anthrax. He also quarantined Kathryn's and Cassidy's on-post family quarters for testing by EPA and CDC investigators. There was some fear that Fort Bragg might have been targeted by anthrax terrorists, but so far all tests had come up negative. There was still no explanation for how Kathryn might have contracted the disease.

The General returned from the ICU and seated himself on the sofa between Cameron and Jameel, an enlisted man who was clearly uncomfortable with being in the presence of a general. He made himself as small as possible in his corner of the couch.

"At ease, son," the General reassured him. He turned his attention to Thornton. Overhead lighting sheened off the agent's shaved head.

"Cassidy's in no condition to answer any questions right now," the General said. "I don't think he can remember his name, rank, and serial number. Besides, haven't you folks already tested every piece of mail in their house? That's where it had to come from, isn't it?"

"It's been the mail in all the other cases," Thornton acknowledged. "However, this case seems different . . ." His voice trailed off, then caught again. "Maybe it'll give us a clue if we can trace her every movement over the past couple of weeks. Has she made any trips, varied her routine somehow, met new people . . . ?"

"I doubt Cassidy can help you," Cameron offered. "He's busy with the Q course. The only time he's been with Kathryn in the past few weeks was at Little Nana's funeral. Kathryn thought she was coming down with the flu then. Rasem and I can probably help you better than anyone else. We see her nearly every day, as we've been taking turns helping her with the shopping, and stopping by with a movie or Chinese takeout. She loves Chinese. She hasn't felt well, what with the baby and everything, and didn't go out much. She went to church Sunday mornings and for Wednesday night worship, and she was at the chapel a few hours on Tuesdays and Saturdays helping with the mailing—"

"The mailing?" Thornton said, looking up.

"We're assisting in a nationwide mail ministry with Reverend Billy Dye—"

"The televangelist? You get large amounts of mail?"

Cameron and Jameel both shook their heads.

"We mail to military personnel stationed all over the country, as well as outside CONUS," Cameron said. "They're small pamphlets about how God moves in the lives of military people. We'll give you the latest copies, if you want."

"The mailings originate where?"

"At the chapel. We receive a master copy once a week from the Dye Foundation. We reprint with facilities donated to the chapel. Jameel has become a competent printer with our old offset press. Kathryn has helped with the stuffing of envelopes and addressing."

Thornton took some notes. Cameron stood up and walked to the long slit window overlooking the scattered lights of the military post. It was raining again.

"God bless and hold her," he said, mostly to himself. "She survived the USS *Randolph* and al-Qaeda, only to . . ."

Rain crawled on the window like black worms.

". . . only to have the terrorists catch up to her like this. God must have His purpose, although it's sometimes difficult for us to comprehend it."

He stared at the dark worms crawling on the window.

"Claude," the General said to Thornton. "Don't the feds have any idea where the anthrax originates?"

"The easy answer would be to say Iraq. We know Saddam Hussein had bioweapons capability before and during Desert Storm and was working on others. Our soldiers were all given anthrax inoculations. But we can't be sure. The production of weapons-grade anthrax is a complicated process. The samples we've recovered were good enough to have been developed here in the United States."

Cameron turned toward him from the window.

"That's right," Thornton said. "Uncle Sam doesn't necessarily have clean hands when it comes to biological and chemical weapons. A bunch of different witch's brews were developed at Fort Detrick during the Cold War."

"The U.S. Army Medical Research Institute of Infectious Diseases at Fort Detrick, Maryland," Cameron said. "Sergeant Jameel was stationed there."

Sergeant Jameel's eyes widened in surprise.

"I looked it up in your 201 file when you first started working with me," Cameron explained. "All commanders check out their men."

"Yes," Jameel agreed. "That was before I go to airborne. I was assigned to military police security detail. There was nothing there at the time."

"He's right," Thornton said. "The Special Operations Division, a secret arm of the U.S. biological weapons program, was dismantled in 1972 in accordance with the Biological Weapons Convention."

The agent had obviously done his homework, the General thought. "You're saying this anthrax may be homegrown and not part of the al-Qaeda plan?" he asked.

"Our world is full of nuts with grudges and grievances. Look at Timothy McVeigh and Oklahoma City. We have all kinds of wacky groups within our borders, including al-Qaeda sleeper cells. With our lax immigration policies, we may have as many al-Qaeda underground in Nebraska and Arkansas as in Afghanistan. What I'm saying is that all during the 1950s and 1960s medical researchers at Detrick designed and experimented with germs to answer the question of what to use against the Soviet Union and the most effective way to deploy it. There were even ten sites across the U.S. playing with VX, a chemical bug spray for humans so potent that one drop of it would kill within fifteen minutes."

The FBI agent stood up, unable to remain seated beneath the weight of what he had discovered about his nation. He went to the window and stood next to Cameron, looking out.

"Chaplain," he said, "it must be hard on God and ministers to see inside men's souls darker than my skin."

He continued speaking with his back to the room. "American scientists would arrange guinea pigs, hogs, monkeys, and sheep out in the desert and dose the whole bunch with deadly clouds of anthrax to see how many became infected. Harmless bacteria meant to simulate anthrax spores were dropped in the New York subway system, sprayed over San Diego from airplanes, and even pumped into the Pentagon's ventilation system. We found out we could kill a whole lot of animals—or people—fairly easily. Today, much of what the biological weapons program learned is locked away in secret libraries at Fort Detrick and in the heads of five or ten scientists who still survive."

"And they know how to manufacture weapons-grade anthrax," the General said.

"We've located several of them, but others have died or disappeared. It's a possible lead, but that's the most that can be said at this point."

Cameron took a deep, sighing breath and lifted his eyes toward the door to the ICU, where Cassidy and Gloria waited at Kathryn's bedside. Waiting for her to die. " 'And I looked, and beheld a pale horse,' " he quoted from some deep well of sadness, " 'and his name that set on him was Death.' "

CHAPTER 15

Afghanistan

It took a few days for Iron Weed 1-Alpha to get the lay of the land and settle into life at the guerrilla camp. Life there was leisurely, all things considered. The team ran a few patrols with the band, nothing serious, mostly just to get their feet wet and get a feel for the country. American bombers flew every day now, and there was land thunder from the bombing toward Kabul and farther south and east. Although there was lots of talk about war at the camp, Bek Gorabic seemed uninterested in pursuing it. He appeared more interested in his horses and in maintaining security than in battle.

Brandon reflected that it had to be obvious to Bek, pig-headed though he might be, that he had to compromise with the red-bearded Abdul if he hoped to remain in command. That didn't mean he had to like it. It was one thing to allow the Americans to operate out of his base camp in exchange for money, food, and weapons; it was quite another to allow them and Abdul to destroy what he had built safely in the mountains. It was curious, Brandon thought, how a man could come to consider even a hole in the rock as a home worth defending and sustaining when he had nothing else.

Abdul, on the other hand, seemed eager to fight and to form a closer working alliance with the Delta detachment. While Iron Weed depended upon SFOB for its CIA and in-country intelligence assets, Brandon saw no benefit in keeping the team's mission secret from the guerrillas. They would have to know sooner or later anyhow. He encouraged Bek and Abdul to cultivate intel contacts in Kabul, Kandahar, and elsewhere in an attempt to pick up the Shake's trail. He was anxious to get on with his job.

Bek didn't like the idea of targeting the terrorist leader. "Such as this will cause the Taliban and al-Qaeda to take stronger actions against my band," he said. Ismael, interpreting, sat with Brandon in the cave, which was illuminated by candles and wick oil lamps. "Here we are left alone to choose when and where to fight. Mullah Omar will send his fighters against us."

"The ground offensive will soon get under way," Abdul Homayan said. "Commander Khalil will lead his fighters across the Shomali Plain and enter Kabul. Kabul cannot resist much longer. American B-52s are dropping so many bombs that you cannot count them. Mullah Omar does not concern himself with you, Commander Bek. You are only the commander of some men and a few boys and horses. Merely a pimple on the ass of the Taliban. The Taliban need not scratch a pimple when boils are breaking out in their crotch."

Bek stiffened. He had a habit of talking with his hands. Now, they shot to his big turbaned head, and he began gesticulating and punching the air as he shouted. His beard squirmed on his face like a skunk with a bellyache.

"I care about my people in this band," he bellowed. "Have I not kept my people fed? We are warm here against the coming winter. My people have lost only one man in the fighting—Shamsher Khan—and only because he was foolish and stepped on a mine. Unlike you, Abdul, who led your people into an ambush and lost many."

"How many Taliban have you killed?" Abdul roared back. "My band are fighters, not old women hiding in a hole in the mountain."

Bek pointed a stiff finger at him. "I think of when the Americans leave again, defeated as were the Russians. The Taliban will seek revenge upon the people who aided the Americans."

Abdul leaped to his feet. "Then why don't you join the Taliban? The Alliance will then hang you alongside Mullah Omar and Osama bin Laden."

"Do not question my loyalty to the Alliance, Abdul. Do not do that."

The guerrilla leaders glared at each other. One of the three women in camp was serving tea. She backed against the cave wall. Only her wide, frightened eyes were visible through her veil. Finally, Abdul shrugged and sat down.

"I do not question your loyalty, Commander Bek," he said. "Only your generalship. We have supplies and ammunition and food from the Americans. I say it is time to fight again so that our band can claim part of the victory. Kabul will fall without us, for we are not prepared. But if we kill Osama with the Americans, al-Qaeda will crumble and we will gain profound status with the Northern Alliance."

Bek, defeated, looked around the cave, his hard pig's eyes glinting dangerously in the oil light. He stood up, shouldered his little machine gun and walked out of the cave without looking back.

"We have spies in the cities," Abdul promised, speaking to Brandon. "We will find Osama for you."

Afterward, Bek seemed more subdued, more accommodating, quiet and withdrawn and content to keep to himself with his horses.

"This is when he is the most dangerous," young Ismael warned. "Bek is a schemer."

Most of the band seemed to fall in with Abdul. The fighters were growing stale and restive from inactivity. Hafiz Saeed the Zarbati, for one, became a permanent fixture among the Americans. A wiry little man with a fierce black beard, his even fiercer black eyes concealed an almost child-like innocence and an open sense of humor. Gloomy Davis began teaching him English.

"He can already talk to purt-near every good ol' boy in Hooker, Oklahoma," Mad Dog chided. "He can say y'all and 'possum, and sing 'Okie from Muskogee.' That's all he needs."

Brandon found Ismael's position and status among the guerrillas difficult to decipher. The smart-mouthed kid was too damned young to enjoy the influence he obviously wielded among the mujahideen. All Brandon could figure was that his linguistics ability made him indispensable.

"This country is going to be overrun with Americans," Ismael explained in his mocking way. "I'll be in demand because I speak English."

One afternoon after Brandon had worked with Mad Dog in compiling a sitrep to be radioed to SFOB, receiving in return a reply that there was still no word on the Shake's whereabouts, he came upon Ismael in the rocks, deep in concentration over a laptop personal computer. It took him aback for a moment—the sight of a little Afghan boy possessing and working a complicated and obviously high-speed piece of technology as if he knew exactly what he was doing. When Ismael looked up and saw him, he closed the PC and returned it to the pack, which he seldom let out of his sight.

Brandon regarded him, puzzled and frowning. He thought he saw something vaguely and disturbingly familiar in the kid's face, mostly in the dark eyes. It was a fleeting sensation.

"Who the hell are you?" he asked. "Where the hell do you come from?"

Ismael smiled mysteriously. "If I told you that, Major Kragle, I'd have to kill you."

There it was again, the "Major Kragle" thing. As if Ismael dropped the name to show how much he knew.

Brandon grabbed him by the collar of his sheepskin coat and jerked him to his feet. He was surprisingly light. "You little shit," he said. "Is it too much to expect a straight answer when I ask you a question?"

Ismael did not struggle. "There are few straight answers in this country, Major."

"How do you know my name and rank?"

"It's my business to know things, Major Kragle. You have my code name, is that correct?"

" 'Dove.' What a misnomer."

"A code name means I've been checked out as reliable at the highest level. You know that. Are you going to keep dangling my feet off the ground or do you want to know about the Shake?"

Brandon took a deep breath, exasperated, but let him go. "What about the Shake?"

The kid even knew Osama's code name. He looked too young to be CIA. He sat down on his rock again and gestured to an adjacent boulder.

Ismael indicated the PC in his pack. "I've received intel that bin Laden and several of his top henchmen are going to meet with Taliban commanders in two days at an al-Qaeda rendezvous house by the river on the south edge of Kabul. . . ."

"Do you know the address?" Brandon asked sarcastically.

"A guide will meet us in Kabul."

He was serious. "How good is this intel?" Brandon asked.

"What do you want—my signature in blood? Look, Major.

I know I said to trust nobody, but you have to trust me or we can't work together. There's nobody else. I'll be with you, so it'll be my ass too if something goes wrong. So, are we going after the Shake or do we hang around playing fuck-fuck with each other's minds? We'll have to move fast. He never stays in any one place too long."

CHAPTER 16

The guerrilla chief, glaring, watched the two Americans and the two Afghans ride out of camp. Brandon felt Bek Gorabic's eyes stabbing him in the back. He pulled up his horse where the trail dipped through a growth of scraggly trees and slipped over the edge of the ridge, down toward the barren flats in the direction of Kabul. Gloomy Davis reined in the gray he had selected because it reminded him of a rodeo horse he owned back in Hooker. Ismael and Hafiz Saeed continued riding, dropping over the edge.

Squat on his short bowlegs, Bek stood in the shadows by the horse pen in the trees. He held the SAW in both hands as though he would like to use it. When he saw the American looking, he turned slowly and disappeared into the pen among his treasured horses.

"That ol' polecat's up to something," Gloomy predicted. His great handlebar mustache quivered separately from the beard he'd begun growing in Colorado.

It made Brandon uneasy to leave 1-Alpha behind in camp, but Ismael and the other Afghans assured him it would be impossible for a large party to enter the city without being spotted and targeted in return. Ismael recommended that no more than four go, counting himself. At a team mission meeting the night before, Brandon selected himself and Gloomy as the two Americans. Saeed had to go because he personally knew the contact and guide in Kabul. It was up to Mother Norman to stay in camp with the rest of the team and maintain a commo watch with Mad Dog.

"The little Motorola radios are hooked up for satellites," Mad Dog had explained. "There are only a couple of hours during the day when the satellites are out of position and you won't be able to reach us. You can always use your cell phones if the Motorolas fail, providing the towers haven't been blown down. Thank God for Motorola and modern technology."

"We have two options," Brandon had said. "Gloomy is the first option. If he gets a shot, he'll take it."

"The Shake shouldn't be hard to spot," Gloomy said. "How many six-foot-four dudes walking on a cane can there be in this country?"

"The second option depends on you, Dog. We're taking the PAQ-10. Keep the PRC-137 warmed up and an open channel to SFOB. We've arranged for strike aircraft to be on standby and in the air for the twenty-four hours we'll be in Kabul. If we determine the Shake's at home. I'll radio in to you, and you relay to the aircraft. We'll laser-direct the strike with the PAQ-10. The KISS principal—keep it simple, stupid. Clear?"

"Clear, sir."

Brandon had been squatting on his haunches, doodling in the dust with a stick. He looked up at Mother Norman.

"I don't trust Bek out of my sight," he said. "Keep an eye on the bastard. Does everybody know the rally point in case everything turns to shit and we have to bug out?"

There were nods. Brandon tossed his doodle stick aside and stood up.

"Gentlemen," he said with a grim smile, "by this time two

days from now, Osama bin Laden will have had his ass waxed and we're outta here for a steak dinner and a beer."

"No more sitting in the dirt watching the goats fuck," Mad Dog said.

KISS always failed to consider Murphy's Law, which stated that anything that could go wrong, would.

Frost stuck to the puny trees, and sprinklings of snow dusted the tops of boulders as the little group of assassins rode out on its mission. The four riders maintained a tiring, mile-eating gait on the tough little Mongol horses. Gloomy the cowboy was in his element. Saeed was full of questions about American life. It came as a great surprise to him to learn that Westerners worshiped God.

"What did he think?" Brandon asked through Ismael. "That we worshiped the Statue of Liberty or the Brooklyn Bridge?"

"You're the first Americans he's ever seen," Ismael explained. "He saw Russians, but only from a distance—and he killed them."

Saeed seemed much amused by American customs. "Do you have wives?" he asked Brandon.

"Neither singular nor plural," Brandon responded.

"Why not?" Ismael asked.

"Is that your question or Saeed's?"

"His, of course."

"It's the job." Brandon left it at that.

"Not even a prospect?" Ismael asked.

An image of Gypsy Iryani flashed through Brandon's thoughts. She was dead. She would have married Cameron anyhow, a matter of honor for all three of them.

Gloomy grinned broadly. "The Major," he interjected, "has cut a swath through womankind like Moses crossing the

Red Sea. Boss, tell them about the stripper at the Pirate's Den, or about the rich widow from Tampa."

Brandon scowled.

"How do you buy a wife in America?" Saeed wanted to know.

Brandon attempted to explain the intricacies of American courtship, how a single man might be introduced to a lady by friends, or how he might go to a club.

Saeed's eyes widened. "Scores of virgins!"

"I wouldn't go that far," Brandon cautioned.

Saeed was stuck on the image of the countless virgins. "Like those Allah will provide for warriors when we die. All in one dance room!"

Brandon laughed. "I doubt if you could find enough virgins to fill a dance room."

"Hafiz wants to know if you have met a virgin," Ismael said.

"I've been too busy recently," Brandon alibied.

"Too busy to find love?" Ismael said. "I thought all Americans believed in love."

"I believe in lust."

They urged their horses up an incline out of a dry wadi. They tried to stay away from well-traveled paths, although they probably wouldn't be noticed in a country where so many rode horses and drove carts and mule wagons.

"Hafiz wants to know if you've lusted recently," Ismael said.

"Not since Israel," Brandon said, for lack of a better response.

"What happened in Israel?"

What was with this kid? Adolescent hormones raging?

"Nothing, really. Just a slit with green eyes and a gorgeous ass in jeans."

"What's her name?"

"Summer."

"Oh? Hafiz wants to know if Summer is a virgin."

Brandon guffawed. "Not too damned likely."

He kicked his horse in the ribs and rode on ahead. The interrogation was getting a bit too personal for him.

They stopped for noon meal at a watering hole hidden in a thick grove of white-barked trees that resembled cottonwoods, only smaller. Chow was MERCs—mobility enhancing ration components. Where did the U.S. Army come up with such names? he wondered. While the horses blew and chewed on bark and tender saplings, Saeed took off his worn sneakers and washed his feet in the freezing water. He dropped his rifle on top of his shoes and took his prayer rug off into the trees. It was a cultural thing. Five times a day the mujahideen dropped everything in order to pray.

"What about you?" Brandon asked Ismael. Gloomy sat cross-legged on the ground between them, eating a MERC.

"I'm a Christian," Ismael said.

"You're not an Afghan?"

"There are Christians in Afghanistan."

"Live ones since Mullah Omar and the Taliban took over?"

"I know what you're trying to do, Major. It won't work. I've told you all you need to know about me. You have your own cover story, I have mine. Let's leave it at that, huh? That way we don't have to kill each other."

Smart-assed kid, he thought.

Snow was falling by the time they reached the sparsely populated outskirts of Kabul. Saeed led the way to an isolated mud hut not far from the river. An old man named Amir lived there alone. He took the horses and put them in a corral out back where he kept a mule and some black sheep.

"It's getting dark," Saeed said. "This man has told me the

way to where Osama will be, but he will also show us tomorrow. There is a curfew tonight. He says we must stay in the house and not be seen. There are many spies in the city."

Electricity was shut off in the capital after nightfall, when the curfew went into effect. Nothing moved in the streets except Taliban troops and women and children flitting about like ghosts scrounging for food. There had been an American airdrop of food packets over the city during the day, and people were defying curfew to continue looking for the rice and bean packets.

Inside the mud hut by the river, the old man, Amir, lit an oil lamp and built a small wood fire in the open fireplace, to cook a meal for his guests. Brandon sat on a low tattered sofa with Ismael and watched Amir's arthritic hands as he knelt in front of the fire and clumsily added goat meat to a boiling pot filled with the contents of an airdrop packet and MERCs contributed by the visitors. He looked up when Gloomy and Saeed entered and closed the door behind them, after having made a security patrol of the area. Brandon insisted on precautions, even though Ismael and Saeed assured him they were safe in the house of Amir.

The old man's face was a muddy road map of wrinkles rearranged by ugly scars around his soiled gray beard and sad dark eyes. One scar ran across his forehead below his dingy turban. Another jagged seam disfigured his nose, thrusting it flat and ugly to one side of his face and exposing his cheekbone. A third started below his left ear and crawled down his neck. He touched his face with the tips of gnarled fingers.

The scars, he explained through Ismael, were compliments of the Soviets. "They took me from my home and told me I would not be alive at the end of an hour. I did not die, so then they said I would be dead by the end of the day. It is not up to the Soviets or anyone else to say when you must die. If

God says you die at eight o'clock of a certain day of a certain year, it will not be ten minutes before or ten minutes after."

Amir sat with his back to the fire, warming his old bones while the meat cooked. He began a story about Kabul and the people of Kabul. Ismael translated using the old man's low tone, as though both feared their voices might disturb the stillness of the night and be heard by spies.

"The Americans come to bomb when it is daylight and when it is dark," Amir said, almost whispering. His eyes lifted toward the ceiling as though it were transparent and he saw the bombers coming. "But what can we in our country do? The whole country is rubble. We have nothing and will have nothing except war and more war. Yet, we are happy that America bombs Afghanistan. We only want to get rid of the Taliban. There is no choice left except to flee if the Taliban remains."

Amir told them he had put up with ten years of drought and tribal wars and the Taliban. Everything became worse after the crazies attacked America. Taliban authorities dragged off young men to serve in the army. Other sons and husbands were shot by militiamen to settle ancient scores. In his village near Rishhore, north of Kabul, the farm families ran away and hid whenever Taliban officials approached. His twenty-four-year-old son was taken away to fight for the Taliban, and his twenty-year-old son, Ramet, was killed.

"I do not know how they put him to death, or why, or where he is buried," Amir said, his eyes glistening. "I saw only that his body was dragged away."

Almost the entire village decided to flee when crops failed and there was nothing left to eat. With his wife and daughter and nearly fifty others from his village, Amir walked through the mountains for fifteen days to reach Quetta, the crossing at the Pakistan border in the wild mountains east of Kandahar. Along the way, eight children, three women, and five elderly men died when they slipped off narrow trails in high mountain passes.

Pakistan had closed its borders, but thousands of people joined in the exodus, hoping to bribe or steal their way out of Afghanistan. Crying babies, women concealed in head-to-toe veils, hobbling old men, boys swathed in bandages . . . ragged and frightened and bringing with them only what they could carry.

"All were people in very bad condition, in poor healthy, with very few possessions, no food, little water, and no shelter. Some were sick, all were hungry, and most of us had sold everything we owned."

Refugees slipped across the border or paid smugglers to guide them across on mud trails or mountain paths. Amir paid 1,500 Pakistan rupees—about thirty dollars of an annual average income of two hundred dollars—as a bribe to get his wife and daughter across to relatives in Islamabad. Then he returned to Afghanistan to join the Northern Alliance and seek revenge for his son. At fifty-five, he was too old to fight, so Commander Khalil put him in Kabul as a spy.

Amir stopped talking. He turned toward the fire and stared into it. The pot bubbled in the quiet as it boiled.

"There are many stories like his," Ismael said after a while.

"I'm curious about yours," Brandon said.

"Mine doesn't matter."

U.S. warplanes returned to the skies over Kabul before they finished eating. Explosions shook the ground and rattled windows. Amir did not move from in front of the fire. Brandon slipped outside and stood in the darkness to watch. It was still snowing, lightly. Ismael and Gloomy soon followed, but Saeed stayed inside with Amir. Eating was more important.

A huge fireball lit up the horizon over the eastern part of the city. More explosions could be heard pounding the Kabul airport to the north and al-Qaeda training camps to the south. Secondary explosions banged and popped from detonations of weapons storage sites. Ineffective and sporadic antiaircraft fire streaked lazily across the low black sky. The B-52s were well out of range of both antiaircraft batteries and SAM missiles, even if the Taliban still had SAMs left. Two-thousand-pound JDAMs—Joint Direct Action Munitions—could be laser-directed to a specific target from as high as 45,000 feet in the air.

Movement near the river drew Brandon's attention away from the awesome display. He spotted figures running up from the banks toward the house, their menacing forms outlined against bright-flashing fireballs on the city horizon.

CHAPTER 17

It was so dark beneath the snow clouds, even with the ground beginning to whiten, that the raiders resembled moving chunks of the night itself, impossible to count and difficult to pinpoint. Brandon estimated four or five militiamen, or perhaps even six. There was no time to consider how they had discovered the Americans' presence. A traitor somewhere. If the Deltas hadn't come outside when they did, chances were they would have been caught by surprise and slaughtered inside the old man's house. The bombing might have saved their lives, although that was an outcome not yet assured.

The attackers hadn't seen them yet. Brandon drew his Sig and dropped to one knee to cut down his silhouette against the flickering backdrop of bomb explosions, pulling Ismael down with him. Gloomy dropped to a knee on the other side, whipping out his pistol. Mr. Blunderbuss rested slung in its case across his back. Ismael was unarmed, having left his carbine inside. That meant two against five or six, but Brandon knew they still had the advantage of surprise. He tasted copper in his mouth, felt his heart pumping. He heard Ismael's breath whistling through his teeth.

A shadow appeared at the corner of the mud hut. It looked

distorted and monstrous in heavy coat, robe, and headdress. Other forms followed closely behind.

At almost that exact moment the door opened. Firelight silhouetted a form in the doorway.

"Now!" Brandon shouted.

In the combat village at Wally World, Delta troopers trained under all lighting conditions, from total darkness to blazing light, learning methodical and accurate shooting with all types of weapons. The shooters practiced picking off alternate targets, starting with the nearest, so that one enemy didn't end up riddled all to hell while others were left unscathed and able to fight back.

Brandon accounted for the first target. It dropped with a shrill otherworldly scream. Gloomy knocked off the second. Then they were both shooting, fast and accurately.

The night suddenly filled with flashes and the chattering bark of firearms and the cries of those hit. An automatic weapon opened up, blasting in their faces. The shooter sprayed the open doorway, mistakenly assuming it to be the source of the ambush. It was his last assumption. Brandon drilled him hard, snap-shooting. The body slammed against the wall of the house before it fell.

Brandon and Gloomy had been involved in other gunfights. They experienced the excitement, confusion, and fear that attended the few seconds that it lasted. Under these conditions, you kept shooting until there was nothing left standing to shoot at or until you ran out of ammo. Strange things sometimes happened during the confusion. You could empty a weapon at point-blank range and never even touch the mark. A stray round might hit a baby lying in a cradle two blocks over. Collateral damage, in the harsh military vernacular.

Eventually, the last attacker panicked and fled. Brandon's shot missed, as did Gloomy's. The militiaman headed back to the river, his form darting back and forth across fires burning in the city. He couldn't be allowed to escape to spread the word, so Brandon sprang after him.

The chase ended as abruptly as it began. The man was going to reach the river ahead of them, where he could either cross at the shallows and disappear into housing on the other side or follow it, concealed by trees and shrubbery growing along the banks. Brandon dropped to his knees in order to etch the darting figure against fires from the bombing raids.

He squeezed off a round, stabbing a spear of flame at the running man. It dropped him. He was running so hard that he hit the ground and tumbled.

Brandon approached cautiously with his pistol in both hands, covering him. Gloomy followed right behind. He nudged the body with his foot. The wounded man stirred and emitted a painful groan, but he was clearly down to stay.

"Major?" Ismael ran toward them.

"Over here."

"Did you get him?"

"Yeah."

Ismael and Saeed came up together and looked down at the body. Snowflakes fell on it. The kid brought disappointing news.

"The old man's dead. He opened the door at the wrong time. We have three bad guys KIA, four with this one."

"Check out the river," Brandon ordered Gloomy. "Then get on back. We have to move ASAP."

Gloomy tapped Saeed's elbow and motioned for him to follow. They trotted off.

"Ismael, did Amir give you enough that you can find the Shake's headquarters?" Brandon demanded tersely.

"Between Saeed and me, I think so."

Brandon was still ragged and on a high from the fight. "Damnit, that's not good enough. Can you find it without him?"

"Yes, yes! Damnit yourself, I can find it."

Bombs still thumped and cracked on various targets around the city. Brandon hoped they'd masked the sounds of the gun battle.

The wounded man moaned and muttered something. Brandon bent over him. "What's he saying?"

"He's praying to Allah. I think he's already counting his virgins. Kill him."

"What?"

"We can't leave him alive to talk. If you haven't noticed, Major, we're behind enemy lines."

The kid was one icy little bastard, he thought, but Brandon knew he was right. They still had one more day to catch Osama with his pants down. When you were in the enemy's backyard, you never took chances you didn't have to. You left no one on your back trail able to talk about you. That was the way it had to be.

Gloomy and Saeed returned from the river. The ground was almost white now, it was snowing so hard. Their outlines showed up against it.

"Shoot him," Ismael insisted.

Brandon flared, "*You* shoot him." He'd had enough of this kid.

"Give me the pistol," Ismael said.

Brandon didn't think he meant it. Shooting a man in a fight was one thing, shooting a helpless wounded man quite another. Brandon handed the kid his Sig, if only to shut him up.

Ismael snatched the weapon. The reverberation of the single additional gunshot echoed over the snowfield. Brandon flinched.

CHAPTER 18

Fort Bragg

The Farm was getting used in this year of the terrorists. Kathryn Burguiere-Kragle had died late on Sunday night of inhalation anthrax. Cassidy sat by her bedside for another hour, holding her lifeless hand while Gloria wept behind him. Cameron came in and offered to pray. Cassidy rebuffed him, saying, "Where was God when we needed Him?" He got up and walked out, still dry-eyed.

On Wednesday they buried Kathryn in the family plot near Little Nana and Rita, the General's wife and the mother-in-law Kathryn never knew. Kathryn's family traveled from Toeterville, Iowa, for the funeral. FBI Agent Thornton, Delta Force Commander Buck Thompson, Sergeant Rasem Jameel, and Bobby Goose Pony were all there. The Kragle clan assembled the day before, except for Brandon. He wouldn't be notified of the death until he was out of Afghanistan and harm's way.

A cold steady drizzle fell, contributing to the bleakness. Cameron opened his Bible beneath the awning and said final words. Cassidy stared straight ahead, his jaw set in the Kragle way, his eyes hard and flinty.

"They will pay for this," he vowed as they left the cemetery in the rain. "It says in the Bible, an eye for an eye—"

"It also says revenge is the Lord's," Cameron pointed out.

Feelings of melancholy and depression accompanied Chaplain Cameron back to Fort Bragg. The weather had been awful and rainy for a week now, which contributed to his mood. The vow of revenge uttered by Cassidy at the funeral disturbed him. He had witnessed Cassidy's rage in Afghanistan against the al-Qaeda terrorist who raped Kathryn. Cassidy had taken Brandon's pistol and deliberately shot off the man's penis while the terrorist cowered naked on the floor.

Killing a man was one thing; deliberate murder was another, and against God's law.

Cassidy's soul in the hereafter concerned Cameron. He was concerned for the violent souls of both his brothers. Perhaps, he thought, he should even be distressed by the future of his own soul. His initial reaction to Kathryn's death jolted him in his realization that God and all America's technology could not protect her from a handful of men with box cutters and plastic knives and from madmen who spread anthrax through the mail. All security systems had failed. Terrorists lived on American soil in a fifth column. They drove around in U.S. Fords and Chevys, like everyone else, drank beer in bars, went to American colleges and trade schools, and duped Americans to unwittingly train them to kill other Americans.

He ached to cry out to God: *Smite them, Lord!*

In his brothers' lives God played only a supporting role as a warrior God. You never turned the other cheek. If someone slapped you, you turned and knocked his dick in the dirt.

Smite them, Lord!

Begone, Satan! He knelt before the altar in his church, beneath the banner of GOD IS GOD IN ALL LANGUAGES, and prayed so hard tears ran down his cheeks. Candles burning on the altar highlighted the blond in his crew cut, his hair the color of his dead mother's. He ordered Satan to begone and leave him a clear communications pathway to the Spirit. He begged God to show him the purpose for His taking of the Kragle women, starting with Cameron's own mother when he was only four and Cassidy was born. He pleaded for understanding, and said entire prayers for his brothers and his father, grandfather, and uncle in their war against terrorists.

God forgive me and lend me patience, understanding, and compassion.

He opened his eyes, and there was Gypsy's face before him. God had taken her too, another who would have been a Kragle woman. Only God knew how much he loved her still. Tears flowed, and he collapsed in great wracking sobs at his altar.

His subject for Sunday's sermon, which he was preparing, was his belief that the United States was about to experience a great spiritual reawakening. There had been three so far, but none within the last century. In his opinion, America had suffered the greatest moral collapse in its history during the previous fifty years, and now that decline was about to end, brought about by the terrorist attack, of all things. A spiritual reawakening generated profound repentance throughout the land and a phenomenal increase in the number of people who became Christians. All such awakenings in the past had produced a dramatic reduction in crime and the divorce rate and a reversal of patterns of general immorality in society.

"I see exact signs that such a great reawakening may be coming," he told Rasem Jameel.

He expected to deliver the sermon to a full house, minus most of the Deltas who were overseas on missions or preparing for missions. The signs of an awakening were clear to him. Wives and mothers of soldiers started pouring into the chapel seeking spiritual solace shortly after 9/11.

"I didn't want to wait for Sunday," said a mother who drove all the way from Wisconsin to see her airborne son. "I never thought in my lifetime to be faced with this. I'm frightened over the tribulations to come in the final days. When you see evil in the world, you want to be with others who believe in the power of God."

What a chaplain needed, Cameron thought, was a reawakening in his own soul to dispel the melancholy of his doubts and inner conflicts. Sometimes he wished he were more like his brothers.

Cassidy had coped with his wife's death by immediately returning to complete the SF Q Course. Colonel Buck Thompson telephoned Cameron on Saturday and asked him to drop by his office at Wally World. Sergeant Jameel offered to type the chaplain's completed sermon while he was gone and have it ready for Sunday morning.

"I won't be long, Rasem," he said.

"I want to help," Rasem told him. "It is like the sermon is dedicated to Kathryn's memory. It is, isn't it? In a way?"

"Yes. In a way."

Rasem was a small man with an earnestness that he brought to everything he undertook. That was especially true when it came to his Christianity. Cameron blessed the day the little man had first come last winter. He simply appeared at the door of the chapel with those black eyes that never seemed to hold still in his narrow face. He took in the sanctuary and the GOD IS GOD IN ALL LANGUAGES banner. He spoke good English but in a quaint, stilted accent.

"I am from Saudi Arabia," he ventured, "but I have become an American citizen and an American soldier. I have been Muslim, but now I desire to become Christian. Will you help me to convert?"

Not only did Rasem prove to be a good student, he selflessly volunteered to help in the maintenance and running of a church with a staff of only one—the pastor. He swept and cleaned. He knew how to type, use a computer, and operate an ancient offset printing press. Often he stayed long into the night to work with Cameron and Kathryn in preparing the Billy Dye ministry pamphlets for next day's mail. He had been a godsend. Cameron baptized the Saudi into his new life in the name of Christ.

"Chaplain Cameron, I work here and I miss her," he said while Cameron was on his way out the door to Wally World.

Cameron stopped and came back.

"I have been emotional like this for whole week," Rasem said in a voice not much louder than a whisper. "I pray I could be so wise to say exactly what must be said the way it needs to be said. I am much fond of Kathryn. I would have died first myself in her place if I know this would happen. Do you believe that, Chaplain Cameron?"

Candles on the altar flickered.

"Anyone who knows war understands civilians are going to be harmed during legitimate military actions," Cameron said. "But intentional targeting of civilians, of women, children, and old people, is out of the realm of God and decent society."

"Yes. It is random with unforeseen consequences."

"We must believe that what was meant for evil will turn to good. What the devil meant to destroy in us will only make us stronger and bring a great revival to this land. That's the subject of my sermon tomorrow."

"I will be in the front pew, as always."

Colonel Thompson wanted to talk about Cassidy. "Your

brother graduates from phase three next week and wins his beret," the Delta Force commander began. "He and Sergeant Pony came to apply for Delta. I turned Cassidy down."

"Cassidy is graduating with honors," Cameron protested mildly, although he thought he already understood Colonel Thompson's reasoning.

"That's true, but he's a walking time bomb right now. All he sees is revenge. He asked to volunteer immediately for the war in Afghanistan."

Cameron thought of the terrorist's penis.

"I told him I thought it best he went into one of the groups, preferably the 7th or the 1st, whose AOs are in Latin America and Southeast Asia. I told him I'd reconsider if he's still interested after a year."

"What did our father say?" Cameron asked.

"The General recommended the delay."

Cameron looked at his hands, then looked up. "Sir, please don't let Cassidy know the General was behind this."

There was already enough friction between father and younger son, who had yet to make their peace with one another.

"It stops here," Colonel Thompson promised. "I told you only because I thought you could help cushion the blow for him."

"Then you don't know the Kragles, sir, with all due respect. My father and my brothers will break first before they accept a cushion from anyone."

Lord, hadn't the Kragles already contributed more than their share of casualties to the war on terror?

Cameron thought Rasem was already gone from the chapel when he returned. He headed toward the office to look over the sermon Rasem promised to type for him, then hesitated when he heard a low voice. Rasem had not heard him return. He was kneeling on the floor in the unlighted office when Cameron opened the door. He immediately sprang to his feet.

"I was praying to Father for Kathryn," he explained, taken aback.

At first Cameron thought what he heard was a Muslim prayer. He smiled at Rasem. He must have been mistaken, he decided.

CHAPTER 19

New York

Former President John Stanton's office on the twenty-first
floor of the Tuttle Building presented a sweeping view of upper Manhattan. At his desk, Stanton thoughtfully puffed on a
thick cheroot while a nubile young woman with a bright
smile served coffee to him and his visitor, Senator Eric B.
Tayloe, chairman of the Armed Services Committee. The
senator sat across the desk from Stanton, leaning forward
with his knees primly pressed together and his briefcase on
top of them. He glanced at the secretary, then at Stanton's cigar. He grinned slyly.

Stanton reddened, annoyed, and stamped out the cigar.
Nasty-minded little fuck, he thought. He looked harmless
enough, like a man who lived with his mother, but looks
could be deceiving. Stanton knew that Tayloe didn't get
where he was through looks and charisma. He got there because he was a scheming little bastard who knew where all
the skeletons were and how to use them. It was said he carried many of the skeletons around with him in his briefcase.

He could be useful, though, as long as you kept an eye on
him.

When they were alone together again, after fresh coffee and a lingering last look at the young woman's departing derriere, the former President tossed a copy of the *New York Times* to his guest.

"Have you seen this?" he asked, getting to the point. "The front page above the fold."

Spread beneath headlines was a chilling tableau of photographs showing Afghan Northern Alliance troops dragging a wounded Taliban soldier out of a ditch and shooting him while he pleaded for his life.

"Our noble allies at work," Tayloe scoffed.

"Look again," the former President countered. "Our noble opportunity at work."

He got up and stared out the window. In the distance, smoke still rose in thin tendrils from where the WTC Towers stood before September 11. When he spoke again, his words sounded sharp and bitter.

"This bunch of cowboys in this administration are scrapping my peace initiative and destroying my historical legacy with their ill-conceived so-called War on Terror," he complained. "I worked harder than I ever worked in my life to remove the causes of strife and conflict and to address the root causes of war. My administration understood the alienation and sense of grievance expressed against us in the Middle East. Because of this understanding, we achieved world peace through globalization efforts within the United Nations. Then this administration won the election and started throwing its weight around like a bunch of drunks in a bar. You didn't see these attacks happening on *my* watch."

"No, sir, Mr. President," Senator Tayloe agreed. "The terrorist attacks under your administration were not nearly of this magnitude."

Stanton turned quickly toward the senator to see if he was being facetious. He could be a sarcastic little fuck. So there had been a few incidents during his eight years in the White House—the bombing of U.S. embassies in Africa, the Somalia fiasco, the blowing up of American military barracks in Saudi Arabia, the first attack on the World Trade Center, and the terrorist bombing of the USS *Randolph* in Aden. He had handled them, hadn't he, without sparking a world war? In fact, with a third term, which the Constitution did not allow, he would have achieved his goal and his ultimate historical legacy of a world that outlawed warfare.

Reasonably satisfied that Senator Tayloe intended no outright disrespect, the former President went back to staring out the window, saying, "This President has embarked on dangerous grounds with his circumvention of the United Nations abroad and his scorning of human rights in the United States. The resolution I had hoped for was that Osama bin Laden and Mullah Omar would be found, arrested, and tried legally before a World Court without the United States murdering innocent civilians in Afghanistan. Now, the President and his underlings are set on trying prisoners in military courts while they cage up innocent immigrants. We're bordering on fascism, Senator Tayloe. Do you realize that?"

"How well I do, Mr. President."

Stanton faced the senator. He bit his lip to check a cynical smile.

"They're playing right into our hands," he said, and the smile broke through. "What we're seeing is the beginning of a bloody conflict that will cause the deaths of thousands of American soldiers before it's over. However, I don't think the American people will stand for it. Public opinion will begin to shift once we're involved in a protracted ground war. Six months or a year from now, there won't be any more flag waving except from the hard core right wing."

"The dissent is already beginning, Mr. President."

"It's our patriotic duty to fan that dissent," Stanton erupted, his face reddening, "to expose to the American people the crimes and atrocities being committed by this administration. These yellow dog sonsofbitches think they can obfuscate and destroy the legacy of peace I worked so hard to build. I still have power in the political arena. I can still make and break."

He caught himself, struggling to control the legendary temper that he had unleashed in the White House for two terms. After a moment, the cynical smile returned and he was biting his lip, watching Tayloe as if he were an experimental laboratory animal.

"Senator Tayloe, with my influence you could be the next President of the United States."

That struck a chord. Tayloe's eyes narrowed with greedy ambition.

"You know where my loyalties lie, Mr. President. I defended you throughout all the hearings and the impeachment."

Stanton winced at Tayloe's reminder of the troubles he had endured from his political enemies. Was it a deliberate remark to put him in his place and warn him of the skeletons the politico supposedly carried in his briefcase? Stanton studied the doughy face across the desk from him, finally deciding the remark had been innocent.

He smiled and selected another cigar from the humidor on his desk. Senator Tayloe carefully avoided looking at it. The former President lit up and peered through the smoke.

"Senator, are you aware of Operation Iron Weed?" he asked with a crafty look.

Tayloe blinked. No politician was ever going to admit outright he wasn't in the know. "That's classified," he ventured, though it was clear to Stanton that he was in the dark.

"I have my reliable sources," Stanton said, his jaw tightening. "USSOCOM and that bastard General Kragle are sending assassination teams to Afghanistan to kill bin Laden and Mullah Omar. Not capture them, *murder* them. That, Senator, is Iron Weed. Did you know that?"

"I know that the CIA attempted to assassinate Mullah Omar on the first day of the bombing," Tayloe said to demonstrate his inside knowledge, that he really was in the know. "Spooks operating a small unmanned aircraft armed with antitank missiles saw the convoy Omar wanders around in. They requested permission to fire. The Judge Advocate General explained the negative legal aspects of an assassination and the shot was not taken. General Kragle almost pounded his desk into splinters when he heard about it."

"The man's a troglodyte, a throwback. If he weren't Irish, he'd be a Cossack." Stanton leaned forward to better bring the senator into his confidence. "Iron Weed was conceived by Kragle to avoid the laws against assassinations. He got away clean the last time he pulled a stunt like this. He won't a second time. We've got the sonofabitch right where we want him."

"How's that? The President must have issued a finding for covert activities."

"Exactly!" Stanton pounded one fist into the palm of the other hand. "Assassinations are against U.S. law, no matter the form they take. If General Kragle goes down for war crimes, the scandal will topple the entire administration. Senator, with your contacts and your inside knowledge of the military, we can make sure Kragle and Iron Weed are exposed, that they fail, and that the stench of it reaches the White House."

Flattered, Senator Tayloe admitted modestly, "Well, I do have certain powerful military people who talk to me."

"And who, no doubt, are indebted to you in various ways."
He glanced meaningfully at the senator's briefcase.

Senator Tayloe smiled.

"How badly do you want to be the next President, Senator Tayloe?"

CHAPTER 20

Kabul

Ismael returned Brandon's pistol without saying a word. The executed militiaman was only so much meat beginning to cool to the surrounding temperature. He and his buddies would be frozen stiff by midnight. The kid engaged in a quick conversation with Hafiz Saeed using the Dari dialect and much pointing and gesticulating. He turned to Brandon.

"He says he knows where he can put the horses so they'll be safe. Snowfall will hide their tracks. There's an abandoned house upriver where we can spend the night. He'll meet us there after he transfers the horses."

"How do you know he won't lead the Taliban to us?" Brandon asked.

"I trust him."

"I thought you trusted no one."

"I trust no one *completely*."

"Somebody snitched on us, or the militia wouldn't have found us so quickly," Brandon pointed out. "We have a traitor inside Bek's camp."

"Quite possibly," Ismael agreed, seemingly unconcerned.

"More likely we were seen riding in and the militia came out to investigate. But I like the way you think. Caution is good."

As though he needed this runt's approval.

Brandon quickly mulled things over. Murphy's Law—anything that could go wrong, would—had reared its scaly head. Things were getting fucked up and getting more fucked up by the minute. The old man, their guide escort, was dead. Brandon found it hard to believe that they had merely been seen riding in, that the attack was coincidence as a result of a chance sighting. If not, it meant the enemy, including Osama bin Laden, knew they were in Kabul and was prepared for them. If ever there was a good cause to abort a mission, this one had causes aplenty.

"It's your call, Major," Ismael prompted. Gloomy and Saeed waited to one side. The bombing continued but seemed to be tapering off, leaving only fires burning here and there.

On the other hand, Brandon thought, Amir had provided directions to the Shake's HQ before he was killed. If the attack had been a chance thing, it meant they still had an opportunity to complete the mission. Or, he pondered, if the enemy thought the mission had been thwarted . . .

What would the General or the Ambassador do under these circumstances? he wondered. He relied on their experiences as a guide and a standard. Surely the General had confronted similar challenges working with the Montagnards during the Vietnam War. The Ambassador had penetrated enemy lines with the Alamo Scouts in the Philippines to lead guerrillas in raids against the Japanese. A third generation Kragle now had to deal with partisans and brigands behind a new enemy's lines.

Osama bin Laden was the most wanted man in the entire world, with a $25 *million* bounty on his head. The General, Brandon decided, would go after him if there was any chance, however slight. He must not fail his father and the Kragle name, he told himself.

"All right," he said to Ismael. "We'll meet Saeed at the house."

But the General would make sure he evened the odds as best he could.

The abandoned house was also located near the Kabul River. The windows were broken out, and the doors and anything else of value had been scavenged. Snow piled up on the windowsills and blew in on the floor. They dared not build a fire that might give them away, even if fuel were available. It was going to be one cold, miserable night.

Gloomy and Ismael kept watch for Saeed's return. Brandon slipped out of their earshot to the opposite corner of the house and raised 1-Alpha base on his Motorola. He didn't want Ismael to know what he was doing. Mad Dog answered.

"Put Mother on." The Motorola had a built-in crypt/decrypt system to allow communications in the clear.

"Mother here," came the response.

Brandon briefly explained about the fight. "They may have been tipped off and were waiting for us," he said. "I want you to spread it around camp that we've scrubbed the mission and are on the way back. Make sure all the Afghans know about it. Clear?"

"Except for one thing," Mother Norman replied. "You have Ismael, and nobody else here speaks English."

"Jesus, I forgot. Vince Lombardi speaks a little." Gloomy had assigned names to each of the guerrillas. He'd called one of them, Bilal, after the famous football coach. "I don't care how you get it across. Draw pictures, if you have to. But somebody in that camp is a snitch and has commo with the Taliban. I want whoever it is to get the all-clear word about us to Kabul, while we actually continue the mission."

"Roger that. Mission is still on. I'll draw pictures if I have to."

Hopefully, the Shake would receive the word—if there was indeed a spy in camp—and let his guard back down.

Saeed soon returned through the falling snow. He hadn't been followed, he said, nor had he seen any other militia out in the storm. Cold and uncomfortable, they relieved each other on watch.

Brandon napped fitfully. He kept waking to go over the next day's operation in his mind. With luck, Iron Weed 1-Alpha would be out of a job tomorrow night. He knew that an operator could always hope for luck, but better never count on it. Murphy was much more reliable.

Sometime during the night, he awoke with a start to find Ismael camped out next to him for warmth. Brandon's arm was around the kid, who felt small and vulnerable while he slept. Like this, it was difficult to associate the kid with the same Ismael who had finished off the wounded militiaman.

Although Brandon kept still to avoid waking Ismael, he felt vaguely uncomfortable for a reason he couldn't quite define. In SpecOps, people got tight. As tight as brothers. Tighter. A few years ago, Delta Troop One parachuted onto the Korean DMZ to pull security for Operation Team Spirit, a joint U.S.-Korean exercise. The South Korean pilot dropped the team into the icy Wan Ju River. To prevent hypothermia, the entire detachment burrowed into an accumulation of manure in an old round barn and piled on top of each other for warmth. That kind of tight.

Unable to shake his discomfort, he changed positions. The kid awoke and quickly moved away. Brandon wondered if he was an orphan.

"Ismael, where is your family?"

"Not everyone has a family."

"You came from somewhere. If my guess is correct, it's not Afghanistan."

The kid paused so long, Brandon thought he must have gone back to sleep. Snow hissed through the open windows and door.

"Israel," Ismael finally said, a shiver in his voice.

"How did you end up in Afghanistan—and why?"

"I came here."

"I was in Jerusalem. Maybe I met you there?"

"I doubt that. We don't run in the same circles."

"We must overlap some of the same circles," Brandon countered. "Nothing about you makes sense. You're nothing but a teenager—you're at least a teen, aren't you?"

"Boys as young as ten or twelve are already combat veterans in this war," Ismael said.

"But boys ten or twelve don't have your kind of experience. Someone had to trust you enough to brief you and send you here as a contact asset for my mission. You even knew my name. You're a hard kid. It's been my observation that even a man doesn't shoot another man in cold blood without a lot of provocation or without previous experience at it."

"Could you have done it, Major?"

"I wasn't convinced it was necessary."

"It was necessary. I prefer not to talk about it. It's my turn to stand watch."

He got up with his rifle. Brandon heard him whisper to Gloomy on guard at the window. Gloomy made his way across the room in the darkness and crowded close to Brandon to share their warmth. Brandon felt no unease at Gloomy's nearness.

"It'll be daylight in another hour," Gloomy reported. "Osama, y'mama should have raised you better. You in a heap of trouble, boy."

CHAPTER 21

Brandon noted an almost medieval quality about daily life in Kabul. Most of the capital lay in ruins, maimed and ravaged by rival armies. It was a land of poor widows and orphans. Women knelt to wash clothes with raw hands along the banks of the freezing, filthy trickle that was the Kabul River. Other people huddled around open fires on street corners. Maimed beggars. Wizened old men struggling with heavy wooden pushcarts. The skies were clear this morning and the sun warm. Last night's snow was quickly melting into slush. Winter had not yet caught the land in its icy grasp.

Bearded and dressed in native garb, weapons concealed beneath their robes, Brandon and his tiny band of assassins passed between mud walls pocked by bullets and shrapnel. Gloomy Davis strode ahead with Saeed, who guided the way. Gloomy affected a serious limp to accommodate the length of Mr. Blunderbuss strapped to his leg underneath his robe and coat. The group walked rapidly while attempting to appear unhurried. A blue truck rumbled by hauling an antiaircraft gun under a black tarp.

"I'll fuck you over first and fast," Brandon warned Ismael and Saeed before departing their cold overnight quarters, "if either of you turns out to be a traitor."

"That's what I'd do," Ismael approved.

Sometimes the boy's eyes looked ancient, as though he had lived many hard lives compressed into fifteen or sixteen years. No kid Brandon ever knew was as worldly and calloused.

Women begging for food sat in the rocket-rutted streets in their giant, sweeping burqas, hands outstretched. A little girl of three or four, her hair tangled and unwashed, scraped a tin dish in the road, then held it out with a pleading little smile.

Brandon kept going, giving her only a glance. Stopping would draw attention to themselves.

"She's just one of thousands like that in the city," Ismael said. "Ignore them. The best thing we can do for them is destroy the Taliban and get rid of al-Qaeda."

The 9/11 terrorist attack and this war could have been averted and thousands of lives saved had he been able to take out Osama bin Laden the last time he was in Afghanistan, Brandon thought. How might history and lives like those of the little girl been changed were Hitler assassinated in 1936? Or Lenin before the Russian Revolution? Or Pol Pot? Or Saddam Hussein? Assassination might not be politically correct, it might not even be legal under U.S. law, but it was effective.

General Kragle had taken his son aside following Iron Weed's mission briefing in Colorado. Both understood that each would be held accountable under military law if the truth ever got out that Iron Weed assassinated a target while pretending to be a SpecOps capture team.

"If you bring him in alive," the General said in confidence, "lawyers and left wingers will make a circus of his trial and a martyr of the man. People like Senator Tayloe and that idiot ex-President are looking for an excuse to get us out of the war before we even start. The only thing they care about is politics and how they can reduce others to enhance their own power. They'll use bin Laden to make a mockery of our government, to weaken it and allow someone like Tayloe to gain the White House so we can start all over again with appeasing every little two-bit terrorist and tyrant like Yasser Arafat who shoves his head out from under a rock. Son, it's in the best interest of our nation that bin Laden not stand trial."

"I understand, sir."

Saeed led the way to a southern neighborhood near the Old City, a warren of mud huts, most of which appeared unoccupied and battle-ruined. Saeed explained how rival factions had engaged in a fierce fight on this street. He had participated in the battle, which was why he knew about the place. A single old man leading a donkey seemed to be the only inhabitant left. He gave the strangers barely a glance, then disappeared as well when jet contrails began inscribing lines high in the incredible blue of the Afghan sky.

The daily U.S. bombing runs began. Huge detonations—smoke, flames, and fireballs—shook dust into the atmosphere. Although none of the bombs landed in the main parts of the city, panicked civilians vacated the streets by any means they could find—donkey carts, bicycles, hand carts.

Saeed picked up his pace but otherwise ignored the air strikes. They were only so much distant land thunder, annoying but not particularly threatening. He turned them down an even more narrow and dilapidated muddy street, with a view and odor of the river. Soon they came to an abandoned mud house that looked like any of the others in the neighborhood. Saeed tried the door. It opened. He looked inside, then nodded at Ismael.

"This is it," Ismael said.

They were unlikely to be noticed, and even if they were, they would be mistaken for locals seeking cover in a vacant building.

The house had a bare dirt floor. The only furnishings were

an overturned chair with a broken leg and a shattered earthenware pot. There was the smell of the river through a broken window; mist and wet soil. A rat's nest of twigs, straw, and mud in the corner was strewn about with tiny bones and nut shells. Saeed solemnly pointed through the window that overlooked a narrow stone bridge spanning the river.

Beyond the bridge, on the far side, on an isolated rise in a grove of trees, stood several houses enclosed within a low mud wall. A long, winding driveway led unkept and muddy up to the compound from the nearest street. There were no vehicles about. The compound appeared unoccupied.

"It looks like Hooker on a Saturday night after they've rolled up the streets," Gloomy observed.

"They will come when the bombs stop," Saeed promised through Ismael. "The old man, Amir, knew things that only he could know."

Maybe. Brandon remained unconvinced and apprehensive. Afghanistan was a vipers' nest of conspirators and deceivers. For all he knew, militiamen might have already set them up for the kill, although he had seen no indications of that. Ismael assured him that everything seemed normal.

Gloomy nursed the same feeling of unease. He caught his commander aside. "Boss, you got any idea what chickens feel like when an ol' owl gets in the hen house and he's just sitting there on the roost looking them over while he decides which one to eat?"

"Are we the owl or the chickens?"

"I feel like the chicken. If a certain somebody knows we're in town for a party, he might be looking us over with big owl's eyes at the same time we're scoping him out."

"Gloomy, we're the owl."

"Yes, sir. I feel like an owl, sir, but my feet want to act like a chicken."

The two Americans studied the target area carefully while

Ismael watched them and Saeed kept guard at the door to the street. Brandon glassed the compound through a pair of binoculars, then handed them to his sniper. They were looking at the backs of three small mud and stone houses. Intact glass in the windows indicated they were still occupied. The driveway from the distant street curved sharply through a gate in the mud wall, then disappeared from view in front of the buildings.

"If they come in vehicles," Gloomy speculated, "they're going to be partially blocked from my scope when they pull up and stop."

Brandon looked again through the binoculars. Gloomy was right. He wouldn't have much of a shot. A footpath across the bridge led past the compound and its mud fence. There was no gate in the wall across the back, but the wall was barely waist high. Other buildings in the vicinity—provided they were empty and available—would not appreciably improve their position. An air strike was probably the surer method of taking out the target, and certainly the most secure for the assassins.

Gloomy accepted the demoted assignment to backup without comment. Standing in the shadows away from the window, he began sighting in his .300 Winchester for two hundred yards, an easy shot at any kind of target. The trick would be getting any kind of target.

Brandon set up the GLTD to laser-fix the main building in the compound and guide in the air strike. He also obtained a geographical fix with his wrist GPS and relayed the coordinates via Motorola to Mad Dog at base camp. The little Motorola, satellite-accessible or not, was stretching its range, but Mad Dog Carson was a wizard when it came to commo. With a little tinkering and jerry-rigging, he could take two tin cans and some string and turn them into a communications system. His voice came in loud and clear.

"Read you five-by-five," Mad Dog said. "Everything here is also five-by."

Sergeant Norman came on and said he and Vince Lombardi together managed to convey the false information about the failed mission, even without drawing pictures.

"Good. How about air cover? Is everything laid on?"

"Carrier F-18s armed with smart-bomb JDAMs went overstation at 0500. They will remain on-target overstation in relays until 0500 tomorrow, or until otherwise released. They're waiting for your signal. Good hunting, sir."

Bombs crumped in banging clusters at distant targets ringing the beleaguered city. There was nothing to do now but wait.

An hour passed. The bombing ceased. Saeed reported the reappearance of the old geezer with the donkey. He continued on down the street and through an alley. Both his head and the donkey's, it seemed, almost touched the ground. It was just another normal day in Kabul.

Brandon kept a wary eye peeled both for the target's arrival and for unexpected company. Ismael looked tight-faced and jumpy as time passed. Saeed affected an elaborate shrug with shoulders, arms, hands, and his entire wiry body, as though to say, "He will come in due time because I want him to come. But if he does not, it is the will of Allah." Gloomy patched up the broken chair and sat on it in the middle of the room, back from the window so he wouldn't be spotted. The deadly Winchester lay ready across his knees. He leaned slightly forward, his flinty blue eyes predatory and watchful.

Two hours. Three.

"Boss?"

"I see 'em. Gloomy."

A convoy of five vehicles turned off the street and onto the drive to the compound. Two were battered Toyota pickups loaded with armed men. A third was a French truck carrying an antiaircraft gun in the back with a Russian heavy .51 machine gun mounted over the cab. Leading the procession came an old flatbed loaded with still more fighters. A black Chevrolet sedan occupied the honored spot in the middle of the cavalcade. Obviously, this was an escort for someone important. Ironic, Brandon thought, how this rabid anti-American Muslim chose an infidel's car for his personal transportation.

The thing was going down. Either the phony all-clear had gotten through or the attack at the old man's house had been a chance coincidence. Brandon felt excitement mounting as the showdown approached. In other less-trained and less-disciplined men, it would have been a dangerous emotion causing rash action and snap decisions. Excitement in Major Kragle acted in the opposite way. He became coldly calculating and as methodical as an accountant.

Ismael stood to one side of the window and peeped around the sill. His face looked pale against the red and green turban and the lock of black hair that fell across his forehead.

The vehicles slowed and passed through the gate and stopped in front of the main house. Men jumped out of the trucks and took posts around the compound. From higher ground and through the binoculars. Brandon still saw only the top of the black sedan glinting back sunlight. But anyone getting out of the car would have to reveal his head and shoulders for at least a couple of minutes.

Gloomy watched through his scope. "It's your call, boss," he said softly.

One shot-one kill. There was little doubt that, given a momentary glimpse of a vital piece of target, say a head, the sniper could pull it off and bring Iron Weed 1-Alpha to a successful climax. The problem was getting the hell out of Dodge afterward. Osama might die, *would* die, but the chance of his assassins making it out alive was about like the proverbial snowball in hell. The single shot would be like poking a stick into a hornet's nest.

Tensions mounted. Saeed's lips were so dry that when he licked them, his tongue actually stuck. Ismael's dark eyes locked on Brandon's. Gloomy remained perfectly still, his eye to the scope and his finger on the trigger.

Iron Weed was no martyrdom mission. Brandon shook his head. "You know what Thumbs always says: Few of life's problems can't be solved by a big bang. Let them get inside. We'll call down air strikes."

He turned on the GLTD. Its invisible laser locked onto the main house. Ismael let out a long slow breath.

A turbaned head moved around the Chevy. Its owner apparently opened a rear door. The head and shoulders of a second man appeared in Brandon's magnified view. It was Osama bin Laden, no doubt of it. Brandon recognized from photographs the white turban, the long mahogany face with the flattened nose, the beefy lips and wild black beard. Brandon observed him all the way down to the pockets of his trademark camouflage BDU coat. He stood exceptionally tall.

Bin Laden looked around, squinting against the bright mid-morning sunlight.

"Major, I can still end it right now," Gloomy offered.

It was tempting. This was the crazy who planned the attacks on the WTC and the Pentagon, among several other American targets over the years. His terrorist hands were red and gory with American blood, including that of Little Nana. Maybe they could kill the cocksucker right here and now and still escape in all the confusion.

The Shake bent over out of sight and reappeared momentarily, hitching an AK-47 onto one shoulder. That accomplished, he hurried into the house, flanked by his inner circle. The opportunity passed.

Brandon radioed Mad Dog, who would in turn alert the air strikes.

"One-Alpha, we have the buzzard in his nest. Bring in the eggs."

"Roger that, Big Daddy. Mother says they're on their way. You got your laser tagging 'em?"

"Roger that, Dog. Get 'em in now."

"Stand by one."

They waited, expecting to see the compound erupting in smoke and flame at any moment. Instead, Mad Dog's voice broke back in over the Motorola.

"Big Daddy, can you read?"

"Roger. What's the delay?"

"The strikes are scrubbed. The strikes are a no go."

Brandon almost crushed the radio in his big hand. "What do you mean, scrubbed? We've got the cocksucker right here, right now. We can end it. Get those airplanes in here. I don't care what it takes."

Mother Norman came on. "Sir, I don't know what the deal is. The pilots are armed and ready, but they tell us higher-higher has ordered them off. Can you read? They've been ordered back to the carriers."

CHAPTER 22

Tampa

General Darren E. Kragle pounded the table in front of him with the meaty part of his fist, making papers flutter and the heavy table dance.

"You *what*?"

A hush fell over the situation room at U.S. Central Command headquarters (CENTCOM) in Tampa, Florida, the nerve center for the war being waged in Afghanistan. A moment before, planners and other specialists were updating wall maps, stamping out orders, hovering over sand tables, watching monitors and TVs tuned to FOX and CNN, and muttering exchanges with banks of high-tech satellite communications radios. It was after midnight, but the War Room was running full blast 24/7. Now, high-ranking officers and enlisted personnel from the various branches of the service, as well as civilian reps from DOD, swiveled heads toward the impending confrontation between USSOCOM and General Abraham Morrison, Chairman of the Joint Chiefs of Staff. General Kragle had transferred some USSOCOM operations to CENTCOM to facilitate coordination within forces committed to Afghanistan, most of which were SpecOps anyhow at this point.

"General Kragle," the CJCS said in a low voice, "must I remind you that you're addressing a superior officer?"

General Morrison, for all his physical appearance of a telemarketing CEO, had distinguished himself in Vietnam combat. Sparks almost flew when his steely blue eyes locked with USSOCOM's hard gray ones.

General Kragle's face looked about to explode from attempting to contain his outrage. "Sir, do I have to remind you that this has happened before? We had Mullah Omar dead to rights—and it was called off."

"General Etheridge had no choice in that, Darren. Pressure was placed on the Defense Department. The Judge Advocate General's office ordered CENTCOM to call off the Predator strike until this could be legally reviewed."

"Sir, this is surreal. What the hell business do a bunch of lawyers have in determining which targets we will or will not strike in a war? If one of my detachments says it needs a strike, it needs it *now*. This could get my men killed, don't they understand that? What the fuck is going on, sir? We had air strikes laid on for Iron Weed, and now they're scrubbed at the last moment, when they need them."

"All I can tell you is that the Senate Armed Services Committee—"

"Tayloe!" General Kragle exploded. "What's that fat fuck of a left-wing egg-sucking—"

"Senator Tayloe claims he learned about Iron Weed and that it's an assassination mission."

"Politicians!" The word felt as if it left scum in his mouth. "These perfumed princes in Washington are so isolated from the real world they have no idea of the consequences of their actions. These bastards live entire lives on the public dole.

Most of them have never lived like real people, never had to pay house payments and grocery bills. They get the big salaries, and on top of everything else the taxpayers give them free quarters, free meals, free parking, free offices. The sonsofbitches don't even pay for their own haircuts—and here they go around sticking their noses in where it doesn't belong and fucking up things."

It wasn't difficult to goad General Kragle into rendering his opinions of politicians.

"Duly noted," the CJCS said with understanding. "I've got a call going through now to the SecDef."

"Sir, it's going to be too late. One-Alpha has a rich target that may not last. Timing is critical. Americans could be killed downrange because of this."

"General Kragle, One-Alpha is your son. Is that correct?"

The General said nothing. CENTCOM's General Etheridge stepped into the office. "Chairman Morrison, the Secretary of Defense is on the phone for you."

"Be right there." The CJCS looked at General Kragle a long, sober moment. "The President and the SecDef won't cave in to JAG on this one," he promised. "I need to tell them Iron Weed, all three detachments, are not primarily assassination squads."

"You know the nature of their missions, sir."

"Iron Weed is not *primarily* assigned to assassinations."

Both men understood the word games they were playing.

"That's right, sir," General Kragle said. "They are not *primarily* assassination missions."

The CJCS turned away, then turned back. "General Kragle, it appears you've generated some powerful enemies. Senator Tayloe is calling for a congressional investigation of USSOCOM's conduct of the war in Afghanistan. He cites you personally and Iron Weed as examples of U.S. law violations. Enduring Freedom is going to get nasty."

"Yes, sir. Just get my men their air strikes. Now."

CHAPTER 23

Kabul

Major Brandon Kragle had no way of knowing why his air strikes had been pulled. A snafu somewhere. Surely the General would fix it if he knew about it. But could he fix it in time?

Brandon understood one thing—the Shake could not be allowed to leave the compound alive. His death was certainly worth the risk of two American soldiers, a Zarbati warrior, and a ruthless Jew boy orphan with a misspent childhood.

Ismael explained the situation to Saeed.

"The two of you can pull on out now," Brandon suggested. "Gloomy and I will handle it. We'll be out of here before the ragheads figure out where the shot came from."

Ismael thought it over and spoke with the Zarbati. He turned back to the Major. "You were lucky in Beit Jalla when the RPG exploded—" he said, then caught himself in mid-sentence.

Brandon blinked. "How did you know . . . ?"

The kid gave him a taut, mysterious smile. "It doesn't matter now how I know. What matters is you can't keep depending on luck or karma. You'll think you've dropped right in the middle of the jihad the minute you fire that shot. They'll be looking for you house-to-house. You don't know Kabul. You'll never find your way back to the horses without Saeed. Saeed and I will stay."

"It is the will of Allah," Saeed added. He grinned at Gloomy. "It is Hooker way," he added in Gloomy-taught English.

They had balls and loyalty. Brandon had to hand them that. He stared into the kid's eyes. He had thought before that there was something familiar about him. Now he was certain of it, but he still couldn't figure out why. The wide mouth and perfectly formed nose. Mad Dog thought he was probably a little light in his Afghan sneakers. "The kid's a fairy god-daughter," he'd said. "He's too pretty to be a boy." Besides, Brandon knew that Ismael had known too much about him from the start to be what he appeared to be.

The kid had some questions to answer after this was over, but for now they had a job to do.

Bin Laden had not shown himself again once he disappeared inside the main house. Other vehicles drove up over the next half hour or so. Old trucks and beat-up Toyotas. They disgorged more men whom Brandon supposed to be Taliban and al-Qaeda troop leaders. Security around the compound expanded. "Sheet sheiks," a Gloomy term, patrolled the mud fence in force and took up defensive positions at the stone bridge. A formless, faceless female figure in black attempted to cross the bridge, but the fighters turned her back and shooed her away.

Wouldn't it be something if Mullah Mohammed Omar showed up? Brandon thought. He was a target almost as valuable and elusive as bin Laden. Brandon studied the face of each new arrival, seeking the Taliban ruler's one-eyed countenance. Rumor had it that the mullah, which translated as "spiritual teacher," had sewn shut the lids of his own eye when he lost it fighting against the Russians. Since then he had grown a little wacky and was rarely seen in public. Only one known photo of him existed. Most Afghans didn't even know what he looked like.

His doctor, who escaped to the West after the American bombing began, reported that the story of Omar locking himself away to receive visions from Allah was a false one. The reality was that he suffered from brain seizures. He rarely left the bomb shelter of his house, inside of which he kept a car. He sat in his car for hours every day, pretending to drive it, turning the wheel and making motor sounds.

If true, the terrorist leadership consisted of a Saudi billionaire intent on making as many martyrs as he could of his followers, and a one-eyed certified nut case. What one accurately delivered JDAM could do to this compound and the terrorist leadership present was a marvelous thing to contemplate.

"If there's real justice in the universe," Gloomy said, his humor intact even under the circumstances, "there won't be any virgins left for ol' Osama and the mullah. Allah'll send them to Hooker, Oklahoma, as some good ol' boy's coon dogs."

They had to be careful inside the abandoned house not to be seen through the window. Gloomy settled into that cocoon of concentration in which everything on the periphery didn't matter; only the target existed. He made minute adjustments to his scope, peering through it and picking out signs of wind direction and wind shift.

They waited. Brandon conferred in low tones with the sniper. "When the Shake exits the house, you have thirty seconds at most while he's getting in the car."

"I won't miss, boss."

"We're outta here as soon as you fire and we confirm a hit. The confusion should give us a few minutes start on them."

"Piece of cake," Gloomy said.

Brandon raised Mad Dog or Mother Norman on the Motorola every few minutes, hoping for a positive change in the air strike situation. His eyes scanned the clear skies for aircraft contrails.

"They're saying the same thing," Norman reported. "They've been ordered back to the carrier. But something else is happening, I don't know what. A couple of the aircraft have turned back toward Kabul. They say they were ordered to stay overtarget until the situation—whatever it is—can be resolved. Keep a laser on the target, sir."

"Keep at them," Brandon urged.

It would be most interesting, Brandon thought, to be a bug on the wall inside Osama's meeting and hear what terrorists discussed among themselves.

The conference dragged on. The rest of the snow melted, turning the streets even muddier and refueling the filthy trickle of river that ran between the observers and the observed in the compound. The meeting ended suddenly and in a totally unexpected manner, catching the observers by surprise.

A battered pickup truck, engine gunning, caromed off the street onto the drive, slinging mud and fishtailing. In a hell of a hurry, it slid sideways at the entrance to the compound, stopped by sentries. Driver and guards held a hurried exchange before the pickup cut a 180 and departed in the same haste with which it arrived. The gate guards bolted toward the house, shouting an alarm.

"Something's going on," Ismael said.

The news produced immediate results. Men poured out of the house and dived into their vehicles as if they'd been warned to get away. Brandon frantically searched the darting figures for Osama bin Laden. Gloomy's rifle swung back and forth as he attempted to find the target in his crosshairs. He trained it on the Shake's black Chevrolet.

"He's not in there, boss—or he's lying on the floorboard."

The sonofabitch had somehow been tipped off, Brandon thought. The bridge sentries ran toward the house, vaulted the mud fence, and caught the last truck as the convoy roared out of the compound, the Chevrolet sandwiched into the middle.

"I don't see him, boss. Want me to stop the Chevrolet? I could nail the driver."

"That still wouldn't get the bastard," Brandon cried in frustration. "Damn. Damn! What happened?"

The compound was completely abandoned in less than two minutes. It lay silent and empty beneath the sun, as though mocking Iron Weed's failure. Brandon glassed the windows for signs of life. There was none. The Shake had escaped.

"I'm going down for a snoop," Brandon said. The intelligence possibilities couldn't be overlooked. "Cover me, Gloomy."

He scrambled over the windowsill and dropped onto the soft turf outside. Ismael piled out directly behind him.

"You'll need a backup," the boy said, slapping his CAR-15 with the palm of his hand. "Don't argue. We have to be quick."

"You're a pushy little fuck," Brandon said, but he secretly admired the kid's spunk.

They scrabbled down the steep mud bank to the bridge. Sunlight glinted off the brown river as they trotted across. To any casual observer, they were merely part of the activity associated with the compound and therefore of only passing interest. Brandon vaulted the walls and led the boy toward the back of the main house, finger on the trigger of the stubby MP-5 submachine gun. They were not challenged.

The recent occupants departed in such haste that doors were left unlocked. Brandon tried one, then stood to the side and nodded at Ismael on the other side of the door, who had his carbine up and ready. He nodded back. The door slapped open before Brandon's kick. He sprang inside, ready for action but not sure what to expect.

A pot of *sholaa*—rice and beans—still boiled on a little field stove. There was also a pot of hot tea. Beyond the nearest door, in another room, were cots or carpet beds scattered on the floor. The house appeared unoccupied. The two intruders checked out all five rooms to be sure, increasingly amazed at their find.

One room contained caches of ammunition, including mortar rounds and grenades. Another, the larger, appeared to be an office or command center. Ismael let out a little whistle of astonishment. The room was filled with high-tech computers and banks of radios, monitors, and cameras. It seemed that Osama and his generals could communicate with each other and their terrorist cells anywhere in the world. Brandon was stunned at the sophistication with which the terrorists seemed to have organized themselves.

Ismael salvaged a backpack from one of the bedrooms and began stuffing papers, maps, manuals, computer software, and other items into it. "This looks like good stuff," he said. "Let's see if we can take some of these hard drives before these guys decide to come back."

On one desk were stacks of what appeared to be graded tests, the subject matter being the Russian-made Dashka antiaircraft weapon. Notebooks contained drawings of Kalishnikov rifles and instructions on building homemade bombs. Ismael read aloud one of the questions: "On the Boeing 767 aircraft, what size bomb would be most effective in inflicting the most damage?" There were several copies of a slick yellow and green book, the title of which Ismael translated as *Call to Jihad*, by Osama bin Laden. Everything went into the backpack.

Brandon's Motorola buzzed from his belt underneath his robe. He expected Gloomy. "Yeah?"

It was Mad Dog. "Major, we have a go on the strike. Repeat, it's a go. Expect birds over the nest in three mikes. Repeat, three mikes."

Three minutes! That meant two, maybe one by now.

"Dog, call them off. Abort the mission. Immediately."

"Fu-uck a duck, sir. I don't think I can. It's too late."

"Try, damnit, try!"

"Yes, sir." He went off.

They had to get out of there. The GLTD with its laser beam was still on and targeting the house. Ismael attempted to stuff final items into the backpack. Brandon yanked him and the pack toward the back door.

They barely got out of the house and were charging toward the stone bridge when they heard the first sighing whistle of falling ordnance, something like a Volkswagen being dropped from the sky. The force and searing heat of the explosion seemed to envelop them. It lifted them off their feet and hurled them through the air. Luckily, they were on the lee side of the rise, below the explosion radius. Most of the fury of the blast went over their heads. They landed in a tangle of arms and legs in the thick rind of mud at the edge of the river. Fire and smoke erupted from the compound. Even with his ears ringing, Brandon heard a second Volkswagen falling.

Ismael appeared stunned. Brandon tucked him underneath one arm—while the kid held onto his precious backpack of intelligence treasures—and dashed for the shelter of the bridge. He threw himself in the stinking mud and crawled, dragging Ismael to the narrowest space where the bridge connected to the bank.

The second JDAM explosion threatened to jolt them off the face of the earth. It finished demolishing the compound. Deadly shrapnel shredded the air. Debris pelted the roadway and bridge above their heads like giant hailstones. They huddled with arms wrapped around each other as follow-up detonations and cook-offs from the stored munitions whizzed and streaked in vicious random paths.

What irony it would have been, Brandon thought, had the delayed bombing caught *them* while the intended target escaped.

It seemed like hours but was actually only several minutes before the worst of it ended. The compound turned into a roaring conflagration. Heat from it seared their eyebrows and Brandon's beard. A few small arms rounds continued to cook off, but most of the danger was over. Ismael lay still on his belly. Brandon turned him over on his back and saw blood from a cut on the kid's face. There was more blood on his coat.

"Ismael. You all right, boy?"

"If you'll quit mauling me."

Brandon felt for wounds, running his hands along the boy's ribs and feeling his chest. He froze. His eyes widened. Ismael slapped his hands away, but not before Brandon confirmed what he was feeling.

"Jesus!"

This kid had— This kid was a *woman*.

CONGRESS INVESTIGATES WAR

WASHINGTON (CPI)—A powerful member of the Senate and chairman of the Armed Services Committee, Senator Eric B. Tayloe, has charged the United States with violating U.S. and international law in its conduct of the war in Afghanistan. In a 23-page document calling for a full investigation by both houses of Congress, Tayloe specifically accuses General Darren E. Kragle, commander of the U.S. Special Operations

Command (USSOCOM), of conducting ground operations in violation of U.S. law.

"War crimes may have been committed and abetted by high-ranking military authority all the way up to the President of the United States," Tayloe said in a news conference on the steps of the Capitol Building. "It begins with General Kragle, who has a record of choosing expediency over established rules of conduct and warfare, and extends into the upper levels of military command."

Former President John Stanton accompanied Senator Tayloe to the news conference.

"We are seeing the onslaught of an ongoing, bloody conflict that, unless carefully monitored and scrutinized, will lead to U.S. atrocities such as those committed at the My Lai massacre in Vietnam by American soldiers," Stanton said. "I don't think the American people will stand for that."

Tayloe and Stanton are calling for General Kragle to either resign command of USSOCOM or face a court-martial. They insist that the President censure General Paul Etheridge of Central Command (CENTCOM), and that the chairman of the Joint Chiefs of Staff, General Abraham Morrison, resign and be replaced.

At the center of allegations lies Iron Weed, a top secret operation by Delta Force, the U.S. counterterrorist unit. Tayloe contends that General Kragle has dispatched teams of assassins into Afghanistan to target top Taliban and al-Qaeda leaders, including Osama bin Laden and Mullah Mohammed Omar. Executive Order 12333, issued by President Ronald Reagan in 1981, states, "No person employed by or acting on behalf of the United States government shall engage in, or conspire to engage in, assassination."

Tayloe and Stanton argue that Omar and bin Laden, as heads of state or representatives of heads of state, are protected by the executive order and therefore cannot be specifically targeted.

During the Cold War the U.S. government attempted assassination a number of times. It reportedly tried everything from mob hits to poison to get rid of Fidel Castro. The CIA also shipped poison to the Congo intended for Patrice Lumumba and supplied weapons to dissidents who shot Dominican Republic dictator Rafael Trujillo. These abuses led to a total ban on assassination.

"There is no question but that the ban does have effect," said Defense Secretary Donald Keating. "It restricts what the government can do."

Officials confirm that Special Forces commandos are in northern and southern Afghanistan seeking Taliban targets to strike, organizing resistance cells, and searching for Osama bin Laden, Mullah Omar, and their Taliban and al-Qaeda lieutenants. USSOCOM commands Special Operations troops.

Chairman General Abraham Morrison denies that Operation Iron Weed is an assassination mission. While the numbers of Delta detachments in Afghanistan and other locations are highly classified, General Morrison confirms that some of the teams are assigned to chase down bin Laden and Omar—but not specifically to assassinate them.

"Such missions are legitimate military exercises," he stated, "but SpecOps is engaged in a variety of diverse operations. For example, operators have been assigned to find and rescue four U.S. Christian aid workers, all women, who have been imprisoned by the Taliban for proselytizing."

General Kragle refused to comment on Iron Weed, saying that to do so would jeopardize his men. Outspoken as always, however, he fired back at Senator Tayloe and ex-President Stanton for putting Americans at risk by their disclosure of classified information concerning operations.

"Everybody from President Stanton to that ragtag bunch of protesters around the White House want us to fight this war 'surgical'" he commented on what he calls "the Catch-22 of political correctness warfare." Kragle explained, "That means we're supposed to know the names of the people we are about to strike. But if we do know their names, that's defined as assassination and against the law. We need commanders running this war, making decisions, not pettifogging lawyers and politicians. They ought to be able to look over a situation and then, if necessary, without having to consult with civilian authorities, make the decision."

CHAPTER 24

Dallas, Texas

A cold, driving, autumn rain that Texans called a "real toad strangler" fell in Dallas. Director Claude Thornton of the FBI's National Domestic Preparedness Office leaned forward over the wheel of the tan Mercury whose engine was idling at the curb. The storefront of the Sacred Land Foundation a half block up the street appeared fluid and diluted through the furious beating of windshield wipers. Big men wearing blue rainproof windbreakers with FBI in yellow letters on the backs made the big car seem crowded.

In preparation for the raid, a second carload of feebies pulled into the alley behind the building in the commercial district. Agent Fred Whiteman radioed Thornton: "The white man be almost ready, massa."

It was an old joke between old friends.

"Let me know when you're there, Fred," Thornton radioed back.

Thornton was tired. He was more than tired. He'd had less than ten hours sleep since last week, when he attended Kathryn Kragle's funeral in Tennessee. He promised General Kragle to use all available resources to track down the killer or killers of the General's daughter-in-law and unborn grandchild. While it was a personal crusade launched out of friendship, it was also a matter of life for thousands, perhaps hundreds of thousands, of faceless Americans. It was also his job.

"Under the right conditions," worried his boss, NHSA director MacArthur Thornbrew, "we could encounter the worst threat to our national security since the Cuban missile crisis. Claude, if we don't find the source of this anthrax, a new Black Death plague could sweep across this land to throw us back to the Middle Ages."

So far, nothing had surfaced on anthrax.

Thornton felt humbled, sometimes even intimidated, at heading the largest criminal investigation in American history. And on so many different fronts! He knew he couldn't spend all his time personally on the anthrax investigations but felt it was his duty to personally participate in at least some of the nationwide forays that had so far rounded up nearly 1,000 suspected terrorists around the country. His office had exposed the rough outlines of a dozen centers of terrorist support on U.S. soil. It was incredible. Osama bin Laden's financial empire encompassed ostrich farms in Kenya, logging interests in Turkey, diamond trading in Africa, bridge construction in the Sudan, agricultural holdings in Tajikistan, beehives and honey shops in Boston . . . All of it helped fund terrorist activities. A number of Palestinian or other Arab "charity" or "relief" organizations like Sacred Land Foundation was discovered to be laundering cash to various terror groups, including al-Qaeda.

A government order had been issued that morning shutting down Mullah Shukri Abu Marzook and Sacred Land Foundation offices in four states: Texas, New Jersey, Illinois, and California. They were being charged with directly supporting al-Qaeda and Hamas under the guise of operating a relief fund for Palestinian refugees.

"The white man is ready."

"The black man is ready, too," Thornton quipped back. He jammed a blue FBI ball cap onto his shaved head. "Let's go!" he said into the mike.

The raid was on, part of a coordinated strike against Sacred Land in all four states. Thornton powered the Mercury away from the curb, moving it directly in front of the objective with all four doors flying open and agents jumping out in the downpour, weapons drawn. Terrorists and those who supported terrorism were dangerous and completely unpredictable. Agents rushed the building underneath the marquee declaring in both English and Arabic that the business was FOR RELIEF & DEVELOPMENT, BOOKS, CRAFTS, PHONE CARDS. It was early morning of a workday, but rain kept most pedestrians indoors or, at most, darting from cars to buildings with umbrellas or newspapers over their heads.

A skinny Middle Easterner of about twenty looked up in surprise from stocking a shelf when the front door burst open. Hefty men charged at him, yelling, "FBI! Freeze!"

Panicked, the kid made a break for the back door, only to run headlong into more hefty men. He jumped up and down in excitement, unsure of whether to run somewhere else or drop down and pray to Allah.

Thornton, who had spent much of his career in Egypt and was fluent in Arabic, shouted, "*Intahit!* It's over. *Raga! Silmee!*"

That stopped the kid. His shoulders slumped. He turned with a resigned half smile. An agent handcuffed his hands behind him while the others spread out to round up employees. After a minute or so of stomping about and calling out to each other, the agents returned empty-handed to the main business area.

"This place is as empty as Grant's tomb," Whiteman said. "You think somebody dropped a quarter on us, Claude?"

"I don't see how. This was kept under wraps until this morning."

The skinny kid stood among the agents shrugging and grinning in confusion. "Do you speak English?" Thornton asked him.

"Yes, sir. I speak very good Winglish."

"What's your name?"

"Mousa."

"How many people work here, Mousa?"

"Uh—seven. If you count me. Sometimes nine or ten."

"Where are they? Where's Mullah Shukri?"

Mousa shrugged. "Mullah Shukri receives a phone call. They all leave in hurry. He tell me to stay here and wait. I ask him what I wait for. He say wait."

Thornton and Whiteman exchanged looks. Somebody *had* tipped him off.

"Sir, I am very good worker. I have papers. I am good American visitor. I am not outlaw."

A few more minutes of interrogation persuaded Thornton the kid was probably telling the truth. He either knew nothing or was a hell of an actor. He claimed he was a simple clerk hired to answer the telephone and handle routine walk-in customers. Thornton placed him in a straight-backed chair in Mullah Shukri's office while he slumped in a swivel chair behind the desk. He leaned forward, elbows on the desk and face in his hands.

"Fred, you handle the search warrant," he instructed. "Take all the computers and software and box up every scrap of paper you can find. Don't leave anything except the rugs, and be sure to look under them."

Weary from lack of sleep, too much black coffee, and hours spent on airplanes and in cars and meetings, Thornton stared unseeingly at the clutter on the desk in front of him. Rain hissed on the windows. Agents worked around him, boxing up papers and other possible evidence of the foundation's illicit activities.

It wasn't until Whiteman brought in an Arabic-language chemistry textbook and a *Bombs and Mines* training manual filled with diagrams and pictures and was thumbing idly through the manual that he noticed the stack of envelopes lying on the desk right in front of him. He'd been too beat to notice before. The top envelope was addressed in block letters to Director MacArthur Thornbrew, National Homeland Security Agency. The return address was a private school in New Jersey.

Thornton jumped back from the desk as though he'd touched a rattlesnake. Mullah Shukri and his gang must have departed in one hell of a hurry to leave *these* behind.

"Fred?" he called out in a grave voice. "Call out HazMat and get our guys out of here. I think we've found anthrax."

CHAPTER 25

Quantico, Virginia

Claude Thornton had a feeling that time was running out. Every time he closed his eyes, he had nightmares of the Black Death of anthrax panicking the nation, infecting its blood and soul, and stacking up rotted corpses like cordwood on street corners. The nightmares might not be farfetched from future reality. He had learned more about anthrax and bioterrorism in the past few weeks than he ever needed to know prior to 9/11.

Before al-Qaeda, the Persian Gulf War produced fears that Iraq and other rogue nations were experimenting with hazardous microorganisms. It was also known that Osama bin Laden wanted to acquire nuclear, biological, and chemical weapons. In 1999 he declared in a television interview that "to seek to possess the weapons that could counter those of the infidels is a religious duty." Subsequent satellite photos revealed dead animals at a terrorist training camp in eastern Afghanistan, indicating experiments with poisons. One of bin Laden's disciples, who was sentenced to prison for plotting to bomb Los Angeles International Airport, testified in court that he and others were taught how to feed cyanide into building air ducts in order to kill masses of people.

NHSA's MacArthur Thornbrew darkly concluded that the use of weapons of mass destruction might be imminent. The use of biological toxins, the poor man's nuclear bomb, could potentially cause more casualties among ordinary Americans than a dozen, a hundred, a *thousand* World Trade Center attacks.

In 1997 the United States had made it illegal to ship deadly microbes within or outside the nation without permission from the Justice Department. Nonetheless, scores of germ banks in the United States and elsewhere in the world maintained dozens of strains of bacillus anthrax, the germ that causes anthrax, for research purposes, along with millions of other potentially deadly bacteria and viruses. Running down leads on all these possible sources proved to be a daunting task for the FBI.

Since Mexico possessed an especially high concentration of potent anthrax spores in its soil, Thornton flew to Mexico City to speak with Professor Hector Villanova, head of the microbiology department at the National School of Biological Science, one of Mexico's two germ banks. There were no armed guards or security cameras. Vials of anthrax were kept in an unlocked closet marked PRIVATE.

Professor Villanova held up a vial. "We use it to develop new and stronger vaccines," he explained. "If I were to open it right now, it wouldn't hurt any of us. Why should we have security when you can find these same anthrax in nature? Someone with the expertise, a microbiologist with time and money, could keep trying different combinations and come up with a deadly weapon. Your own government developed it as a weapon during the Cold War. For weaponized anthrax of the quality indicated, I would be looking for the source, if I were you, somewhere around Fort Detrick, Maryland."

America was going to suffer civilian casualties—men, women, children, the old and young—within weeks, even days. The FBI and Homeland Security had little to go on in order to stop it. Claude Thornton listened to the ticking of the clock on the wall of his office. It seemed to throb inside his head.

The Centers of Disease Control and Prevention confirmed that the letters seized in the Dallas raid contained a fine grade of weaponized anthrax. There were five envelopes, each addressed to a prominent counterterrorist official, congressman, or news media personality. Each envelope came with a virtual carbon of previous anthrax letters: "You cannot stop us. You die now. Allah is great."

All agents involved in the raid immediately went on antibiotics to counter likely exposure to the deadly organism. After CDC decontaminated the letters and other materials found in the offices, agents and crime scene lab experts began going through the mass of it, searching for clues. Thornton was particularly interested in one of a long list of telephone numbers that might have had some bearing on Kathryn Kragle and how she contracted the disease. It turned out to be the number of a pay telephone in front of a 7-Eleven store on Hays Street in Fayetteville, North Carolina, near the main gate at Fort Bragg.

Thornton sent agents to ask questions and place a temporary stakeout and a tap on the phone. Nothing developed. It was unlikely the terrorists would use the same pay phone every time. He hadn't expected much. The raids scattered all the Sacred Land conspirators. Shukri Abu Marzook and his accomplices deserted their homes, pulled up stakes, and were on the lam. Pictures of them appeared on TV and were displayed at all border crossings and international airports. Shukri's capture promised to provide a link to the source of anthrax being unleashed upon a frightened America.

Skinny Mousa, the only prisoner nabbed during the Dallas

operation, was held for immigration violations and possession of anthrax. He seemed eager to talk to save his own neck. Thornton and Fred Whiteman interrogated him at length.

"I want to be American," he insisted.

"Yeah, right," Thornton replied, short on time and patience. "The letters were on the desk. Where did they come from?"

"They were delivered in the morning before you come. I swear on the name of Allah and Jesus Christ, I did not know what they were."

"Who delivered them?"

"He has been there before. I heard Mullah Shukri refer to him as 'Otta.' That means 'cat.' "

"How many times has he come?" Whiteman asked.

Mousa wet his lips and looked around the interrogation room. "Two times, maybe three times, that I see myself. He never says anything to me. He leaves a package and I am to pass it to Mullah Shukri when the mullah is not in. I opened the package this time to see if it was important only because Mullah Shukri and the others had to leave in such a rush."

"What does Otta look like?"

"He wears the sun shades and a red ball cap pulled down on his head so that you cannot see his hair, but it is short. He is not very big and he is dark like an Egyptian of the South Nile. He comes in, leaves the package, and leaves again. It is all very mysterious."

"I'll bet," Thornton said.

Under more grilling, Mousa recalled a conversation he overheard between Mullah Shukri and Otta. "It was not intentional. I was curious, so I pass by the office real close when Otta is inside."

His dark eyes darted guiltily from side to side.

"And you heard . . . ?" Whiteman prompted.

"They speak Winglish. I hear 'jihad' and I hear Mullah Shukri ask if more can be deliver. I don't know more of *what*. Otta ask how much more. Mullah Shukri say he require perhaps one hundred pounds. Otta say he thought his man can provide it—"

Thornton stopped him. "Did you get 'his man's' name?"

"He just say 'my man.' I think they maybe are talking about drugs. You know—dope. Mullah Shukri laugh like he pleased and I heard him say, 'Good. One hundred pounds. It will take out a city and awake the Great Satan to his sins. I warn you. See that you get it, Otta.' "

Thornton's blood seemed to freeze in his veins. "Did he name the city?"

Mousa shrugged.

One hundred pounds of anthrax! Thornton dropped his head into his big hands. It was enough anthrax, effectively dispersed, to wipe out much of the population of Atlanta, Miami, or Washington, D.C.

CHAPTER 26

Afghanistan

The little bitch had looked familiar to him from the beginning. Nonetheless, he wondered how he could have been so deceived. The only way he could explain it was that he hadn't *really* known her in Israel, that he'd only seen her on two occasions. Once at Army HQ in Jerusalem, and again that same night in Beit Jalla when the RPG explosion killed Major Landau and the machine gunners and wounded him. Besides, he knew that you saw only what you expected to see. You didn't see a slit-tail when it was a kid in front of you.

The last time he saw him—*her*—she had long sunburned hair and bright emerald eyes that reminded him of Gypsy's. Her hair was black now—dyed, no doubt—and wrapped inside a man's turban. Brandon looked closely into her eyes as the bombing fires crackled and popped at the Shake's compound. Colored contact lenses.

"I'll explain," she snapped as they huddled together underneath the bridge. "Now get your hands off. You're enjoying it too much."

"How do you explain tits . . . Summer?"

"I had a job to do and it was the only way to do it."

He grabbed her and shook her the way he should have shaken Gypsy, who he believed would still be alive if he had left her behind—and probably married to Cameron by now.

"Women complicate lives," he growled. "Women complicate war. Women complicate the world."

"Well, just get rid of them all, then. Now that we've got that worked out, Major," she came back with sarcasm, "why don't we go on to something less complicated, like nuclear proliferation treaties or the moral dilemma of cloning?"

"Keep your smart mouth shut, Summer. Let me think."

"Can you think while we're getting our asses out of here? Remember one thing, Major—you *need* me. Call me Ishmael."

It was Murphy's fault. As in Murphy's Law. Brandon considered all the things that could go wrong, and *had*, as they retrieved the horses and headed on a hard ride back to the mountain refuge. Fortunately, they picked up no trackers. They kept the horses to the wadis and streambeds and valleys not only to avoid Taliban patrols, but to minimize detection from the air. American warplanes, having bombed everything of significance around Kabul, were now switching to targets of opportunity.

Summer kept trying to catch his eye as they rode, as though to ask by her look what he was going to do about her secret. He ignored her. Christ! Bek's band was split almost down the middle and verging on the brink of internecine violence. He had been so close to killing bin Laden, until some asshole in CENTCOM blew it with the air strikes. Somebody among the guerrillas had tipped off the enemy militia about their arrival in Kabul, and then, at the last moment warned bin Laden so he could escape. Now, on top of all that, he had to learn that his in-country contact and interpreter was a *woman*.

Murphy, you sonofabitch, he thought.

"For a hundred years," Gloomy said, "we've saved these shit-pot countries from sitting in the dirt, drinking stagnant water, wearing loincloths, and watching the goats fuck. They'll hate us no matter what we do. You can't trust a one of the fuckers."

Brandon glared at Summer, whom he formerly thought of as Ismael. "Not a one of them," he agreed.

Summer cornered him when they stopped to rest the horses. Brandon swung down from the saddle with the MP-5 he carried across the cantle and loosened the cinch. Summer did the same thing and led her mount close to his. Gloomy and Saeed were on the other side of a little glade, watering their animals at a stream.

Brandon avoided looking at her. He said, "Who all knows about your little charade? How high up does it go?" He knew the General wouldn't send a woman with him again, not after Gypsy.

"As high as it needs to," she said, as cryptic as always.

"Do our people know about it?"

"*Our* people? If by that you mean the U.S. military, the answer is no."

"Are you American? CIA?" he asked point-blank.

"Major, it's better I don't answer these questions yet."

"It's okay that you know about me, but I'm not to know anything about you?"

"Look, Brandon—"

"It's *Major* Kragle."

"*Major* Kragle. You've seen how Islam treats women in this country. You can't expose me. A disguise is necessary."

"You'd look good in a burqa," he said, and led his horse off.

He still hadn't decided what to do about her when purple dusk settled and the four horsemen climbed off the flats into the Hindu Kush. He was still undecided by black dark. Cold bright stars shone on them as they came in through the copse of trees below the camp and the cave. The ground was frozen but clear of snow except beneath the trees, where the sun failed to reach. The horses' hoof beats in the hard soil should have attracted attention. Instead, Saeed had to ride ahead and awaken the sentry to let him know they were returning.

"Major?" a voice challenged from the darkness.

Ice Man stepped out of the shadows. Mother Norman had Iron Weed encamped in the rocks higher up. The Delta sentries weren't sleeping.

"You knew we were coming?" Brandon said.

"Yes."

Soon, the excitement of the return had the entire camp up. All the Americans except two sentries—Ice Man, who rarely spoke anyhow, and Thumbs Jones—gathered around to hear the disappointing news about the Shake as the horses were unsaddled and fed.

"Fu-uck," Mad Dog said in disgust. "Major, I was on the radio constantly trying to prod somebody up the ass to get them moving. Them rear-echelon REMF motherfuckers—"

It was up to Saeed and Summer-Ismael to inform the clan. The fighters gathered around until Bek Gorabic appeared with his skunk's beard bristling, barking orders and waving his hands to disperse the curious mujahideen and, Brandon suspected, reinforce his position as leader while he diverted attention from the Americans. Brandon gave him a long, searching look in the light of an oil lamp carried by one of the warriors. Deceitful bastard. Could he be the traitor?

Bek returned the American's raw scrutiny, his beady pig's eyes hard and hostile. The corner of his beard nearest the lips lifted in a sneer. He laughed with a guttural sound, slapped the receiver side of his SAW with the thick palm of his hand, and walked back to the cave. A flash of light escaped into the darkness as he pushed aside the skin covering to the cave's entrance and went inside without looking back.

"That one," said the red-bearded Abdul Homayan, looking after Bek, "will have to be disposed of."

Summer translated for Brandon. It made him realize how indispensable to the team a translator was in this environment. Although among the eight men of 1-Alpha there were six different languages, excluding what Mad Dog called Gloomy's "Okie-ese," not one spoke the relatively rare dialects of the Afghan mountains. Like Gypsy, Summer had a facility with the singular languages of the Middle East.

"You need me, Major," she said in English, smiling up at him.

As usual, Summer prepared her bedroll next to Brandon's in the open crisp air among the rocks. In case she were needed during the night. Nothing must change to give her away until Brandon decided what to do. It was an awkward situation, but it seemed more awkward for Brandon than for her. The only difference was that she seemed quieter now than she had as Ismael. Bushed from the physical and emotional strain of past days, Brandon nonetheless left her to her ministrations while he made a tour of camp. He hoped she was asleep when he returned. He didn't know what to say to her.

He wasted as much time as he could, stopping to visit with the genial young giant, Doc TB, who was now on watch. As team medic, Doc had been treating the Afghans' infections, ailments, and injuries and had built up a loyal following among the mujahideen warriors.

Then he stopped at Mother Norman's bedroll for a brief conversation about routine detachment matters.

"Sir, do you think Bek snitched you off to the al-Qaeda in Kabul?"

"I don't know what to think," Brandon replied. "Someone did. The only place I can think it could have come from is here."

"Right after you left camp, sir, Bek rode out too."

"When did he get back?"

"This morning, early."

Brandon knew that Bek didn't have to leave the camp to communicate a warning. He had radios for that—old PRC-77s and -25s and some Russian models—all of which were capable of using extended antenna to reach Kabul. The Shake certainly had communications capability. But he had been alerted by the messenger in the pickup, not by radio.

"Did anyone else leave camp while we were gone?" Brandon asked.

"Abdul sent out horse patrols, but they were never out for long. He rode out about noon, but came back before dark. The best I can figure is, he went south toward Kandahar to scout out a new campsite."

Brandon thought about it. "I don't know," he admitted. "We'd better keep an eye on both of them."

"Sir, I don't know if we can trust any of these diaper heads, except Ismael, of course, and maybe Saeed."

"Yeah."

Tired as he was, he would have to postpone thinking about it tonight. The chase for the Shake, which had seemed so uncomplicated and near its end this morning, was actually only starting. And Murphy was right there in the middle of everything.

It occurred to him as he continued to make his rounds that he was doing everything he could to delay returning to his bedroll next to Summer's. It made him angry at himself. For God's sake, he was acting like a virgin bridegroom on his wedding night.

Summer was already deep inside her bedroll when he returned. Her face was the only thing that showed. There was a moon now. It illuminated her black hair and the closed eyes and the pulse beating in the delicate curve of her throat. Her breathing made little balloons of mist in the cold night air. He remembered how she looked back in Jerusalem the night at the Lutheran church, when she was carrying the baby and leading orphans to safety in the basement. Her face had been the first thing he saw when he regained consciousness. Still groggy from the explosion, he'd opened his eyes and saw emerald ones directly above. He couldn't believe it.

"Gypsy?"

"You're alive."

"You're not. You must be an angel."

How could he ever have been fooled into taking her for a boy? He studied her face in the moonlight while she slept, her dyed-black hair loose on the folded coat she used for a pillow. He would never again be fooled by those strong, clean features, the wide mouth, the pert little nose. The Ice Maiden. God, how could a woman so beautiful execute a man so ruthlessly and set up other men to be killed? What had happened to her?

His throat felt dry and tight. He would like to see her in jeans again. He would like to see her naked.

What the hell was the matter with him? This was the kind of trouble slits caused when you put them in the field with fighting men. He and Cameron, his own brother, had almost come to blows over Gypsy during Punitive Strike. How did he keep getting women assigned to his detachments? Bad karma?

Disturbed by his mixed feelings, he walked off, sat on a boulder and looked out across the meadow in front of the cave below. Frost turned it silver under the moon. There was snow in the trees farther down. He tucked his hands underneath his sheik sheet and into his armpits to keep them warm.

She approached silently from behind. "Major?"

She sat next to him on the boulder. She had put on her turban.

"I never intended you to find out," she said. "We would have done the mission and gone our separate ways without ever knowing or seeing each other again."

The sexual tension with her sitting so near was too intense. Brandon stood up.

"You've told so many lies on top of lies. Tell me, is Summer your real name?"

"It's 'Ismael' as long as we're in-country. You understand cover stories, Major. They're necessary."

"All right, Ismael. Are you Israeli, or is that also part of the cover?"

"You saw me in Israel."

"With you, that doesn't mean anything. You showed up here too. Nobody in Jerusalem seemed to know who you really were and where you came from. You're very good at mystery. The Ice Maiden who, like the black widow, kills her mates. It's said that everybody you sleep with ends up as dead as the old PLO, Abu Mustafa."

"Not *everyone*," she mocked.

"I wouldn't touch you, lady, with a snake stick."

"I haven't asked you," she flared. "We're both professionals, Major Kragle. We're alike."

"God protect us both, then," he said.

The air between them crackled. She sighed and stood up in front of him. She was tiny, but God help anyone who made the mistake of thinking her vulnerable.

She tried to soften the sarcasm in her voice when she spoke. "I was warned of how you feel about women in *your* military, Major. I even understand why you feel the way you do. I'm not Gypsy Iryani, Major. But she was a soldier too. You take your chances and shit sometimes happens. It's not becoming of you, Major, to be stuck in the past with a dead woman."

"Fuck you." He glared at her through the darkness.

"I don't think so," she said. "I want you to stay alive, at least until Iron Weed is over."

"Why were you assigned to me?"

She let him stand there fuming for a moment before she explained. "Like Gypsy, I speak the local dialects—and there are damned few of us who do, male or female. I had to come disguised as Ismael because of the Taliban attitudes toward women, a sentiment you apparently share with them. The main reason is I was needed here, for this mission, and I'm good at what I do."

"So I've heard," Brandon scoffed.

She let it go by. "So, what have you decided to do about Ismael?"

"I don't want broads in my outfit, *Ismael*. It's that simple. You're nothing but trouble. Sergeant Carson will send a commo request for a replacement tomorrow. As soon as *he* gets here—and he had better be a man this time—your pretty ass is gone like snow on a warm rock."

"Until then," she replied in a controlled tone, "I suppose we have no choice but to work together. Unless, of course, you learn to speak the language overnight."

She was infuriating enough as Ismael and doubly infuriating now. She turned and walked off, saying sweetly over her shoulder, "Are you coming to bed now, honey?"

CHAPTER 27

The guerrillas were in a holiday mood, having been generously resupplied with American paradrops of food, and were eagerly looking forward to the fall of Kabul. They made bets on exactly the day and hour when al-Qaeda and the Taliban took off to the mountains in flight. In a big kettle over a fire vented through a fissure leading out of the cave, the Afghans mixed packaged U.S. combat rations with beans and rice to concoct a fiery *sholaa*. The cave smelled rich of spices, wood smoke, locally brewed wine, dampness, and unwashed bodies.

Although fighting bonds were established by participating with hosts in observance of special occasions, Brandon's thoughts were not on feast and fun. It galled him that his detachment had to depend on locals for intelligence, as so often was necessary in clandestine, behind-the-lines ops, or upon SFOB-maintained contacts with the CIA and other intelligence operatives. Iron Weed 1-Alpha couldn't move until sooner or later, hopefully sooner, someone sniffed out the Shake's filthy ass again.

It also galled him that it was Summer and her contacts who had located bin Laden before, and would probably do so again. He was convinced now that she was CIA, or at least a CIA operative, what with her "Dove" code name and her seemingly inexhaustible reservoir of information and intelligence about the Iron Weed mission. Nonetheless, he sent a radio request to SFOB asking that "Ismael" be replaced, providing no reason why he thought it necessary. So far there had been no response. He suspected silence was higher-higher's way of turning him down. That galled him too. Would he have to send another message explaining that she was a woman in an Islam society and therefore a danger to herself and everyone else?

Most of the band crammed into the cave to eat and drink were yakking it up and having a great time. Gloomy Davis and his new buddy Saeed gobbled down food and were a little high on wine. Although frowned upon by Muslims, home brew remained a form of cheap escape throughout Afghanistan, especially in rural areas. Gloomy was telling Saeed a Hooker story, which Saeed listened to with enthusiasm, although he understood not a word.

The Baby Huey medic, Doc TB, and skinny Harvard-talking Winnie Brown attracted an audience of their own. Mad Dog Carson sidled up to a female wearing a black burqa and started teasing her to show him her face and, undoubtedly, her tits, drawing disapproving looks from the mujahideen. Mother Norman gave him a hard look and motioned him over to the CO.

"What's the matter with you, Sergeant?" Brandon reprimanded. "Do you want to get our throats cut?"

"I've had gook pussy, sir, spic pussy, and once tried me a nigger," the commo man slurred. "I was wondering what a little mooja-din nookie was like."

Politically correct the commo man wasn't.

"It doesn't run crossways," Ismael-Summer said. "You're

lucky she doesn't take off her veil. She's got more hair on her legs and chest than you have on your face."

"*My* kind of woman," Mad Dog applauded. "I like hairy twats."

"You've had too much wine, Sergeant," Brandon said. "Go and relieve Thumbs Jones on watch."

Topkick Norman, as befitted his role as detachment mother, kept vigil near the cave exit. His gray burnt-orange beard made him look like a watchful porcupine. Abdul walked by and rubbed Norman's beard for luck. Norman grinned and buffed the other's red beard in return. They both laughed.

Smelling of alcohol, laughing happily, Abdul cornered Brandon with a no-shit-there-I-was tale about a battle his band had engaged in prior to its link-up with Bek and its subsequent inactivity. Naturally, Abdul made himself the hero. He and his warriors charged a tank on horseback and took it out.

"He says he has balls as big as an American's," Summer translated impishly. "Do Americans have big balls, Major?"

"I don't need your crude commentary. I'm not shocked."

"Major, it's only Ismael's nature."

"Ismael is a wiseass who should know when to keep his mouth shut."

"Like any good Afghan woman? After this is over, Major, I'll start wearing a veil and get you an honorary membership in the Taliban."

Abdul listened to the English exchange with a quizzical expression. Summer said something to him in Arabic. He laughed heartily through his great red bush.

"I told him you said he had big balls indeed," Summer said with an innocent expression.

Only Bek Gorabic sat aloof from the fun. The stocky commander ate in sullen silence by the fire, his eyes glowering reflected firelight. The longer he sat there and the more wine he drank, the surlier he became. In his drunken state, it must have seemed his authority, already undermined by the redbeard, was being further eroded by the presence of the Americans and their abundance of food and supplies.

He got up suddenly, his eyes locked on Brandon and Abdul, and tossed his tin plate toward the fire for the women to pick up. Wiping his mouth on his sleeve, he picked up his light machine gun and swaggered across the cave, pushing men out of his way. He stopped in front of Abdul. Both men bristled. Bek stuck out his huge head and barked out what was obviously a challenge.

Summer translated.

"He's challenging Abdul to a game of bushkazi. Bek was a feared and well-known competitor in the days before the Russians. For Abdul not to accept would be an admission of cowardice."

Abdul glared back at his rival. Bek burst out in a roar of harsh laughter.

"Abdul accepts."

Still laughing, Bek turned slyly toward Brandon. Summer hesitated in translating.

"Bek thinks he's found a way to regain face and reclaim what he thinks is his lost authority," she said. "Major, the man is particularly ruthless on the field. He'll hurt you and hurt you badly if he gets the chance."

"What did he say?"

"Did you hear what I said, Major?"

"I heard. What did he say?"

She took a breath. "He challenges you also. He wonders if you and perhaps one of your men have the courage to play on Abdul's team against him. Don't do it, Major."

"Wouldn't that be cowardice, *Ismael*?"

Summer said nothing. Every eye in the cave fixed on the two men. It was a challenge issued before the entire band.

"Tell him I accept. It looks like we have no other choice if we want to continue working with these people."

"Major—"

Gloomy had overheard the transaction and walked over. "When I was a kid back in Hooker, boss," he said, "some of the good ol' boys would get together for field polo with long sticks and a baseball, riding bareback. A goat ain't nothing compared to a baseball flying through the air at eighty miles an hour. Major, you and me, we're gonna tear up that goat and stretch its asshole over Bek's head."

Brandon grinned tightly at Bek. "You sly hound," he said.

Somebody turned a live goat loose on the playing field, a scrawny black and tan billy with a curved rack of horns and a gagging piss-in-his-beard stench. The confused beast tiptoed hesitatingly into the middle of the field. It wandered in circles, bleating fearfully, surrounded and trapped by horsemen at either end and spectators on both sides. From where his team of six horsemen lined up at his goalpost, Bek Gorabic released a diabolical laugh that made the goat jump.

Gloomy rode the gray he used on the mission to Kabul. Abdul helped Brandon select a chestnut stallion a bit larger than the normal run of doglike Afghan ponies. The little horses skittered and danced in anticipation. Snow began falling lightly from a dark overcast that promised heavier snow. There would be no American bombing today.

"*Live* footballs. These ol' boys play rough," Gloomy commented. "Boss, remember Bek is after you. Try to stay away from him. He'll maul you if he gets a chance."

Brandon had played tailback in the Army-Navy game. Them ol' boys played rough too, he thought.

There was only one rule in bushkazi as far as Brandon could tell—get the goat, or at least the larger part of him—past the opposing side's goalpost more times than the other team got it past yours. Team captains Abdul on one side and Bek on the other established the winning game point at four. It was the same game, primitive and savage, that had amused Genghis Khan and his Mongol hordes when they swept across Asia and onto the Russian Steppes. Except the Khan might have used a man as the football instead of a goat.

Bek stood up in his stirrups, waved a hand in a circle above his head and yelped a signal. Ungainly on the ground with his short bowlegs and thick body, looking as grotesque in his skunk-striped beard as a monstrous dwarf, Commander Bek turned to fluid grace in the saddle. The two sides charged each other like cavalry.

The opposing forces clashed in the center of the field with the goat trapped between them. Horses screamed. Men shouted. There was the sound of thundering hooves, the meaty thunking of horses colliding. A mount went down in the melee, but the rider stayed with the animal as it lunged back to its feet.

Snorting with triumphant laughter, Bek emerged grasping the goat by one horn while the terrified creature kicked and struggled like a hare held by its ears. He broke free of the skirmish line and galloped toward Abdul's goal.

Gloomy and Saeed teamed to save the point. They blocked him from the front while Abdul came in from the rear, pounding his mount with his heels and lunging at Bek. He succeeded in catching the goat's hind leg. He veered off, almost jerking Bek's horse off its feet as they stretched the screaming goat between them.

Blood spurted from the animal's abdomen. A leg bone cracked like a dried tree branch. The goat bellowed in pain and terror.

Bek broke free, still in possession of the prize. Brandon spotted an opening, yanked his chestnut around and urged it into the fray of pounding hooves, bawling goat, spraying blood, screaming horses, and shouting men. He got enough of the goat in one hand to check Bek's headlong rush to score.

Bek surprised him by going on the attack rather than playing tug-of-war. He crashed his bay into Brandon's mount, at the same time unleashing a vicious kick that caught the stallion in its balls. The chestnut dropped to its knees with a grunt, but Brandon held onto the goat. The stallion regained its feet. The hot odor of blood, the kick to the nuts, and all the excitement was too much for the animal. He plunged his head between his front legs and took off upfield bucking and farting and bellowing.

Brandon was too busy trying to stay on his horse to worry about the point. Bek ended up in possession of the goat. He bolted toward the goalpost, pursued by Abdul's team. Skirmishes broke out all over the field as Abdul's players pursued and Bek's ran interference for him.

In the meantime, Brandon sailed off the stallion's back and hit the frozen ground. He was no cowboy, in spite of Slim and Toothless in Colorado. Stunned, he lay on his back looking up into snowflakes swirling in front of his eyes and causing pinpricks of cold on his face.

Summer bent over him. "You all right, Major? When you fall, you fall hard."

He caught his breath and got up. "Disappointed?" he asked.

She smiled at him. "Surprised. I like a man who falls at my feet."

No witty response came immediately to mind. He grunted something unintelligible.

Somebody caught his horse and led it back to him. Bek made it to the goalpost with the goat and looked back at him, laughing at him, mocking.

"I suppose it'll do no good to warn you to stay away from him," Summer said. She saw the look on his face. "I didn't think so."

The mutilated goat was back in the middle of the field, pulling itself around on its remaining functional legs, leaving smears of blood staining the accumulating snow. It mercifully died during the second play.

Gloomy proved every bit the equal in horsemanship of any of the mujahideen. He and Saeed teamed to chalk a point, tying the score.

The next points were hard won by both sides. The battle moved furiously from one end of the playing field to the other, with each team blocking, checking, passing, and brawling like a pack of wolves over the goat's bloody remains. Abdul lost one man due to a severely wrenched elbow, giving Bek the advantage until one of his horses went down and was led off, limping on three legs. Brandon managed to hold his own. He neither avoided Bek nor made an effort to retaliate. Bek seemed frustrated by his inability, so far, to put the American out of commission.

There were no substitutes in the game, no time-outs, and no half-time show. Each side scored again, making it two to two.

Gloomy reined up alongside his commander during a brief lull in the action between face-offs. The horses were blowing from exertion. The riders were almost as winded.

"Boss, take a gander at Bek. If looks could kill, we'd be using you instead of the goat. He expected this to be a piece of cake."

"We're going to beat the bastard, Gloomy."

"Hoo-ya!"

Summer waved at them from the sidelines.

"That's an odd kid," Gloomy said. "Reckon he's a fag?"

"What do we care if he screws camels, as long as he does his job?"

"I didn't mean anything, boss." A half grin spread over his countenance. "I don't know, but he sure seems to have a crush on you."

"Jesus Christ, Gloomy."

Bek made it clear during the struggle for the final points that he intended to win at any cost, that this was as much a personal mano-a-mano between him and the American leader as it was a contest between the camp's two factions. He cast aside even the pretense of civility and went for Brandon with everything he had.

Brandon's stallion was strong and quick on its feet, enabling its less skillful rider to avoid most of the guerrilla chief's bullish charges and attempts to knock him to the ground and trample him. Bek possessed outstanding horsemanship and had scored both of his team's points. Brandon hadn't touched the flesh ball since the first time.

The guerrilla chief laughed and yelled insults at the Americans, reveling in humbling his rivals. So confident was he in winning that he deliberately gave up scoring a point in order to give himself more chances to catch Brandon or Abdul vulnerable at the line of scrimmage.

The score was tied again, three to three, with the winning point at stake.

Bek emerged from a clash with the goat. Abdul's red beard flashed as he checked Bek and caught the animal's remaining hind leg. The haunch ripped off in his hand when a Bek player crashed into him.

In the clear with a cook's share of the dead beast, Bek took off at a hard gallop for the goalpost. Brandon and his chestnut stallion presented the only obstacle to prevent the guerrilla leader from taking the game.

Brandon whooped at his horse and dug his heels into its ribs. The startled animal leaped forward. The two riders thundered toward each other like jousting knights. The evil grin on Bek's face suggested this was exactly what he wanted. He was going to finish off the American in a big way, hurt him bad, and *then* score to win.

Brandon felt like Rooster Coburn in *True Grit*. "You son of a bitch!" he roared.

He resisted the urge to transfer his reins to his teeth and John Wayne into battle with both hands free.

Bek feinted his mount to the left to draw out Brandon and expose the chestnut's flank. He was so much a part of his animal that they appeared permanently joined. Through luck and because he expected the move this time, Brandon dodged with him and blocked. The horses crashed. The chestnut stumbled back but kept his footing.

Shouting and red-faced above his skunk beard, Bek began kicking with his near foot, attempting to catch Brandon's knee or ankle and disable him.

Brandon drove in and snatched a piece of the goat's ragged hide. But instead of pulling back with it, as Bek expected, the American continued forward, driving the chestnut deep and hard into Bek's bay. That caught the guerrilla chief by surprise and gave Brandon a momentary advantage.

He used it.

Sensing his opponent and his horse both off balance, Brandon yanked on the goat and at the same time twisted the stallion in a tight circle. He almost lost his saddle, but held on out of sheer determination. He counterkicked as soon as he recovered, tagging Bek painfully on the thigh.

Bek cried out. The look on his face said he knew he'd been had. The force of the unexpected kick, the loss of balance by

Bek's horse, and the opposite heave on the dead goat did the trick. The bay fell hard on its side, throwing Bek free and facedown in the beaten muddy muck of the fresh snow.

Gloomy and Saeed shouted in triumph and raced in to block for Brandon and lead the blitzkrieg toward the opponent's goal. Nothing could stop them now. Brandon flew past the post for the winning point.

Bek remained alone on the field, standing spread-legged in the snowfall and glowering in humiliation while his freed horse trotted off. Brandon looked back. While he couldn't help feeling elated, he also felt he might have made a final dangerous mistake in disgracing the guerrilla leader in front of his men.

BIN LADEN NAMES TARGETS

ISLAMABAD, PAKISTAN (CPI)—The U.S. State Department has released a 33-minute video in which Osama bin Laden discusses the September 11 terror attack. On the tape, bin Laden is seen speaking with aides and a Saudi Arabian sheik.

"We calculated in advance the number of casualties from the enemy, who would be killed based on the position of the tower," Osama was heard saying. "I was thinking that the fire from the gas in the plane would melt the iron structure of the building and collapse the area where the plane hit and all the floors above it only. This is all that we had hoped for . . ."

It is unknown who made the tape, which is of amateur quality. It was reportedly recovered in Kabul by a U.S. Special Forces Delta detachment working with Northern Alliance fighters. Among other materials secreted out of Afghanistan were parts of an 11-volume *Manual of Afghan Jihad*. It instructs in chilling terms that attack sites should include targets of "high human intensity" such as skyscrapers, nuclear plants, and football stadiums, and targets of "sentimental value," such as the Statue of Liberty.

"In every country," the manual reads, "we should hit their organizations, institutions, clubs, and hospitals. The targets must be identified, carefully chosen, and include their largest gatherings so that any strike should cause thousands of deaths."

Other documents found in Afghanistan include diagrams of American nuclear plants and city water supplies. There is also material discussing how to use bioterrorism and the best and most effective agents to use.

To date, nearly a dozen Americans have died of inhalation anthrax. Many more have been contaminated and are under treatment. Authorities warn that anthrax or smallpox, if successfully infused into cities, could cause thousands, even millions, of deaths.

MacArthur Thornbrew, chairman of the National Homeland Security Agency, cautioned that large terror attacks could still take place and called for continued vigilance. He said that it is only a matter of time until America experiences the same kind of suicide bombings that occur in Israel in malls and restaurants, schools and churches. America, he said, is at war as much in its states and cities as in Afghanistan.

While the Osama materials from Afghanistan have shocked and horrified the world, many remain skeptical.

"This administration is trying to scare hell out of us," said former President John Stanton, "telling us we are at war and can expect to be for a very long time. We are at war, but must we give up our civil liberties at the same time? For eight years when I was in the White House I worked hard to maintain the peace—and succeeded. The world is today a more dangerous place than it has been in more than sixty years."

Senator Eric B. Tayloe, chairman of the Senate Armed Services Committee, was also critical.

"I'm not implying that the bin Laden tape is a forgery," he asserted in a printed statement. "However, I have two Muslim-Americans on my staff who said the translation is not completely accurate. The administration may be using the tape as part of a scare tactic to implicate Muslims and round up thousands of honest people and detain them out of panic, as we did Japanese citizens during World War II. Our government is trampling their human rights.

"Only this week," the statement went on, "the FBI raided offices of the charity-based Sacred Land Foundation and arrested Muslims. The founder of the foundation, Mullah Shukri Abu Marzook, is a friend and colleague of my Muslim staff members. I don't personally know him, but I am told he is a good and decent man who was forced to become a fugitive as a result of the raids. He fears for his life if he tries to turn himself in. The FBI's National Domestic Preparedness Office refuses to say what evidence, if any, there is against Mullah Shukri and the foundation. It is a witch hunt that should appall and horrify all fair-minded Americans."

The former President and Senator Tayloe have called for a congressional investigation of U.S. Special Forces activities in Afghanistan. They claim Special Operations has targeted bin Laden and other officials in Afghanistan for assassination, which is currently against U.S. law.

CHAPTER 28

Fort Bragg

Sergeant Cassidy Kragle's eyes abruptly opened and he sat upright in bed, sweating and blinking rapidly in the darkness. The nightmare returned night after night. It always began in the tomb blackness of his al-Qaeda cell in Afghanistan, that dreary land of death and incessant warfare where Kathryn and he were held hostage following the bombing of the USS *Randolph*. Amal—"Rat Man," as Cassidy dubbed him—had Kathryn in the guards' room, raping her. Cassidy bellowed and threatened and threw himself against the barred doors until his hands were torn and bleeding. Rat Man laughed at him and kept pumping at Kathryn on the cot against the wall while the other guards watched.

"We'll be rescued. My brothers will come," he tried to reassure her each night, holding her on the cold stone floor of their filthy cage. "You'll see. When we're home, I'll never let anything hurt you again."

"Cassidy, you have to promise me. Do you promise?"

He married her, but he could not keep his promise. Osama bin Laden, from whom they escaped once, reached out again and indifferently took her life. Cassidy was glad he did what needed to be done to Amal and that the Rat Man was dead. He burned to do the same thing to bin Laden. Shoot him in the nuts and watch while he bled to death. It might be God's job to forgive Osama bin Laden, but Cassidy trusted his brother Brandon to arrange the meeting. Cassidy felt he should be in Afghanistan with Brandon now.

How could a just God let such things happen to a sweet human being like his wife? And to their unborn child? If there was a heaven and a hell, Cassidy swore he would consign to those fires his own soul in order to see dead the lunatics who poisoned his wife.

He swung his legs over the side of his bunk and sat there breathing deeply to bring back the present reality. As an NCO, he rated a single cadre room in Training Group billeting on base. He had tried for a while after Kathryn's death to stay in the little house they shared, but there were too many memories there.

Their baby was going to be a boy. Kathryn fixed up the nursery in blue. The wallpaper was sky blue with army paratroopers floating below cloudlike parachutes. Now it would never be used. Sometimes when the nightmares first started, Cassidy got up and stood in the nursery, his angled face stony and his dark high and tight haircut bristling. Gloria, who stayed with him after the funeral, padded up behind in her old flannel robe and rabbit ear house shoes and put her arms around him.

"It be all right to cry, baby, if'n you feels like it," she whispered.

Cassidy had never seen the General cry. Nor Brandon either. Not even when they were kids and got hurt. Kragle men didn't cry. Except for Cameron maybe. Cameron wept when Gypsy Iryani died in Afghanistan. Cameron was different than the rest of the Kragles.

"They's some things you can't hold all inside until it starts to rot and rots you with it," Gloria said. "Baby, I knows you a big Special Forces trooper now, just like you daddy and big brothers, but it ain't no weakness to grieve for somebody you loves."

"The General looks down on weakness," Cassidy responded with a bitter edge. "He thinks I'm weak. Why else would he block me from going to Delta? Nobody'll tell me it was him who did it. Colonel Buck denies it, but I know it was him. In Delta, I would have had a chance to do something about crazies."

"We don't know it was you daddy. Cassidy. Even if he did, I is sure it was for a good reason."

"None of us will ever live up to what the General expects of us," Cassidy flared.

"Cass, he be you *father*, baby."

"He was never a real father."

He turned toward her. The black woman tiptoed and put her heavy arms tightly around his neck. Tears rolled down her fat dark cheeks, but the young soldier she thought of as her own son still did not cry.

"Brown Sugar Doll," he said, "you go on back to Florida to be with the General."

He put his fingers against her lips to stifle her protest. He had to leave this house. He saw Kathryn all through it, smelled her, felt her.

"You're the only person the General has ever needed since our mother died, Sugar Doll," he said. "He depends on you. Especially now when he has so much pressure on him from the war and the congressional investigation."

"But— But what you gone do, honey?" Gloria pleaded.

"I can't stay here and think about Kathryn. I'm moving back on-post. I'll be all right, Sugar Doll. Honest. You can count on it. We Kragles are tough."

"Sometimes, honey, tough just ain't enough."

Cassidy took nothing of Kathryn's with him from the

house except some old navy photos, the pictures of their wedding, and a scarf she liked to wear when it was windy. He could smell her on it. He became something of a barracks rat, hanging around doing make-work chickenshit details with Training Group at the JFK Center. His buddy Bobby Goose Pony went over to Wally World to go through Delta counterterrorist training. Clerking and jerking made Cassidy feel helpless, useless. He had graduated as an honor candidate from the SF Q Course. He felt he should have gone to Delta with Pony to join his brothers.

Cameron tried to ease things for him. He was always around with his chaplain's Bible, his spouting of scripture, and his good intentions.

> *"I will be glad and rejoice in thy mercy:*
> *for thou hast considered my trouble:*
> *thou hast known my soul in adversities . . ."*

"Cameron, leave me alone."

"Little brother, don't judge our father if he tries to protect you. It is difficult for us to see the way without God's help when we sorrow."

"Cameron, sometimes I see God and the General in the same face."

The chaplain was a gentle soul always eager to forgive others and overlook their transgressions. It was his way. It was not the Kragle way. When the nightmares were really bad, as they were tonight, Cassidy depended on Goose Pony.

Sitting in the dark, sweating through his T-shirt, Cassidy glanced at the illuminated dial of his wristwatch: 11:00 P.M. He hated to disturb Pony, considering the long hours of training the Arapaho was putting in at Wally World.

"If you *don't* call me, paleface," Pony scolded, "I'll have your scalp."

Cassidy got up, slipped on jeans, a sweatshirt, and sneakers, went downstairs to the dayroom and dialed Pony's quarters at the Delta compound. They arranged to meet at a Fayetteville bar called De Libre, run by a retired SF sergeant.

He really didn't *depend* on Goose Pony, Cassidy corrected himself. They were just buddies.

Hays Street was almost deserted, since it was late and in the middle of the week. The bars were open, along with a few gas stations and all-night convenience stores, but everything else was shut down. A figure at a pay phone outside a ratty soldiers' bar caught Cassidy's eye as he drove past in his blue Mustang. It looked familiar, one of the men who might need a lift, so he took a right at the next intersection and circled the block.

Rasem Jameel was just finishing on the phone. Odd, Cassidy thought, that Jameel, who devoted so much time and energy to Cameron's chapel, who showed up to pray every time the church doors opened, should be hanging out late downtown around the bars. Curious, Cassidy turned off his headlights and eased up at the corner in the shadow of a dark warehouse.

Glancing in both directions, as though cautious of being seen, the Saudi hurried toward his vehicle, parked nearby. A new red Mazda. An expensive car to support on a sergeant E-5's pay, Cassidy reflected. Still curious about what Jameel was doing out so late and why he appeared so secretive, he decided to tail him for a distance.

They proceeded out Hays toward Fort Bragg. Cassidy was about to pull off, thinking Jameel was heading toward the 82nd Airborne billets, when the Saudi took a different turn and sped on out of town. Cassidy followed. The Mazda soon pulled into the parking lot of a twenty-four-hour Super Wal-Mart on Ramsey Street. Maybe he needed a new toothbrush or something, Cassidy thought, castigating himself. He had a right to be out and about, after all.

In the few times they'd encountered each other, Cassidy had never taken to Jameel. He had shifty eyes. Now Cassidy wondered if his suspicion might merely be fueled by his dislike and by recent events. People were prone to be wary of Muslims since 9/11, to mistrust their darker skins, their accents, their very foreignness. It was called "racial profiling" when cops did it.

He was about to call off his surveillance when the Mazda pulled up alongside a black Chrysler in the parking lot. Cassidy scowled. Strange that they would meet like this in the middle of the night. Was it a tryst between gays?

Cassidy eased onto the Wal-Mart lot. A few customers pushed carts or walked to and from the store with their purchases. A man was getting out of the Chrysler. Cassidy drove past with his head averted and his hand held up to his face, to avoid Jameel recognizing him. He got a good look at the stranger in the glow of the sodium security lights.

The man was of average size, in his mid-thirties or early forties, and was dark like a Middle Easterner. He was clean-shaved, his black hair styled and combed, and looked powerfully built. He wore dark slacks, shined shoes, and an expensive black leather jacket.

Jameel and the Chrysler man appeared to be quarreling by the time Cassidy picked a parking space behind another car near the store. The stranger grabbed Jameel by his lapels with both fists and slammed him hard against the side of the Mazda.

Cassidy got out, peered across the top of his car and the one parked next to him. Relative shadow away from the nearest security light provided him some concealment. Besides, Jameel seemed so busy trying to appease the guy who was roughing him up that he probably wouldn't have noticed a freight train cutting across the parking lot. Cassidy wished he could hear what was being said.

After a minute or so the man cooled off and let go of Jameel, but his body language said he was still upset. Jameel held up both palms. They talked some more. The man shook his finger in Jameel's face, as though issuing a warning or an ultimatum, then got into the Chrysler and slammed the door. Jameel watched him leave before he got back into his Mazda and headed out in the direction of the army post.

What the hell was that all about? Cassidy wondered.

He told himself this was none of his business. Still, it was out of character for a God-fearing Christian convert. He felt vaguely troubled as he left the Wal-Mart and drove to meet Goose Pony at De Libre.

CHAPTER 29

Quantico

Alone in his office, Claude Thornton raked big hands across his shaved head in exasperation. So far, even after finding anthrax at the Dallas Sacred Land Foundation, the FBI kept turning into blind alleys in its search for the source of the deadly anthrax powder. Apparently, this Otta character was the go-between from the source to Mullah Shukri. Where it went from there was anybody's guess. And now it seemed a hundred pounds of it was out there in terrorist hands, waiting to be used. Telephone numbers, addresses, and other evidence seized during the raids provided few clues to date. Terrorist sleepers working in the U.S. knew how to cover and protect themselves in small cells the guerrilla warfare way.

People were starting to panic over the anthrax scare. An airliner emergency landed because a passenger opened a greeting card containing confetti. Another airliner banned Sweet 'N Low because it looked like anthrax powder. An entire town went on alert when somebody found dried bird poop on a parked car at city hall. A tunnel was closed during an ice storm because somebody mistook road salt for anthrax.

The whole country would shut down if people knew how imminent the threat really was. MacArthur Thornbrew over at NHSA swore everyone to secrecy about the possible bioattack against an as yet unknown city. The people, he said, were like what Jack Nicholson said in the movie *A Few Good Men*: "You can't handle the truth."

Thornton's secretary buzzed his desk from the outer office. He picked up the phone, expecting a report from Fred Whiteman on an al-Qaeda lead in Atlanta. "Thornton here."

"Sir, this is Sergeant Cassidy Kragle, General Kragle's son . . ."

"Sure. How are you doing?"

"Sir, I didn't want to bother you, but I saw something a couple of nights ago that I keep thinking about. I'm probably just paranoid, but the whole thing was so out of character. Do you remember Rasem Jameel?"

"From Saudi Arabia, right? Thin-faced sergeant with the 82nd Airborne. He does a lot of volunteer chaplain work for your brother. I talked to him about the Reverend Billy Dye mailings your wife worked on with him."

"I don't want to say anything to Cameron just yet," Cassidy said. "Like I say, it's probably nothing, but I thought you should know, what with Kathryn and all. . . . I'm sure you're getting a lot of calls these days about suspicious-acting Arabs."

In fact, every FBI regional office in the country was besieged by them.

Cassidy described the incident he'd observed between Jameel and the powerfully built man in the Wal-Mart lot.

It was probably nothing, like most such tips, Thornton assumed when Cassidy was finished. There was nothing inherently suspicious about two guys quarreling in a parking lot. Nonetheless, a long shot was better than nothing. He said, "I'm coming to Bragg on Thursday to meet Mr. Thornbrew and the commanding staff at the JFK Center for a briefing. We'll get together then and discuss it."

Seeing Sergeant Cassidy Kragle striding across the foyer at the fortresslike headquarters of U.S. Army Special Forces Command reminded Thornton that his own son was now in military uniform. Claude Jr. had begun classes at the U.S. Naval Academy shortly before 9/11. He wondered why the General's youngest son had not chosen to be an officer instead of following the enlisted career path.

Cassidy was in uniform, wearing his green beret and Training Group flash. Thornton reflected that Training Group must be a disappointment for him. Cassidy was a tall, tanned young man, a less worn copy of both his older brother and the General. He even walked like the General, with long, purposeful strides and braced shoulders. They shook hands warmly, then went to the canteen for coffee and a place to talk in relative privacy. They selected a table toward the back. It was still early on a duty day, and the canteen was nearly empty.

"I've brought along some pictures I want you to look at," Thornton said. "Can you ID the guy if you saw his photo?"

"I got a good look at him."

Thornton opened his briefcase and extracted a thick stack of what appeared to be enlarged passport photos.

"These are compliments of your granddaddy," he said. "The Ambassador is a remarkable old gentleman when it comes to dealing with Muslims and Middle Easterners. He persuaded Saudi Arabia to provide a list of suspected terrorists who may have entered the United States and are moled-in waiting for orders to strike—like they did on 9/11."

"There must be three hundred of them here," Cassidy exclaimed, hefting the photographs before taking some off the top.

"That's only on the surface. We don't really know what we

do have in this country. Our government has been so wrapped up in political correctness when it comes to immigration policy that it wouldn't have turned down Osama bin Laden's visa for fear of being considered discriminatory. Some good old-fashioned discrimination and racial profiling might have been a good thing."

Cassidy started through the pictures slowly, taking a long look at each before discarding it. The FBI agent sipped his coffee, not too hopeful. He was going through the steps because he was at Bragg anyhow and because this was his friend's son.

To Thornton's surprise, Cassidy hadn't gone halfway through the first stack before he flipped a photo across the table and leaned back in his chair.

Thornton stared at it. "Are you sure?"

"That's him. Who is he?"

"I'll be damned for a Mississippi sharecropper." He shook his head, marveling. "His name is Mullah Shukri Abu Marzook. He's been in the United States since 1998 organizing terrorist cells under the guise of the Sacred Land Foundation. We suspected him, but we really didn't understand all his terrorist connections until the Ambassador came through with his list of names. We have arrest warrants out for him now. He's a Saudi, like fifteen of the nineteen tangos who crashed into the Trade Center and the Pentagon."

"What's he doing in Fayetteville with Sergeant Jameel?"

The agent stood up. "That's what we're going to find out."

KABUL FALLS

KABUL (CPI)—Northern Alliance forces armed with rifles and rocket launchers and riding in pickup trucks moved into the Afghan capital after a series of stunning victories. The streets were empty of Taliban soldiers and the military compounds deserted when they arrived, with sporadic small arms fire coming from the hills outside the city. Residents honking car horns and ringing bicycle bells shouted congratulations.

Taliban military forces deserted Kabul on Tuesday, taking with them eight foreign aid workers, including four American women who were accused of spreading Christianity in Muslim Afghanistan.

"I saw them leaving," a witness told CPI. "They put the women in a truck and left at midnight. They said they were going to Kandahar."

Weeks of bombing by the United States weakened the Taliban and forced the surrender of the capital. At least 600 U.S. Marines are on the ground, with 400 more on the way. Pentagon officials said they would be used to choke off escape routes for Taliban leaders and fighters loyal to al-Qaeda.

The collapse of Taliban resistance in the north now focuses attention around Kandahar in the south and the mountain base of Tora Bora in the White Mountains south of Jalalabad near the Pakistan border. Authorities speculate that al-Qaeda leader Osama bin Laden may have moved his headquarters to the Tora Bora area. U.S. Special Forces continue to pursue bin Laden and Mullah Mohammed Omar, the Taliban leader.

"I can be eliminated, but not my mission," bin Laden was quoted as saying in the Pakistani newspaper *Ausef*.

Western speculation is that bin Laden has likely prepared his last rites to assure his legacy and his legend. In anticipation of his death, money and operators may already have been moved out across a global grid. It is possible that "sleepers" in the U.S. and elsewhere have received orders on how to continue the campaign, guided by bin Laden's dead hand.

The likely scenario of the terrorist mastermind's death could take either of two paths. He could immolate himself and those closing in on him, or bin Laden might flee to a remote cave, detonate an explosive device, and bury himself in the mountains. Were he to take the latter course, a U.S. government spokesman notes, his legend would continue to grow. Bin Laden would be seen and suspected in every subsequent terrorist action against the West.

CHAPTER 30

Afghanistan

Turban wrapped low over his brow and covering his ears, snow and ice crusted in his beard, Major Brandon Kragle shielded his eyes from the light, blowing snow and strained to make out anything moving in the soupy sky. He half expected the choppers to scrub because of weather, but they had sent the code word a half hour ago. They were on their way in to airlift 1-Alpha and selected guerrilla assets to a new base camp. Iron Weed screwed up its first attempt against the Shake, but the war and the chase were still a long way from over.

His orders arrived two days after the fall of Kabul. SFOB and whomever Summer contacted over her little solar-powered SAT PC came to the same conclusion: Kandahar was the next major objective for American air power. Iron Weed 1A's target, the Shake, was expected to set up in the Tora Bora region of the White Mountains near Kandahar, from which he would continue to direct his share of the war. He and his lieutenants apparently valued their own lives enough to hole up in caves while others did the fighting. According to the verbal coded orders, 1-Alpha, with Northern

Alliance assets, would be helo-lifted from their present location and be reinserted in the White Mountains. There, they would continue their mission to find and deal with Osama bin Laden.

"We have a mole in bin Laden's organization," Summer confided to the Delta commander, once again confirming Brandon's suspicions that she was far from being merely an interpreter and AO expert.

"We?" Brandon said, short of temper, disliking the elevated status she assumed in the mission. She and her secret PC contacts had put a pin on the Shake the first time. Now it looked like she was going to do it again. Iron Weed's success might well depend on her, as Punitive Strike had depended on Gypsy Iryani. The déjà vu made Brandon nervous.

Summer, still pretending to be Ismael, smiled. "We're working this mole," she said, not explaining *we*. "We'll be notified when the target is stationary. This time, Major, we— that's you and I—are expected to complete the assignment."

There it was, his subjection to outside intelligence sources over which he had no control. It wasn't so much that it went against his grain as the fact that she was a woman and therefore his team's weak link. He had already tried to have her replaced.

There was not enough time, SFOB had told him. No other asset was available.

"Damnit!" Brandon exclaimed. Did SFOB know that Ismael was a woman?

Ismael has access to valuable Afghan network, SFOB's message informed him. *Work closely with him in next phase*.

"Major," she whispered with a teasing smile, "it looks like you and I are stuck in the same bed after all."

She knew it all along. He glared at her.

The rest of the detachment knew their CO was trying to get rid of Ismael, but not why.

"Sometimes I don't think that Ismael is a kid at all," Gloomy opined.

Summer walked away in deep conversation with Abdul Homayan and Saeed the Zarbati.

"He's got a smart mouth," Thumbs Jones said. "He needs his dick knocked in the dirt."

"The more we see of him," Winnie Brown interjected, "the less certain I am that he even possesses that appendage. Have any of you noticed the manner in which he walks?"

"You're the intel specialist, Winnie," Doc TB said. "Grab his crotch and see if he's got one."

"Fu-uck. Let Thumbs grab his crotch," Mad Dog suggested. "Thumbs don't look nigger anymore. He looks like a genuine A-rab, and I understand you diaper heads relish young boys more than you do women."

"That's *African-American* to you, hairball," Thumbs shot back, and the team was, as always, ready for a little fun and the rough give-and-take of men who liked and respected each other.

"Whether he's got a dick or not," Gloomy Davis concluded, having witnessed Ismael in action in Kabul, "I can tell you one thing—that boy's got a big set of Oklahoma *cojones* and I'd go into a fight with him anywhere."

The detachment received digital photos and a target area study of its new AO by hooking Summer's PC and software to the PRC-137 radio with its built-in encryption device. The materials revealed a daunting portrait of the Tora Bora mountain refuge. It was rugged country, jagged and ridged and rubbled with rock. What forest existed there grew stunted and deformed in the draws and canyons. Summer said Tora Bora translated as "Black Dust." A good breeze could blow at sixty miles an hour, howling and shrieking among the pinnacles and precipices and filling the air with black grit. Old people said there were malignant spirits in the mountains.

"There's at least one, if we're lucky—the Shake," Mother Norman said.

The mountains were honeycombed with networks of natural and man-made caves and underground tunnels that had been used to fight invaders since the time of Genghis Khan. Caves allowed Afghans to stage surprise attacks, spot attacking military forces, and hide troops for months at a time. It was rumored that some of the lairs extended thousands of feet under mountains, beyond the reach of bunker-busting bombs. They were four or five stories deep and had dozens of rooms large enough to house tanks, trucks, and ammunition. One of bin Laden's underground sanctuaries supposedly had an Islamic library, artillery and communications rooms, computers, faxes, and telephones. Steel doors reinforced with concrete sealed all entries, and mortar and machine-gun emplacements protected them.

And Iron Weed was going into that mess to find one man!

"Fu-ucked up!" Mad Dog Carson opined, slapping his sides with his arms to keep warm while he stood over his radio and scanned the snow-swirling sky for the arrival of the helicopters. "I swore I'd never go to a war if it was north of Miami Beach. Where do I end up? Siberia."

"It's not Siberia," Ice Man corrected, using up his allotment of conversation for the day. He rubbed a scar high on his cheek, where he'd been wounded during Punitive Strike. It was particularly susceptible to cold.

"If it ain't Siberia, it's still too damned close."

On one side of the bushkazi field in front of the cave, Abdul Homayan and five of his selected fighters stamped their feet and rubbed their hands together, as much from nervousness as from the cold. None of them had ever flown in a helicopter before. The red-beard sat on a case of mortar rounds, trying to look nonchalant, as though he were an old hand at flying.

Bek Gorabic and his fighter selection, also six, encamped on the other side of the field. The two factions had grown more openly hostile toward each other after the unexpected outcome of the bushkazi game. Bek made it a point of ignoring the Americans, as though they did not exist and everything that happened concerning them was a result of his own decisions and motivation.

Brandon especially distrusted Bek after the game and couldn't help thinking he was plotting some sort of retaliation. He wanted to exclude Bek and his men from moving with the band, but Summer pointed out that to reject one leader over the other would likely trigger into violence the longstanding hostility between the two camps.

"You had your chance to get rid of Bek the day you arrived," Summer said. "You blew it."

In the end, a compromise selected an equal number of fighters from each bloc, for a total of twelve, while the others stayed behind with the two or three women to take care of the horses and eventually move their headquarters into liberated Kabul. The camp as it transferred into the White Mountains was almost equally split into three elements, two of which were hostile toward each other and one of which, Bek's, was at least sour on the American contingent.

Major Brandon, Summer, and 1-Alpha waited for the choppers in a separate group upwind, in order to direct the birds in. Sergeant Gloomy Davis lapsed into one of his stories.

"The Dog and this ol' boy from the 7th had their eyes on the same piece of snatch at the NCO Club," he recited in his deadpan voice. "So this guy wants to go outside and fight. Mad Dog says to him, 'I propose a contest.' 'A contest?' says the other guy. 'What kinda contest?' 'Well,' the Dog drawls, 'I propose we go outside. You take out your pee-pee and I'll take out mine.' The guy is staring at Mad Dog like he's either crazy or the meanest SOB in the valley. The Dog goes on, 'We rub the heads of our pee-pees together and the first one who smiles loses.' "

Gloomy let it hang like that until Doc TB had to know. "What happened?"

"Mad Dog won."

"It's the God's honest truth," Thumbs swore. "I was there. Gloomy, you still haven't told us what happened when Arachna Phoebe jumped off the Beaver River Bridge—"

Summer laughed. *"Who?"*

"Arachna Phoebe," Gloomy said morosely, as though it was the saddest story he knew.

Mad Dog squatted and placed both radio earphones over his ears. He listened, keyed his mike, spoke, and listened again.

"It's the choppers, Major," he said. "They're going to circle once to take a look before they come in. I think they're cautious of RPGs."

Brandon nodded. "Arachna will have to wait. Get those birds in and get the troops on."

The helicopters were an agile Pave Hawk gunship and a huge, double-rotared MH-47 Chinook from the 160th SOAR—the Nightstalkers. The Pave Hawk came over low and the Chinook high to take a look, igniting a burst of energy among the guerrillas. Saeed waved both hands and shouted until he was hoarse; he had never been so near to such magnificent flying machines, and now he was about to fly in one. A gunner in the side door of the Chinook leaned out over a 30mm chain gun and waved. The birds whirled up snow and ground clutter, then swung out wide to complete their area recon.

Mad Dog hurriedly packed his radio gear, slung the rucksack on his back, and picked up his M-16 rifle. Gloomy guided in the MH-47 while the Hawk continued to fly in tight circles. The Chinook set down quickly in the high rare air and the tailgate dropped. Brandon and Mother Norman ushered the guerrillas aboard up the ramp, everyone bent double in the rotor windstorm. Bek's men took one side of the aircraft, Abdul's the other. The bird jumped back into the falling snow even before the ramp closed.

Summer squeezed onto the canvas next to Brandon. Her breath made clouds around her face. Very much aware of the pressure of her curves against him, he studied a map of their new base camp site and AO to take his mind off her.

"Interesting?" she asked. She said it twice before he heard her above engine roar.

He looked at her, her face only inches from his. The straight nose, the full lips, the eyes dark from the contact lenses but rich emerald green underneath . . . His throat thickened.

"You really know how to show a girl a good time," she said with impish mischief.

CHAPTER 31

The new camp was at an even higher altitude than the old one, but there was no snow there yet, only the wind, which started out as a cold breeze in the morning and built into a bitter gale by midday, tufting and swirling black dust. They built camp in the shelter of a long ledge that was like a porch. It ran along the lee side of a lofty ridge and was protected at either end by blind canyons. It was well-hidden, easy to defend, and provided a breathtaking view of the White Mountains and the Tora Bora area that was ultimately Iron Weed 1A's objective.

Forced inactivity made Brandon and the detachment restless. It wasn't the team's job on this mission to know about spies and clandestine operatives, CIA spooks and moles. It was Iron Weed's job to act upon information fed it. Such missions required a direct action mentality, which chafed at idleness.

When and where the detachment moved depended upon intelligence from SFOB, Ismael-Summer's secret SAT PC channels, or the contact her "people" had supposedly cultivated inside bin Laden's organization.

"There are literally thousands of caves up there," Summer

said, pointing toward the Tora Bora. "It would be insane and futile to go in there without knowing which cave is bin Laden's command post."

Brandon understood the logic, but it made the waiting no easier.

Northern Alliance forces were starting to make their push on the Tora Bora. U.S. B-2 Stealth bombers prepped the mountain redoubts for them, pounding away with 5,000-pound "bunker buster" bombs and 15,000-pound "daisy cutters." The ledge camp provided box seats for the spectacle of dark clouds roiling over the serrated horizon like an approaching hurricane, while in its midst explosions crackled and flashed like lightning. The storm was nearly twenty klicks away, but the earth shuddered at the camp so violently that the spectators, it seemed, were sometimes almost shaken off their feet.

"Jesus God, how could *anything* live through that?" Thumbs Jones exclaimed. "If I could carry *that* kind of bang in my ruck . . ."

"They've burrowed deep inside, like rats," Brandon said.

Doc TB blew a sigh through his lips. "Pity the poor bastards that have to go in there to root 'em out."

"You idiot," Mad Dog said. "Them poor bastards are *us*."

The medic's eyes widened.

Brandon feared the Shake would run again if pressed too hard. That meant that he might escape to continue his reign of terror against the Western world and Iron Weed 1-Alpha would fail its mission. He, Brandon, would fail.

Then again, where would bin Laden go? His back was up against Pakistan. The U.S. 10th Mountain Division, U.S. Marines, Army Special Forces, and even the SEALs were cutting off the border and blocking the terrorist king's escape routes. Brandon found it ironic that one of the richest men in the world, although he was a terrorist, was about to end his days hiding in a hole in the mountain. Brandon knew that he and his Delta detachment had to make sure that happened.

Bek came and stood next to the American commander and watched the bombing. Since the move to the new camp, his bellicosity seemed to have diminished somewhat. Witnessing day after day the power of the U.S. appeared to have instilled in him a new awe and respect for the winning side. He was still no Norman Vincent Peale, would not be winning friends and influencing people, and Brandon still did not trust him, but the belligerence of his earlier days had receded. It was almost a new era of accommodation.

He appeared about to say something. Brandon called Summer over.

"You think you can trust Abdul," Bek said gruffly, watching the bombing and not looking at Brandon. "You are a fool."

"What does he mean by that?" Brandon asked.

"The men of Abdul's band were not killed fighting the Taliban," Bek said, and Summer translated. "They were fighting Commander Khalil of the Northern Alliance. That is true."

He turned and walked off, leaving both Brandon and Summer puzzled. What was that all about?

Who *could* you trust in this crazy, shit-pot country?

"Bek is up to something," Summer predicted.

"How good is your intel on Abdul?" Brandon asked, thinking.

"You're not going to believe Bek!"

"You trust Abdul?"

"Like I said, I trust no one completely, not even you. I merely trust Abdul more than I trust Bek."

Things were further complicated and muddled the next day on a patrol down toward a valley where Northern Alliance troops were attempting to advance on Tora Bora. The patrol consisted of Abdul and Saeed the Zarbati along with Major Kragle, Gloomy Davis, and Summer. They stopped for mid-meal in the shelter of some scrubby trees. Sounds of the Northern Alliance advance one valley over—mules braying, engines roaring, shouting—came to them on the wind. Brandon questioned Saeed about Abdul when Abdul borrowed his binoculars and climbed to some high ground to take a look.

"Have you been with Abdul's band all along?" he asked.

"I was with Commander Khalil at first. That was before the Americans. All the bands were fighting each other as well as the Taliban."

"And Abdul?"

"When I was with Commander Khalil, we had an engagement against some rebel tribesmen. I was wounded and left behind. I was contemplating my virgins when Abdul found me lying near death. He had lost some of his men in another engagement and was weakened from fighting. I came into the mountains with him to Commander Bek's camp, where we could recover to fight again."

It gave Brandon something to think about.

The patrol continued to the edge of the valley, where Northern Alliance fighters were slowly moving up. A long column of foot soldiers, mules, horses, old pickup trucks loaded with troops, and an early model T-64 battle tank captured from the Russians, its 125mm main gun snouting from side to side, came to a clogged halt as a machine gun opened up on point elements.

Through his binoculars Brandon spotted muzzle flash and thin blue smoke threading out of a thicket of stunted trees on the opposite ridgeline. Below it, a squad of Alliance soldiers attempted to maneuver against it. None of the warriors appeared too eager to close on the gun.

"The tank can't get to it," Abdul observed. "Tanks are not

good in the mountains. That is why we took so many of them from the Russians."

Brandon glassed the progress of three Alliance soldiers who worked up enough courage to go against the enemy machine gun. The steepness of the climb slowed their charge. They digressed from a run to a shambling trot and finally to a laborious trudging walk. Robes beneath their worn winter coats whipped around their pantaloons.

Summer tensed. "They can't see the gun, but it can see them."

The machine gun chattered, banging in hard reverberating echoes through the windswept mountains. Bullets chewed a path toward the first Alliance soldier.

All three fighters fell to the ground.

"I don't think he's hit," Brandon observed, watching through the binoculars.

The man lifted his head to look around for cover. His two comrades farther below sprang to their feet. One fired his rifle uphill. It was a Chicom AK with its distinctive harder, looser sound. Then he sprinted for the cover of some boulders.

The other fled, running back downhill until momentum threatened to overcome him and send him rolling head over heels. Machine gun fire chased him, gouging furiously at his heels. The little dirt tornadoes swept over and through the retreating man, literally exploding him in a pink mist. He tumbled and kept tumbling on the decline until a bush stopped his body.

Brandon dropped the binoculars from his eyes. No one said a word for a while as the life-and-death drama continued to play itself out on the opposite ridge.

The machine gun returned to seek out the first man, banging at him. He jumped up and, through a hail of fire, reached the cover of a larger flat rock behind which rain and erosion had hollowed a shallow depression. He curled up in the hole like a fetus in a womb, looking downhill toward his dead friend with a pathetic look. Brandon, using the binoculars, focused on his face. It was a dark, eroded face with an unkempt beard gray-black with dust. The horror of war was reflected in the terrified eyes.

"Can you get the machine gun from here?" Brandon asked Gloomy.

Gloomy lay on his belly and unsheathed Mr. Blunderbuss. His blue eyes glinted like slivers of ice in his thin tanned face as they contemplated the range and automatically sought signs of wind velocity and direction. The range was a good twelve hundred yards. Shooting across the valley meant three, maybe four, changes of wind.

"Piece of cake," he decided.

The .300 Winchester was a beautiful piece of work, blued steel and scope set in a walnut stock and fore grip. Gloomy handled it like he was handling a woman as he got himself set, going into what he called his cocoon. All his energy, his total concentration, his entire focus, went into preparing for the shot. An eternity seemed to pass while the little Okie peered through his scope, making allowances for conditions, taking adjustments on the scope, waiting for a piece of target to reveal itself.

Summer sprawled at Brandon's side with Saeed and Abdul. They hardly breathed. There was something compelling about the way Gloomy went about coolly, calculatedly preparing himself. To look into another human being's unknowing eyes through the scope and then deliberately snuff out his candle was a difficult thing for most people to do. Brandon had witnessed Summer execute the semiconscious militiaman in Kabul, but he wasn't sure even she could kill like this. He wouldn't want to put it to the test, however, with himself downrange of her as the target.

Gloomy fired, smoothly squeezing the trigger.

The special match-grade 173-grain projectile, traveling at a speed of over 2,500 feet per second, arched more than fifteen feet in the air and remained there for two seconds, the amount of time it took to recite "Now is the time for all good men to come to the aid . . ." before it reached the target over one-half mile away.

The machine gun fell silent. Blue smoke from the nest dissipated in the wind. Gloomy remained in his cocoon, waiting for the second man, the assistant gunner, to show himself. It didn't take long. Gloomy killed him too.

Friendlies in the valley didn't understand what was going on except that the enemy machine gun was knocked out. A big cheer went up. A few exhilarated soldiers squeezed off shots into the air. Someone from the column went up to help bring down the dead soldier. The convoy began moving forward again, until it would meet increased resistance and engage in a real battle.

Gloomy scooted out of his firing position. He seemed introspective as he dug out materials to clean his remarkable weapon.

"Can your man shoot so well all the time?" Abdul asked Brandon through Summer.

"If necessary."

"It may be necessary," Abdul said. He looked up at Brandon through bushy eyebrows while he built himself a cigarette, as though contemplating whether to go on or not. He finally decided as he broke out a match. "Commander Bek is a traitor," he revealed.

Brandon waited.

"Your presence here was already known by Mullah Omar and Osama bin Laden even as you arrived. Be very aware of Bek. He follows orders that come from Osama himself. He is al-Qaeda. Soon he will make his move."

CHAPTER 32

Major Kragle's refined instincts for danger sensed a sudden change of environment even while he slept. He opened his eyes in time to see a shadow slipping away from the ledge camp and down into the rock scree and stunted evergreens. He reached and felt Summer's bedroll. It was empty. She might be going out to answer a call of nature, except it was customary at such times to check in with the sentry. She was headed away from where Ice Man stood guard. Ice Man would be looking for someone approaching the bivouac area, not leaving it.

Brandon quickly crawled out of his bag and followed her, also avoiding Ice Man. As per standard operating procedure, the detachment always slept fully clothed in what they called Indian country, or hostile territory. You never knew when you might have to bug out, and you didn't want to have to go barefoot.

Summer skirted the edges of the guerrilla camp, keeping concealed in the shadows. It was a moonless night, dark and cold, and the wind lay still, seemingly frozen. Brandon had a hard time keeping her in sight. She was skilled at this sort of thing, but so, obviously, was he.

The mujahideen sentry suddenly loomed ahead, suspicious and looking about. Summer froze. Brandon dropped to one knee to avoid silhouetting himself. He refused to let himself speculate on her mission. *Just when you thought you could trust someone . . .*

You trusted *no one* in this country. It seemed everyone had his own agenda. It was every man's hand turned against the other.

Presently, seeing nothing, the guard sat back down and pulled his coat and robe around him against the cold, hunching down into them. Brandon tailed Summer's shadow on downhill out of camp, toward the blind canyon to the south. There, she stopped next to a dry streambed crawling through a little forest of stunted trees. After a while he realized that she was waiting for someone.

About fifteen minutes passed before the scuff of a sneaker on rocky soil alerted Brandon. He waited, watching until a formless figure in Arab garb appeared, advancing cautiously down the streambed, assault rifle held at the ready. Summer hissed to him. He jumped, startled, then recognized her and rushed over.

They wasted no time in getting down to business. They dropped to the ground in the shadow of a tree. A hooded red-lensed flashlight glowed. They appeared to discuss some papers, perhaps a map. Brandon dared not try to get closer.

Whatever the purpose of the meet, it lasted only a short time. The man had to be al-Qaeda, Brandon thought. Otherwise, why the secrecy? What were they plotting? Brandon felt rage and a sense of betrayal building up in him like a head of steam. *Who* was she, really? What was going on?

He slung the stubby MP-5 submachine gun across his back and drew his grandfather's Marine Ka-Bar. He kept the good steel sharp enough to shave the hair off his arms—or to sever a head from its body. He considered taking out the

Arab, but just as quickly reconsidered. No use alerting the enemy that he was on to them.

He crouched in ambush and waited until the two split up and Summer started back to camp in the darkness. He sprang out behind her as she passed, snaking out one hand to clasp over her mouth and prevent her from crying out. In the same motion, he yanked her backward off balance, exposing her tender throat to his big knife. The blade drew a thin trickle of blood.

"Give me one good reason why I shouldn't cut through your spine," he seethed. "It had better be good."

She dared not struggle. She hung in the vise of his arms, signaling her surrender. He eased his grip on her mouth, but kept the knife at her throat.

"All right, lady. What's with the blind date?"

"You fool!"

The response took him aback. He gave her a good shake.

"Okay, okay," she conceded in a more reasonable tone. "Let me go."

He shook her again. He was in no mood to be trifled with.

"That's the mole," she said after a moment. "That's the guy we had inside al-Qaeda."

"How did you make contact with him? The PC?"

"Reach out and touch someone," she said.

"If you haven't noticed, it's no time to be a wiseass."

"Yes, yes, the PC. The guy's a communications whiz at bin Laden's command center. That's how he knows so much. We have a secret code. I asked him to meet me. It's not that hard. We're close to Osama, real close."

"How do I know I can believe you?"

"You'll be getting this same info through SFOB," she said. "That'll confirm it."

"He's a CIA informant?"

"Let's just say he gets paid well for doing his job. You forget, there's a $25 million reward on bin Laden's head."

He knew that a lot of people would turn in their own mothers for that kind of dough. "Can he lead us to the Shake?" he asked.

"He gave me a map. Just as good. You're hurting me," she protested.

Her story had the ring of truth to it, but Brandon's anger wasn't yet spent. "I warned you before not to keep things from me," he threatened.

"You had no need to know, Major. The fewer people who know about a source, the safer he is. It's my training."

"You're about to be retrained, or you're out of the operation even if I have to tie you up and put a guard on you. That had better be understood. I have a need to know about anything that affects this mission, my men, or me."

"Understood," she acquiesced, her voice strained to prevent her throat from coming into contact with the blade at her throat. "Providing . . ." she added, growing cockier. Ismael coming through.

"Providing what? I'm the guy with the bargaining power."

"Providing you take the knife off my throat and get your dick out of my ass. Or is it that you're just happy to see me?"

"It's called an involuntary vascular reaction to a stimuli," he said, mildly embarrassed. He released her and stepped back.

That was his mistake. As soon as she felt him let go, she whirled and lashed out with a front kick at his groin. He blocked instinctively with a cross wrist, catching her foot in midair. He jerked and twisted at the same time. She landed hard on her back, momentarily knocking the wind out of her. He jumped astraddle, grabbing her flailing hands and pinning her to the ground.

"You sonofabitch!" she raved when she regained her breath. "What right do you have to treat me like a—like a—"

"Some tight-assed bitch out of her element?"

"Get off me, you big bastard. *Get off me!*"

She lost her turban. Her eyes flashed dark and fiery in the starlight. Brandon held her while she continued to fight him. She felt tough and strong for so small a woman, and at the same time rounded and distractingly vulnerable. His face was only inches above hers. She twisted her head to one side to deny him her lips.

"You flatter yourself," he taunted. "I'd rather kiss the back-side of a mule."

That started the struggle over. Brandon laughed in her face.

"You *bastard*!" she cried.

"You can do better than that, Summer."

"You sonofabitch. Bastard. Cocksucker. Polecat son of a—"

"Weasel and a rat?" he suggested, still laughing silently in her face.

She ceased resisting. Their eyes locked. "Yes," she said.

It happened very quickly. It wasn't her and it wasn't him. It was a mutual attraction, a raw animal hunger. He bent close, impulsively, and kissed her brutally on her open mouth, a hard, searching kiss. She returned it in the same manner, pressing herself up against him with a craving that matched his.

He collapsed on top and her legs tried to close themselves around his waist and their mouths were open and devouring and she pushed into him with her hips.

"Sonofabitch . . . sonofabitch . . ." she gasped between kisses.

He rose to his knees over her. She clung to him desperately. He picked her up in his arms and carried her beneath some low-branched trees where it was safer and darker and there was a soft mat of leaves and needles. She helped him tear off her sheepskin coat and spread it on the ground for her. Then, lying between her coat and his, they disrobed feverishly until they were naked.

Gasping for air, they explored each other's bodies with hands, lips, and tongues. Brandon licked the salty taste of blood from her throat where his knife nicked her. He trailed his lips down to her breasts. They were full and rounded, and he took her nipples into his mouth one by one and rolled them between his teeth like ripe raspberries while he slipped his hand up her inner thighs to the thick patch of hair and the opening, which he found moist and ready.

The odors between the coats and then in the open air when they kicked off the coats were musky and sweaty and it was incredibly erotic. After tonight, he knew he would never think of her again as the Ice Maiden.

Then it flashed through his mind that it was said in Israel that anyone Summer slept with ended up dead.

Brandon had no time for women. One-night stands, okay, and maybe a few more times if a woman was particularly good in the sheets, but then he'd be gone before she started making plans for next weekend. Often, he rolled over after his partner went to sleep, looked at her, then got up silently in the middle of the night, put on his clothes, and went home. He didn't believe in attachments. They made a man vulnerable.

He thought he might have been in love with Gypsy Iryani. No one before, no one after. If you believed in something as illusory as *love*. Love was painful; Gypsy was going to marry Cameron. There was never going to be another Gypsy—he would make sure of that.

Yet here he was, back in Afghanistan and sacked out with

another warrior princess whose eyes, when she wasn't wearing contacts, reminded him of Gypsy's. "Fu-ucked up," as Mad Dog would put it.

He lay under the low branches of the evergreens, warm with Summer nude in his arms and wrapped in their discarded clothing. Her breath felt heated and they tentatively explored each other's mouths. Then he touched her face and cupped her breasts and felt himself aroused again. He ran hands down her skin, over the curves, cupping her wonderful breasts some more, feeling her smooth belly and finding where the soft hair began. He put his hand in the warm, moist place between her thighs. She squeezed her thighs against his hand, and he inserted a finger to her quick intake of breath.

He rolled over and penetrated her again and moved in her, deeply and slowly, while she breathed hard and deep and clasped his hips to pull him even deeper. Her ass was small and rounded and tight, and with a cheek in each hand he eased in and out of her slowly to prolong the pleasure of it. They came together, rushing, gasping. Brandon lay his sweaty beard next to her cheek and drew her smell through his nostrils.

He knew that if he had any sense, he would notify SFOB, explain that Ismael was actually a woman, and insist she be flown out at daylight. Females in combat distracted a man, made him careless.

"I like your beard against my breasts," she whispered, stroking his hair and then down the side of his face to the thick growth that covered his jaw. "But I liked you better I think the way I saw you in Israel with only the mustache."

Israel. He wondered how many men she had slept with there and elsewhere in order to lure them to their deaths.

"You're quiet," she said, breathing against his ear.

"It's a dirty business for a woman," he said. "Why do you do it?"

He felt her tense. She sensed what he was talking about. It had been between them since he first learned she wasn't Ismael.

"Do you believe it?" she asked.

They were suddenly far apart. She relaxed and lay quietly for a long time.

"What do you want me to do?" she asked presently, an edge of bitterness and scorn to her voice. "So I'm no virgin. Neither were you. I did what I thought had to be done to save innocent lives. If that makes me a whore, then I guess I'm a whore."

She seemed to be mulling something over.

"So you want to know about Summer?" she said, still with an edge. "I'll tell you about Summer. My father was an Israeli officer. He fought in the Six Day War and the war with Egypt in 1974. My mother was a little Christian country girl from Longview, Texas. They met when my mother came over on a tour of the Holy Land. They married and had three kids, all of us girls. I was the oldest."

Her voice broke with the first emotion Brandon had ever detected in her. He automatically tightened his arm as protection and comfort.

"I know you thought me a monster when I shot the militiaman," she said. Her voice broke again. "Maybe I am a monster, but what do you think he would have done to us? What he might already have done to little kids and old people, and what acts of terror he might commit in the name of Allah in the future? He was a terrorist and, yes, I have no mercy for terrorists. Let me tell you why."

It seemed to all come out in a rush, and she couldn't stop herself.

"When I was sixteen years old and Sarai was fourteen and Rachel thirteen, Mom took us to Jaffa Street, the main commercial strip in West Jerusalem, to shop for my father's birthday. We were having lunch in a crowded pizzeria when a Palestinian suicide bomber blew himself up. Twenty-seven people were wounded. Six were killed, including Sarai and Rachel."

Brandon understood at that moment how she became the Ice Maiden.

"It's nothing like the numbers of people killed at the World Trade Center," Summer went on, "but if it's personal, it's an equal tragedy."

"Yes." Brandon felt inadequate in expressing sympathy. "My grandmother was on United 175 when it crashed into the south tower."

He hadn't been informed yet of Kathryn's death from anthrax.

"It's difficult for Americans to understand what it's like to live every day under the threat of terrorism," Summer said. "When you can be attacked anywhere, anytime, and killed for no other reason than who you are, when no one from a tiny baby to an elderly woman in a wheelchair is immune from these crazies."

"I think Americans are going to find out. How did you end up here as Ismael?"

She gave a wry Ismael-type laugh. "Just lucky, I guess. I have a gift for languages. They say I'm a genius when it comes to Middle Eastern and Arab dialects. Mom couldn't take living in Israel after what happened. I remember seeing her crying every day until we finally moved to the United States. I was going to college at Yale when I was recruited—"

"By the CIA?"

"When I was recruited," she said, dancing around the question, "I'd been working in the Middle East for the past five years, a year of that in Afghanistan keeping tabs on al-Qaeda and Osama bin Laden. I had just returned from Kabul on an assignment to Jerusalem when I met you in Beit Jalla. I came back to Afghanistan after the September eleventh attacks to work with you as your 'boy Friday.' I was fortunate to have already established myself in-country as Ismael and to have cultivated a number of contacts."

"Such as the guy tonight?"

"He's become disillusioned with al-Qaeda and its martyrdom culture of suicide attacks. We've got the map to where bin Laden is, but we're going to have to move fast."

They lay together talking for another hour, since nothing could be done about the Shake tonight anyhow. Brandon felt unusually content to stay with her. Uneasiness accompanied the thought that her personal vendetta against the terrorism that consumed her sisters might in the end also consume her.

"Tonight changes nothing," she assured him. "I expect nothing from you except professionalism in carrying out this mission. I don't want you to expect anything from me. Just because we made love, or had sex, whatever you want to call it, doesn't mean we have an investment in each other. We can't afford to make investments in our line of work. Agreed?"

He hesitated. "Agreed," he said finally.

"Agreed," she repeated, sounding less sure of herself and maybe even, uncharacteristically, a bit frightened.

NEW CAVE WEAPON DEVELOPED

WASHINGTON (CPI)—The Pentagon has developed a new weapon in its search for Osama bin Laden and his al-Qaeda holdouts in the Tora Bora region of the White Mountains of Afghanistan. According to General Paul Etheridge, head of U.S. Central Command, military researchers tested a "thermobaric" bomb in Nevada last week. It is to be used against caves and bunkers.

While the shock wave of a thermobaric weapon is powerful, it does not collapse a cave or tunnel as "bunker buster" bombs do. Rather, it produces shock waves amplified in enclosed spaces, which reverberate throughout an underground complex. It destroys life inside a tunnel, cave, or bunker without collapsing them.

"In other words," General Etheridge said, "you kill people but you can still look at them to figure out who you killed."

In the meantime, U.S. Special Operations troops are in the Tora Bora region helping Afghan tribal forces wipe out Taliban and al-Qaeda resistance and search caves for enemy forces. Green Berets and clandestine Delta troops, working with CIA officers, are coordinating intelligence-gathering efforts with local Afghans, searching caves and bunkers, and interrogating prisoners in an effort to snare al-Qaeda leader Osama bin Laden and Taliban Supreme Leader Mullah Mohammed Omar.

Senator Eric B. Tayloe, with the backing of other lawmakers and former President John Stanton, charges that Delta units have been assigned as assassination forces against the Afghan leadership. A congressional investigation has been convened to probe his charges. General Darren E. Kragle, commander of the U.S. Special Operations Command (USSOCOM), has been called to testify this week. . . .

CHAPTER 33

Washington, D.C.

General Darren Kragle knew the intricate steps of what he derisively called the "D.C. Tango." The idea of the dance was to dazzle the opposition while heaping it with bullshit, to pretend to dance to the music selected by your partner while you were actually making up your own hustle. In D.C. politics, you either learned the tango or the predators cut you down.

He arrived at the capitol to be questioned by a congressional committee. He wore class A's complete with full medals, not the ribbons. They covered the left breast of his tunic in metal and ribbon rows from the pocket to his shoulder. For those few military veterans on the panel or in the small gallery who might recognize them, his awards included the Distinguished Service Cross, the Silver Star with three oak leaf clusters, the Bronze Star with clusters, and, above all, the stars-on-a-blue-background Congressional Medal of Honor, the nation's highest award for valor. Ordinarily, the CMH was worn alone on a sash around the neck, but the General came here to dazzle. The man was the genuine thing, a war hero, and he wanted the press to make the contrast, intentionally or unintentionally, between himself and the politicians.

He cast an imposing figure as he entered—six feet six inches; salt and pepper crew cut; trimmed mustache; square, tanned jaw. The chamber fell silent. Flanked by CENTCOM General Paul Etheridge on his left and CJCS General Abraham Morrison on his right, he walked straight to the table up front that had been arranged to face the panel elevated on its diocese. He stood at attention a moment before he sat down, letting his hard gray eyes rake across each of the eight members of the panel, starting with the chair, Senator Eric B. Tayloe. It was obvious Tayloe had stacked the odds in his favor. Nearly every member of the panel had come out publicly in opposition to the War on Terror in general and action in Afghanistan in particular, or had been critical of the way it was being conducted.

Keenly watching the show from the gallery sat former President John Stanton, next to another senator whose mistress had mysteriously disappeared last spring after she began pressuring him to leave his wife. Stanton and Tayloe seemed tight buddies of late. Like Siamese twins. Where you saw one, you saw the other.

Also in the gallery sat FBI Senior Agent Claude Thornton, his shaved black head in contrast to the carefully coiffed and perfumed men and women of politics and the media who largely populated the chamber. Thornton had also been subpoenaed to testify before the committee about what its members had already determined to be the illegal detention of illegal immigrants. The General and Thornton had exchanged a few words outside in the hallway before entering the chamber.

"Where you go, others will undoubtedly follow," the agent commented, indicating the investigation room with a nod.

"Yell racial discrimination," the General advised.

"Won't work. Justice Clarence Thomas and me—we're Uncle Toms and not *real* African-Americans. They're waiting in there for you like a school of piranha, General."

"I've been in them waters before, Claude. Have you come up with any leads on how my daughter-in-law contracted anthrax?"

"Maybe. Have you talked to Cassidy?"

"Cassidy and I sometimes don't talk much."

"He was the one who actually supplied the lead."

Thornton briefed him on the FBI raids against the Sacred Land Foundation offices and the seizure of anthrax letters. He concluded with Cassidy's tailing Rasem Jameel to a rendezvous with Shukri Abu Marzook, the fugitive head of the foundation.

"We can't prove it yet, General, but it looks like your son Cameron's chaplain assistant may be the middleman between the anthrax source and anthrax terrorists. It's partly conjecture at this point, but it appears Jameel picked up the stuff from the source and stored it somewhere on Fort Bragg. He parceled it out in letters and delivered the letters to Abu Marzook in Dallas. He was ID'd from photos by a Dallas employee of Sacred Land. From there, the letters arrived in New Jersey and elsewhere, to be addressed and sent to selected victims. It's a clever maze intended to isolate and protect each layer of the process."

He paused and shook his head. "Our best guess on how Kathryn became infected is that one of the Billy Dye evangelical mailings became contaminated. Jameel may have been sending anthrax mailings to some of his buddies and it leaked."

The General scowled. "Then Cameron and Cassidy . . . ?"

"Don't worry, General. They're okay. We've tested them both, along with the chaplain's congregation and anyone else associated with the chapel. So far, no one else has come up positive, although our suspicions were confirmed when CDC found minute traces of anthrax in the chapel. It's been decontaminated."

"Is Jameel talking? The sonofabitch."

"He found out we were asking questions and went AWOL before we could get our hands on him."

"How in *hell* did he get in our army?"

"It's complicated," said the FBI agent, "but then it's also simple. We've learned since this all started that Jameel was involved in training members of bin Laden's al-Qaeda organization for the 1993 World Trade Center bombing. The CIA developed a relationship with him after he offered to turn snitch and provide information about terrorist groups in the Middle East. His loyalties obviously lay elsewhere."

"Obviously. He became a sleeper and a double agent."

"Uh-huh. Jameel obtained a legitimate U.S. visa in 1996. He enlisted in the U.S. Army under the sponsorship of the CIA and was eventually assigned to the 82nd Airborne Division at Fort Bragg as a parachute rigger. More significantly, before that he served a year on an MP detachment pulling security at Fort Detrick, Maryland. That's where the U.S. conducted biochemical warfare experiments during the Cold War. We suspect Jameel somehow developed a contact source for anthrax through Fort Detrick while he was there."

"How? And who?"

Thornton shrugged. "We're following some leads. When we find that out, we'll have a big piece of the puzzle."

"So Jameel's been lying low all these years, soldiering and pretending to be a CIA informant while actually awaiting orders from bin Laden?"

"He's not the only one. There may be hundreds of them, all just waiting for the signal. Jameel was supposed to have delivered one hundred pounds of anthrax—"

The General stiffened.

"That's right. One hundred *pounds*. That's some deep, serious shit. If we don't intercept it . . ."

His voice trailed off. He looked at the closed double doors leading to the investigation chambers and made a scoffing sound. "Your ol' buddy in there, Senator Tayloe, came out in the press and vouched for Mullah Shukri as a 'good and decent man' persecuted by the big bad government. It seems you *can* fool some of the people all the time."

"The good senator has a history of backing scoundrels," the General said.

The War on Terror was extracting a heavy toll in American civilian casualties and was likely to extract many more if Agent Thornton's anthrax fears materialized.

Flashbulbs popped all around and TV cameramen jockeyed for position as General Kragle stood before the Congressional Investigation Committee and defiantly eyed the panel. All the major media was represented. Tayloe and Stanton were making sure General Kragle's exposure as a Hitler-like character sanctioning illegal acts of war received the widest possible coverage. It didn't help his image any that anyone who appeared as a subject of an investigation before Congress was inevitably viewed as suspect by the public.

Public opinion at the moment supported the War on Terror. That could rapidly change. The General was all too well aware of 1965, when the 101st Airborne left for Vietnam with the ringing endorsements of President Lyndon Johnson, Congress, and the public. Nearly ninety percent of Americans told pollsters they were "All the way with LBJ." Airborne survivors of the war returned a year later to many of the same people chanting, "Hey, hey, LBJ. How many kids did you kill today?"

Were Senator Tayloe and ex-President Stanton attempting to instigate a replay of those antiwar times? the General wondered. What was the benefit to them of tarnishing military leaders and clouding necessary actions against terrorist networks who were even now preparing to strike again? Their motivation, the General cynically decided, had to do with political advantage and power.

Senator Tayloe averted his watery eyes from the steely eyes of his intended prey. He opened his briefcase and rummaged through it, as if rattling the skeletons. He found what he was looking for. He took out his notes.

"Will everyone please be seated," he said. He then began his opening remarks, looking unself-consciously self-important and playing to the press.

"This panel," he said, "is assembled to look both into the necessity of this so-called War on Terror and how it is being conducted. The loyal opposition in Congress feels that we may be in danger of sacrificing our standards and values in the name of expediency, that we may be committing war atrocities in seeking revenge against those we accuse—but have not yet proved—to be responsible for the attacks of September eleventh . . ."

He went on for another fifteen minutes, enumerating his various grievances against the war and bringing up what he alleged to be possible war crimes committed by American forces: bombing of a Red Cross building in Kabul; bombing and slaughter of civilians; sanctioning or ignoring summary executions of Taliban and al-Qaeda members by the Northern Alliance; deprivations and hardships of the Afghan population exacerbated by American actions; use of U.S. Special Operations troops as assassins and as guerrillas operating behind enemy lines, out of uniform, under conditions contrary to the Geneva Conventions and U.S. law . . .

"The war is certainly going a lot worse than we expected," the senator pontificated, "and is continuing to deteriorate. It's becoming an unwelcome specter from an unhappy past. Can anyone say 'quagmire'? This is a war in trouble, and it's a war searching for its own justification . . ."

A member of the panel held up his hand during a pause and informed the media that copies of Senator Tayloe's remarks would be made available to the press.

"While this administration attempts to push a Reaganist agenda at home to unbalance the federal budget on the backs of poor people," Tayloe continued, "it sends our military to search the globe for presumed evil—in terrorist cells this time rather than in evil empires. It is the duty of statesmen, the press, and citizens to respond to indications that there are, first, U.S. atrocities and illegalities being committed, and second, that our policies are leading us to military disaster.

"General Darren Kragle, who appears before this august panel today is commander of the United States Special Operations Command, whose Special Forces are conducting much of the ground operations in Afghanistan. We will question him on two points. The first concerns Operation Iron Weed and its mission to illegally conduct assassination missions against foreign heads of state."

It was still unclear to the General how Tayloe found out about Iron Weed.

"The second point concerns a detachment of his men who called in a bombing strike on a civilian compound in Kabul where thirteen civilians were killed, including four children."

What the hell was he talking about? The General stared. Both General Morrison and General Etheridge looked jolted.

Senator Tayloe looked at the witness over the tops of his glasses, as though the General were an insect about to be dissected.

"First question, General Kragle. Before the fall of Kabul, U.S. aircraft were made available on a twenty-four-hour cover for a Delta detachment on a secret mission into the capital to assassinate a state leader. Is that correct?"

General Kragle stood up.

"Please remain seated, sir."

"I'll stand. I won't be here long. To begin with, Osama bin Laden is a wanted criminal who masterminded the murders of thousands of American citizens. He is *not* a state leader—"

"The Taliban is the sanctioned government of Afghanistan," Tayloe interjected. "Mr. bin Laden has not been convicted of any crimes. Until at such time as this occurs, as I understand it, he is an advisor to Mullah Omar—"

"Bin Laden is a terrorist, sir," General Kragle shot back. "Anyone who would suggest otherwise is the same kind of fool who believes Yasser Arafat is a statesman. American policy and American lives are going to be further endangered by these public proceedings. On that ground, I decline to answer any questions put before me by this panel in the presence of the world's press. I'm not sure I would trust the confidentiality of this panel even without the presence of the media."

Tayloe blushed like a schoolboy whose mother had been insulted by the playground bully. He recovered and pushed on. "The Delta detachment called in an air strike on what it presumed to be Mr. bin Laden's quarters but which was actually a residential family compound. The youngest killed was a three-year-old girl."

"Where did you get this information, sir? Because it's a damned pack of lies."

"It was in the European press. You admit it occurred?"

"I admit nothing, sir."

"You will concede that you have inserted assassination teams into Afghanistan?"

"Special Operations is conducting a war in conjunction with other American forces."

"Does that war include assassinations?"

"It's a fact of history," the General said, "that world bullies will abuse other countries and other peoples until they are stopped. Our past indulgences of Osama bin Laden under previous presidential administrations did not bring us respect, much less sympathy."

He turned to look squarely at ex-President Stanton. He wanted to make sure that Stanton, the press, the panel, and everyone else present realized who his following comments were about.

"Human nature being what it is, our official forbearance of bin Laden's terror attacks against the United States simply invited more contempt and audacity until we've ended up letting him kill thousands of us in one sweep. If you don't realize it, you don't realize the nature of the dangers we face. We are at war for our survival and the survival of Western civilization. Terrorists must understand that it is wrong and it is dangerous to blow up our people in the streets of our cities. The harsh defeat of our terrorist enemies will serve as a profound teacher to those who would follow their lead."

He paused for a single heartbeat.

"Sirs, this is a fishing expedition meant to bring discredit upon me personally and upon the fine young soldiers of my command. Their lives lie in your hands, in mine, and in what is revealed here today. For the sake of decency, I would ask that you close down this investigation. You can play politics after the war is won. Having said that, I decline, respectfully or otherwise, to further participate in these hearings."

Flushing wildly, Tayloe leaped to his feet, a stubby, agitated little man whose jowls quivered in anger. Ex-President Stanton in the gallery also jumped to his feet but remained tight-lipped. The news media hustled to catch the action.

"General Kragle!" Tayloe shouted above the melee. "This committee will reconvene first thing Monday morning. I'm advising you now that you have until then to get yourself a lawyer and to withdraw Iron Weed from its illegal and immoral mission or face criminal contempt charges from this body."

On his way out of the chamber, General Kragle overheard a news anchor asking Tayloe if it were true he intended to run for President of the United States, since he'd been seen stumping in New Hampshire earlier in the week.

Outside in the hallway, General Morrison said, "I might have put it a bit more diplomatically, Darren, but I support your decision not to answer before that lynch mob. However, it may cost us in the long run. Tayloe has some clout in Congress. He's not bluffing. He'll most certainly charge you with contempt of Congress. Darren, you have four days to complete Iron Weed's mission. Can you do it?"

CHAPTER 34

Fort Bragg

Rasem Jameel had already printed the month's Billy Dye bulletins before he disappeared. The mailing still had to be prepared. Now, lacking assistance from either Jameel or Kathryn, Chaplain Cameron Kragle stayed late at the church to get it out. As he worked he prayed and wrestled with his faith, as he often did when alone and the spirit seemed weak within him.

Sometimes he thought he was like Peter. Peter became afraid when he started to walk on the sea to go to Jesus. "O thou of little faith," Jesus rebuked him, "wherefore didst thou doubt?"

Wherefore did he doubt? Cameron wondered.

The ways of God sometimes troubled him. God had permitted evil disguised to come into his chapel. To test his faith? To teach him a lesson the nature of which escaped him? For months, Rasem Jameel came to the church regularly, always with a smile and a *"salaam alaikan"*—peace be with you. He pretended to be a Christian, to have washed himself anew in the blood of the Lamb. He cried at Kathryn's funeral. And all the time he plotted war and acts of terrorism. Cameron felt betrayed not only by Jameel, but also by God.

Jameel's faith in an Allah of the jihad had never wavered, no matter how he pretended otherwise. While America was being assured that Islam had nothing to do with the 9/11 terror attacks, Osama bin Laden, Rasem Jameel, the nineteen who committed martyrdom in the hijacked airliners, and millions of other Muslims worldwide demonstrated otherwise. Cameron had come to the conclusion that America was in a religious war but wouldn't acknowledge it because Americans disapproved of religious wars. He knew that much of Western society, including the clergy, no longer believed in a God who played a role in the affairs of men. Muslims, on the other hand, worshiped a warrior Old Testament Allah for whom they willingly sacrificed their own lives and the lives of everyone else.

That was faith. Misguided, perhaps, but they *believed*. Deep somewhere in his soul Cameron envied that kind of faith.

How could he have been so blind about Jameel? His blindness led directly to Kathryn's death. He knelt at his altar in the empty church beneath the sign GOD IS GOD IN ALL LANGUAGES and prayed fervently for greater faith so he could understand why God let this happen to him and the ones he loved, so that he could forgive himself for his shortsightedness. He lifted his head and opened his eyes as the chapel door opened and closed.

Cassidy walked down the aisle toward him, wearing BDUs and his beret. Cameron's heart went out to his little brother's suffering. He was already a widower at age twenty-three. Cameron stifled an impulse to stand and embrace him. Such a gesture, he knew, would not be received. Kragles were not huggers. They suffered alone and mostly in silence.

The dim ceiling lights and the guttering candles on the altar scudded shadows beneath Cassidy's eyes and in the cheeks gone hollow since his wife's death. Candle flames reflected in his blue eyes gave him a fierce, vengeful look. He sat down in one of the pews in the front row, removed his beret, and watched the candles solemnly without speaking. Cameron took the chair next to him and hoped his presence, if not his words, might offer some comfort.

"She prayed every night while we were being held in Afghanistan that we would be rescued," Cassidy said at last, his voice low and bleak. "She liked to come here to the chapel because she got a great deal of strength from it."

Cameron understood. After Gypsy's death, he spent many hours in her apartment among her things, feeling where she had been. Cassidy was feeling where Kathryn had been, but it seemed to bring him no solace. Hate and a desire for vengeance were eating him up from the inside.

" 'To me belongeth vengeance, and recompose,' " Cameron quoted softly, somehow feeling called to that passage, " 'their foot shall slide in due time. . . . And if ye forgive men their trespasses, your heavenly Father will also forgive you.' "

"God may forgive," Cassidy said in a hollow voice. "I don't. Not in this I don't."

Cameron saw a flashback of Cassidy with the pistol in the terrorist camp, aiming it at Amal's penis. Kragle men were not readily forgiving of transgressions against them, especially transgressions of magnitude. Cameron knew he would have to pray hard for the poison to be washed from Cassidy's soul.

"Agent Thornton said Jameel may have also contracted anthrax," the chaplain said, to reassure his little brother that God did not overlook evil deeds.

God's revenge was not enough for Cassidy. Cameron felt

helpless and uncomfortable in the presence of such intense malice. Since Cassidy seemed to want to be alone, Cameron got up and went into his office to resume work on the Billy Dye mailings.

The printed bulletins were stacked in boxes waiting to be addressed. The FBI had gone through them seeking clues, and the CDC had tested them for anthrax. They were clean. Cameron scooped up a stack and pressed it into the addressing machine. The machine was antiquated, slow, noisy, and often jammed, necessitating close supervision.

Cassidy came to the doorway and leaned against the jamb, watching. "Do you know where he is?" he asked. "The FBI can't seem to find him."

"My guess is he's gone back to Saudi Arabia by this time, or somewhere else in the Middle East."

"He can't hide forever."

"Cassidy, let Agent Thornton handle it. He'll find him."

Cassidy stood there with a dark expression of grief and hatred on his face. What did you say to a man who rejected comforting? While Cameron was trying to think of something, the address machine came to his rescue and started growling, flapping and flinging bulletins into the air. He hit the off switch and knelt to gather up bulletins scattered on the floor. Cassidy squatted to help him.

Cameron picked up a thin pink slip of paper that apparently had fallen from one of the bulletins. He was surprised to find a traffic citation for speeding issued to Rasem Jameel in Fort Worth, Texas. The date on it, if Cameron recalled correctly, was the day before the FBI raided Mullah Shukri's Sacred Land Foundation office in Dallas. The traffic cop issuing the citation had jotted down a passenger's name in the notes section: Zaccarias al-Tawwah.

"What is it?" Cassidy asked.

Cameron showed him the citation. "Jameel must have

misplaced the ticket in the bulletins. The FBI also over-looked it."

"How careless of them. What's the writing on the back?"

Jameel had used the back of the ticket as an expedient notepad, scribbling several notations on it in English, including a date.

"The nineteenth," Cassidy observed. "Something must be happening on the nineteenth. That's the day after tomorrow."

Underneath the date there appeared a shopping list: eggs, glue, pack. For most shoppers *eggs* went with *bacon* or *ham* or *milk*. There was also a crude hand-drawn map with street names and locations Cameron failed to recognize: *Eastland Apts, Kneeland St., Kingston T.*

"He got this ticket just a few days before he bugged out," Cassidy said. "These are directions to a destination. This is where he might go. Wait a minute. . . ." He took another look at the notes. His face lit up with recognition.

"Cassidy, you know where it is, don't you? We'd better call Claude."

"You call Claude." He copied the information off the ticket onto the margin of one of the Billy Dye bulletins. He headed for the door.

"Cassidy?"

He was already gone, the front door of the chapel slamming behind him. Cameron immediately dialed Agent Thornton's private number at Quantico. Phones at the FBI's National Domestic Preparedness Office were manned twenty-four hours a day, but it was late and Claude was not in. The receptionist told him Agent Thornton was in Washington, D.C.

"This is extremely important," Cameron told her. "This is Chaplain Kragle at Fort Bragg, North Carolina."

"Give me your phone number. I'll get hold of his page and have him call."

Cameron continued to work on the mailing while he waited on the agent's return call. The address machine temporarily worked, so he opened the front door and looked down toward the sprinkling of lights where Training Group enlisted and junior NCOs were billeted. What was Cassidy up to?

The phone rang. Cameron hurried to answer it. It was Cassidy's friend, Sergeant Bobby Goose Pony.

"Sir, if you see Cass, would you tell him that everything's taken care of. I'd have told him myself, but he's already gone."

"Gone where?"

"He didn't say, sir. He was in a big hurry. He called the duty officer and requested emergency leave. He asked me to go over and fill out the papers for him. Then he took off."

"In his car?"

"Yes, sir."

Cameron experienced a gnawing feeling in his gut. *Eastland Apartments on Kneeland Street.*

"Sir?" Pony said. "I'm worried about him. You know how hardheaded he can be. He wouldn't say where he was going, and he didn't think I saw . . ."

"Saw what?"

"Well . . . He was in civvies and wore a loose jacket. When he bent over, I saw he had a pistol stuck down in the belt of his jeans."

CHAPTER 35

Baltimore

Illumination from a residential street lamp on the corner in the Baltimore suburb of Rosedale barely touched the two FBI agents sitting quietly in their unmarked car. A dog barked from somewhere beyond the comfortable-looking suburban Tudor the agents had placed under surveillance shortly after nightfall. The porch light at the house was off and there was no car in the drive or in the closed garage. Agent Fred Whiteman had sneaked up earlier and peeped through a crack around the garage door to make sure it was empty, while Claude Thornton kept watch from the car. Dr. Tobias Martfeld, Ph.D. in chemistry and biological sciences, was not at home.

The director of the FBI's National Domestic Preparedness Office checked his watch.

"It's five minutes later than it was five minutes ago when you checked," Whiteman chided with a dry chuckle. "You haven't changed much, have you, Claude?"

"I'm still black, if that's what you mean."

"I was referring to patience—of which you still have none, big man."

"We've been here five hours already. I deserve a merit raise for patience."

Thornton had disliked stakeouts since his junior FBI days when the new guys drew them all—hours of sitting on your butt guzzling strong coffee and watching some bookie parlor or suspected bank robber's girlfriend's mother's house. What made this one marginally bearable was the chance to catch up on an old friendship. Whiteman and he attended the same academy class over twenty years ago. They still ran into each other occasionally, the last time being in Dallas at the raid on the Sacred Land Foundation. Whiteman had put on a few pounds over the years and lost much of his curly brown hair, but he was still the same beefy, blustery white man with a sense of humor he had always been. And a damn good investigator.

Thornton listened to the hum of traffic from nearby U.S. 95. John F. Kennedy Memorial Highway linked the entire East Coast in a four-lane ribbon from Miami to New Brunswick in Canada. It showed how bored he was, he thought, listening to traffic.

Car lights turned into the far end of the block. The agents slid low in the seat. The car went on by. Thornton sighed. Whiteman chuckled.

In the beginning, Thornton considered it almost a waste of time and resources to assign agents to tracking down scientists who helped build, direct, and run experiments on biochemical agents at Fort Detrick during the 1960s and 1970s. The survivors had to be getting old by now, and besides, it was unlikely that scientists who worked for the U.S. government would become terrorists. The long shot seemed more tenable, however, after it surfaced that Rasem Jameel was a possible middleman between the anthrax source and anthrax terrorists—*and* that he was once assigned to a security detachment at Fort Detrick where he could have cultivated a contact.

Whiteman had telephoned Thornton's office shortly after noon. "Claude, I've found Tobias Martfeld," he said. "He's on your list of the old Detrick scientists. Didn't you arrest the Unabomber?"

"I was in on the bust when I was still almost a rookie. Why?"

"Wasn't it Ted Kaczynski's brother who turned him in?"

"Cut to the chase, white man."

"Right. It seems the good Dr. Martfeld is a big fan of the mad bomber's tactics of blowing up people to get public attention."

"Is he, now?"

"Is he now ever. Agent Steve Ecker—the guy from Minnesota with the accent?—picked up a tip on Martfeld's brother, who turned out to be just as willing as the Unabomber's brother to talk to the feds. Elias Martfeld says his brother stood up and cheered when the World Trade Center collapsed on TV. He told Elias that the best was yet to come."

"You've got my attention."

"Elias thinks Dr. Martfeld is a bit off his plumb, a few bricks shy of a shithouse, if you know what I mean. The old man has a lab at home. Elias thinks he's experimenting with germs. Claude, did you ever read the Unabomber's manifesto?"

"What about it? It's taught at the training academy in criminal profiling."

"Kaczynski sent out bombs through the mail for what—seven years?—just so when he got caught he'd be famous enough that his manifesto would be published. Elias turned over a briefcase belonging to the mad scientist. Among some other stuff was a copy of the Unabomber's manifesto. You need to read the parts the old bird underlined."

What was with this country in the last half of the twentieth century and into the twenty-first that it produced so many genuine nut cases? It must be something in the water, Thornton decided.

A hands-on administrator, Thornton liked getting out in the field with his men. Whiteman obtained a search warrant for the old Ph.D.'s residence, and Thornton drove out to Baltimore to get in on the action. They ended up on a stakeout because they didn't want to hit his house until they were sure he was inside. It made it easier if you served a warrant and made the arrest at the same time. It kept the "Ten Most Wanted" list manageable.

Thornton reached the same conclusion as Whiteman after going through the scientist's copy of the manifesto: Dr. Martfeld and Ted Kaczynski were soulmates. The Unabomber's enemy was Western technology, which he desired to eventually destroy. Dr. Martfeld underlined all the good parts and made notations in the margins, concurring with the Unabomber's conclusion that society had to somehow be made aware of the evils of modernization.

"We hope," the Unabomber wrote, "we have convinced the reader that the system cannot be reformed in such a way as to reconcile freedom and technology . . . The only way out is to dispense with the industrial-technological system altogether . . . and once this technology has been lost for a generation or so it would take centuries to rebuild it. . . .

"Revolutionaries," Kaczynski went on, "work to gain a powerful reward: fulfillment of their revolutionary vision— and therefore work harder and more persistently than reformers do. . . ."

Thornton knew there was certainly no shortage of true believers willing to sacrifice themselves for the cause, whether that cause be protection of the kangaroo rat in California or the destruction of Israel and the West. Dr. Martfeld highlighted a select manifesto phrase with emphasis, then copied it again and added his own notes to show how much he agreed with it. The paragraph drew a chilling conclusion:

> *If we had never done anything violent and had sub-mitted the present writings to a publisher, they proba-bly would not have been accepted. If they had been accepted and published, they probably would not have attracted many readers, because it's more fun to watch the entertainment put out by the media than to read a sober essay . . . In order to get our message before the public with some chance of a lasting impression, we've had to kill people.*

The street that ran past the scientist's house was quiet, bathed in the soft glow of streetlights and humming a kind of peacefulness in the distant traffic sounds from I–95. It could have been a scene from any one of hundreds, thou-sands, of cities from Maine to California, Florida to Wash-ington State. It was so familiar, so *normal*. Yet, behind the American facade conspiracies were under way to destroy it all.

The car phone rang. Whiteman answered and passed it to Thornton. It was his office, with an urgent message to tele-phone Chaplain Cameron Kragle at Fort Bragg.

The news relayed to him by the chaplain added to the level of his anxiety. He agreed with Cameron that something was about to happen on the nineteenth. It didn't take much to in-terpolate what it would be. Rasem Jameel might already have taken delivery of one hundred pounds of anthrax and could even now be distributing it to terrorists in an American city containing an Eastland Apartments on Kneeland Street near Kingston T.

"I'll have an agent stop by and pick up the citation, Chaplain," Thornton said. "Don't handle it any more than necessary."

"Eggs, glue, pack?" Cameron speculated. "Any idea what that can mean?"

"I don't know. It's too early to tell, but we may have found the source of the bacteria. If we're in luck, he hasn't delivered the shipment yet."

"And if we're not?"

The agent almost heard the ticking of a clock inside his head, ticking down to H-hour when plague released on a U.S. city started killing men and women, grandmas and infants . . . just like in his nightmares. Rotting corpses stacked up like cordwood.

"I read this article in *Time*," Cameron said. "Back in 1966, scientists from the Special Operations Division out at Fort Detrick got on a New York subway and walked through the train, pausing between cars to drop objects on the track. They were ordinary lightbulbs pumped full of harmless bacteria meant to simulate anthrax spores."

Thornton picked up on the thought. "Eggs—like lightbulbs. They'd both work."

"In the study, it was determined that most of New York could have been fatally infected," Cameron said.

"But *which* city will it be? I'll have our office run a database on 'Kneeland Street' and 'Kingston T' and see what comes up."

"I think my brother Cassidy knows where it is. He left Bragg a couple of hours ago. He took a pistol with him. I think he's going after Jameel. He's hurting enough right now to shoot him on sight."

Thornton cursed to himself. These Kragles were single-minded, action-directed, exasperating . . . "Have you notified your dad yet?" he asked.

"Not yet. I will."

"In the meantime, try to think of where your brother might have gone. I don't have to tell you—we may not have much time left."

So Thornton sat on his ass in the dark while the clock continued to tick down. The mad scientist was a big gamble, but he was the best hand they had been dealt so far. With luck, they would find that one hundred pounds of anthrax in his home lab before he delivered it.

Headlights washed onto the block. It was nearly midnight. "Claude?" Whiteman said.

It was the blue Cherokee SUV they were told he drove. It turned into Martfeld's driveway. A security light above the garage door automatically came on and illuminated the well-kept lawn. An elderly man with a stereotypical scientist's white beard and wearing a tweed coat with elbow patches got out of the car. Although thin enough to be the figment of Thornton's imagination, he seemed spry and active enough. The man looked up and down the street, then walked toward the front door, fumbling for his keys.

"Let's go," Thornton said.

Dr. Martfeld made no attempt to escape. He slowly turned when the agents jumped out of their car. His dark eyes flinted with a hint of madness as he threw back his withered head and cackled fiendishly.

"You're too late!" he shouted. "Nothing can save you now!"

CHAPTER 36

Afghanistan

Brandon couldn't be sure that last night with Summer had actually happened. It was like one of those dreams in which it was difficult to distinguish fantasy from reality when he awoke. He had little time to sort it out, however, for bedlam aroused the entire camp almost as soon as he opened his eyes. One of the mujahideen going out to relieve himself discovered the sentry missing. Worse yet, there was a dead man down near the dry streambed with his throat slit. Brandon quickly figured out it was the al-Qaeda snitch with whom Summer rendezvoused last night.

The camp was further rattled when Abdul Homayan was found inside his bedroll beneath the ledge with his throat cut, blood turning his massive beard even redder. It was a fresh murder, not more than an hour or so old. The camp went on a war footing until the situation could be resolved, Brandon dispatching the Deltas to defensive positions above and below.

Saeed ran to Brandon and Summer. "Commander Bek is not down by the water hole!" he exclaimed. "He is gone! He left in the night with some of the men. They slipped out without anyone knowing."

Doc TB had had the last two-hour watch for the Americans. He was stationed toward the northern blind canyon, the most likely avenue of enemy approach, while the mujahideen covered the southern approach along the dry streambed. The sentry there had apparently abandoned his post and departed with Bek, the entire band slipping out by that route under cover of the moonless night. It was flawlessly planned and executed.

Brandon reasoned that the al-Qaeda operative was spotted leaving the area and killed because Bek thought he was there to expose him as the band's traitor. Abdul's murder was a gimme, Bek exacting his revenge on a personal enemy before he fled. More than half the Afghan force, seven fighters, had absconded with Bek, reducing the unit both in number and effectiveness. Only Saeed the Zarbati, Vince Lombardi, and two other Afghans remained with the Delta detachment. Moreover, Bek knew Iron Weed's mission against the Shake. He would undoubtedly warn bin Laden, thereby multiplying the risk to 1-Alpha.

He should have killed him at the beginning, Brandon thought.

"Sir, I didn't see anything," Doc TB said, shattered by what he considered his personal failing. "Nothing passed in my area, and I couldn't see under the ledge because it was dark. Besides, there's only two ways to get to the camp. I covered one approach, and the Afghans covered the other—"

"It wasn't your fault, Doc."

The mujahideen sentry was slack. Brandon had observed that the night before, when both he and Summer slipped out of camp and then back in without being challenged. And he was obviously in cahoots with Bek, since he'd left when Bek did.

Brandon accepted the fault; if it was anyone's, it was his. He was the commander. Instead of devoting full attention to business and mission, he let himself be distracted and was therefore off guard and susceptible to mistakes. It proved to him once again that you couldn't put men and women together in a combat environment. The temptation of nature was just too strong. Not that either he or Summer could have necessarily prevented what happened, but they certainly could do nothing while naked and sweating over each other in the bushes.

Summer avoided meeting his eyes, as he avoided hers. Like him, he knew she must be mentally beating herself up.

Saeed, ever loyal to Abdul, worked himself and the other Jijak fighters into going after Bek. His sense of humor was gone. "Bek went over to the Taliban dogs," he declared hotly. "A blood crime requires blood revenge."

"It has to wait," Brandon countered through Summer. "We have more important matters to attend to."

He should have remembered that last night, he told himself.

It was time for damage control, to reconsolidate after an action. Shit happened in war. Murphy's Law was always at work.

They could still pull off the mission. He had his Deltas, which, along with the map to the Shake's command post, was all he needed. Even assuming Bek *was* heading to bin Laden, did he know exactly where to go? Maybe not. Bek possessed a radio to warn the terrorist leader, but most knowledgeable and competent military commanders changed frequencies and codes regularly to prevent communications compromise. It was doubtful Bek was current with the command post. Tribesmen were too easily corrupted to let them into the inner circle. Brandon doubted bin Laden could be warned in time—if 1-Alpha moved quickly.

The only assets he needed were locals who knew the mountains, which the Zarbati did. Saeed was cooling down, forsaking revenge until afterward. Good man, Brandon thought. All Saeed demanded was time to give Abdul a proper Islam funeral.

"Major?" Mad Dog huddled over the PRC-137. "You better take a look."

The decrypted radio message was routed through CENT-COM and SFOB from USSOCOM. It stated simply, without explanation, that Iron Weed would be extracted from its AO on Monday, in four days.

Completion of mission before then is essential, it concluded.

"We're already moving. Send back that message," Brandon ordered. It was what his father expected; it was what he expected of himself.

Brandon placed the hand-drawn map Summer received from her snitch before he was killed on the ground. Next to it he flattened a 1000:1 map of the region downloaded from Summer's PC and the PRC-137. Without questioning the source of Summer's map, Saeed got down on his hands and knees with the American major. Winnie Brown, Sergeant Norman, and Ismael-Summer studied it and compared it to the topographical map. The rest of the Deltas stood or knelt behind the inner circle, looking over shoulders. A stiff cold wind full of gritty black dust snatched at the corners of the map. Summer placed rocks on the corners to hold them down.

"Yes, yes," Saeed said through Summer. "It is not an easy trip, but we can get there. I have been in these mountains."

Brandon pointed out the Shake's command post. "It's about fifteen klicks—kilometers. How long will it take in this terrain?"

"We cannot go direct. Three days, maybe as few as two if everything goes well with us," Saeed responded. "It is ugly country. Here there is an old camel and mule path used by flower smugglers." He'd used the word "flower," which Summer translated as *heroin*. "It is the fastest way, but it is very high and dangerous. There may be storms this time of year."

"What's the alternative?" Brandon asked.

Saeed turned to Summer. "Ismael, you have been to the Tora Bora?"

"No."

"Explain to the American that this is not a dance club where there are virgins to meet. The Taliban has fought in these mountains since the Russian war and longer. They know them well, with which we must contend."

He traced a valley on the map with his finger, the same one where Gloomy shot the machine gunners and through which the Northern Alliance was attempting to advance. Although Alliance patrols were being sent out into the surrounding mountains to root out pockets of resistance and search caves, the advance had bogged down in the valley against heavy opposition. It was the last friendly outpost on the way to the Shake's fortress.

"It is easier going here in the valley," Saeed acknowledged, "but there will be enemy and they know the terrain well. Nonetheless, we must travel in the valley before we can climb up to the camel trail. We will be exposed for that time. It is as the Gloomy one says—sitting the ducks."

"Sitting ducks," Summer corrected.

"Then we should travel at night," Mother Norman put in. His orange-red beard was gray around the edges and gray around the mouth where his breath froze.

"We should travel in the valley when it is night," Saeed agreed, "but not even the Zarbati travel the camel trail in darkness. There have been many camels and mules lost on that trail, as well as men, when it was also know as the Silk Road."

He stood, and Brandon stood with him. They studied the country to the south. The terrain looked as though some great celestial giant had crumpled the crust of the earth like a sheet of paper. Wind pulled a swirling gray scud across the sky like a curtain. There would probably be no bombing today because of the weather.

Saeed pointed. "That is your mountain where the big cave is," he said. "Perhaps Osama bin Laden is there, as we found him in Kabul. Perhaps he is not. Or perhaps he already knows we are coming and is waiting. They are many and we are few." His lips tightened. "We are even fewer now after what the traitor Bek has done. How will we kill him if we do get there?"

"Leave that to us," Brandon said.

He had discussed the plan with SFOB by radio and received a go-ahead. Assets would be in place given a six-hour heads-up. The plan depended on 1-Alpha locating the entrance to Osama's cave, which bombers and land scouts had been unable to do so far. Once the detachment laser-painted the entrance with the PAQ-10, B-2s with thermobaric bombs would place several of them deep inside. The thermobaric bomb was the latest in American technology. It destroyed all life inside a cave for hundreds of feet. It seemed the surest, and perhaps only, way to get to the Shake now that he had gone underground.

The mountain rose purple-hazed beyond a nearer range of mountains, sandwiched between snowcaps. It was not a great distance away—a good training run for the Deltas at Wally World, except the terrain at Fort Bragg had not been as brutal.

"All right," Brandon decided. "If no one has a better plan,

we'll move into the valley tonight and climb up to the camel trail at first light."

He looked from man to man, seeking input. Mother Norman made a gesture. "Looks like a go," he said.

Mad Dog gazed at the mountain. "Verily, though I walk through the Valley of the Shadow of Death," he misquoted, "I shall fear no evil—for we're the baddest motherfuckers in the valley."

Saeed swallowed. He grinned at his friend Gloomy Davis. "Is piece of cake?" he asked in English.

"As easy as Arachna Phoebe. Onward to the bat cave, brave knights."

"Batman and Robin and the Seven Stooges," Summer murmured, and walked off.

"The more I'm around that Ismael," Mad Dog remarked, "the more he acts like a cunt on PMS."

"Hoo-ya!" Thumbs Jones agreed.

If they only knew. Brandon's gray eyes narrowed as he studied the distant mountain. He didn't like it, but he had to depend upon Summer and her now dead informant. Nothing was ever certain in the fog of war. The most you could ask for was a slight advantage. His Deltas gave him that in superior physical conditioning, skill, and raw guts. An opportunity was all he asked for.

The screeching of the rising wind seemed the voice of the mountain itself issuing a challenge.

Don't worry. We're coming.

CHAPTER 37

The killings compromised the ledge campsite. The detachment and its remaining four mujahideen buried Abdul in the rocky soil facing Mecca, rucked up, and set out to reach the valley in order to rest before nightfall. Gloomy looked back.

"Ol' Abdul is already cavorting with his seventy-two virgins," he said. "Maybe I'll revert to Islam."

"Good idea," Mad Dog allowed. "There probably ain't seventy-two virgins left in Hooker anyhow."

"There aren't seventy-two nonvirgins."

"Perverts," Winnie Brown hissed.

Wind rose throughout the day, churning up black dust, transforming the landscape into restless molecular patterns and keeping Doc TB busy washing grit out of the detachment's reddened eyes. One-Alpha and the remnants of Bek's band reached the ridge above the valley before noon and sought refuge among the cliffs and rocks while they awaited sunset and, with luck, the laying of the wind. Mother Norman established a duty and watch list with his usual quiet efficiency and ordered everyone else to crawl into shelters and get as much sleep as they could. Rest would be a short commodity for the next few days as Iron Weed 1A made what would hopefully be its final push against the terrorist leader. America would have justice.

"Osama, yo mama is coming," Mad Dog recited, squinting as he hunkered over commo gear and complained how the fine black sand blasted into the seams and connections of his high-tech radio equipment, causing minor malfunctions. Commo was a team's lifeline, without which it was left on its own to survive or perish.

"We can rig up two tin cans and a length of string," Ice Man laconically suggested, then pulled his poncho over his head and lapsed into his normal taciturnity.

Brandon sent Vince Lombardi down into the valley as a messenger to make connection with friendlies. There would have to be a passage of lines after nightfall, and he didn't want trigger-happy sentries making sound shots. Glassing from above, he watched the runner approach the Northern Alliance defensive perimeter, through which he was soon escorted under guard. Old pickup trucks used as transports and a couple of Russian-made BMTs sat scattered about. Nothing much seemed to be happening. The near-sandstorm put a crimp in the war.

He scanned the route his detachment must take after nightfall, committing as much of it as he could to memory and to notations on his map. He inspected draws and ravines and ridgelines. He looked for signs that Bek or other enemy forces were waiting for Iron Weed to commit itself to no-man's-land. Nothing moved out there.

Summer slid belly down next to him in the protected site he selected overlooking the valley. "Saeed says there may be snow later," she said.

Brandon ignored her and continued to glass the valley. Last night might never have occurred had he kept his mind on business rather than on a rounded piece of female ass.

They had not spoken to each other all day, other than by the necessity of her translating for him. Ismael was a fake, and as far as he was concerned, everything about Summer except the mole below her belly button was equally fake, to match her hair, eyes, and Ismael persona.

"There was nothing we could have done," she reasoned.

"You mean, even if we hadn't been screwing in the bushes?"

"Yes. Even if we hadn't been screwing in the bushes."

"So far I guess I'm luckier than most of the men you've bedded."

"You bastard!" she blazed. "You're a fool if you didn't see that last night was different."

"We're both fools," he said.

She said nothing for a moment, and when she did, the wiseass Ismael was back. "It could have been worse. What if Mad Dog or Gloomy or one of the others had seen? How would you explain that? They'd have you marching in Gay Pride Day—and I'd let them."

The thought amused Brandon in spite of himself. He was about to crack back that he'd strip her first, let them see for themselves, but restrained himself. He didn't want to provide her, or himself, an opening for another episode. He knew he'd made a mistake. It was up to him now to limit the fallout, and to hell with his emotions. Feelings didn't count in this situation. He was a professional soldier, a Delta warrior, and mission came first, above everything else.

It didn't matter that he wanted to grab her right now, taste those lips reddened and puffed by the weather, and drag her off to his cave like a modern day Neanderthal.

Damn her.

A tall man walking across the Alliance encampment below caught his attention. The man was clearly a Westerner. He kept his head ducked against blowing sand. He looked clean-shaved and wore heavy olive drab woolen trousers, a tan safari jacket, and carried a heavy camera bag slung from one shoulder. He ducked out of sight into a desert tent.

Summer lay silently at his side, fuming. Brandon kept his glasses focused on the tent until the Westerner reemerged. He recognized the tall man with a pleasant start. A grin slid across his bearded face.

"That crazy old fart," he murmured with open admiration.

He should have realized his old uncle would never be content with hanging around a reporter's pool in Kabul waiting for the Five O'clock Follies—the daily briefing by some public information officer from the State Department or the military. Uncle Mike had to be out where the action was, and right now most of it occurred in the Tora Bora area where both the one-eyed Taliban leader and Osama bin Laden were holed up.

Uncle Mike Kragle had been chasing wars for CPI for at least fifty years on and off—Korea, Vietnam (where he had also been a soldier), Central America, Afghanistan when the Russians were here, Desert Storm, and Bosnia. He was shot twice in Vietnam, wounded in Somalia with the Rangers, and couldn't pass through airport security without setting off alarms from all the lead and steel embedded in his scarred body. And now here he was, over seventy years old, and still the war chaser. Aunt Brigette, the Eurasian girl he brought back from Vietnam and married, always said before she died that Mike, "for goo'ness sake," would chase wars right up to the Pearly Gates.

"I'm going down there," Brandon said. "I'll need an interpreter to get through the lines."

"Yes, sir. Yes, sir, three bags full, sir."

Still the wiseass.

Uncle Mike shook hands warmly with his nephew as soon as he recognized him through the beard and mujahideen garb. Brandon reluctantly introduced Summer.

"This is Ismael. She's my interpreter."

Uncle Mike caught the slip. *"She?"*

"He," Brandon quickly amended. "What are you doing in these woods, you old fox?"

Uncle Mike grinned. "I won't ask you the same question, but my guess is you have something to do with Iron Weed. Let's just say I heard my nephew was up here looking like Lawrence of Arabia."

"How did you know about Iron Weed?"

"Two and two add up to four. Besides, I'll tell you something, Brandon—Iron Weed is cocktail talk back in the States. Hell, it seems the whole world knows you're out here—and a lot of folks are trying to stop you. Starting in Washington."

Little news other than what directly concerned Iron Weed had reached 1-Alpha since it became isolated in the Hindu Kush with the mujahideen. Uncle Mike summarized events involving the General and USSOCOM and the congressional investigation of SpecOps activities in Afghanistan.

"It was all unity and nonpartisan cooperation among the pols right after 9/11," he explained. "But now the politicians are slinging mud and trying to make an opening for themselves in the next election. Fucking career politicians are like a bunch of lice feeding on America's blood."

Strong conviction was a Kragle trait. Uncle Mike always said objectivity and moderation were for idiots with minds so open nothing stayed in them.

"A couple of dirtbags—Senator Eric Tayloe and John Stanton—found out about Delta Force being assigned to capture or kill Taliban and al-Qaeda leaders. You can imagine the ruckus that started. The last I heard, your dad was given until Monday to extract Iron Weed from Afghanistan or face contempt of Congress charges."

"So that's why we were suddenly given a mission deadline," Brandon said. "It's my bet that contempt charges won't nearly match the contempt the General feels for that bunch."

Uncle Mike laughed. "I imagine the old boy is as furious as an elephant with musk. What makes things worse is that the enemy is also aware of Iron Weed."

Several hundred Taliban and al-Qaeda prisoners held at the northern Afghan fortress of Kali Jangi near Mazar-e-Sherif had revolted with smuggled-in arms, he went on to explain, and a lot of people were killed in the uprising, including a CIA agent sent there to question captives.

"Some of the prisoners, mostly the leaders, were talking about an op called Iron Weed. They were bragging about how al-Qaeda had contacts in America that keep bin Laden informed about everything that's going on in Special Operations," Uncle Mike concluded.

Brandon thought of how it seemed the enemy had been forewarned about his movements from almost the moment the detachment parachuted in-country. First it was the militia attack in Kabul, then the mysterious warning that allowed bin Laden to escape when 1-Alpha initially targeted him. And after what happened the night before to Abdul, Brandon was more willing than ever to look at Bek as the leak.

But there were certain things Bek could not have known and passed on, like the air strike that was laid on to catch the Shake in Kabul. Bek couldn't have warned bin Laden about that. If not him, then who did?

Brandon knew he couldn't concern himself with that now. He had a job to do.

"We have to move out, Uncle Mike."

They shook hands. "Take care, son. Keep an eye on your back trail. They're back there, and I suspect they know about you. I'll pass on to the General and your brothers—and Gloria, of course—that I saw you and you're okay."

"How about them?" Brandon asked. "Did Cassidy honor-grad the Q course? Is Kathryn looking forward to having the baby?"

"You can see for yourself soon," Mike said, deciding not to tell him about Kathryn's death. Brandon had enough to worry about without burdening him with that and the anthrax scare back in the States.

Mike turned to Summer. "Take care of him—Ismael, is it?"

"Yes. Ismael."

Uncle Mike chuckled.

CHAPTER 38

The near-total blackness of the Afghan night felt almost solid with blowing matter. Visibility was reduced to near zero. The point element, consisting of Ice Man and Saeed, literally felt its way forward in order to make any progress at all, while the dial on Brandon's wrist GPS fluttered, losing its satellite signal but still catching often enough to provide a general fix. Brandon bent close to the ground to cover the beam of his red-lensed flashlight. He consulted the GPS, compared it to the map, showed it to Saeed, then folded the map and put it away. He peered through the blackness as though he actually saw their destination.

"Sir, I suggest we hole up till daybreak." Mother Norman advised, whispering loudly to be heard above the howling of the dry wind and blasting sand. He coughed, smothering the sound in his fist. "We're wandering around in dark space. The GPSes are going crazy trying to pick up an SAT signal, and the radios are about to blink out because of all the sand."

Delta Force teams were carefully selected so that individuals on a detachment complimented each other in abilities and temperament. For every hard charger like Major Kragle, who literally stormed through hell to pull off missions, there was an older, cooler head to moderate him.

Brandon conceded it was risky to continue under these conditions. It might even be suicidal. Although SpecOps C-130 Specters had started flying the unfriendly skies of Afghanistan with their 20mm BOFORS, miniguns, and 105 howitzers, the detachment had no access to their air cover and support as long as the weather remained unflyable. Mad Dog warned for the third time that the radios might not work, although he wrapped the PRC-137 in his poncho to protect it and stuffed it into his rucksack.

"I thought they were built to take any kind of weather and conditions," Brandon chafed.

"This ain't just any kind of weather, sir," Mad Dog said. "This sand is almost like talcum powder. Any kind of small opening and it gets into the works and jams things, then connections have to be taken apart and cleaned. We've already missed our last scheduled sitrep contact with SFOB."

"How long will it take to fix?"

"Twenty minutes or so to take it apart and get the sand out. That should give us another hour before it clogs again."

"How about the Motorolas?"

"Same problem. This shit's so fine it even gets into the fillings of your teeth. Plus, it's easier to squeeze water out of a rock than a SATCOM signal through this atmosphere. Satellite commo is okay when it works, Major, but it's highly overrated."

Into the best-laid plans of mice and men—there was always Murphy.

"Major?" Mother Norman pressed.

Brandon turned to Summer. "Ask Saeed if he thinks he can find the trail."

She spoke to the Zarbati, her voice taut and weary even when speaking the clipped guttural dialect of Saeed's Jajik tribe, then turned back after he answered.

"He says he can," Summer said. "He says we'll start to

climb out of the valley up to the camel trail at the place where
there is a narrows and an iron-oxide wall. We'll have to climb
like goats, it's almost straight up a mountain, but we should
reach the camel Silk Road trail high up by the time it gets
daylight."

"That's good enough for me," Brandon replied. "We have
three days left to complete the mission. Give the troops a five
minute break. Top. Then we're moving out."

"Let's do it, sir," Norman said. He always voiced his opinion, but resolutely trusted his CO with the final decision.

Iron Weed was the most important mission of Major Brandon Kragle's career, perhaps of his lifetime. He was selected
to command it because the mission always came first and because he had a history of daring military successes. This
might also prove to be his most challenging mission. He
lifted his eyes in the direction of the unseen mountain where
the Shake hid with his terrorist lieutenants and advisors,
where Brandon assumed he must feel secure, deep inside the
mountain bowels with his forces protecting him. His command posts were likely equipped with the best communications and computers available to a billionaire renegade with
money to burn in the name of the jihad. They would keep him
in constant contact with the outside world and his leagues of
terrorists and sympathizers. Possessing such technology, it
was no difficult matter for him to receive warnings and intelligence from operators inside America and elsewhere. If Uncle Mike was right, he might even be in contact with sleepers
inside U.S. Special Operations.

Cutting off al-Qaeda's treacherous head was essential to
destroying the terrorist network. Brandon's jaw tightened.
He could not fail the General, his father. He could not fail his
grandfather, or Little Nana, who perished in the World Trade
Center disaster. He could not fail himself. Most of all he
could not fail America.

Get to the mountain, laser-direct bombs onto it, confirm the Shake's death, then get out again, he told himself, focusing on his task.

Brandon's posse picked up his urgency. To a man, they seemed to feel that if they passed through the Valley of the Shadow of Death quickly enough and reached the Silk Road, they would be on more even ground. Saeed located the iron-oxide wall, and the detachment climbed in lung-searing stretches. The footing proved loose and treacherous, and everyone soon had skinned knees and bruised hands and elbows. Brandon moved up and down the line of march in the wind-howling darkness, checking on his people and ensuring that no one strayed away in exhaustion. They stepped into the footprints of the person ahead of them in order to keep to the trail and maintain visual with each other.

Gloomy, on drag with one of the mujahideen, passed up a chilling signal: *Danger enemy near!* The patrol dropped on alert to either side of the trail, weapons at the ready, while Brandon hustled to the rear to check.

"Boss, I thought I was hearing things at first," Gloomy whispered, his voice cracked and hoarse from the elements. "I'm not. I keep hearing it. I can *feel* them. I thought I even heard engines."

"They can't get vehicles up this mountain."

"I know that, boss. But I'm telling you what I heard."

In spite of his good-ol'-boy Okie affectations, Gloomy Davis was an expert outdoorsman with a finely honed set of senses he claimed to have inherited from Comanche ancestors. "My great-great-granddaddy was ol' Man with Bare Butt. He had visions." No one knew whether to take him seriously, but Brandon learned through experience that his talents, premonitions—whatever he wanted to call them—were not to be ignored.

"All right. Let's drop a stay-behind."

It was risky, as dark and unsettled as the night was, but the main element required maximum security.

"I'll do it, boss. I'll take Vince Lombardi with me." He indicated the scrawny, rawhide strip of a mujahideen who knelt beside him.

"Don't drop back more than fifty meters in this stuff," Brandon cautioned. "I'll put Winnie on drag to take your place. You have a Motorola. We don't need an SAT at close range. Keep in contact with him."

"Roger that, boss."

How an enemy possibly stayed on this mountainside with them, much less tracked them under these conditions, was beyond Brandon's comprehension. Still, Gloomy insisted there were people back there, sometimes to one side or another. Maybe they really were *dukhi*, the Russian word for ghosts, which was what the Soviets called the Afghans.

"Boss, I got it figgered out," Gloomy announced. "When we used to hunt pheasant back in Hooker, one bunch of us would be the drivers. We drove the birds into blockers, who shot them when they jumped up to fly. You didn't actually have to see the pheasants to drive them. You just had to know they were in the field."

"Then someone knew we were going to be in the field?"

"That's how I figure it. They ain't just one bunch of 'em or we would have lost 'em way back. They got bunches scattered out all over the side of this mountain and everybody's heading uphill. When one bunch loses us, another picks us up."

Brandon drew a deep breath and let it out slowly. He squinted up into the whirling night. "We'll find out soon enough," he said. "It'll be daylight in another hour or so. Keep your eyes peeled. Saeed says we should be getting near the camel trail."

Dawn was a long time penetrating the living curtain of

blown black sand. Gradually, however, as if in defiance, the sky lightened. The jagged and serrated knife edges of mountain ridges, spires, and pinnacles slowly emerged higher up in silhouette against the sky, a formidable, cold wall of granite and old lava. Patches of snow lay blown up in piles at this higher altitude. It was savage country, with weather conditions to match, all too capable of exacting a toll from anything living.

From the looks of things, it was going to be another no-fly day except for the high-flying B-52s and B-2s. That troubled Brandon. Without tactical air cover, they were literally out here on their own.

He scanned their back trail with the binoculars but saw nothing moving except the shadowy, laboring outlines of his own people. Summer staggered from exhaustion as she climbed. She fell to her knees, refused Brandon's offer of help, then recovered and clambered to her feet. She picked up her dropped carbine and continued the struggle to put one foot in front of the other.

"Ismael is almost done in," Mother Norman noticed. "We're all dragging."

Mad Dog scoffed. "Ismael is a puss."

A single rifle shot suddenly penetrated the awful gloom. It reverberated and echoed throughout the mountains from peak to pinnacle, ridge to moraine. Brandon recognized in it the deadly crack of Gloomy's .300 Winchester. Enemy contact had undoubtedly been made; somebody was dead.

Though nearly spent, the patrol hustled into a watchful defensive perimeter as the echoes died away into silence. Brandon glassed the terrain in the direction of the shot. It was lighter now. He made out the terrain all the way down to the valley floor, but he still saw nothing moving. Saeed dropped down next to him, talking excitedly and pointing uphill.

"What's with him?" Brandon asked Summer.

"He says hurry. They can't get us if we reach the trail. It's too narrow."

Saeed pointed up toward what appeared to be a cleft in an otherwise solid wall of stone. It was about three hundred meters away at the top of an incline almost steep enough to qualify as a cliff.

"I'd say it's just in the nick of time," Mother Norman said. He had his own binoculars out. "Look farther down toward the bottom, Major."

Brandon shifted focus. Deep in the crease of the valley out of which 1-Alpha had climbed during the night sat a battered pickup truck. Another was partly hidden behind a pile of boulders, next to a copse of withered gray trees where horses were picketed. Gloomy *had* heard engines last night.

As Brandon counted the horses, pickups, and two half-ton trucks in order to estimate the size of the enemy force, a boat-shaped BMP nosed into view. One of the old Soviet infantry fighting vehicles developed for Warsaw Pact forces, the BMP was a formidable armored car equipped with both cannon and antitank AT-3 Sagger missiles. Brandon doubted the Taliban had Saggers, but the 73mm gun was nothing to spit at. It was capable of hurling an HEAT round out to a maximum effective range of about 1,500 meters, a klick and a half, with enough force to penetrate a foot and a half of solid steel.

You didn't want to fight it with small arms. Plus, it climbed pretty good. It scooted on out of the trees like a dark and dangerous beetle. Its snout of a gun slowly elevated until Brandon stared directly down its barrel through his binoculars. He and his men, he calculated, were within its range.

Shit!

He dropped the binoculars on a thong around his neck. Gloomy fired a second round at almost the same instant. Brandon felt a wave of relief as Vince Lombardi scrambled up through the boulders and scree, his coat and robe whipped by the wicked wind and his eyes wild. He paused long enough to turn and rattle off a burst downhill from his AK-47 to cover Gloomy's withdrawal. Both came running.

Gloomy's breath whistled and his dirty blond beard bristled almost white in the new morning light. "Boss, we've done gone and stirred up a hornets' nest," he panted. "I estimate company size. I put their heads down, but they'll be popping up like prairie dogs soon enough I reckon."

The BMP belched a puff of smoke and a tongue of white flame. The *craaaaack!* of the heavy gun was magnified by the surrounding mountains and echoed and reechoed. Along with the added explosion when the round hit, short of target, the echoes merged into one continuous sound like the earth splitting at the seams.

"Holy shit!" Gloomy gulped.

Brandon jumped to his feet. "Sergeant Norman, get them moving! Everybody follow Saeed."

The Zarbati didn't have to be told twice. He was already on his way clawing up the steep hillside, yelling and waving his arms. Summer hesitated.

"Get the hell out of here, Summer! Move it!" Brandon bellowed.

Gloomy caught the name and shot the major a quick look. There wasn't time for anything else. The rest of the small force, Americans and Afghans, scrambled through the rocks as though blown like scattered debris toward the safety of the Silk Road.

They failed to make it. All hell broke loose from the boulders ahead. There was rifle fire, a clatter of it reverberating, sounding in the echoing reiteration like at least a battalion firing in force. A machine gun stabbed green tracers. Flames licked into the bolting Iron Weed fighters. Brandon heard a woman scream, and his blood ran cold. He recalled another time when a woman screamed like that in this same land not so long ago.

Gloomy shouted, "Jesus to God, it's the blockers!"

CHAPTER 39

New York

Former President John Stanton touched a flame to his cheroot, then irritably stamped it out and tossed it in the trash basket as his secretary showed in Senator Eric B. Tayloe and his ever-present briefcase. Stanton swiveled his desk chair so that his back was to the chubby senator and he faced the window overlooking upper Manhattan.

"Sit down," he snapped.

"Pardon?" Tayloe flashed back, ruffling.

Stanton took a deep breath. What was with this little hairball today? "Sit down, please."

He swiveled around to his desk and watched the scheming little senator, mollified, settle himself into an overstuffed chair like a hen onto her nest. He knew that the senator had to be handled skillfully.

"You weren't at the hearings today," Tayloe accused.

"I've been there almost every other day. I shouldn't appear to be too interested or involved," Stanton explained. "The media is starting to pick up on it. CPI was always hostile to my administration. They're a bunch of right-wing fanatics that'd love to catch me dirty at something, which they won't."

"General Kragle's brother is a big shot reporter at CPI," Tayloe pointed out.

Stanton uttered a swear word beneath his breath, then asked, "How'd it go with MacArthur Thornbrew today?"

"He pulled a Kragle and refused to answer questions about the activities of the Homeland Security Agency," Tayloe said. "That bunch of shit kickers in the White House act like they think they're above the law."

"They're playing right into our hands. There's lots of ways to skin a cat." The former President held up a thumb the way he always did to make a point. "What you might do is plant a rumor in the press that the President and Thornbrew knew about 9/11 before it happened and chose not to stop it for political reasons. What did they know and when did they know it?"

"Nobody would believe that."

"Let Senator Boxley from California bring it up. She's an airhead, but it'll start the talking. In the meantime, subpoena the President and ask him that question in a casual way but in such a manner that the media picks up on it."

"He'll refuse the congressional subpoena—"

"Just as good. It will appear he has something to hide."

Tayloe thought about it. "I don't know. His polls are shooting off the charts. Higher than yours ever were," he added, unable to resist the dig.

Stanton looked annoyed but let the remark pass. "Did you read the piece in the *New Yorker*?" he asked. "A year ago eighty-nine percent of American men and ninety-four percent of American women thought the United States was the greatest country on earth. Those numbers have dropped to fifty-eight percent for men and fifty-one percent for women. We can use that, especially if we were to have an incident."

Senator Tayloe frowned. "Every time there's another anthrax scare, the President and Thornbrew come out and tell people how hard they're working to make America safe again and the President's numbers climb another point."

"Such things concern folks, scares the peewaddley out of them, but what scares them worse is an open-ended war on terror that could lead to World War Three or terrorism on the scale of Israel. The tide is turning against the war, buddy, and in favor of peace in our time. Our friends in the media are already suggesting that it's cowardly of America to keep bombing Afghanistan without getting down on the ground mano-a-mano, so to speak. If we were to have an embarrassing incident . . ."

This time Tayloe asked it, his expression blank. "What kind of incident?"

"General Kragle has all those Iron Weed teams inside Afghanistan—"

"But only until Monday, or he'll be charged with contempt of Congress."

"You think that bothers him?"

"It's personal between you and General Kragle, isn't it, Mr. President?"

Stanton's jaw knotted. "Nothing would give me greater pleasure than to see the bastard court-martialed, then hung."

Tayloe delicately crossed his legs. His expensive gray suit had creases sharp enough to cause paper cuts. An expression came across his fleshy face that was part cat watching a mouse, part spectator at a bloody highway accident.

"I heard you gave orders to have one of our Air Force planes shot down over Afghanistan during Operation Punitive Strike. That took balls," the senator acknowledged with an oily smile.

"Kragle was a rogue taking matters into his own hands and had to be stopped. First rule of politics—transfer blame and never admit anything. "Besides, it was shot down by Afghan missiles."

"It was shot down by American fighter planes from the USS *Abe Lincoln*," Tayloe corrected him, still smiling. "Mr. President, what you must understand is that I know which closets to look in when it comes to Washington."

"What you must understand," Stanton shot back, "is that you'll need an issue more than a social agenda if you ever hope to be President of the United States."

That sobered Senator Tayloe. Stanton knew that Tayloe wanted to be President badly enough to sell his soul to hell to get it. Nevertheless, the round little man still seemed to have something stuck in his craw.

"Mr. President, before we go any further," he said casually, "I would like to know what your former National Security Advisor, Mr. Clarence Todwell, is engaged in these days?"

Stanton stiffened. "Why do you ask that?"

"He did manage to avoid going to the federal penitentiary, I understand, although he paid a high price in everything else for his association with you."

Todwell bore the blame for the scandal that followed Punitive Strike. Washington rumor mills hinted that then-President Stanton set him up as the fall guy if anything went wrong with their scheming.

"I didn't know what he was doing when we did it," Stanton said, flushing angrily. "So when he did it, whatever he did—at least from my point of view—I can tell you we didn't mean to do it."

Senator Tayloe placed his briefcase across his knees. "It won't happen to me," he promised, patting the briefcase. "I have taken precautions. I won't go alone down that bad road like Clarence Todwell did."

The arrogant little primfuck, Stanton fumed. He thinks he's going to be President. When I get through using him, he'll be lucky to get a job washing dishes in the congressional cafeteria.

"It was all a conspiracy by Kragle and the right-wingers at the Pentagon and in the FBI," Stanton alibied, fighting to control his anger.

"Just so we have an understanding," Senator Tayloe said.

Neither trusted the other. That much was understood.

"We were speaking of an 'incident,' " Tayloe reminded the former President. "We can be friends again now that we understand that neither will attempt to, well, take *advantage* of the other, and that we have mutual interests."

"Of course."

Stanton stood up, having had enough of Tayloe's company. Then his cooler side prevailed. He needed Tayloe. Everything had been thought out, from the congressional investigation to Afghanistan. Besides, Tayloe wasn't smart enough to outwit him in the long run. It was fun manipulating him.

Stanton sat down, relaxed. He even smiled. He propped his elbows on his desk and leaned forward, tenting his hands beneath his chin.

"Now that we've cleared the air, let's get down to business," he said smoothly, choosing his words carefully and parsing them for any overt illegality, a practice at which he'd had experience. "Suppose we have an incident with the war that exposes the illegality of how it's being conducted in Afghanistan by General Kragle's USSOCOM and the White House? Won't people turn even more against the war? People are gullible. They want to believe that everything will be all right without war. We've got perfect timing, what with everybody in the administration refusing to testify before the hearings and making the public think they have something to hide. An incident that creates a full-fledged scandal is an issue we can use to return honesty to government and end the war, to get back the White House and both houses of Congress and ensure the survival of my presidential legacy."

"As well as run the shaft into some old enemies?"

Stanton smiled without humor. "I call it collateral damage."

He paused before deciding to go on. If they were both equally involved, equally dirty, didn't that protect both? In for a penny, in for a pound.

"Surely, as chairman of the Armed Services Committee, you have contacts that can expose Special Operations inside Afghanistan for what they are?" he said.

Tayloe remained silent for a long while, as though contemplating his own risk. In the end he was as greedy to obtain power as Stanton was to ensure his legacy, as he'd called it.

"I have people who are both loyal to me and ambitious at the same time," he said. "It's a very good combination. It gives me the ability to intercept all messages coming out of the Afghan theater and know what's going on *before* the messages reach CENTCOM himself, General Kragle, the Joint Chiefs, or the White House."

Stanton looked pleased. His eyes narrowed. He *had* cultivated the right man for the job.

"For example," Senator Tayloe said, "I know that one of the Iron Weed detachments, which just happens to be commanded by General Kragle's son, has been out of communications with SFOB in Uzbekistan since early last night. It's in the Tora Bora area on an assassination mission against Osama bin Laden. Is that the kind of incident you have in mind?"

Stanton exhaled and rubbed his palms together. "It couldn't be more perfect. How many men?"

"Eight, ten maybe. SFOB fears they may be in trouble."

"If ten Americans can be exposed as engaged in a mission that U.S. law specifically forbids, and orders for it can be

traced back through General Kragle to the White House . . .
That's a scandal, a big issue that the press can use to beat this
administration over the head with. Senator, we have to be
blunt. Can you make sure any messages that may come from
this lost detachment, if it's still alive, is either delayed or, better yet, lost coming out of SSOF?"

"That's SFOB," Tayloe corrected. "Special Forces Operational Base."

"Whatever. We need that detachment to remain lost until it
makes headlines and the press discovers that its true mission
is against U.S. law. A week of that kind of front page and
people will be demanding new leadership and a new direction for peace."

He stood up, looking altogether satisfied with the way
things were going.

"These sheep stickers in this administration are amateurs
when it comes to big-time politics," Stanton gloated. "We
have the opportunity to build a lasting world peace and return
compassion, social justice, and peace to the American government. It's a big order for a big man, *President* Tayloe."

CHAPTER 40

Tampa

Wearing her robe and rabbit ear slippers, Gloria brought two coffees into General Kragle's upper-floor study and office as dawn illuminated the window-framed scene of Tampa Bay. Her haggard appearance suggested she had slept even less than the General. Getting older and grayer by the minute, she complained. Worrying about her boys was going to be the death of her. Brandon and his men in "A-rab camel land" had been out of radio contact for almost eighteen hours. Cassidy ran off on his own to "Lawd only knows where"; she was as anxious about him in his present state of mind as she was about Brandon. Cameron went out searching for Cassidy somewhere. Lawdy, Lawdy, she hoped the chaplain took his Bible, 'cause if these weren't the end times, the Lawd was missing his best opportunity.

She set the coffee tray on the corner of the General's desk. He glanced up and rubbed his eyes. Chubby arms akimbo, she was about to unleash her deadly finger and give him hell over their boys. The worn-down look on his face changed her mind.

"You looks like death warmed over, Darren," she said gently. "I is getting you some breakfast."

In Gloria's mind, the right food cured everything.

"Coffee's enough, Gloria. I have to catch the 0915 flight to D.C."

"I done got your bags packed and you is ready to go. That ain't no excuse. You gots to keep your strength up. You ain't leaving this house till you has your breakfast. Is that clear, Darren?"

He rose, towering over her, and stooped to envelop her in an enormous bear hug. Brown Sugar Doll provided one of the few exceptions in the lives of the Kragle men where open affection was accepted.

"Yes, ma'am, sergeant major," he joked wearily. "Brown Sugar, you've always been the backbone of this family."

The unexpected compliment flustered her. "Oh, pshaw and hog dumplings," she murmured, blushing as she squirmed to extricate herself from his embrace. "Now go on with you, Darren. What decent folks gonna say if they sees me letting some big white man drool all over my head rag?"

"Are these decent folks standing out there looking through our window?"

He patted her cheek as he released her. She hurried out, fussing, "Eggs over easy, grits and toast, the way you likes it, and you done better eat every bite of it too."

The General sat back down and took a deep, bone-tired breath. He'd left CENTCOM at the air base after 0300. General Etheridge had persuaded him to go home by promising to have the duty officer call immediately when commo was reestablished with Iron Weed 1-Alpha.

"Neither of us can continue to conduct this war on three hours' sleep a night," Etheridge had said. "We both need some rest. There's probably a good explanation for why we've lost contact. Weather has moved into the Tora Bora.

That sometimes causes problems with satellite communications."

Teams on mission also carried backup conventional radios, but the General saw no point in bringing it up.

"There's little either of us can do here the rest of the night," General Etheridge had gone on. "We need to be fresh for tomorrow's—today's—meeting with the SecDef and Chairman Thornbrew. Iron Weed 3-Alpha will help, but nothing is going to stifle Senator Tayloe until he embarrasses the President and chops off our heads, starting with yours."

The General's itinerary included a stop by Fort Bragg on his way back from D.C., where he would welcome Major Keith Laub's Iron Weed-3A back from Afghanistan and congratulate him on a mission accomplished. Three-Alpha had successfully rescued the four American women missionaries held by the Taliban. Two-Alpha was still southeast of Kandahar on Mullah Omar's trail. One-Alpha, presumably, was somewhere in the White Mountains chasing Osama bin Laden. In a telephone patch, the General learned that his brother Mike had seen Brandon yesterday before the detachment headed out into no-man's-land.

The story of 3-Alpha and the rescue of the missionaries covered the front pages. The General saw to it. It refuted Tayloe's accusations that Iron Weed was primarily dedicated to political assassination, and temporarily silenced the voices of Senator Tayloe and Stanton. But he knew they'd be back, and that they wouldn't quit until they soiled everything they touched.

"I can't imagine what you could have done to piss off Tayloe," General Etheridge commented, then grinned. "I'd have thought your charming disposition and accommodating personality would have won him over."

"It's Stanton I've pissed off," the General said.

"So I've heard."

It was now 0700, and the duty officer still hadn't called.

As usual when the General was home, the TVs were on in his study and tuned to the news stations—one to CNN and the other to Fox. On Fox, the President addressed high school students in Minnesota.

"People say, well, how long is this war going to last? And the answer is, for however long it takes to make sure America is secure. The nation will defend ourselves and freedom at any price. It is too precious a gift for future generations to give up to terrorists."

On CNN, former President Stanton held forth at the World Congress: "This is a brief moment in history when the United States has preeminent military, economic, and political power. We should not waste it chasing shadows around the globe."

What was this guy smoking? the General asked himself. Didn't he and his bunch realize how serious things were?

For years, long before he became head of USSOCOM, General Kragle warned of a new kind of war more insidious and bloody than any America had yet fought. That war did not start with the 9/11 attacks. It actually started more than a decade earlier, when terrorists organized to strike against American interests in other parts of the world; 9/11 simply brought the war to America's shores.

He was convinced that battles would now be fought in Milwaukee and San Francisco, in New York and Arizona. A mindless war of terrorism waged by America's self-proclaimed enemies, fanatical and devoted to annihilation, men who considered a five-year-old kid confined to a wheelchair as legitimate a target as a uniformed soldier or cop, and who would use any weapon, including nuclear devices or anthrax germs.

"It is gonna be the Battle of Armageddon," Gloria solemnly predicted. "Folks better get they house in order, 'cause Jesus is about to come back."

Kragle railed to himself about the peaceniks-at-any-cost crowd, as he thought of them, always harping about World War III, who wanted to call a victory now and bring the troops home. To him, it was like Franklin Roosevelt declaring victory at Tarawa following Pearl Harbor. In Netanya, Israel, a suicide Hamas bomber burst into a hotel dining room and blew himself up, killing nineteen Israelis and injuring more than 120. That would be the United States if the War on Terror was not pursued to real victory, daily terrorist activity from Maine to California. As far as he was concerned, World War III had already started, and it was going to be fought literally everywhere. Delta Force was going to be busy.

All you had to do was look at world events to see the war unfolding.

A grenade blast in the Philippines ripped through a market and a movie theater, killing eight people as U.S. Special Forces arrived to open a new front in the campaign against terror. In Iran, hundreds of thousands of Iranians chanted "Death to America!" Iraqi strongman Saddam Hussein was paying $25,000 to the families of each suicide bomber who struck Israeli, American, or other Western targets; the surviving kin of the 9/11 martyrs received their checks. Jihad videos went on sale in Birmingham, England, where a third of the city's population was Muslim; the videos celebrated the 9/11 attacks while referring to Jews and Americans as monkeys and pigs. The polls he'd seen indicated that nearly one-half of all immigrant and naturalized citizens of Muslim countries considered the attack on America to be justified.

General Kragle muted the sounds on both TVs but left the pictures on. He rose from his desk and stood looking out his picture window toward Tampa Bay. In his agitated frame of mind, he wouldn't have been surprised to see a Denny's restaurant or a Methodist church go up in a sudden explosion.

Gloria entered the study and interrupted his reveried

thoughts. "Here they is—eggs and grits." She attempted to remain cheerful and keep the household functioning in spite of his fears.

"Put it on the desk, please, Sugar Doll," he said.

"You be sure to eat. I gonna come back and check on you, hear? Then you better get ready to go. I done put your bag by the front door."

The General continued to gaze out the window. Thinking about his political enemies, men elected by the people to represent them and lead, he recalled a passage from a book by the ex-Trotskyite James Burnham.

I do not know what the cause is of the West's extraordinarily rapid decline, which is most profoundly shown by the deepening loss, among the leaders of the West, of confidence in themselves and in the unique quality of their own civilization, and by a correlated weakness of the Western will to survive.

GOVERNMENT ISSUES BIOTERRORISM ALERT

WASHINGTON (CPI)—American cities could be targeted as early as this weekend by extremist groups, the U.S. government warned today. Americans face increased danger as terrorists search for vulnerable targets, said MacArthur Thornbrew, chairman of the National Homeland Security Agency. He called for increased vigilance against bioterrorism, such as anthrax, and warned people to be wary of or to avoid places this weekend where large numbers of people congregate. The intended target is still unknown, he said. An entire city may be targeted.

After weeks of anthrax-tainted letters, the FBI said its investigators do not have a prime suspect. However, FBI agents under the direction of Claude Thornton arrested a former scientist, Dr. Tobias Martfeld, who was among those conducting bio- and chemical research at Fort Detrick, Maryland, more than three decades ago. Martfeld was arrested last night at his residence in the Baltimore suburb of Rosedale. He has not yet been charged with a crime.

The Homeland Security Agency released the photographs of two men whom FBI say may be implicated in this week's terrorist plot. They are Shukri Abu Marzook, 38, president of the Sacred Land Foundation, and U.S. Army Sergeant Rasem Jameel, 29.

Marzook had been sought by the FBI following a raid on his Dallas office, which authorities say was a cover organization supplying funds and other support for "sleeper" terrorists of al-Qaeda and Palestinian terror groups within the U.S.

Jameel, also known as "Otta," is a naturalized U.S. citizen from Saudi Arabia who enlisted in the U.S. Army and is a sergeant with the 82nd Airborne Division at Fort Bragg, North Carolina. He reportedly deserted following a clandestine meeting with Marzook in Fayetteville, North Carolina. He is believed to have taken possession of a large quantity of "weaponized" anthrax from Dr. Martfeld.

Anyone spotting either of these two men should immediately contact local police and the nearest FBI office.

Government medical authorities have found that one of the September 11 skyjackers was treated three months before the terrorist attack for lesions that could have been caused by exposure to anthrax. FBI Agent Thornton has alerted hospitals nationwide to be on the lookout for new cases, as other terrorists may also be infected. There is some indication, he said that the fugitive Rasem Jameel was exposed to the deadly disease. He was a church volunteer at a Fort Bragg chapel where another volunteer, Kathryn Kragle, is believed to have contracted the disease that led to her death.

CHAPTER 41

Quantico, Virginia

The ticking of the clock inside Claude Thornton's shaved head grew progressively louder as its countdown demolished the hours minute by minute, second by second. Today was the nineteenth of the month, the presumed target date for whatever plan the terrorists had concocted. The agent almost heard the busting of eggshells filled with lethal anthrax spores.

The only thing old Dr. Martfeld confirmed as he huddled in his jail cell sniggering into his white beard and quoting the Unabomber was that, yes, he delivered one hundred pounds of anthrax—"Finely powdered and of a grade unequaled in the world," he added with pride—to a Middle Easterner he knew only as "Otta." Some of the deadly dust was recovered by HazMat in the search of the old man's home laboratory.

"Where did you deliver it?" Thornton demanded.

"Someplace."

"Where was Otta taking it?"

The old man cackled. It seemed he was truly a mad scientist. "Once technology has been destroyed and lost for a generation or two," he raved, "it won't be coming back in any foreseeable lifetimes. . . ."

Thornton stifled the impulse to grab him by the beard and shake him to his senses. "Don't you understand what you've done?" he asked. "Thousands of people, perhaps even millions, may die because of you."

"Don't *you* understand? They're expendable if we can save the world."

"He's mad as a hatter," Agent Whiteman declared.

He probably *was* certifiable, Thornton thought. But Martfeld's lack of sanity concerned him less than the location of the terrorists' next target. The old man wasn't going to tell. Chances were he didn't know and didn't really care.

Even an FBI database on the clues discovered in Rasem Jameel's handwriting on the back of his traffic ticket proved less than revealing in locating the site of the intended attack.

"There are 104 cities listed containing an Eastland Apartments," research clerks informed Thornton. "Sixty-five have a Kneeland Street and 308 have some form of Kingston T— Kingston Thoroughfare, Kingston Turnpike, Kingston Tunnel. . . ."

"How many have all three features?"

"Let's see . . . uh, twenty-six."

"Get me a printout of those twenty-six cities," he requested.

When Thornton had the printout, he notified law enforcement in all twenty-six cities to check their Eastland Apartments for Shukri Abu Marzook and Rasem Jameel and notify the FBI immediately if they were located. The police were also told to attempt to identify any other Middle Easterners who might occupy Eastland Apartments or houses and apartments in the vicinity. They were to be detained if they so much as dropped a cigarette on the sidewalk.

Thornton assumed that ACLU attorneys, human rights groups, and other attack dogs led by men such as Senator Tayloe and former-President John Stanton were already howling about "racial profiling." But how else did you stop Middle Eastern terrorists without racial profiling? he wondered. As a black man, he knew that if the situation pointed to blacks, he wouldn't have his agents hounding Italians or Jews. They would be taking a close look at every African-American they saw in the wrong place.

Political correctness disgusted Thornton, particularly while the United States literally fought for its survival as a free nation.

He scanned the city database printout for perhaps the twentieth time, as though to witch the correct city as his grandpa used to witch water wells down in Mississippi. Edgy and eager to be in action, he glared at the paper, daring it to hide anything from him. His secretary came on the intercom.

"Chaplain Kragle is here."

"Good. Send him right in."

Cameron strode in wearing jeans and a flannel shirt, with an open jacket over it to ward off the autumn Atlantic chill. His blond crew cut looked moist from the Virginia coastal fog.

"Is this the federal government in action, you and your secretary on the job before daybreak?" he asked with a smile.

"Four people my daddy always said you never keep waiting—the Father, the Son, the Holy Ghost, and the preacher. How you doing, Chaplain?"

Cameron had driven up from Fort Bragg in the hopes of helping the agent brainstorm where Cassidy might have gone in pursuit of Jameel. Surely there was some clue, if they could just uncover it.

"Could you use some coffee?" Thornton asked. "Did you drive all night?"

After some quick catch-up and promise of breakfast, they got down to business. There was no time to waste.

"I think best when I'm driving," Cameron said. "I've

thought about it until 'Kingston T' has worn a groove in my brain, but I can't come up with anything. I'm sorry. I'm not sure I'm going to be much help."

"Look at this and see if anything strikes a bell." Thornton handed him the printout. "There are twenty-six cities that contain all three features."

Sipping coffee to give himself a boost after a sleepless night, Cameron sat down on the chair in front of the desk, crossed his legs, and started down the column of names. He went over the list twice before he set his coffee cup on the edge of the desk.

"Anything?" Thornton asked.

"I don't know." He tapped a city name with his finger. "I keep coming back to Boston. Gloria took us there when we were kids to visit some of her relatives. Cassidy and Kathryn went there on their honeymoon for a couple of days before they continued on to Niagara Falls and Canada. But I don't see what Jameel—"

He caught himself. Thornton leaned forward across his desk.

"You remembered something?"

"Maybe. When Cassidy and Kathryn returned from their honeymoon, they gave a slide show at their new house for friends. Jameel and I went. I remember Jameel saying he had never been to Boston but had always wanted to go. He called it the 'cradle of democracy,' the 'Athens of America.' He asked a lot of questions. I don't know if that means anything now or not."

"It apparently meant something to Cassidy," Thornton said, pondering. He stood up. "If you were a terrorist, where would you make your statement—the Athens of America, Porkopolis, or City of the Big Shoulders?"

CHAPTER 42

Boston

The 9mm Glock semiautomatic pistol snugged into the back waistband of his jeans exerted a comforting feeling against Cassidy's bare skin, a constant reminder of what he had to do. In his pocket, he carried the scarf Kathryn had liked to wear on windy days.

Eastland Apartments weren't difficult to locate. Last spring after Kathryn and he were married, they came to Boston as part of their honeymoon trip. They walked Freedom Trail to see the colonial historic sites—Paul Revere's house, Samuel Adams's grave, the birthplace of Benjamin Franklin, the site of the Boston Massacre . . . They drove to the New England Aquarium and the site of the Boston Tea Party, taking the Fitzgerald Expressway to the Kingston Tunnel and getting lost on Kneeland Street trying to find their way back to Boston Common. These names on the back of Jameel's speeding citation, plus all the questions he recalled Jameel asking about Boston the night of the side show, cued Cassidy as to where the Saudi might be going into hiding. It was worth coming up to find out. With his gun.

Cassidy gave a friendly smile to the elfin apartment manager. He had a pencil-line mustache and hair grown long on one side and brushed to cover baldness on top. Cassidy wore a ball cap pulled low above his eyes and some lightly tinted sunglasses to help disguise his features.

"I'm looking for an old buddy, sir," Cassidy said. "I wasn't sure your office was open this early."

The tidy man smiled back. "We're open all night. We have the motel there where you first came in. What's your buddy's name?"

"Rasem Jameel."

"Nope. Don't think so. Sounds like Lebanese or something."

"Actually, sir, he's a Saudi."

"We only got one Middle Eastern type and that's not his name. He's had a couple of visitors, though, the past few days. They're quiet and don't cause nobody any problems, so I haven't said anything."

"My buddy's a skinny kind of a little guy with a thin face and a military haircut."

"Hmmm. Could be, son. The other guy's older and wears an expensive black leather jacket."

"Shorter but stocky, muscular?"

"That's him all right."

Cassidy felt a sense of exultation. It seemed his hunch had paid off.

"I hope your friends aren't in trouble," the manager said.

"Why's that, sir?"

"Some cops were in here before daylight asking questions." He walked over to the office window and made a gesture. "That's their car down there by the motel. Cops think just because they wear plainclothes, nobody knows who they are. They've been sitting down there watching the apartment for about two hours now."

"Thank you, sir. I'm sure they have the wrong people. What apartment are they in, sir?"

"That's 221. It's upstairs. You can see the front door from here. They don't act like terrorists or anything."

Sergeant Rasem Jameel didn't act like a terrorist at Fort Bragg either, but Cassidy believed that he'd murdered Kathryn as surely as if he placed a gun to her head and pulled the trigger.

He gave the unmarked police car at the motel a casual passing glance as he went out, sufficient to see that the two plainclothesmen inside paid him little attention. He didn't fit the stereotype. He readjusted the pistol underneath his shirt, got into his blue Mustang, and slowly drove down the street, which curved deeper into the complex of two-story brick and wood town houses and apartments. They all had balconies. He quickly located 221's upstairs balcony. It overlooked another parking lot out of sight of the cops.

Sliding glass doors reflected the red sky of the coming sunrise. The drapes were pulled and there was no sign of movement. It was early enough on a Friday that the mostly young residents of the complex weren't up yet, getting ready for work or to go to college classes. Cassidy parked and waited a few minutes, observing. He took Kathryn's scarf out of his pocket and drew in her scent from it. It brought back memories. Memories were all he had of her now. Thanks to Rasem Jameel.

"You and the baby we're going to have are the only good things that came out of Afghanistan," she often remarked. "You are what kept me sane in that dreadful place among those horrible people."

They escaped al-Qaeda once, only for Kathryn to fall victim to the terrorists in her own country. Cassidy had exacted a terrible revenge against the rat-faced Amal who raped Kathryn. He intended taking a similar reprisal against

Jameel, and to hell with his own soul, if that was what it took, he thought, and to hell with whatever became of him before the hereafter got there. Cameron could pray for him if that made him feel better.

The General's youngest son was about to commit murder. Get in, get the job done, get the hell out again, and establish an alibi. With luck, the police and the FBI would think Jameel was killed in a dispute with another terrorist. Terrorists were unstable people, after all.

Committed to the path, the young Green Beret left the car and shimmied up a drainpipe. At the top, he caught hold of the porch railing around the balcony by gripping the pipe with one hand and stretching with the other. He swung loose underneath, then quickly pulled himself up and over the railing. He looked around to make sure he hadn't been seen. A young woman walked across the parking lot to her Volkswagen, but she seemed absorbed in reading a newspaper.

Cassidy tried the sliding glass doors. They were unlocked. He drew his pistol, chambered a round, then slipped into the apartment with the weapon ready to fire. He found himself alone inside the kitchenette dining room. He paused, alert and watchful, to let his eyes adjust to the dimness. All the lights were off, and shades appeared to be drawn throughout. He heard nothing other than the hum of the refrigerator and the ticking of a clock on the wall.

As he became accustomed to the dim light, he could see that the wallpaper was blue and the tile floor littered with scraps of food. Like the floor, the kitchen table was cluttered with debris. These people lived like pigs, he thought. On the table sat a large lidded jar containing remnants of a white powder. Curious, he edged around the table, keeping the door leading into the darkened living room covered with his gun. He saw several empty egg cartons stacked on a chair, while broken eggshells lay scattered on the floor and underneath the table. The floor felt sticky to his feet from the breakage. A large bowl on the stove was full of the contents of the eggshells. Two hot glue guns rested on the counter next to the bowl.

These people had messy cooking habits. So many eggs!

Then it dawned on him. The shopping list on the back of the Jameel citation: eggs, glue, pack. What he discovered here was a bomb-making factory of sorts. The "bombs" were eggs out of which the insides had been sucked, replaced with anthrax powder and glued closed again. The enormity of what he saw, the pure evil of it, caused his gun hand to tremble.

Today, he realized with a jolt, was the nineteenth, a date that apparently meant enough to Jameel to write it down with his shopping list and his directions to Eastland Apartments. Something was about to happen today, in Boston, and Cassidy thought he knew what it was. Boston with all its American history was the perfect site for terrorists to make a statement in corpses.

He took a deep breath and sprang into the living room, weapon at the ready. The living room was also a mess, with clothing, pizza boxes, beer cans, and other clutter strewn about. A man lay on the sofa, faceup, unmoving. A blanket covered him from the waist down, leaving his bare chest exposed. Cassidy strode over and thrust the muzzle of the Glock against the guy's temple.

"Wake up, Cinderella!" he snapped.

The man was as stiff as a board—dead. Stunned, Cassidy backed away.

He searched the rest of the apartment, finding it unoccupied, before he returned to the dead man. Something about him looked familiar. His eyes remained half open and staring sightlessly—into Mecca or Valhalla, he thought, or wherever it was dead Muslim tangos went to claim their virgins. The cheeks were sunken and unshaved. The skin had lost its tone and healthy coloring. Dried puke smeared his lips, and dried blood formed a large scab on his upper lip and nose.

Nonetheless, Cassidy recognized him as the dark, slick-haired man in the black leather coat with whom Jameel had quarreled that night in the Wal-Mart parking lot. Agent Thornton called him Mullah Shukri something-or-other. From the looks of things, the poor bastard got sick and died from his own poison. Served him right, Cassidy thought.

He returned to the kitchen to search for clues as to where Jameel and his friends might go to deliver their diabolical hatches of eggs. He was still driven by personal desire for revenge, but another thought slowly took form. This thing was becoming much bigger than he and Jameel. Thousands of other lives had entered the equation.

They would want to strike at some event, some attraction that drew large crowds. A concert, perhaps, or a racetrack or ball game. A political gathering, rally, or celebration. Cassidy tossed aside some public transportation schedules, but went back to them when he discovered nothing else of interest. This time he noticed that certain stations on both the subway and the Amtrak schedule were circled in red ink, while the front of each was marked with an initial: R on the subway, Z on the Amtrak. R for Rasem? he wondered. Z for . . . Zaccarias? Wasn't that the other name on Jameel's citation?

The morning rush hour to work and school peaked in about an hour. Nearly three million people lived in the Greater Boston area. Each weekday, more than 500,000 passengers were transported on buses, streetcars, subways, trains, and trolley cars. How simple it would be for a few passengers innocently carrying bags of groceries or book packs to surreptitiously bust an egg now and then in opportune places where the spread of anthrax would reach the greatest number of victims. Hundreds of thousands of people could easily become infected, far too many to be treated in time. It would be an epidemic unlike anything seen in the world since the Bubonic Plague of the Middle Ages.

It seemed that Rasem and Zaccarias had made no attempt to cover their tracks. Were they also terminally ill from anthrax? Had they chosen to pull a martyrdom mission like the airliner hijackers and meet Allah in a blaze of glory? What else could it be?

Was it already too late to stop them?

Sobered by the prospect of so many people getting sick and dying the same way Kathryn died, Cassidy changed his plans. He still intended to go after Jameel, but he needed some help to stop "Z" and whoever else might be involved in the plot. He couldn't simply think of his own selfish motives when confronted with this kind of evil in the making.

Working rapidly, driven by renewed energy, he copied down the red-coded "R" subway stations on a piece of paper, then scrawled a note on one of the schedules: *Call FBI. Agent Thornton. Urgent.* He placed both schedules on the dead man's chest where they were sure to be found. He didn't have time to hang around and explain.

He opened the front door so the stakeout police were certain to observe movement. Staying out of sight, he fired two shots into the ceiling to make sure the cops came running. He glanced through the window curtains to be positive. Satisfied, he returned the gun to his waistband, dashed out the back of the apartment and across the balcony, hanging momentarily from his fingertips before dropping to the flower beds below.

Cassidy sprinted for the Mustang. His personal revenge had become much more. He knew that thousands of lives depended on what he did within the next hour or so.

PRESIDENT ACCUSES CONGRESS

WASHINGTON (CPI)—In the wake of a controversy surrounding U.S. Special Operations forces in Afghanistan, the President of the United States yesterday accused members of Congress of leaking military secrets to the news media for political advantage.

"It is unacceptable behavior to leak classified information when we have troops at risk," he said. "It's a serious matter, very serious. I intend to protect our troops."

Although he did not mention names, the President was speaking particularly of Operation Iron Weed. Senator Eric B. Tayloe, head of the powerful Armed Services Committee, is chairing investigations into Iron Weed, which he claims may be committing "possible illegal acts and war crimes" in targeting top Taliban and al-Qaeda leaders.

At issue is Executive Order 12333 of 1981, which forbids the U.S. government from "engaging in, or conspiring to engage in, assassination." Secretary of Defense Donald Keating has asked the U.S. Supreme Court for a decision on whether the U.S. can legally "assassinate people in foreign countries who commit terrorist acts."

"As it stands," Keating said, "there is no question but that the ban does have some effects. It restricts certain things the government can and cannot do."

In response to the President's charges, Senator Tayloe said the leaks came from the administration itself, not from members of Congress. He demanded that the President keep congressional leaders informed about Operation Enduring Freedom and the war on terrorism rather than restricting their access.

During congressional hearings this week, Tayloe issued a warning that General Darren E. Kragle, commander of U.S. Special Operations Command, will be held in contempt of Congress unless he withdraws assassination teams operating in Afghanistan. His deadline for withdrawal ends Monday.

Senator Tayloe is seen as a likely presidential contender for the next election.

"He's attempting to fill the void as the peace candidate alternative to the destructive war policies of the President," former President John Stanton said. "He has the right as well as the duty to criticize. That is the role of Congress. Congress is a coequal branch of government, and I don't think it ought to rubber-stamp any President as we get into these very difficult decisions. This war is a failure, a disaster waiting to happen, and it's up to the loyal opposition to point it out in time to avert another world war."

The President sent a memo to Capitol Hill restricting top secret congressional briefings to only the House and Senate majority and minority leaders. The chairman of the Senate Armed Services Committee would be excluded from the briefings. Senator Tayloe said his office would release a statement later in the day, in which he is expected to criticize the President's decision.

CHAPTER 43

Afghanistan

The man the Americans called Vince Lombardi went down hard in the ambush's first volley, falling and rolling back downhill until Ice Man caught him. Ice Man switched his M-60 machine gun to his left hand to leave his right free. He grabbed the fallen mujahideen by his battle harness and started dragging him to the side like a sack of wheat. Summer, who had screamed with alarm when the fusillade exploded in their faces, was otherwise unharmed and ran to help.

Ahead and to the left lay a small relatively level area strewn with large boulders, a natural fortress snugged into the base of a sheer cliff that towered eighty feet above. Major Kragle spotted it and selected it as the only hasty defensive position within reach. He stood upright at its edge, yelling and directing his men toward it while bullets shrieked past, kicked up geysers at his feet and ricocheted off rock.

Several of the Deltas and at least one other Afghan limped or grasped limbs or other body wounds as the patrol swarmed into the fortress and took cover behind boulders. Brandon glanced out toward the kill zone to make sure no one was left behind. If not for the steepness of the incline, which partially masked the detachment from the blocking force, and the enemy's overeagerness to open fire, half of them would be dead or dying by now. As it was, only a couple of dropped rucksacks and Vince Lombardi's rifle remained out there.

A bullet tugged at Brandon's robe. He dove for cover.

Green tracers from enemy machine guns streaked and flared, making a spectacular spiderweb of pulsating psychedelic color as they bounced off the cliff. The men were banging back now, shouting and burning up ammo at an alarming rate. Winnie Brown had the M-203 unlimbered. He lobbed grenades toward the blocking force as fast as he could fire, breach, reload, and pull the trigger again. Bright explosions stamped among the enemy uphill.

Ice Man, though wounded during the mad rush, set up the M-60 on a bipod to cover the most likely avenue of enemy approach from below. A fresh belt of bright 7.62 trailed into a box attached to the gun. Grim-faced and tight-lipped as always, the former kick boxer posed as though waiting for an opening to end the fight in the first round.

Doc TB threw down his weapon and went to work with his aid bag. Lying prone next to Vince Lombardi behind a cluster of rock, he spiked an IV into a vein. He opened the wounded man's clothing and slapped the plastic container from a MERC ration over the sucking chest wound. He felt underneath for an exit wound. Finding none, he shouted at Summer.

"Ismael? Yeah, over here. Put your hands over this and press. Keep it airtight or his lungs will deflate."

The big medic was already covered with blood up to his elbows. More blood smeared his beard. Calmly nodding his approval of Summer's ministration, he looked around for his next patient.

The critical and most deadly minute of the initial ambush was over. The blocking force went to hole, as did the enemy force moving up from below to apply pincers.

"Hold your fire! Hold your fire!" Brandon ordered, a command quickly taken up by Mother Norman. Every bullet counted in a long fight.

Firing spattered off to an occasional round. Even the attackers ceased shooting. An eerie quiet settled over the mountainside, as though everyone opted to take a breather in between rounds.

"Save ammo for when they rush us," Brandon called out as he assessed the situation.

The fortress, he saw now, was semicircular against the cliff face, about fifty feet in circumference, and soft with gravel and sand. Oddly enough, large rocks and boulders appeared to have been moved out of the center and piled around it, as though another outfit had once made a stand there.

"Dig in deep," he encouraged, although little encouragement was needed. "Two-man fighting holes. One of you dig, the other maintain defense. Winnie, you team with the Dog. Mad Dog, get to work on those radios. Sergeant Norman, I need a damage and assessment. I'm going to take a look along the cliff."

As the men dug in behind the boulders, scraping and mining with rifle butts, knives, or, like gophers, with their bare hands, Brandon crawled on his belly along the base of the cliff. It rose so sheer above him that even a tree toad with its suction cup toes might have taken a second look. Escape downhill was also out of the question. The ground was too exposed and under the command of the attackers. Uphill appeared the only hope.

He eased forward until, by raising his head an inch or so, he saw the cleft in the wall Saeed had pointed out earlier. That was where the camel trail began. From the looks of it, the trail was cut into the visage of the cliff itself. One side of the rock rose like a sheet of rough glass, while it dropped off from the path on the other side into an abyss.

He raised his head another inch to get a better look. A rifle rattled on full auto. He ducked instinctively. The firing came from a mound of rock near the entrance to the Silk Road. Lead thumped and shrieked. A bullet bit his cheek. He felt a sting and blood, but it was nothing serious. A mere scratch. He backed off.

There was no soft-soaping it. They were in a fix, surrounded by a superior force with their backs literally between a rock and a hard place.

"We're pinned down. I don't see a way out," Brandon confided to his top sergeant. "We're going to be here awhile. Prepare for a siege."

Norman's rusty beard looked grayer than ever. "Your face is bleeding, sir."

"I'm okay. What about the others?"

"Doc was hit in the arm, a flesh wound. The kid has grit. He patched himself up and wouldn't have said anything about it except I saw him bleeding. Ice Man was grazed across the chest, but he's back in the fight. So is Thumbs. One of the moojies got hit in the buttocks. As for Vince Lombardi, I don't think he'll make it. The ground's soft enough that everybody's almost dug in. Gloomy's digging one for you now."

He paused in his report to look out over the battleground, still quiet at the moment.

"They'll know they've been in a fight, sir."

They were doubly SOL without commo and the capability to call in air support—*if* the weather lifted and airplanes flew. Right now it looked like the weather intended to worsen instead of get better. Brandon rolled over onto his back and studied the morning gray. The wind was lifting with the coming of daylight, and sand grit was diminishing. However, the ceiling hovered lower than ever and looked ominous. A light snow swirled before his eyes, and his breath condensed into a cloud and formed ice crystals in his beard. If the temperature kept dropping, it was going to get as cold as a well digger's ass.

Summer came up after helping Doc TB, crawling fast.

"Vince Lombardi is dead," she said without emotion. Saeed translated the news for the mujahideen. Uddin let out a single painful wail and dropped his head. Bilal—Vince Lombardi—was his brother.

Brandon had a feeling Bilal wasn't going to be the only casualty before this fight was over.

The slam of the BMP's 73mm cannon brought them back to the reality of their predicament. It reverberated through the mountain passes. The first round, earlier, had been short. This one was long, pocking into the cliff above their heads and exploding stinging rock down onto them. Brandon saw what the gunner was doing, bracketing until he found their range. The next round should land right in the middle of the fortress. Winnie Brown jumped down in the bottom of his hole and began digging with both hands like a dog burying a bone.

Then the gun stopped firing.

"What the hell's going on?" Mad Dog called out.

Brandon recognized the strategy. Ammunition for the big gun was apparently limited. It had got its target's range and now it would wait until the assault elements were in place for an attack before it opened up final prep fire to soften the objective. Classic infantry–artillery tactics.

Glassing through the haze of smoke and dust hanging over the defenses, Brandon watched the squatty armored vehicle sitting confidently in the open while its crew leisurely went about the business of preparing another shot. The tank commander had his head and shoulders sticking up out of the forward hatch. He also peered through binoculars. Snow swirled around his wind-whipped blue headdress and stuck to his heavy beard.

Closer, al-Qaeda soldiers maneuvered on the stronghold, using available cover and concealment, occasionally firing but mostly ducking and dodging.

"Easy, lads, easy," Brandon counseled, his voice steady and controlled. "Hold your fire."

No sense wasting ammunition at this range, which was what the enemy wanted them to do.

"I can smell their armpits already, boss," Gloomy remarked.

"Wait until you can smell what they had for breakfast. The BMP will fire for effect before the attack. As soon as it quits, expect hell to break loose. Make every shot count."

Summer worked frantically on deepening the fighting hole she shared with the Delta commander. Brandon had never seen her looking so crunched before. He caught her eye. Her eyes were the bright emerald he remembered from the West Bank in Israel, so like Gypsy's that they made him catch his breath.

"Your eyes . . . ?"

"I had to remove my contacts during the sandstorm if I wanted to see," she explained. "What difference does it make now? Isn't this where it's the fourth quarter, fourth down coming up, one minute to go, we're behind in the big game, and Knute Rockne steps up with his pep talk?"

"I guess I'm fresh out. Do you need one?"

She stood up in the hole and shrugged. The depth came up to her shoulders. "Will you be here with me when . . . when it happens?"

"Why're you talking that way?"

"I've taken off my rose-colored contacts, Major. I can see

how things are." She lowered her voice. "I'm glad it happened," she said. "You know, the other night."

Brandon felt a sudden tenderness toward her that he had rarely experienced. She still looked tough, with the determined set of her jaw, but he recognized in her the vulnerability that often lay underneath the exteriors of tough women. He realized he'd been aware of that quality in her, and excited by it, when they were together in the trees.

He regretted she had to be here.

Feeling uncomfortable and distracted by the direction the conversation took, Brandon looked for a way out. Ice Man and Doc TB continued to dig loudly, the sounds they made echoing against the backdrop of the cliff. Winnie Brown stacked a little pile of 40mm grenades on a constructed ledge inside his hole so he could reach them easily and quickly. Gloomy Davis settled in with Mr. Blunderbuss and methodically went about adjusting its sights and preparing for the killing to begin. Mad Dog dismantled the radios and was cleaning parts and blowing into them.

Summer touched Brandon's cheek. "You're still bleeding." Her hand lingered. Gloomy noticed the exchange and looked puzzled.

"It's only a scratch."

"Another Purple Heart. How many does that make?"

"You're the one who seems to know everything. You tell me. What was it? Did the CIA brief you?"

"Only as far as it affected the mission," she admitted.

"You knew about Gypsy Iryani. She has nothing to do with the mission."

"I accessed that little piece of history out of personal interest. I wondered what type of woman a man like you would want."

"And what kind of a man am I?"

She cocked her head to one side in thought. "Resourceful,

tough, a good small-unit commander, maybe the best there is in Delta or Special Forces. And a real sonofabitch at times. From what I hear, you must be a lot like your father."

"Nobody's like the General. In Vietnam, the gooks broke both his legs for trying to escape from a POW camp—and he still escaped and made it out. *That* is tough."

"What was your mother like?"

"She's dead."

"I know she's dead, but what was she like?"

She had a way of drawing things out of him.

"I think I must have been about six when she died. What I remember the most is the funeral at the Farm."

"The Farm?"

"It's been in the family for generations. It's in Tennessee. The original cabin is still there. The main house—at least the central core of it—is over a hundred years old. I love it there. Maybe you'll see it sometime."

"I'd like that. Will you take me? How did your mom die? An accident?"

"Childbirth. She died when my brother Cassidy was born. The General led the way down through the trees to the family cemetery while Gloria carried Cassidy."

"Who's Gloria?"

"I thought you knew everything."

Brandon smiled. He almost saw the chubby black woman fussing around the General, ordering him about, wagging her finger at him and scolding him that he had better not let anything happen to *her* boys.

"How to describe Gloria?" he mused. "Gloria is who kept us from growing up on motherless biscuits."

"You love her like a mother, don't you?"

The Kragle men rarely talked of love. That was private and kept hidden in their innermost feelings. He changed the subject.

"And what kind of woman did you decide I would like?" he asked.

She looked at him out of those incredible green eyes. They were honest and wide, and he saw the wiseass Ismael nowhere in them. "Someone like me," she said before they were interrupted by a *craaaack!* and a shrill whine ripping through the air, superheating the atmosphere with the projectile's passage.

"Incoming!" someone shouted.

Brandon threw Summer to the bottom of the pit and covered her body with his. The shell landed with a terrific bang. The earth shook like a dog trying to shake off fleas. The air filled with dust and choking smoke.

More shells landed in the middle of the fortress, detonating in tremendous deadly geysers of blasting gravel and shrieking shrapnel. It was then that the Deltas became aware of old bones raining down on top of them. A human skull bounced and fell into Gloomy's hole on top of him.

"Jesus Christ—!"

He hefted the yellowed skull. Dried strips of skin and hanks of hair remained attached to the cranium. It grimaced eerily back at him.

Elsewhere, Winnie Brown complained of being pelted with skeleton parts. Even Ice Man broke his silence to protest.

"Major, we're in a graveyard."

"How appropriate," Gloomy commented wryly. He tossed the skull at Mad Dog's position. The Dog cursed—"Fuuck!"—when it hit him. "Dog, is this one of your old girlfriends? She reminds me a little of Arachna Phoebe—"

"We don't need your Hooker shit," Mad Dog growled. "Besides, look at the bright side. We're already in the graveyard. Saves all that crying bullshit at our funerals."

CHAPTER 44

Prep fire mauled and savaged the little graveyard fortress against the cliff and its band of defenders. A shell landed directly on Bilal's corpse where it lay stretched on the ground behind rocks, IV lines still in place. It erupted in a central bloody core that chunked scraps of flesh, bone, blood, and hair in all directions. Gore rained down, splattering. Part of a hand landed in the hole with Brandon and Summer. An eye attached to skin and hair hit Winnie Brown's turban. He brushed it off like it was an annoying insect.

Bilal's brother, Uddin, screamed as though the shell had exploded in his own vitals. Overcome with grief and rage, he scrambled from his hole as explosions cracked all around and charged the advancing enemy. The blaze of his AK on full auto added depth and substance to his otherworldly howling. Machine-gun fire cut him down, chewing one arm completely off. It took him a minute or two to die. His screaming slowly subsided with his rapid loss of blood. He thumped and writhed against the ground until nothing remained except a long, final drawn-out moan.

It was a hell of a messy way to die—but in battle there were many messy ways to die.

There was no time to dwell on one man's death. Taliban

and al-Qaeda warriors hiding in the rocks along the hillside and below the fortress were getting ready to attack. Brandon heard them talking and giving orders. Premature firing broke out here and there. The hidden machine gun uphill laced the area with streams of green tracers.

One-Alpha seemed momentarily stunned by the shelling and the sudden dying. Brandon knew that a loss of morale and fighting spirit could prove disastrous. Even hardened combat soldiers sometimes succumbed to it. Thinking quickly, he forced himself to laugh loudly and raucously. Summer stared at him as if he'd lost his mind.

"Laugh!" he shouted. "Laugh, damn you! *Everybody laugh!*"

Mother Norman understood. He added a shrill cackle to his commander's laughter. Summer laughed, joined by Mad Dog. It was contagious. It was inspired. Snickers and sniggers, chortles and guffaws and loud hooting. It broke the psychological hold the enemy expected to exert over its victims. Not only that, but the reverse psychology of it unnerved the enemy and broke the momentum of the forthcoming attack. The detachment hurled catcalls, insults, and taunts, all punctuated by the wild mirth.

"You are *all* crazy!" Summer decreed.

The BMP lobbed in a curtain of fire, the explosions stamping back and forth across the target. It ceased abruptly, leaving acrid clouds of smoke and dust oozing into the thickening veil of falling snow.

"Here they come!"

The terrorist horde burst out of the rocks firing their weapons, bellowing war cries and shouting to Allah, leaders up front attempting to restore energy. Laughter ceased, but the defenders were once more determined, focused, and deadly professional. Tongues of flame stabbed back into the attackers. Juking and fencing, crazed by blood and faith in receiving their virgins if they died, flitting bearded dervishes in turbans, headdresses and billowing filthy robes leaped and raced toward the defensive perimeter. A scene right out of Kipling, Brandon thought, and a phrase came to his mind.

Stand up and take the war.
The Hun is at the gate . . .

The Hun was indeed at the gate. Point-blank range, coming for the throat. The discordant cacophony of the battle surged to deafening levels in waves of opposing rifle and machine-gun fire. But while battles are won or lost by troops, individual men do the fighting.

Ice Man's M-60 chewed a swath into the onslaught, tracers red and stabbing at such close range, leaving men shattered and broken and screeching in agony.

Sergeant Winnie Brown launched 40mm grenades from his M-203 as fast as he could fire and reload.

Doc TB relinquished his aid bag for his M-16 and engaged in a one-on-one duel with a rifleman in the rocks almost directly in front of him.

The detachment's demo man, Thumbs Jones, with his partiality for demolitions and things that went bang, hurled frag grenades at targets concealed in the boulders.

Brandon and Summer fought side by side from their shared fighting hole.

"The family that fights together stays together," she managed, her uncharacteristic depression having been replaced by Ismael's old spirit.

The fight immediately disintegrated into individual contests as the enemy closed and broke through the lines here and there. An Arab leaped high out of the turmoil, flailing his arms and screaming his hatred as he landed on top of Mad Dog. Although not exceptionally tall, the Dog was built like a gorilla. He flung the smaller man from him, vaulted out of his hole on top of him, and with a quick twist of his thick hands snapped the man's neck.

Two fighters charged Brandon and Summer. She coolly blasted one with her carbine, the high-velocity slugs ripping a pink mist from his body and stopping him in his tracks. Brandon disposed of the second, his stubby MP-5 making the sound of ripping cloth. The body dropped not an arm's length away from the rucksacks that formed the position's bulwarks.

The attack broke against such deadly resistance. The terrorist army turned and ran. Firing crackled down to an occasionally pop-off from the less disciplined enemy fighters. A number of bodies lay strewn among the rocks like old bags of bloody clothing. Screams and moans issued from the tortured throats of the wounded.

"Sergeant Norman, assess and redistribute ammo," Brandon called out, already crawling from hole to hole to check men and equipment.

Gloomy Davis suffered a grazing scalp wound, painful and bloody but not serious. His fighting buddy Saeed had taken a round through the fleshy part of his upper arm, also painful but not dangerous.

The detachment was getting itself shot all to hell.

"Mother Norman . . . ?"

"Major . . . over here . . ."

Overtaken by icy dread, Brandon scrabbled to the hole Mother Norman had shared with Uddin before the Afghan sacrificed himself in anguish over his brother. The red-bearded team sergeant lay crumpled low in the pit. Breath rattled in his throat.

"Sorry I can't . . . get up right now, sir."

Doc TB arrived. His look told Brandon everything as soon as he completed a cursory examination. The senior NCO had taken a bullet directly in the center of his sternum, a lung shot that also clipped the aortal artery. Blood gurgled in his throat as he attempted to speak.

"Doc . . . you're a good man. Patch—" He swallowed a mouthful of blood. "Patch me up . . . then get back to your post. . . ."

Lying on his belly at the edge of the pit, Brandon reached down and grasped the older man's rough hand. It was wet and sticky. "We'll get you out of here, Top."

"Sir . . . I know how bad I'm hit. Worry . . . Worry about the others. Put my . . . my weapon in my hand." He managed a weak grin. "I'll take . . . some of them with me when I go."

Brandon batted his eyes and pretended it was because of melting snowfall. Men working together in the teams and detachments got tight, real tight. He looked up at Doc.

"Give him morphine, Doc, and make him as comfortable as you can. Then put his weapon in his hands and get back to your position. They'll be coming again."

And this time, he thought, they won't be stopped.

During the lull, an eerie, echoing murmur rose from the ranks of the surrounding enemy. Saeed and the surviving Afghan, Kamla, got down on their hands and knees in the cover of the rocks and started bobbing, bowing and chanting toward the direction of Mecca.

"Dear God," Mad Dog prayed, "save us from the assholes who believe in You."

"The radios?" Brandon asked Mad Dog.

"The cell phones and Motorolas ain't getting a signal. We might have used Ismael's PC, except it's fucked up too. Especially now since it's got a bullet hole through it. That leaves the Turkey-43 and the PRC-137. Give me a few more minutes and I think I'll have the 137 going."

Without the radios, Brandon knew, they were in this fight, alone—and no one harbored any illusions about surviving it.

Even if Northern Alliance troops down the valley heard the battle—even with his uncle Mike there encouraging them—they weren't apt to commit themselves. All they could do was send to Allah as many of the bad guys as possible, Brandon thought, and laughed softly—he hoped there weren't enough virgins to go around.

The mercury dropped by the minute. The fall of snow thickened and skimmed a thin layer across the ground, with the promise of more to come. A brief period had ensued between the end of the blowing sand and the start of the snow when the cloud ceiling lifted and tactical aircraft could fly out of Bagram. Brandon surmised the window of opportunity had now closed. Thick, gray clouds hung almost low enough to touch.

Gloomy shivered. "It's gonna get *cold* tonight. Reminds me of the winter of 'ninety back in Hooker. My mama yelled at me out in the barn to come to the house, but her words froze in the air. We had to put them in a frying pan to thaw them out."

"You are so full of shit," said Ice Man, which was a major speech for him.

It was quiet now. The prayers were over. The men were alert and waiting for the next round. It was the waiting, Brandon knew, that destroyed you.

He watched snow lightly falling on the face of the al-Qaeda he'd killed in front of the rucksack bulwarks of his hole. It melted on the skin because the body still retained heat, but it accumulated in his beard and in the long black hair exposed when he'd lost his headgear.

Snow would be falling like that on Summer's dyed-black hair after the next charge, he thought. Virtually every defender was wounded. Two of the Afghans were dead and an American operator, Mother Norman, would soon join them. Brandon listened to stealthy movements all around as the terrorist army worked into position. Falling snow absorbed sound and allowed them to get close. The BMP remained quiet, but he knew it was loaded and ready.

There was no way they could hold out much longer. He'd failed his mission, he thought. He had failed his father.

Winnie Brown placed the disinterred skull on top of a rock to construct a grisly shrine looking out at the enemy.

"Ismael?" Gloomy called out. "Saeed is trying to tell me something about this place. What's he saying?"

Summer translated, her voice reaching every silent defender. He had heard about this place, Saeed said. They were at the site of a mass grave where about fifty members of the Hazara minority were brought in 1998 and slaughtered by the Taliban. Sunni Muslims, who made up most of the Taliban, considered the Hazara a flawed version of Islam and attempted to eradicate them wherever they were found.

"When they come for us," Seed concluded, "do not expect any more mercy from them than they gave the Hazara. Always it is wise to save one bullet for yourself."

"Major?" Gloomy consulted.

Brandon swallowed. He throat felt parched. It was advice he didn't want to give. "That's up to you."

"They'll torture us if we're captured alive."

"If it's inevitable, I'd rather shoot myself," Summer inserted.

Brandon looked at her, then quickly looked away.

She softly spoke his first name. "Brandon." She said it again, "Brandon." It took her a moment to continue. "Will you do it for me if it must be done?" she asked. "I'd consider it an act of kindness, even an act of love."

The thought horrified him. He swallowed the lump of emotion in his throat and nodded, once, without looking at her.

"It's Rhodeman," Summer said, staring straight ahead over the dead man's body in the snowfall. Snow clung to her long lashes.

Brandon started. "What?"

"Summer Marie Rhodeman. I wanted you to know my name."

Brandon could think of nothing to say in return.

"It's true that I slept with terrorists in order to trap them," she confessed. "It was very ugly and sometimes I hate myself for it. It was only twice. They were monsters and deserved to die. Does that make me a monster too?"

The Ice Maiden was thawing in this her final hour. Brandon knew strong men, tough men, who broke down and cried under similar circumstances. Still, he wondered, even if they survived would there be room in her heart for anything other than revenge for the terrorist murders of her sisters? He hesitated before answering her, then slowly shook his head.

"You are no monster," he said.

"I never *made love* before you," she said, whispering and still not looking at him. "Do you believe that? I wanted you to know that it was different with you."

He reached out, took her hand and squeezed it hard before letting it go again. There was not much time left.

CHAPTER 45

"Fu-uck a duck!" Mad Dog suddenly sang out in jubilation. "Major. I got through! I got SFOB on the hook."

He and Winnie made room for Brandon to jump into their hole with them. They were positioned at the V of an ancient lava mass, in the shelter of which Mad Dog had erected his antenna. Grinning, Dog thrust the mike at his CO.

Brandon hesitated a moment to control the excitement in his voice. "Iron Weed Red, this is Iron Weed Green, over."

"Weed Green, this is Red."

"Request air support ASAP. Anything you have. Enemy near. Repeat, enemy near. I'm giving you the grid coordinates of our position in case we lose commo again. Prepare to copy."

"Go ahead, Green."

Brandon read the coordinates and the radio operator on the other end read the grid back.

"Affirmative," Brandon said. "Did you copy the situation is desperate? The bastards are all around us."

"Roger that. The bastards are all around you. We have some fast movers in the Gulf that may be able to get through the ceiling."

"Negative, Red. That's two hours. We can't hold out for

two hours. Do you have a Specter or something at Bagram
Air Base? Choppers maybe? Choppers are best. The wind is
down, but we have a ceiling of less than five hundred. If we
don't get air support, you can mark us off."

"Stand by, Green."

The Special Forces Operational Base in Uzbekistan exerted immediate control only of its own deployed elements in
the field. All other military assets had to be requested in a cir-
cuitous route through the U.S. Central Command in Tampa,
Florida. If CENTCOM approved, the request went to USSO-
COM for action. USSOCOM requested the desired assets directly from the Joint Task Force and the theater commander
of Afghanistan operations.

Brandon hoped all lines were functioning.

"Weed Green? Weed Red."

"Go ahead, Red."

"We're having a problem making contact. Give me an
hour and I'll try to have you something. We're also having
another problem. The weather is socking in everywhere."

An *hour*? They had to buy time somehow.

"Keep the channel open," Brandon admonished Mad Dog
as he sprang out to return to his own fighting hole.

"Like a drowning man on a rope, sir."

Brandon glassed the BMP. The tank commander in the
forward hatch glassed him back. It gave him an idea. He
tossed his binoculars to Gloomy and indicated the distant vehicle with a nod of his head.

"I make it eleven hundred meters," he said.

Gloomy looked and returned the binoculars. "More like
thirteen, boss." He made adjustments to the opticals on his
Winchester. "The visibility is poor through the snow. Wind's
coming uphill. It'll sheer off down there and change directions. But it's moderate. Shooting downhill into a canyon—"

"Can you do it?"

"Boss, you're asking the impossible—but I'll do it."

Brandon turned to Ice Man. "When Gloomy picks off the TC, it'll send the BMP scuttling for cover. It'll be cautious and less accurate from now on. At the same time, I want you to open up with the M-60 on the ragheads down there in the rocks. That'll make 'em less enthused about taking us on direct."

He raised his voice. "The rest of you! I want a mad minute. Spray everything out there. I want 'em disorganized and thinking about what's waiting for them the next time they attack. We need to buy as much time as we can get."

It seemed to take the sniper an eternity to get into his cocoon. He sighted in on his target, using the rucksack in front of his hole as a bench rest. Brandon kept his glasses on the tank commander, who was oblivious to the fact that in a few more seconds he would be on his way to Islam heaven.

Mr. Blunderbuss cracked spitefully. Brandon counted, still glassing the target. "One . . . two . . . three . . ." The tank commander's body jerked as if an invisible baseball bat had whacked him across the chest. He dropped into the vehicle, out of sight.

Brandon watched the BMP scurrying for cover behind a rock ledge as Ice Man led the chorus in a violent concerto, playing the lead instrument in three-burst rhythms, weaving a pattern of red tracers into the rocks among the hiding enemy soldiers. The rest of the detachment and the two Afghans released pent-up tensions through their triggers.

"Cease fire!"

That had to hold things for a while, Brandon hoped. Now 1-Alpha would wait.

"Major?" Mad Dog looked puzzled. "I still got SFOB on, but Weed Red says CENTCOM is cutting out on him. He says it's like somebody in Florida keeps hanging up."

That didn't make sense.

"That's what Red says. That's all I know."

"Sergeant, ask Red if he can circumvent CENTCOM."

Mad Dog held a conversation through his mike. "Sir, he says he no can do. Nothing moves unless it's approved first by CENTCOM and USSOCOM. It'll be his ass if he even tries."

"It'll be ours if he doesn't. Okay, okay. Try this. Can we get a SATCOM direct to CENTCOM ourselves?"

"I can try. If we got some satellites in position."

Long minutes dragged. From the sound of things out there, Mr. Blunderbuss and the mad minute had sown some confusion. Commanders yelled at their men and the men yelled back.

"They don't want to attack until the BMP has somebody else to replace the dead guy on the gun," Saeed explained through Summer.

Good. Brandon glanced at his watch.

"Sir, I got through."

Brandon crawled to the radio and snatched the mike.

"Iron Weed," said a voice. "You are out of your chain of command. We have orders to accept no communications without authentication. Are you prepared to copy? Authenticate—"

Brandon interrupted him. "We've been off the net because of battle complications. Besides, we don't have access to your CEOI."

"Authenticate bravo, tango, alpha, mike—"

"Did you hear me? We can't."

"Then we can't talk to you unless you go through proper channels—"

Brandon lost it. "Listen to me, you insufferable little prick. You contact USSOCOM right away—that's USSOCOM Six *personally*—and tell him what's happening. Understood?"

"This connection is terminated. Out."

Brandon stared at the mike and listened to dead air. The silence in the fortification turned even colder than the air temperature.

The attack began a half hour later, while Mad Dog still tried to insinuate communications through a different route. It was a tremendous salvo of rifle and automatic fire, but without prep from the BMP cannon. Brandon popped up, ready to give an accounting of himself. To his surprise, nothing moved out front.

His heart sank as, confused and disoriented, he realized what had happened. The shooting came from *behind* and high, from the top of the cliff. The enemy had flanked them and climbed to the top of the bluff in order to bring fire directly down onto them. Like shooting proverbial fish in a barrel.

He rolled around, bringing up his MP-5. The entire edge of the precipice sparked and crackled. A man up there jumped to his feet, waving and shouting. Brandon recognized the stocky figure and skunk-stripe beard of the traitor Bek Gorabic. It seemed he'd brought his pirates back to be in on the finish.

Brandon drew a bead on him and felt a surge of elation as his finger tightened on the trigger. Summer knocked his weapon aside.

"Wait! *Don't fire!*" she yelled. *"Don't fire. Don't fire!"*

Brandon failed to understand at first. Then he did. *"Hold your fire!"*

Bek was still howling at them.

"He's killing the Taliban!" Summer exclaimed. "He's telling us he's cleared the camel trail. We can get out. He's made an opening for us."

There was no time for questions. Commander Bek might be a sonofabitch, Brandon thought, but for the moment, and just in time, it seemed he was *their* sonofabitch.

CIA SUSPECTS TERRORISTS IN U.S. GOVERNMENT

KABUL (CPI)—The CIA has uncovered information that Taliban and al-Qaeda leaders may have inside sources within the U.S. government. The CIA is heavily involved in the Afghan conflict, working covertly to provide weapons, money, and intelligence to rebel groups opposing the Taliban and al-Qaeda. Paul Thomas, a paramilitary officer with the CIA's Special Activities Division, made a report stating that at least some al-Qaeda captives were aware of clandestine missions by U.S. Special Operations targeting Taliban ruler Mohammed Omar and al-Qaeda leader Osama bin Laden.

"We have many heroes inside the infidel American government," one captured al-Qaeda reportedly boasted. "Osama knows about Iron Weed. He is kept informed. Iron Weed will be stopped and all of them destroyed."

Shortly after he made this report. Thomas was killed during the bloody prison uprising at the northern Afghan fortress of Kala Jangi, where he was interrogating prisoners.

As of this writing, a detachment of Special Forces Delta troops operating under the code name Iron Weed has been out of contact for nearly twenty-four hours. It is feared the detachment may have been surrounded and cut off by the enemy in the Tora Bora region of the White Mountains.

"The destructive policies of this administration is leading to disaster," said former President John Stanton in a news conference earlier today.

"The loss of these brave young men in the Afghan mountains is only the beginning. Perhaps the American people, for whom I worked so hard to bring peace when I was President, will understand now how this administration is leading America blindly into body bags and pain."

Sources within the American delegation assigned to Saudi Arabia confirm that there may be leaks to al-Qaeda in Washington. According to this unnamed source, a man suspected of funneling intelligence from connections in Washington to Osama bin Laden through Saudi Arabia is being interrogated in Riyadh.

CHAPTER 46

Boston

"The white stuff in the jar on the table is anthrax, right?" The Boston plainclothesman, Sergeant Wheeler, rubbed his hand on the seam of his trousers. He'd actually *touched* the dead guy. "Does that mean we're contaminated?"

Wheeler glanced anxiously back at FBI Agent Claude Thornton and army chaplain Cameron Kragle as he led them upstairs to Room 221.

"There's nothing to be alarmed about if it's caught in time," Thornton assured the cop. "CDC and HazMat are on the way. They'll have medical people with antibiotics. Everyone in the apartment complex may have to be treated. But right now we have smellier skunks to skin. Sergeant, I want your people to evacuate the apartments and isolate this entire area without causing a panic. Lie if the news media gets wind of it. Tell them we have a gas leak."

He knew that story wouldn't last long. Police brass would soon be swarming all over the place, along with guys in white space suits driving big white step vans. The media wasn't going to believe that kind of turnout for an ordinary gas leak and the death of some guy who wasn't a celebrity.

To Thornton's relief, Boston looked to have been a good guess. It got better with additional facts. First of all, there was the suspected anthrax in the apartment of some Middle Easterners, one of whom was now dead. Second, the apartment manager with the wipe-over hair described his dawn visitor as a tall good-looking kid wearing tinted glasses and a dark military haircut underneath a baseball cap. The description matched Cassidy, in spite of his hasty attempt to disguise himself.

Wheeler explained how he and his partner happened to be at the complex. "We were on stakeout because of the FBI alert about Eastland Apartments and these two perps, Rasem Jameel and Shooker. Some guy named Zaccarias what's-his-name leased the apartment—"

"Zaccarias al-Tawwah," Cameron supplied.

"Whatever. These camel jock names all sound Greek to me. A couple of other Arab types were seen up here, so George and I were waiting for them to come out this morning so we could have a talk with them. Well, the door opened and we heard two gunshots."

"Did you see who fired them?" Thornton asked.

"We didn't see nobody. The shooter must have gone off the back balcony, because when we got up here there was just the stiff on the couch, and he wasn't getting up and talking."

Cameron's heart pounded. "The deceased . . . ? Was he shot?"

"Nah. He's stiff as a board. Been dead eight or ten hours."

The chaplain released a deep sigh of relief. Sergeant Wheeler opened the door to 221 but refused to go inside. "You guys go on in. It's your crime scene. I'm staying out here to start evacuating people. They ain't going to like it, even if there is a gas leak."

He looked inside, as if to make sure the victim hadn't gotten up and walked off.

"We left everything just like you see it now, including the note on the dead guy saying to call you. The guy who broke in must have left it."

Thornton and Cameron stepped inside. The shades were drawn. Cameron didn't know whether to hope the dead man was Jameel or not. Just what he needed, his brother charged with murder. He barely made out the still form in the dimness. They walked closer. It was the second time he felt relieved in almost as many minutes—first that there were no bullet holes in the corpse, second that it wasn't Jameel.

"Do you know him?" Cameron asked.

"I never had the pleasure of meeting him in person," Thornton replied. "He was missing in action when we raided his Sacred Land office in Dallas. But, yeah, I recognize him from his photos—Mullah Shukri."

He shook his shaved head, looking down on the remains. The note still lay on the man's chest, but Thornton had been a federal cop too long to go handling things at a crime scene without looking them over first.

"Died as a result of his own folly, most likely," he mused. "These fuckers are all nuts. Sorry about the French, Chaplain. Do you suppose there really are virgins in the afterlife?"

"It's a mistranslation," Cameron said dully.

"How's that?"

"In the Syra-Aramaic reading of the Koran, the word now written as *houri*, meaning virgin, is really *hur*, meaning white raisin."

Thornton chuckled. "You mean all these assholes dying as martyrs are gonna be given seventy-two white raisins instead of seventy-two virgins when they get to heaven? I'd like to see their faces."

As he spoke he slipped on a pair of rubber surgical gloves and picked up the note on the dead man's chest. *Call FBI. Agent Thornton. Urgent.* He studied it, frowning, as though it contained some hidden message he should understand but didn't. He showed it to Cameron.

"That's Cassidy's handwriting. He's been here."

Thornton nodded. "The question is, where is he now? And where's Jameel and whoever else is with him? Apparently, they were already gone when your brother got here."

The eggshells in the kitchen, the powder residue, today being the nineteenth . . . It all added up, Cameron realized. It meant that Jameel and his terrorist accomplices were about to strike somewhere in Boston, at some crowded place. Apparently, Cassidy discovered the plot for himself and was on his way to break it up and kill Jameel.

He knew Cassidy wouldn't have left the note behind and made sure the body was discovered unless he also intended to leave a clue.

"Claude, let me see that again. It's written on a subway schedule. The other is Amtrak. Here, look at this. Certain stations are circled in red ink."

They looked at each other, grim as the realization dawned on them.

"That's where they're gonna hatch their eggs!" Thornton exclaimed.

"There are only two schedules. One is marked R, the other Z. R for Rasem. Z for Zaccarias. Claude, Jameel is heading for the subway. That's where Cassidy will go."

Thornton looked at his watch. "Rush hour is just starting. Commuters will be boarding. . . . We don't have much time. We don't have *any* time."

They rushed from the apartment, Thornton on his cell phone with the police chief, issuing orders in his capacity as director of the National Domestic Preparedness Office.

"Chief, I'm sorry. I don't have time to explain. Trust me on this. Shut down all public transportation immediately. Send officers to every subway, Amtrak, and bus station everywhere in the Boston area . . . What're they looking for? Chief, my ass is as black as a lump of coal, and I'm telling you to do some racial profiling. If a guy looks like he's got a camel tied up outside, drag the poor bastard in and hold him . . . I know. I understand. But don't worry about the ACLU and lawsuits now unless you want half the population of Boston sick and dying because we can't treat them fast enough. We'll sort everything out later and apologize if we have to . . . Eggs. That's right, Chief. That's what we're looking for. Eggs."

Cameron knew that everyone who entered Apartment 221 had come in contact with deadly anthrax bacteria, including Cassidy. In Cassidy's current state of mind, he might succeed in stopping Jameel, but he would also destroy his army career and the rest of his life. Chances were he would run after he accomplished his mission and not seek medical aid until it was too late.

The horror of considering that as well as contemplating the release of plague upon the city made Cameron's heart race with dread. Finding either Cassidy or the terrorists in time seemed an impossible task. Public transportation in Boston involved thousands of miles of track and hundreds of carriers.

He muttered a prayer as he and Thornton sprinted toward the agent's car. Sergeant Wheeler cut across from the manager's office to intercept them, the tail of his sport coat flapping.

"Agent? Hold up a minute. We just got something on the radio you might be interested in. A scout car found an Arab at Amtrak. He was sick and vomiting and couldn't move. He'll be room temperature pretty quick from the sound of it, just like the crud upstairs. He had a backpack full of eggs."

"Unbusted?"

"So far."

"Keep 'em that way. Did he have a name?"

"He wasn't trying to hide it. He had a pocket full of ID. He's that Zaccarias guy."

That left Rasem Jameel and the subway.

CHAPTER 47

The fury of Cassidy Kragle's vengeance remained focused on the man who had weaseled himself into the Kragle trust zone and then betrayed it to kill Kathryn and her unborn child. That's how he saw it. It wasn't good enough that Jameel might himself be dying of anthrax infection. Cassidy needed to personally see him die. So much the better if he were stopped before he busted the eggs and fatally contaminated Boston.

Surely by now, he thought, the police and FBI had reached Eastland Apartments and realized that Boston was ground zero. Let them stop Zaccarias. He couldn't do it all.

He pulled into a convenience store to buy a city map. On it he located the nearest subway station the terrorists had circled in red on the schedule. It was logical to assume that Jameel would start at a convenient point and then deliver his lethal missiles in a consistent pattern. If he were to miss Jameel at the starting point, Cassidy reasoned, he might not catch up until after the Saudi ran out of eggs, dropping them at red-circled stations throughout the metropolitan area.

Everything depended on when Jameel and Zaccarias left the apartment—on how much of a head start they had.

As he drove, he heard MacArthur Thornbrew on the morning news warning the nation of weekend terrorist activity, particularly of bioterrorism. Although he warned people not to congregate, the Boston streets were congested with normal morning commuters. People hurried, and in their haste honked horns and mouthed insults at each other. An accident occurred in the subway station parking lot when two cars tried for a remaining parking place and reached it simultaneously. The drivers jumped out of their vehicles shouting at each other and causing a traffic jam. They might still be there quarreling, Cassidy reflected, when they sucked in the first anthrax bacteria.

Inextricably caught in the glut, Cassidy abandoned his car, leaving the engine running so cops could move it when they arrived. Afraid he might be too late, he sprinted along the parked lanes of traffic, his eyes frantically darting in search of Jameel's red Mazda. He refused to think of alternatives the terrorist might have selected, such as changing vehicles. He had to go with what he had—and if he was wrong . . .

Time was running out for the citizens of Boston. Cassidy readjusted the Glock in his waistband as he turned into another lane and saw the top of a red vehicle at the other end. He raced toward it.

"God's word says that we should not *murder*, not that we shouldn't kill under any conditions," Chaplain Cameron had preached to his warrior congregation at Fort Bragg. "The difference between *murder* and *kill* may lie in your heart. No matter how justified we might be in taking another human life, it becomes murder before God and therefore a violation of His commandments when we take life out of hate or jealousy or revenge."

Cassidy retained no illusions about his motivations.

The red car was a Honda Accord. Sweating from exertion and disappointment, he continued his search. He shimmied up a light pole to get an overall look at the giant parking lot.

The number of red cars dismayed him. Almost sure that a car a couple of lanes over was a Mazda, he dropped to the pavement and ran toward it. Commuters hurrying to catch their trains leaped out of his way, shouting. He caused several other near fender benders as motorists slammed on brakes to avoid hitting him.

This red car *was* a Mazda. Its doors were locked. If it was Jameel's, the Fort Bragg base sticker had been removed and nothing visible inside on the seats or floorboards identified the owner. It looked like Jameel's, but Cassidy knew he had to be sure. He drew the Glock and smashed out a side window with the butt. The sound of breaking glass attracted passersby.

"I'm calling the police!" someone threatened.

A burly guy rushed forward. Cassidy turned the gun on him. "Back off, hero. There's no time to explain."

The man turned and ran toward the station while Cassidy quickly rummaged through the glove compartment. The title and registration were in the name of James Conroy. Christ! Cassidy was stuffing everything back when he saw an envelope underneath the front seat. What attracted him to it was the return address: *Billy Dye Ministries*. It was too much of a coincidence, he thought. This had to be Jameel's car.

Vengeful and bitter and driven by a sense of urgency, Cassidy charged toward the train station, brandishing the gun to ward off interference from those whose attentions were drawn to his crime of car burglary. Swept ahead by honking cars and yelling people in his wake, he shoved people out of his way and vaulted the turnstile. Ticket clerks ran out of their booths but ran back in again when they saw that he was armed.

His military boots pounded against concrete and tile, echoing in the passageway. Emerging onto the crowded loading platform, he pushed his way through the crowd. A couple of men protested, but panic ensued when they saw the gun.

"He's got a gun!"

The subway cars in the station were filling up and the doors were about to close. Cassidy's head swiveled and his eyes darted. He trotted alongside the train, looking into the cars through the windows. Frightened eyes stared back at his gun.

There was no Jameel.

Too late! Too late! The phrase beat a rhythm in his head.

He spotted a uniformed transit authority cop running toward him, accompanied by the burly hero from the parking lot. People scattered, opening a lane of fire. The cop whipped out his sidearm and shouted a command.

At the same time, from the other direction, a slim familiar figure wearing a red ball cap and sun shades staggered from the men's room. Rasem Jameel carried a school backpack and seemed disoriented.

Attracted by the commotion, Jameel looked up and saw Cassidy. At first he didn't seem to recognize the young Green Beret. Then his eyes snapped wide with panic and he drew upon some deep reservoir of strength and dashed for the train with his pack full of death. He managed to squeeze through a door before it closed. The subway train jerked then, and rapidly gained speed as it pulled away from the station.

Cassidy darted a look at the transit cop, who still pounded toward him, yelling at him to stop. Desperation can sometimes prompt men to do foolish and dangerous things, and Cassidy, acting upon impulse and the immediacy of the chase, raced for the departing train. He saw Jameel's face pressed against the window of the car two coaches ahead.

With a leap of faith and desperation, Cassidy flung himself into space, grabbing for the handhold bar next to the door of the last car. With good timing and luck, mostly luck, he caught the bar with his free hand. His body slammed against the door and the speed of the train almost wrenched his arm from its socket. His dangling legs whipped against the loading platform and he felt waves of pain as the platform ripped jeans, scraped skin, and dug gashes into his flesh.

Then they were free of the platform and into the open tunnel. Frames of light from the train's windows speed-flashed against the walls of the tunnel. People inside the coach stared out at him and bunched up at the other end like chicks threatened by a raider owl.

Brandon stuck his pistol into his jeans. He held on with both hands and attempted to kick open the door. He cried out in rage and pain. All he could think of was that Jameel, his wife's killer, was getting away.

To obtain more leverage and force, he bounced back from the door with his legs and used his arms to jerk power into his kicks. He rebounded, and at that moment the train suddenly braked. Losing his grip, he flew through the air, landing in gravel next to the track.

He hit on his face, hands, and belly, then tumbled until, stunned and bleeding, he came to rest blinking up into the lights of the halted coach. He felt like every bone in his body was broken and all the skin torn off his face. Blood blurred his vision.

The fall might have killed him had he not been in excellent physical condition. Nonetheless, he had trouble getting up. He struggled to his feet, staggering and panting, and lurched toward the front of the train, looking for Jameel's coach. He still had a mission to perform before either he or his dead wife rested.

Cassidy heard glass breaking on the other side of the train. All the coach doors had been frozen closed when the train cut power and stopped dead. A woman screamed. Dropping to his hands and knees, Cassidy looked underneath the car. A man appeared, falling feet first from the car's broken window. Cassidy heard him grunt and collapse on the rail bed. He recognized Jameel attempting to escape on foot.

He drew the Glock and battle-rolled underneath the coach, coming up near the fallen Saudi. Looking terrified and ill, Jameel clawed with his free hand, the other hand dragging a red backpack as he managed to scramble to his feet.

"It is Allah's will! Don't you understand that?" Jameel screamed.

The time for talk was over. Cassidy cocked the hammer on the double-action semiautomatic and thrust it out ahead of him, holding it steady with both bleeding hands. He could hardly see because of his injuries, and knew he had to get close to be sure. Jameel backed off, cringing and muttering his death prayers to Allah. The backpack still dangled from his hand. He reached into it and started throwing eggs at the train.

He threw the eggs and they broke while he muttered and blubbered because he had failed to kill the thousands and even millions of enemies he and his fellow warriors of God envisioned. He had been defeated in his portion of the great crusade to drive back and destroy the corrupt infidels of the West. For years he had hid under the enemy's own nose, in the enemy's *military*, waiting for this day—and now he was sick and weak and weeping from pain and frustration. Had Allah deserted him in the hour of his victorious martyrdom?

He stumbled on the uneven footing of the track and fell on his back. He had an egg in his hand. He hurled it at the merciless American, threw it with all his strength, but that was not much now, and the egg fell and cracked at Cassidy's feet.

Cassidy kept coming, Jameel stared wide-eyed into the barrel of the gun. Cassidy stood above him.

"I'm going to kill you now," he said. He took out Kathryn's scarf and held it up to his nose so he could smell her.

Jameel covered his face with his hands and sobbed. This was not the way he was supposed to die.

CHAPTER 48

At FBI insistence, the Boston police chief had simultaneously shut down all public transportation in the city. Buses pulled off the roads and killed their engines. Trolleys, subway, and Amtrak trains stopped, wherever they happened to be. Private traffic clotted the city. The mayor and the governor got on radio and TV and urged patience as rumors flew and the city verged on panic. One man with an amplifier strapped to his back hurried through the streets of South Boston bellowing through an electronic bullhorn: "God has sent plague to destroy the wickedness in our cities. You breathe it now. None will escape!"

Chaplain Cameron Kragle feared Agent Thornton and he would arrive only in time to arrest his brother for criminal homicide. A single act of revenge could destroy the rest of his life. His fear intensified when he saw the train stalled on the track ahead. Thornton had commandeered a second train at the station in order to pursue the one on which a transit authority cop saw an armed man fleeing.

"He was plumb crazy or something," the cop said, still red-faced from his heart-pounding run the length of the boarding platform. "You guys must have been just around the corner when it happened, you got here so fast."

"We were," Thornton said. "Can you get us another train? We need to go after it."

"Let me use my radio." He did. "It'll be right here. It's coming from Market Street. Like I said, the guy was nuts. The last I seen of him, he was hanging onto the outside of the car, getting beat against the platform. I think he was chasing this other guy, an Arab-looking fella carrying a backpack. This Arab looked sick, but not too sick to come out of the bathroom and start running to catch the train when he seen this young fella with the gun. He really stunk up the bathroom though, puking all over the stalls. He must have been real sick."

The train arrived with an air hiss of brakes. It pulled up and the door to the control car opened. The operator looked out, frowning.

"These fellas are FBI," the transit cop said. "Do whatever they ask."

Cameron stepped into the train. Thornton paused a moment to give the cop instructions.

"Police and other FBI are on the way," he said. "Seal off the men's room toilet and confine everyone to the station. The police chief'll give you further instructions."

"Okay. That other train couldn't have gone far before they were all shut down," the cop said.

A few minutes later, Cameron closed his eyes and uttered a quick prayer when they spotted the back of the train. Its lights were on, but it sat still. When they were near enough, they saw people crowding the windows on one side, looking out at the tracks.

"God in heaven, forgive him for he knows not what he does. . . ."

Cameron leaped out and ran as soon as the operator opened the door. Thornton pounded along behind him. They spotted the two figures at the same time in the bleached-out light coming from coach windows. It barely illuminated the tall outline of a man in jeans and jacket wearing a ball cap. One hand clutched something to his lower face while the other pointed a pistol at another man lying on the ground as though frozen in place.

He was too late, Cameron thought. "Lord . . ." He could think of nothing else to say. God had not listened. God had either not heard his pleas or had ignored them. Did that not prove God took no interest in the petty personal affairs of men on earth?

"Cassidy!" Thornton called out. He clutched Cameron's arm to keep him from rushing the scene and upsetting the delicate equilibrium. "Don't do it, Cassidy. Believe me, son, this scumbag's not worth it."

Jameel's hands dropped away from his face. A band of diluted light slashed across his stricken countenance. Cameron could see that he was still alive. God *was* listening.

Thank you, Lord! he cried silently, with feeling so profound that it seemed his entire being elevated into the air.

Thornton brought him back down. The agent had his pistol out but held it along his side, out of sight. Cautiously, the two men walked forward until they were only a few feet away. Neither Cassidy nor Jameel stirred. They were like wax figures in a crime tableau at Madam Tussaud's—Cassidy with the pistol pointed and cocked, finger on the trigger, Kathryn's scarf over his lower face, breathing her in, his face smeared with blood; Jameel on the gravel looking up at him with a face twisted into a caricature of himself, dirty white powder blowing carelessly in a slight tunnel breeze, eggshells broken and scattered all around.

"Drop the gun, Cassidy," Thornton ordered gently. "It's all over."

A shock seemed to course through the Green Beret's body, as though only now he became aware of an external world populated by other people.

"No," he replied in a lifeless voice. "It's not over until I've killed him."

"Cassidy, this is your brother." Cameron eased forward until he was in view of both men.

Jameel looked up at him and tears rolled down his cheeks. It might be godly to forgive, but Cameron had no forgiveness left for this man after what he'd done.

"You have to understand, Cassidy," Cameron said. "God won't let you do it. If it goes no further than this, you've saved the lives of countless people. Because of you, the FBI tracked these people to Boston in time to prevent another 9/11. Zaccarias is in custody and dying. We have all his eggs, unbroken. We think Jameel is the only one left. We can contain his damage if it goes no further—but he will have succeeded, at least partly, if you kill him now and go to prison because of it. Don't let him do that, little brother. Our family has sacrificed enough to this war."

"Look at him," Cassidy snarled. "Kathryn was a good human being who should have lived with me until we had grandchildren, and longer."

Thornton remained silent and out of the picture, letting the chaplain handle it, at least until it seemed he might not be effective. Perhaps a bullet through Cassidy's leg would stop him, the FBI agent thought. But he knew he could not bring himself to shoot the younger son of his friend.

"Cassidy, this happened once before in Afghanistan," Cameron reminded him in a calmer voice. "Do you remember what Kathryn said to you? She said that what Amal did to her was something that would heal, but that what he did to you when you killed him left a scar in your soul that will never heal. What do you think this will do if you pull that trigger now? To your soul before God, and to the rest of your earthly life in jail? Cassidy, please put the gun down. The General would tell you the same thing."

"The General is not here. He has never been *here*."

"Our father loves and cares for us in ways none of us will understand. You don't see that now, but someday, with God's help, you will."

"I don't want to talk about him."

Cameron moved forward carefully until he was almost within arm's reach. Cassidy's resolve did not waver. He seemed to hesitate only because he knew he had Jameel a finger's squeeze away and he wanted him to suffer as long as possible.

Jameel coughed. Cameron flinched. Cassidy jabbed the gun as though about to pull the trigger. Thornton's weapon flew up to readiness.

Jameel laughed almost hysterically until coughing arrested it. He hacked and spat to the side.

"Let him kill me," he pleaded in a voice grown tired of it all. "I am dying anyhow. The same way Kathryn died, if that is any victory for you. Her death was an accident, if you will believe it. She became infected when I stored some of our stuff at the chapel and the Billy Dye letters got contaminated. I also contracted my death at the same time, I think."

He broke into more coughing. He laughed another phlegmy laugh. "Is that not the supreme irony of all times?"

"Shut up!" Cassidy growled. "You have thirty seconds to pray to Allah."

"Allah sees. Allah understands."

That was too much even for Cameron. "How can you kill mass numbers of unsuspecting innocents and say Allah will understand? How can you live brazenly among us for years, accepting our friendship, mocking our hospitality, exploiting our freedoms—"

"Chaplain . . ." Thornton said softly, to keep him from making Cassidy's case for him.

"For you I am sorry for believing me your friend when I was not," Jameel said. "But there is a higher purpose in Allah. The scholars in al-Qaeda, they discuss it and they make a *fatwa*. With God's help, they call on every Muslim who believes in God and wishes to be rewarded to comply with God's orders to kill Americans and plunder their money. We are ordered to fight the infidels until they say there is no God but Allah and his Prophet Mohammed."

He lowered his head and began to chant.

*"When the darkness comes upon us and we are bit by a
Sharp tooth, I say . . .
'Our homes are flooded with blood and the tyrant is freely
wandering in our homes.' "*

"Say hello to Allah," Cassidy said, and it was clear he intended to fire.

Cameron sprang at his brother then, and the Glock barked once. Spectators watching the drama from the coaches screamed.

Cassidy went down underneath the train with his brother on top of him, struggling to hold him. Thornton rushed forward, wrenched the pistol from Cassidy's fist, then stepped back. Cassidy ceased fighting and lay on the gravel with his brother's arms around him, holding him.

"Did I kill him?" he asked.

"I think I deflected the bullet. God was looking out for us."

The younger Kragle slowly seemed to wilt. Then, abruptly, unexpectedly, great sobs convulsed the strong young body.

"Kathryn . . . Kathryn . . ."

The chaplain held his brother for a long time until he was through crying. It was the first time he recalled seeing either of his brothers cry.

CHAPTER 49

Tampa

General Darren Kragle came up through the officer ranks by way of Officer Candidate School, a "shake 'n' bake" route often looked upon with disdain by the ring knockers from West Point. The smug look on the handsome face of Lieutenant Colonel Ross Canfield as he stood at attention before General Kragle's desk implied he might share that view with other Westies. He'd graduated eighth in his class and was now one of the youngest light colonels in the army, on a fast track to career success. Punching all the right cards.

"It was correct communications procedure, sir," he said crisply, knowing he was correct by the book and therefore protected by the book. Nevertheless, he felt uneasy. The smirk on his face was more or less permanent, not something he'd consciously chosen to wear for this occasion. Both Colonel Buck Thompson, CO of Delta Force, and CENTCOM commander General Paul Etheridge regarded him like predators over a soon-to-be fresh kill. General Kragle was the gray-eyed hawk who intended to do the killing.

"Sir, I have explained all this to General Etheridge," Canfield said. "With all due respect, sir, this is highly extraordinary and not within military procedure. USSOCOM is not in my chain of command, sir, and as such—"

"Colonel!" General Kragle barked, fighting to control his temper. "Do you see this tall gentleman to my right? That is Colonel Thompson. The men you left out there to die by your 'proper communications procedure' belong to him and to me."

"Sir, we attempted to authenticate—"

"Damn your authentication. These men identified themselves as Iron Weed 1-Alpha and asked to speak to me personally. You personally took over instead and cut them off."

"Sir, as you know, due to possible enemy interception on the battlefield and compromise of communications, I followed proper procedure and—"

"But not common sense. Why didn't you at least push this on up to General Etheridge? Why did you personally take over the line? You were overheard cutting commo with our people in the field, even though you knew they were in danger."

Canfield swallowed. The smirk on his face faded fast, permanent or not. "Sir, it was late at night. I followed the book—"

"I don't want to hear 'the book' again!"

SFOB in Uzbekistan had received a sitrep from 1-Alpha early that morning noting that the detachment was out of danger and proceeding on its mission. That was before the senior enlisted operator who had inadvertently overheard the exchange between Colonel Canfield and 1-Alpha went over his colonel's head to General Etheridge about it. Enraged and embarrassed by the incident, General Etheridge relieved Canfield immediately and gave orders that any commo originating from Iron Weed—and damn authentication—was hereafter accorded top priority. Iron Weed frequencies were to be constantly monitored.

General Kragle held a thick file in his hands which he opened and closed to distraction. In spite of eyes locked precisely one inch above the General's head, Canfield couldn't help glancing nervously at the file. The General opened it and this time splayed it on his desk in full view. Canfield saw his name on a cover sheet. Sweat popped onto his forehead and he felt it running down his spine and into the crack of his ass.

"Do you recognize this name?" General Kragle asked, showing Canfield the file.

Canfield looked. He swallowed.

"What did he promise you for your cooperation?" General Kragle asked.

Canfield licked his lips.

The General pulled a sheaf of papers from the file. "Or did you think you had no other choice, Colonel? Everybody has skeletons in his closet, and this guy is a wizard at exploiting them for his personal aggrandizement and advantage. It's called blackmail, if you don't care to be polite about it."

There was no smirk left. His look had turned to horror.

"Colonel, did you really think you could hide Miss Kandy Kane when you have a top secret crypto clearance and a critical slot? Let's see . . . I think the report says you're into S and M and golden showers. Is that right? You lie underneath and let her pee on you . . . ? What does your wife think about that?"

Colonel Canfield's entire body trembled. Wet circles appeared at his armpits.

"We're going to ask you some questions about what you were promised," General Kragle said, "and you're going to answer them as though your career and your ass itself depend on the truth. . . ."

CHAPTER 50

Afghanistan

They buried Mother Norman at noon. Bilal, whom the Americans had dubbed "Vince Lombardi," had been blown all to pieces, and his brother Uddin's body lay on disputed ground where it could not be recovered. They buried Norman high on a cold, windy sweep in the White Mountains where there was a view of a land as rugged as the old top sergeant had been. Bek and his mujahideen band, which had grown to ten, respectfully withdrew to allow the Americans to take care of their own. The warriors kept guard, although Sergeant Thumbs Jones blew the camel trail closed with C-4, thereby barring pursuit.

They dug the hole shallow because of rock, but no animals lived this high to dig him up again. His body would have to be reclaimed later anyhow and returned to family in the United States. The Deltas and Ismael, whom only Brandon knew to be an American, stood in a circle around the open grave in the blowing snow. Brandon spoke the words.

"Master Sergeant Roger 'Mother' Norman. He was a soldier, Lord, and maybe you ought to keep him in heaven to take care of other Special Forces soldiers when they get there. He's good at that. Amen."

Then they covered him.

Doc TB rebandaged the wounded from the savage fighting at the cemetery. Gloomy assumed Mother Norman's place as top NCO to reconsolidate the team. Fortunately, the detachment had escaped the trap with most of its rucksacks, which contained equipment, food, and ammunition. Brandon took the opportunity to question Bek about the motive behind his daring rescue of the lost detachment. Curiosity almost consumed him during the cold and dangerous flight along the precipitous trail, but there had been no time for talk then.

Bek now sat alone on a rock, the SAW across his knees and his skunk's beard thrust out belligerently as he gazed off in the direction of Osama bin Laden's Tora Bora retreat. He had spoken not a single word since his bold deed, and it was clear he didn't intend to speak to the Americans now until they came to him. His mien said he knew he had accomplished something heroic today and that his action had redeemed honor lost in the bushkazi game. Commander Bek was a leader again, undisputed, and he held his massive head erect with pride.

"Now what do you say?" Brandon chided Summer, looking at Bek from a new perspective.

"What do you want me to say—that I was wrong about the crazy old bastard? He gave us every reason to be suspicious. Even our background on him warned that he was unreliable."

"I'm not laying blame, Summer. I was going to kill him."

"I pushed you to do it. If you had, well, we'd still be back there in the graveyard. When I looked up and saw him at the top of the cliff, I could have fainted."

"You? The Ice Maiden? Faint?"

"It's not funny. Don't call me that again."

"That was a cheap shot," he admitted. "What we have to

figure out now is why he did it and what he wants. One thing's a cinch—he doesn't want us dead, or he'd have left us to the Huns at the gate."

She smiled halfheartedly. "Then we go to him? No more halfway. We probably ought to crawl. Especially me."

"Let's not go that far."

Commander Bek proved as irascible as ever. He sat on his boulder like a king on a throne, peering regally down upon his subjects as Brandon and Summer approached. He looked away, chin up, as proud and haughty as a gamecock.

"Tell him we thank him," Brandon began. "Also, we would like to hear what he would like to tell us about why he left the camp with his men. Tell him it's important that we know these things."

"Hah!" Bek snorted angrily, after the questions had been conveyed, Summer translating his reply. "*Now* you will listen, when before I was only a crazy old man. American, I do not like you any more than I like the Russians or any others who come to our country uninvited. But I have seen what you Americans can do. For years the Northern Alliance sat in the mountains on the border and starved while the Taliban and Osama bin Laden brought death and fear to the people and destruction to our country. In three weeks, you Americans toppled Kabul, and now you will do the same to Kandahar and Mazar-e-Sherif in even less time. I do not like you. I do not want you to stay, but . . ." His voice trailed off and his eyes narrowed as though it pained him to admit the truth. "But we need you here, and we can use you even as you use us."

"Fair enough," Brandon said. "Now ask him about Abdul."

Summer conveyed his question.

"Abdul!" Commander Bek roared, and spat to the side as though even the name in his mouth tasted of bile. "I attempted to warn you that Abdul's men were killed fighting against our Northern Alliance. But would you listen? Nah! You are as hard-headed as this kid Ismael. Abdul was a traitor and deserved to die. If I had had a pig, I would have wrapped his body in its hide so that he could never enter heaven."

After a few minutes of throwing his hands about and seething, he calmed down and narrated how he discovered the truth about the red-beard. Bek had suspected Abdul when he first arrived with a few men to join his band. There had been two or three suspicious occasions when Bek's patrols were intercepted by the enemy. Once, the enemy even raided the guerrillas' base camp. Bek moved it after that to the big cave where Ismael had come and then the Americans had joined.

"We were ordered by Commander Khalil of the Northern Alliance to accept Ismael as an interpreter for Americans who would come and fight with us," Bek explained. "But you did not come to fight with us. You came to use my people for your own missions. Our enemy is the Taliban, not al-Qaeda, although I have come now to see that they are one and the same."

Against his better judgment, Bek accepted Ismael and the detachment in exchange for provisions of food, weapons, and money. Abdul was in favor of it, as were most of the guerrillas. For the first time in at least three years, they had plenty of food in their bellies, and many of them began to side with Abdul and whisper that perhaps Abdul should lead.

"And then we also sided with Abdul against Bek when we came," Brandon added.

That made Bek's leadership even more uncertain. Bek resented it. He resented the Americans and even went so far as to contemplate killing them.

"What stopped you?" Brandon asked.

Bek looked directly at him. "More Americans would come, and they would bomb us," he frankly admitted.

On the day Brandon led the excursion into Kabul to attempt to target the Shake, Abdul slipped out of camp. Bek followed him to where he had a radio hidden.

"It was a good radio that uses satellites. I have it now if you care to look at it. Abdul was speaking Arabic on the radio like a Saudi Arabian. I understand because Osama attracted many Saudis here to fight with the mujahideen against the Russians. They were talking about Iron Weed, which I did not understand at the time. Now I know it must be the code name for you."

Bek overheard only parts of the conversation before Abdul discovered his presence.

"They were talking about America. The person on the other end of the radio said there were mujahideen in America who called to report on Iron Weed. That was all I heard."

Abdul explained away his secret possession of the radio by saying it was necessary that he maintain contact with Commander Khalil north of Bagram, who promised to give him command of a unit to fight with the Northern Alliance again. Later, Bek realized that Abdul must have been either alerting someone or receiving orders. His awakening came on the night that ended in Abdul's death.

"Because I was suspicious of Abdul," Bek said, "I detailed men to keep an eye on him at all times. Kafi saw the al-Qaeda sneak up to camp and talk with Ismael."

Brandon and Summer exchanged sheepish looks. Apparently, however, Kafi missed what transpired between the two of them afterward.

The al-Qaeda circled the camp and waited at another place until Abdul came. After a short conversation, Abdul returned to his sleeping bed at the ledge.

"The al-Qaeda was what I think you call a double agent," Bek said. "He told us everything before Kafi slit his throat. He provided Ismael a map to Osama bin Laden's headquarters, but at the same time he and Abdul had already arranged a trap. You Americans and my fighters were to walk into a company of militia that would kill us and protect Osama."

Summer sat with bowed head. She had been taken in and looked crushed by it. You really couldn't trust anybody in this shit-pot country, Brandon thought, not for the first time.

"So I cut Abdul's throat while the pig pretended to be asleep."

"And you neglected to warn us?"

"It seemed the simple solution. Abdul was dead, the militia would kill you. The problem was solved."

"All neat and wrapped up. What changed your mind?"

Bek shrugged and threw out his arms in one of his elaborate gestures. "What can I say? I have a kind heart."

"Like a tiger has a kind heart."

Bek laughed, not displeased at the comparison. "This war will end soon," he said, "and there will be a new government. If I were to destroy Osama and al-Qaeda. I would be a great person and have a title in the government again. There is also a great deal of reward money for his head. All the bombing there is cannot kill him. He simply rolls over and goes back to sleep inside his deep caves. I need you and your men and your explosives. You know how to use them the most effective way. There is but one way to kill Osama—go *inside* his cave and blow him up."

Brandon looked at him. Was he serious? "You said yourself militia was sent out to stop us," he pointed out. "What are we supposed to do? Get on horses and charge the entrance like cavalry through machine guns and mortars?"

Bek winked. "You have courage. I like that. How did *you* intend to kill him?"

Brandon saw no benefit in holding back now. He explained the GLTD and thermobaric bombs. The weather was not a factor, as it was in strategic air cover and in personnel extraction. B-2s could fly under virtually any conditions, flying as high as they did, and deliver their loads with pinpoint accuracy once the target was laser-designated.

"Can such a bomb reach one thousand feet deep past tunnels and air locks and sealed chambers?" Bek asked. "Can it reach into your tunnels in the mountains at your Strategic Air Command? If it cannot, it cannot touch Osama. The command post for the Taliban and al-Qaeda was constructed and enlarged over a period of ten years. Communications rooms and air defense systems, quarters for perhaps one thousand troops, a motor pool for trucks and tanks, ammunition depots. It has eating halls and officer quarters. It supports almost a brigade in a military complex completely underground."

"How do you know all this?"

Bek stood up and motioned to a fighter, a rawboned older man with a grayish-yellow beard.

"Will your thermobaric bomb kill such a cave?" Bek insisted again.

Brandon didn't think so.

"We must kill Osama from the inside, then," Bek stressed. "This man is Bacha. Bacha has lived in these mountains since he was a child. He knows a secret entrance to Osama's cave that even Osama does not know. It is difficult, but a small party of determined saboteurs could enter and—"

"There are few of life's problems that can't be solved with the proper explosive," Brandon finished for him.

Summer's hand trembled when it reached to brush snow off her eyebrows.

CHAPTER 51

Nightfall was approaching by the time 1-Alpha and Bek's Afghans reached the secret access to the Shake's cave. But as Gloomy pointed out, what difference did it make if the sun shone outside or not if you were inside the earth's bowels? The grueling march to get there along snow-swept pathways known only to Bacha and a few other old mountain nomads like him all but exhausted the entire band. There was no time to rest now, though.

The opening proved barely large enough to accommodate one man at a time. No wonder no one knew about it, Brandon thought. It was hidden high on the mountain crest among slabs of stone and erosion, through solid rock that looked as if God had reached down, scraped His fingers across it, pounded it, tossed it about, and all but pulverized it, all because of intense American bombing.

For a while Brandon feared the entrance might have been permanently blocked. But then Bacha found it concealed beneath a plug of fresh snow. Brandon flopped down on his belly and looked inside, able to see only a few feet before the passageway disappeared into darkness. It seemed to go almost straight down.

Faint sounds of activity rumbled up from inside, like from

the center of a hungry giant's stomach. Summer plopped down next to Brandon. "It's digesting," she said, reaching the same analogy.

"Let's see it doesn't digest *us*."

Some of Bek's men brought up a rope, secured one end around a boulder, further anchored it to a scrubby tree, and paid the free end down the hole.

"The first drop is about ten feet," Bacha explained to Brandon through Summer. "Then it is steep and tight but walkable until you come to a passage where you have to crawl. You will find the door at the end."

The assault team got ready by stripping down to bare essentials, including leaving their coats outside. The soldiers inside with whom they expected to mingle would not be wearing wraps. Thumbs Jones prepared a single rucksack. It contained a heavy load of demolitions, a spare rope, and other possibles. He hefted it to the cave opening, slung his M-16 across his back in preparation for his descent, and winked at Brandon.

"Let's go blow up something."

"Let's do it."

The assault team consisted of Thumbs Jones; Saeed the Zarbati, who volunteered and had since made his peace with Bek; Commander Bek, who insisted he go since it was the heroic thing to do to regain a title; Summer; and Brandon. The plan was hastily conceived, as many such plans are in the fog and changing fortunes of battle. Murphy, as in Murphy's Law, had to be considered.

Since Mad Dog and Winnie Brown were the only team members not wounded in the morning's fight, Brandon had left them at the cave's main entrance to cover it with the PAQ-10 laser. The entrance, though large enough to accommodate troop trucks and tanks, was all but invisible from the air and protected by overhanging rocks. The PAQ-10 would take care of locating it for attack aircraft. Mad Dog and Winnie had orders to stuff the cave full of ordnance from the sky, then bug out for the extraction landing zone if for some reason the saboteur assault failed. It might not kill Osama, but maybe it would bury him—along with Brandon and the assault element.

The only sure way of blowing up the cave and cutting off the snake's head, as Bek successfully argued, was to go inside after the snake. Air strikes afterward would finish the job.

"If something goes wrong in there, I'll give you the signal," Brandon advised Mad Dog.

"Fu-uck, sir. Blow you up? I don't like it."

"You don't have to like it, Dog. Just do it."

"What if we can't get your signal from here?"

"Ice Man will relay from up top at the other opening."

Brandon slapped Mad Dog on the shoulder before leaving him and Winnie in a hidden observation post with a direct view of the cave's main entrance. There was little activity down there now. Most of the troops either hid inside during daylight hours or were distributed in defensive positions prepared for battle. Concealed mortar and machine-gun emplacements in the rocks to either side and above the cave promised hell to any direct attack attempting to storm the command post.

"Don't worry, Dog," Brandon said. "We're coming back out of there. It's not a martyr mission. See you on the LZ tonight. I'll buy all of you a steak dinner tomorrow night."

"That's a deal, sir."

Brandon shook hands with both fighters.

"Good luck, sir," Winnie said. "Keep your powder dry. Isn't that what one's supposed to say at a time like this?"

Ice Man and Doc TB would remain outside at the second entrance to the cave with Bek's mujahideen to provide security and maintain commo with Winnie and Mad Dog.

Gloomy argued for the privilege of accompanying his boss into the cave, but Brandon needed him and Mr. Blunderbuss in a strategic location to cover the withdrawal to the LZ once the job was finished. He would set up his post about three hundred yards south of the cave, where his rifle could lay command over both the entrance and a flat place farther south that would serve as an LZ for extraction helicopters— providing the choppers could get in through the snow and soup.

As the demolitions man, Thumbs Jones had to be included in the cave mission. Summer pointed out that it was not only her duty but also her obligation to go as the element's fifth member in order to redeem herself after her misunderstanding of Bek.

"Besides, how are you going to speak to the others without me to translate?"

Brandon hesitated. He saw Gypsy making that same argument before she was killed.

Summer said, "We have no investment in each other. Remember?"

He remembered.

Gloomy overheard the exchange. "You're not an Ismael," he blurted. "You're a woman!"

Both of them looked at him.

"Your eyes changed color," he explained. "Plus, I graduated at the top of my Hooker high school class. I can tell the difference between a boy and a girl eighty percent of the time. Does one of you want to explain this?"

"Wait until this is over," they said in unison.

Gloomy shook his head. "What a relief. I was afraid the major was about to change his luck and go funny on us."

Brandon knew that his luck had changed, all right. For the worse, ever since Ismael showed up at the DZ reception. He had to admit he had no choice but to include her. But how could he concentrate on a mission when he had a woman to protect? He didn't think he would survive with another woman's death on his conscience.

"This is not Punitive Strike and I'm not Gypsy Iryani," she said. "Brandon, look at me. We're both coming back. Okay?"

Saeed dropped into the cave first while the security element and designated ready reaction force led by Ice Man and Doc TB deployed around the entrance. Brandon slid down the rope next, followed by Summer, Thumbs, and then Bek.

They landed in a small chamber where the only light came from the round hole above. Snow swirled down on top of them, and the snow in the chamber was a foot deep. The floor dropped off steeply into total blackness. Saeed switched on a flashlight. Its beam lit up a narrow damp passageway. As they descended one behind the other, sometimes sliding against the steepness of the decline, the passageway narrowed until they had to proceed on hands and knees for what seemed at least a half mile. While they had been shivering when they first started, sweat now sheened their faces in the yellow illumination of the single flashlight. The giant's belly sounds grew louder.

The tunnel ended abruptly. Puzzled, Saeed played the flashlight beam against a blind rock wall where a thin trickle of water dripped from an opening the size of a rabbit hole. Had the old nomad Bacha been wrong about the tunnel joining with the main cave?

Brandon took the flashlight and shone the beam over every inch of the wall, ceiling, and floor. Nothing. Noise from the big cave sounded louder than ever, however. He distinguished the hum of generators, a motor revving, and someone shouting orders.

"It's got to be here," he said. "Feel around. Erosion might have covered it."

Water had to go somewhere. He shined the light on the water ooze. It reflected back the beam as Brandon followed it to where it disappeared through a crack in the floor. He dug his fingers into the fissure and heard dirt sprinkling onto the floor below. He caught his breath and they all remained perfectly still until certain that no one below saw or heard.

Brandon switched off the light. In a moment he'd cleared an opening big enough for his head to fit through. He looked out carefully, extending his head until he saw that this branch of the cave was only about four feet high. Artificial lighting glowed at its open end, providing enough light for him to see that they were in an unused dead-end grotto.

Brandon enlarged the hole, letting in a weak shaft of light. He tapped Saeed, indicating that he was to follow. Saeed gripped Brandon's arm, assenting.

Brandon eased down through the opening until his boots touched. He crouched, submachine gun at the ready, while the others joined him one at a time. Thumbs dropped through and reached up to accept his rucksack full of explosives from Bek. Then Bek eased down.

Now came the major test of their disguises. Brandon felt gratitude for Colonel Thompson's and the General's foresight in ordering the detachment to start growing beards when they were in Colorado. They now had to venture into the cave's general population and mingle while they looked around to locate the best place for Thumbs to set his charges. An arms magazine, Thumbs recommended. It would be the ideal place to generate secondary explosions that would ensure the cave's total collapse.

With a final glance at Summer, which she returned, even smiling a little, Brandon squared his shoulders and walked to the end of the corridor, Summer on one side and Bek on the other. Thumbs followed with the rucksack and Saeed.

Their first exposure to the underground fortress cavern almost took their breath away. It was enormous, roughly the size of the Super Dome. It was like walking onto a James Bond movie set. Electric lights run by generators illuminated it, but it was so huge that, fortunately, there were lots of dark corners and areas of dimness.

Three bearded militiamen in filthy Afghan garb and carrying AK rifles ambled past. Brandon tensed, but the men kept walking, chatting among themselves as they proceeded along a wide rock-ledge catwalk running all the way around a monumental central area nearly forty feet below. A motor pool of armored personnel carriers, pickup trucks, wheeled howitzers, and a few Russian tanks were in the central area. At least a hundred soldiers appeared employed at various tasks.

Closed steel doors, some of which were immense, indicated corridors leading off the common area. Brandon could only guess at the cave's actual size.

Trying to appear as casual as the three militiamen they'd passed, the saboteurs strolled the catwalk, past open guarded grottos containing food stuffs, equipment parts, weapons, and other stores. Guards greeted them without interest.

"Salam alaikam."

The only way Brandon could explain the apparent disinterest in them was that the bombing and fighting up north had driven Taliban and al-Qaeda strangers into the mountains for a final stand. Everyone entering the cave had to be cleared by gate pickets, which meant if you were inside, you belonged there. It reinforced the old gold-bricking scam that you could take a clipboard and go anywhere you wanted on a military post without challenge.

"This is going to be easier than I thought," Thumbs Jones whispered in excitement. "Let's go around one more time. That hole over there has boxes of small arms ammo, and I think the one on the opposite side is full of mortar rounds. I need to take another look. Can you *imagine* the boom this is going to make! All I have to do is plant some plastic in with all that other stuff and we can drop a million or two tons of rock right down in the center of this rat's nest."

From a tactical standpoint, Brandon observed two narrow stairways carved out of solid rock leading down into the common. They appeared to be the only way to access the catwalk, unless some of the upper caverns compartmented with those below, which was a good possibility. Nonetheless, he thought they could hold out long enough for Thumbs to do his work if it became necessary.

He counted only eight guards upstairs, plus a few mujahideen wandering about, obviously awed newcomers themselves.

"We'll work it this way," Brandon said, letting Summer translate to the Afghans as they continued their slow walk. "Bek and Thumbs take out the guard at the mortar cave. Do it silently so nobody sees or hears. Bek takes his place at the door while Thumbs rigs a charge. Okay?"

Bek started to object but, under the circumstances, thought of nothing better. He nodded.

"Good. Saeed and I will do the same at the ammo cache. Summer comes with us. Thumbs gives the okay to light the fuses. Any questions?"

"It'll have to be a time fuse," Thumbs said. "Thirty minutes?"

"Better make it twenty. We'll have to hustle to get out, but any longer than that and someone may notice."

He scanned the large area below, looking for a tall figure with a cane and a telltale camouflage jacket. How would they ever know if Osama bin Laden was in here when the mountain collapsed?

"Let's get to work."

The words were barely out of his mouth when two militia-men trotted toward them, calling out a challenge. Damn that Murphy.

A good defense was a good offense. Bek confronted the approaching mujahideen, his fierce skunk's beard thrust forward, his little pig's eyes glaring. Brandon accepted his example and stepped forward with the same demeanor. The militiamen faltered. Bek berated them soundly, accustomed as he was to command and expecting obedience from such men. In a moment his scathing voice reduced them to obsequiousness. Bek laughed. He tore them down, then built them back up. The militiamen were laughing and joking with him when they took their leave, going back downstairs.

It looked skillfully accomplished. Summer explained when the two were out of hearing, "They said they had never seen us before. Bek said he had never seen *them* before and demanded they identify themselves. I think Bek is a better friend than enemy."

He was. Once he had regained his mantle of leadership.

"We had better get this done and get out of here before somebody else gets suspicious," Summer added.

They casually continued their stroll along the catwalk, pretending to laugh and talk among themselves. Brandon's eyes searched the main cave below, looking for signs of Osama. A pair of rooms near the bottom of one set of rock stairs appeared particularly active. Men came and went out of the first room, darting about and delivering papers. They looked cleaner and better dressed than ordinary soldiers. Brandon assumed he had pinpointed the terrorist command center. But there was still no sign of the Shake. Maybe he wasn't even here.

With feigned indifference, the little band approached the entrance of the cave room that contained mortar tubes and crates of rounds. Laughing as though at a joke, Brandon took a last quick look around. The catwalk was deserted except for the bored guards, one of whom sat on the floor sleeping. The mortar sentry still stood, but looked equally bored as he leaned against the wall smoking a cigarette. His rifle rested against the wall on the other side of the door from him. Anyone looking up from below would be partly blinded by the high overhead lights.

Brandon nodded at Bek. The squat Afghan approached the guard, saying something. The guard straightened and twisted around to look inside the room. Bek shoved him inside, Saeed springing inside directly behind them. In short order the sentry had his throat soundly cut and was dragged out of sight. Bek took his place as guard and Thumbs went to work.

He retrieved soft blocks of C-4 and other supplies from his rucksack and handed the pack with the rest of the explosives to Brandon.

"Save a few blocks for when we withdraw," he advised. "We may need them."

From outside the door Bek gave Brandon the all-clear signal. Brandon stepped back onto the catwalk with Summer and Saeed and the trio headed nonchalantly toward the small arms room. None of the other guards appeared to have noticed what happened, it had occurred so swiftly.

They pulled the same chicanery on the other guard. Pretending friendliness, Saeed pushed him into the room, then Brandon leaped on him. He clapped one hand over the victim's mouth and jerked his head back, exposing the jugular, then sliced to the spinal cord with his grandfather's Ka-Bar, all but decapitating the man. The sour coppery odor of blood filled the darkened grotto. Brandon felt blood gush hot across his hand and heard gurgles coming from the corpse. He had never killed like this before, close up and personal, and the

ease with which he accomplished it left him momentarily
pale and shaken.

He quickly recovered. Summer was already taking explosives from the rucksack. Saeed assumed the guard's place at
the door, while Brandon dragged the dead man deeper into
the subcavern, then commenced work.

The force of the blasts needed to be diverted away from
openings where it would dissipate and into the heart of the
mountain in order to get total collapse. Some boxes of frag-
mentation grenades along with another of incendiaries proved
perfect for tamping blocks of C-4 against the cavern's rear
wall. Brandon pushed two mechanical blasting caps into the
malleable explosives, one as backup for the other. To these he
secured a Y of time fuse and measured out twenty minutes
worth. He attached an igniter to the end, and the chain was
ready to go. He and Summer quickly piled more munitions
around the C-4 and grenades. More bang for the buck.

Saeed stuck his head inside, his face tense and set. Brandon nodded and picked up the igniter to set it off on
Thumbs's signal. Then he laid it down again and walked to
the entrance, where he saw Thumbs and Bek look question-
ingly at him from the other side of the circled catwalk. Below
and between, activity continued in the common cave.

"Brandon, let's do it and get out of here," Summer encouraged him.

Brandon examined the bustle below, seeking the Shake's
trademark height, cane, camouflage jacket, and white headdress. Summer tugged on his sleeve, fearful they were going
to be noticed. Saeed's hands trembled from apprehension
and anticipation. Thumbs threw him an inquiring look from
the mortar room.

"What if he's not here?" Brandon hissed. "Our mission is
to get him, not blow up a cave."

"Bek says he's here," Summer hissed back. "That's the intel we have from everywhere."

"Now Bek is the paragon of trustworthiness?"

"I deserve that. We'll talk about it later. Set it off."

He took a deep breath, his mind made up. "I'm going down to make sure the Shake is here."

"Major, you can't do that. It's insane. He's here. I know he's here. Let's go."

Brandon signaled Thumbs to hold up. He quickly rigged a half-pound block of C-4 with a short fuse and stuffed it under his robe, pulled his turban low above his eyes and, with his MP-5 slung over his shoulder, strode determinedly toward the stairs leading down into the heart of the enemy command center. He simply could not leave the job half done. He had to know for sure that Osama bin Laden went up with the cave.

Summer caught up with him before he started down the stairs. He stopped.

"You don't want to create a scene, do you?" she warned, as stubborn as he was.

He deliberated it in his mind. "I know," he said finally. "Who's going to talk for me? I never thought it'd be a woman."

CHAPTER 52

The big cave had about it the air of a National Guard armory in Wichita or Des Moines on a drill weekend, except the soldiers all wore sheets and beards. Recognizing that he was pushing their luck and tweaking Murphy's tail by insisting on confirming the Shake's presence, Brandon nevertheless felt it his duty to make sure that the Iron Weed mission succeeded. He and Summer mingled with the terrorists and helped load a truck and carry some cheese and fruit into a grotto chow hall near the two command center rooms. Meanwhile, he'd looked around. There was still no sign of the intended target.

Summer's smooth, beardless face attracted some attention. Most boys had at least some hair on their faces. One man laughed and patted her cheek. Summer blazed back at him in apparent indignation.

"Don't you think you might have overdone it?" Brandon whispered as they walked on.

"I told him you were my father and you took offense at men insulting his sons."

"You didn't challenge him to a duel or anything?"

"That was the next step."

They resumed their quest feeling a bit like ducks tossed

into a kennel of starving wolfhounds. Sooner or later one of the hounds would discover that the ducks weren't a different breed of dog.

Lights throughout the cavern system blinked, dimming. Some men worked on huge generators inside a room. Apparently, this was the cave's power source. Brandon glanced up, and had to look hard into even the dimmed lights to make out features on the catwalk high above. Obviously no one went up there unless he had specific business. He knew Thumbs Jones was watching over them.

Summer nudged him and indicated a young kid carrying a tray of food. Only important people, very important people, rated room service. They followed him while trying to appear not to.

The kid hurried across the cave, dodging soldiers and weaving in and out of vehicles. He started trotting in order to get the food to its destination while it was still hot. Brandon picked up their pace. He glimpsed the kid turning into a long tunnel. Summer breathed from excitement and exertion. They both sweated.

"Why can't you take me out for dinner and dancing like a normal date?" she puffed.

"You're not a normal girl."

"Glad you noticed."

Brandon paused at the entrance to the tunnel and looked down it. A row of overhead lights illuminated it with renewed brightness as the generators kicked back in. The tunnel curved to the left, but before the curve the servant stopped at a closed iron door and knocked.

This had to be it. Brandon's heart pounded at the prospect of coming face-to-face with perhaps the most notorious criminal mastermind in the world. He was so engrossed in waiting for the door to open that he overlooked the pair of militiamen trotting across the main cave toward them.

The door opened, and at the same time, a sentry wearing a pistol belt strode around the curve in the tunnel and the two militiamen shouted a warning. Brandon knew the ducks' cover was blown; the wolfhounds were alert.

Osama bin Laden looked out the open door. Brandon took in the long, narrow face, black beard, meaty lips, and cruel dark eyes. Their gazes locked and both men froze, as though each recognized the approach of his violent destiny.

The sentry's hand snaked for his pistol. Behind Brandon iron bolts snapped as weapons were charged. Brandon had one target in mind. A Kragle never failed his mission. He swung up the short barrel of the MP-5 and pointed it directly at the Shake. Sayonara, motherfucker, he thought.

The next moments before he fired occurred so quickly that it seemed he went on autopilot and functioned from instinct and emotion rather than from his usual cool detachment.

Summer leaped out in front to place herself between Brandon and the pistol-pointing sentry. She was going to accept the sentry's bullet so he could take his shot at Osama. The sentry's finger tightened on the trigger, the pistol pointing directly at Summer's heart.

Brandon had a choice, and only an instant in which to make it. Either the Shake and the mission—or Summer.

He knew he'd failed Gypsy. He'd let her get killed while she was under his command.

It wasn't Gypsy he saw, though. It was Summer, and it was Summer's life. It was her name, *"Summer!"* he bellowed as he tilted the barrel away from Osama, a sure kill. The little submachine gun burped, loud and ripping inside the tunnel. The guard's body jerked like a puppet controlled by spastic strings as bullets ripped into his chest. His reaction flung the unfired pistol against the cave wall, and he dropped where he stood.

Finger still on the trigger, Brandon sprayed the door as it was closing. The iron door slammed and locked home.

He became aware of rifle shots from the cave. A ricochet screamed past his head and kept ricocheting all the way down the tunnel. Summer pivoted with her carbine and pinged at the militiamen, sending them scurrying for cover.

Pandemonium erupted inside the cave. It would work to the intruders' advantage as long as it continued. But Brandon knew it wouldn't last long.

The first two mujahideen, now hiding behind a pickup truck, shouted and waved their arms and pointed at the tunnel. Brandon forced them to dive to the floor with a quick burst. Summer popped away at a couple of other targets. Confused and disoriented, soldiers ducked and dodged and got their heads down until they figured out what was going on or until someone took charge and issued orders.

No matter, the Americans knew they were in shit up to their necks. For them, there was only one way out, which was the way they'd come in. But escaping to the catwalk assumed the probability of a trip to Mars.

"Light it up! Pull the fuse!" Brandon roared up at Thumbs Jones on the catwalk.

He and Summer would die together in the explosion. Along with the Shake. Damn. What a hell of a way to end things.

Workmen from the generator room stuck their heads out to see what was happening. It gave Brandon an idea. It was a long shot, but what did they have to lose?

He grabbed Summer's arm. "Come on!"

Summer realized what he was up to. They raced toward the power grotto. The unarmed workmen fled. Bullets shrieked and firearms banged throughout the huge cavern as the terrorists homed in on the genesis of all the excitement.

For Brandon, it was like running through raindrops of lead and steel while underneath a huge tub upon which a thousand infuriated giants beat with clubs.

A pickup exploded in a brilliant core of light. A platoon of fighters double-timing into action scattered in confusion as another detonation took out its leaders.

Good ol' Thumbs, Brandon thought as he ran. He and the two Afghans must have taken out the rest of the guards and were now hurling grenades from the catwalk as fast as they could pull pins and toss them. Explosions sowed further confusion. Wounded men screamed.

Brandon darted into the generator room ahead of Summer. Massive gasoline machines rumbled away, producing electricity. Wires ran from them, out the top of the door, then splayed throughout the complex, affirming Brandon's suspicion that this was the main power source.

"Cover me!" he barked. "This'll only take a minute."

"Better make it a second." She fired off a couple of rounds at a bold mujahideen who tried to better his position. "Why didn't you shoot Osama?" she asked.

"I want you alive. I'm in love with you, you crazy bitch."

There, he'd said it.

"What?" she shouted.

"Shut up and shoot."

He took out the C-4 with the short fuse and pushed it into the motor of the largest generator. He popped the igniter and scrambled to the entrance, where he crouched next to Summer.

"Thirty seconds," he said. "When I say *jump*, you'd better be a frog. Go to the left toward the stairs. Wait until you have my hand. If I'm right, it's going to get darker in this bat cave than you can imagine."

"If you're wrong?"

The carbine *bark-barked*.

"You'd better hope I'm not."

"I love you too."

"What?"

"Shut up and shoot."

He started the countdown. "Fifteen . . . fourteen . . . thirteen . . ."

When there were two seconds left before the explosive detonated, he said, *"Now!"*

Together, they tumbled out the door to flatten themselves to the floor against the outer wall. A hail of bullets sought flesh. The C-4 went off, and lights went out so instantaneously that the flash of the explosion was the only point of light anywhere. Then it was gone too and the darkness was complete, so thick it was almost palpable. A blind man's darkness.

"Summer?"

"Here."

"Quick. Come to my voice."

They bumped into each other. He grabbed her hand. "The stairs are this way."

Slinging his submachine gun in order to free both hands, he felt his way along the wall at a trot, dragging her with him. Firing ceased, except for an isolated jittery round. Men shouted orders and questions and ran blindly about. An insane game of blind man's bluff, Brandon thought. Three blind mice and all that . . . It seemed everyone in the cave, a battalion of voices, all started talking and yelling at once. Good. It covered their escape. Thumbs and the Afghans stopped tossing grenades.

They were on their way out of there. He'd collect the others and then they would flee back up the chimney tunnel before hell and fire erupted. Get ready, Osama. Your virgins are waiting.

Someone bumped into them in the total darkness. Summer scolded him in Arabic.

"What did you say?" Brandon asked.

"I told him to watch where he was going."

OSAMA BIN LADEN DEAD?

KABUL (CPI)—Reports from the Tora Bora region of Afghanistan say terrorist leader Osama bin Laden and as many as 1,000 of his followers may have been killed in savage U.S. bombing that all but demolished a mountaintop and a command cave network.

The U.S. air raids began shortly before midnight last night. Witnesses say they were preceded by a series of underground explosions inside the cave itself. It is believed that arms and ammunition magazines inside the cave were ignited.

U.S. planes have bombed Tora Bora for days. Before this apparent detonation, however, it was believed that ground troops would have to fight their way into the mountains' command bunkers in a bloody battle that was sure to result in many casualties on both sides.

Recent satellite photos show smoke still rising from fissures blown in the earth's crust. Battle damage estimates conclude that nothing inside could have survived.

General Paul Etheridge of CENTCOM, the U.S. central command, said that bin Laden's presence in the cave at the time of the bombing was confirmed.

"Obviously, we will be unable to recover the body to corroborate his death," he said. "Could he have escaped? It is possible, but unlikely, that he had an escape route laid out in advance. Does this signify the end of al-Qaeda and terrorism? Hardly. Even though the head may have been stepped on, others will arise to assume command until terrorists and the outlaw governments that support them are wiped out worldwide."

U.S. terrorism experts speculate that bin Laden prepared in advance for his death by seeding money and terrorist cells in countries around the globe in order to maintain his legacy.

Shortly after the first explosions occurred, and before air strikes began, U.S. CH-47 Chinook helicopters reportedly extracted a Delta Force detachment and an unknown number of Northern Alliance guerrillas from near the top of the mountain. Neither CENTCOM nor General Darren E. Kragle of the U.S. Special Operations Command will confirm or deny that an Iron Weed detachment was in the area and may have played a role in the operation.

The use of Delta Force to track down Taliban and al-Qaeda leaders led to a congressional investigation that began last week in Washington on charges that the elite counterterrorism unit was conducting assassination missions.

HEARINGS CANCELED FOLLOWING SENATOR'S DEATH

WASHINGTON, D.C. (CPI)—A shocking twist yesterday ended the so-called Iron Weed congressional hearings into alleged American war crimes and atrocities in Afghanistan. Senator Eric B. Tayloe, chair of the congressional investigations committee, was found dead in Washington's Rock Creek

Park by an early morning jogger. Police say he died of an apparent self-inflicted gunshot wound. Police found a pistol in his hand.

The powerful head of the Senate Armed Services Committee and presidential contender died the same way he lived, shrouded in mystery and controversy.

Reports indicate Tayloe's office recently came under investigation as a result of its ties to purported terrorists connected to al-Qaeda. Agents of the FBI's National Domestic Preparedness Office, led by Senior Agent Claude Thornton, arrested three of Tayloe's top aides Monday at the Capitol Building. Arrested were Isam Faraj, 27; Roger Carlton, 29; and Tariq Awadallah, 31. All were charged with espionage and conspiracy to commit terrorism.

Authorities say Senator Tayloe was not involved in the spy network, that he was merely being used by the spies.

According to documents made available to CPI, the spy network began unraveling due to information developed in Afghanistan and in Saudi Arabia. CPI veteran war correspondents reportedly uncovered information that Osama bin Laden was receiving advance notice and warnings about U.S. Special Operations movements, including those of the top secret mission code-named Iron Weed.

Mission detachments from Delta Force, the elite U.S. counterterrorism unit, were assigned to Afghanistan to track down Taliban and al-Qaeda leaders. The detachments were reportedly involved in the destruction of bin Laden's central command post in the Tora Bora region, in which bin Laden himself may have perished.

A harsh critic of the war, Senator Tayloe accused Iron Weed of assassinations, which is against U.S. law, and initiated a congressional hearing.

According to sources, information funneled into Afghanistan through Saudi Arabia enabled bin Laden to avoid his pursuers on several occasions and almost resulted in the loss of a Delta detachment.

In Saudi Arabia, state police arrested the head of its diplomatic delegation, 40-year-old Agha Mir, as a middleman in the plot. Mir is accused of receiving sensitive intelligence from contacts in the United States and funneling it through an elaborate communications system to the al-Qaeda network in Afghanistan.

Authorities say Mir received intelligence from Shukri Abu Marzook, 38. Marzook, in turn, was kept informed by Senator Tayloe's aides, Faraj, Carlton, and Awadallah, who were privy to Tayloe's communications and other intelligence files. Sources disclose that the three men worked for Senator Tayloe for more than four years and that Senator Tayloe considered them trustworthy. The FBI contends they were "sleepers," underground terrorists who insinuated themselves into a position to spy on military matters. As chairman of the Senate Armed Services Committee, Tayloe was kept abreast of important war developments and movements. The sleepers allegedly obtained such information without Tayloe's awareness.

Tayloe's aides were reportedly infected in September when his office received anthrax-tainted letters through the mail. It has since been discovered that the letters contained a less virulent form of the bacteria and may have been used to throw any investigation of them off track.

Shukri Abu Marzook ran the Sacred Land Foundation, a cover organization the FBI says laundered money to terrorist groups. Marzook became a fugitive following FBI raids on his organization. He was found dead last Friday in a Boston apartment, the result of inhalation anthrax disease.

Federal sources say Marzook, in addition to being a middleman between Tayloe's office and Agha Mir in Saudi Arabia, was involved in a desperate attempt to spread more than one hundred pounds of anthrax through Boston's public transportation system. A scientist who once worked with U.S. biochemical experiments, Dr. Tobias Martfeld, is in custody for manufacturing weaponized anthrax.

The plot to poison Boston was foiled, and no details of the plot have been disclosed, but it was learned that Rasem Jameel and Zaccarias al-Tawwah died in Boston from anthrax poisoning after they were apprehended.

Some anthrax had apparently been distributed in the city, but authorities were reportedly able to contain it and successfully treat all who may have come in contact with it.

All future congressional hearings were canceled as "counterproductive" following Tayloe's death. The day before police discovered Tayloe's body in Rock Creek Park, General Darren E. Kragle agreed to answer questions before the hearings providing he could introduce a surprise witness. Inside sources identify the witness as Army Lt. Colonel Ross Canfield, a communications officer specialist at Central Command (CENTCOM).

Canfield was expected to testify that Senator Tayloe blackmailed him into blocking communications with Iron Weed elements in Afghanistan in an effort to discredit the War on Terror and provide himself a platform upon which to run for the office of President in the next election. Tayloe's wife, Eleanor, described him as being despondent the night before he was found dead.

"He was talking very strangely," Eleanor Tayloe told police. "He kept saying that if he went down, he wasn't going down by himself, he would take someone else important down with him."

Senator Tayloe was last seen leaving home for work at about 6:00 A.M. He was found dead less than two hours later.

His wife's statement has fed suspicion that Tayloe's death may not be suicide.

"I have known Eric for nearly twelve years," said Senator Kenneth Call of the Armed Services Committee. "I don't believe he would kill himself. If it was suicide, where is his briefcase? He never went anywhere without it. He had it when he left home that morning. Police have been unable to find it anywhere."

Tayloe and former President John Stanton were often seen together following 9/11 in their vocal opposition against the war on terror.

"I'm afraid I didn't know Senator Tayloe very well at all," Stanton said in a brief press release. "We spoke together a few times. We agreed that the policies of the administration were destructive and could lead to a world war. I know he had presidential ambitions, but in my opinion he wasn't presidential material. Other than this, I express my condolences to his family for his untimely death. It is a sad thing when a human being chooses to end his life at his own hand, and I feel his family's pain."

A reporter asked General Darren Kragle as he left the Capitol Building if the war on terror might now wind down with the decline of al-Qaeda and the Taliban in Afghanistan and the exposure of the anthrax plot in America.

"Afghanistan is an important first step," he responded. "But it's of little importance when compared to states that support terrorism while controlling great wealth, territory, resources, and population. Iran, part of the axis of evil with Iraq and North Korea, has a population greater than that of Britain, France, Spain, or Italy. Some terrorist states have influential allies, large armies, and they possess biological, chemical, and nuclear weapons with the means to deliver them. We haven't yet come up against state support for terrorism when it turns to weapons of mass destruction. I'm afraid what we have seen so far is only the opening campaign of the War on Terror."

Afterword

Collierville, Tennessee

The Farm had served as the axis, the center of gravity, for the Irish Kragle clan for over three hundred years. Ambassador Kragle, the family patriarch, liked to say that the land endured and the Kragles endured with it. Over the generations, Kragles gathered at the Farm to pay tribute to those who were buried in the family plot, to seek solace in the land, and to recuperate from battles they had fought since the French and Indian Wars.

Except for Gloria, the present generation was male again, following the terrorism deaths of Kathryn Burguiere-Kragle and Little Nana and their burial in the family cemetery behind the old log cabin. The clan gathered in the aftermath of Afghanistan and Boston, New York, and Washington, D.C.—the Ambassador, Uncle Mike, the General, his three Green Beret sons, and, of course, Gloria, who attempted to add a feminine touch.

The others who came were also male—FBI agent Claude Thornton and his Naval Academy son; Colonel Buck Thompson; Sergeant Bobby Goose Pony; and the members of Delta Detachment 1-Alpha minus Mother Norman, who fell in the mountains. Gloria clung to her Kragles and gathered all the others into her fold as well by fussing over them and feeding them and saying, "Lawdy, Lawdy, how can a lady be so lucky with all these big strong men. And my sons be home again all safe and sound! Thank the Lawd!"

"Gloria, them two younger sons of yours," Gloomy Davis teased, "don't look so much like you, but the older one, the Major . . . you don't suppose there might really be a Brown Sugar Doll in the woodpile, do you?"

She giggled and laughed and hugged him hard enough to make him wince.

All the men and Gloria walked back to the cemetery, and Chaplain Cameron read from his Bible. They had a moment of silence. The men visited the graves of mothers, fathers, wives, children, grandparents, and grandchildren. Then they slowly returned down the long lane in pairs or small groups, the detachment members freshly shaved and looking gaunt and worn from the weight they lost during Iron Weed. Most of them wore bandages on parts of their anatomy.

Cassidy looked as beaten-up as the others, from his fall off the Boston subway. After saving the city, he was something of a national hero. And you couldn't charge a national hero with any of the minor crimes he might have committed in the process. Buck Thompson even promised he would accept Cassidy's application to Delta Force, providing he passed a one-year probation period after training.

The men conversed in low tones beneath the pecans and sweetgum. Gloomy Davis walked with Brandon.

"Have you heard from her?" he asked.

"Who?"

"Boss, you know who."

As soon as the C-141 transporting the detachment from Kabul to CONUS touched down at Pope AFB, men in suits hustled Summer off the airplane and into a black car. She barely had time to say good-bye to the men who had accepted her as the wiseass Ismael and were just now getting used to her as Summer.

"I'll be back," she said to Brandon, looking deep into his eyes.

"MacArthur already said that."

"He came back, didn't he?"

"Boss?" Gloomy prompted.

"No, I haven't heard from her," he snapped.

It had been three days.

They came out of the trees on the pathway as a yellow cab from Memphis negotiated the long winding drive up to the main house. It stopped and a small figure got out. It was clad head to toe in a black Afghan burqa. A veil covered the face, except for the eyes, which were an incredible emerald as Summer looked up and saw Brandon running toward her, laughing.